*To DG, another lost too soon. Thank you for all those memories of playing mage, wizard, dragon as children. And thanks for reminding me that my time is not limitless and love transcends all.*

# Contents

# ACKNOWLEDGEMENTS

I would like to thank my editor, Elizabeth Nover of Razor Sharp Editing, for helping me to see (and write) more clearly.

Thanks to my beta readers, Vanessa Kristoff and Jeff Hoskinson, whose valuable feedback gave me courage while also making this book far better.

And last but not least, thanks so much to my mom and dad for telling me I could do anything I put my mind to. I listened. To all my family and friends, I appreciate your unwavering stability and support.

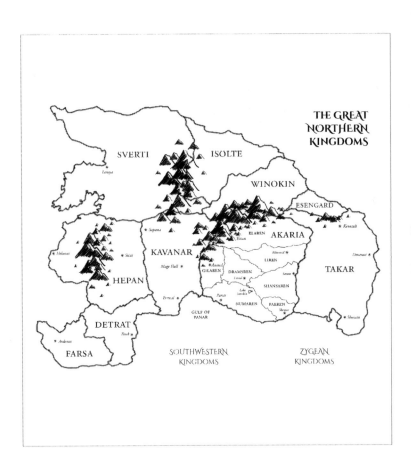

THE GREAT
NORTHERN
KINGDOMS

SVERTI

ISOLTE

WINOKIN

ESENGARD

Leuya

Kenatall

Supana

ELAREN

Estun

AKARIA

Helanas

Sicat

KAVANAR

LIREN

Demreset

Rokeresal

Mage Hall

TAKAR

Anoni

GILAREN

Senate

HEPAN

DRAMSREN

Lorsal

SHANSAREN

Lake
Sevoden

Panas

Evrical

NUMAREN

PARREN

Shester

GULF OF
PANAR

Shousin

DETRAT

Trosch

FARSA

Ardonis

SOUTHWESTERN
KINGDOMS

ZYGEAN
KINGDOMS

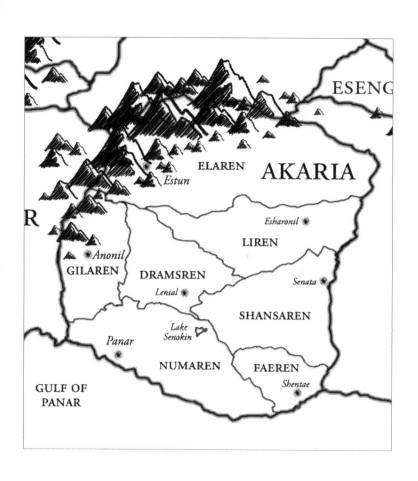

# MAGE
# STRIKE

# I    ASSEMBLY

"It's going to be fine. I'm sure everyone will listen to reason," Aven said. He and Miara had crested the ridge, and the long, narrow bridge to Estun stretched out before them. That expanse of stone was all that stood between them and his home.

If only he could be sure it would be a cheerful homecoming. He'd practiced confessing he was a mage and tried to figure the chances of being exiled on the spot but had given up without drawing any conclusions. The only thing he knew for sure was that no one would want to hear his news.

"Are you trying to convince me or yourself?" She gave him a crooked smile.

"You know me too well."

"You know people rarely listen to reason."

Aven hung his head as they rode forward, knowing it was true. He owed his people the details of their journey and all that had transpired. Everything they thought about mages needed to change, lest they face war woefully underprepared. Knowing he needed to tell them this didn't stop him from dreading it, however.

"If reason doesn't work, there's always appealing to their hearts. Or bribery. Or threats," she said.

He snorted.

"That seems to work well for King Demikin."

Aven shook his head at the Kavanarian king. Of course, neither of them wanted to mimic that fool's methods.

"You also have a veteran kidnapper on your side now," she continued. "That has to count for something."

"You're joking, right? To help me relax?" They'd taken an extra day as he'd tried to gather his thoughts. They could have flown back, had it been urgent. Instead, they'd lingered as long as he'd dared.

She smiled mischievously, eyes intent on the bridge before them.

"Right?"

"Don't forget your ability to set them on fire or strike them with lightning. If they won't listen to anything else, maybe that will get through to them."

"I can't even do that yet." He laughed.

"They don't know that." She flashed a broader grin and then returned her eyes to the approaching fortress. The pale stone bridge crossed a deep valley and offered a promenade wide enough for two wagons to pass side by side, a marvel of construction. Estun itself sat pewter gray and regal on the side of the mountain. Towers flew the same midnight and steel flags as the watchtowers they'd passed, the symbol of sword and shield adorning each. Eyes from those heights tracked their approach. He hoped he was recognizable enough to avoid any arrows nocked in his direction. Miara had sent word ahead via a bird and a scroll that Aven had penned, sharing the news that they'd escaped and were returning. These tower guards *should* be expecting them.

The great oak doors stood open, splitting the wooden inlay of a roaring bear, another of Akaria's royal symbols. Through the gatehouse and its three portcullises, the courtyard and stables lay beyond, its cobblestones as welcoming as flat, gray stones could be.

His mother swept into the courtyard and spotted them. She waved, the wind snapping the sapphire-blue fabric of her gown.

The weak winter sun sank toward the tops of the peaks. Midday had passed, but dinner was not yet near. Aven and Miara dismounted and handed off their horses to a stable girl. His mother attacked him with a fierce hug before he could even take a step into Estun.

"It's good to see you again too," he murmured in her ear. "Think everyone will be happy to see me?"

She pulled away, pressing her lips together in annoyance. "Your father asked the Assembly members to meet here when we received your missive. Lord Alikar has just arrived—even though he came the shortest distance, mind you. He's causing trouble already."

"No rest for the weary, eh?"

"Apparently. But no matter." His mother turned

toward Miara now. "I believe we haven't yet been formally introduced."

Miara had been hovering behind his shoulder, and now she blushed. Huh, that wasn't an expression he'd seen before. He stepped aside so the two could face each other.

"Mother, Miara Floren. Miara, Elise Lanuken, queen of Akaria."

The two exchanged slight bows, Miara's appropriately deeper than his mother's.

"It is… good to actually meet you," his mother said. The awkwardness in the air around them was far greater than Aven had expected. Perhaps it *was* odd to have only met someone via magic before. Especially when, at the time, they happened to be kidnapping your son.

"Let's head in," Aven said to break the tension. "Might as well get this over with." The women nodded, and they headed inside.

The sounds of shouts and tense voices rose, followed by the angered murmurs of a large group. A quarrel was apparently already well underway. Aven and Miara hurried after his mother down the beautifully arched corridor that led to his father's meeting chamber. Ah, familiar sights. It was good to be home. Mostly.

"Even the *thought* of a mage as king is an outrage—"

Well, that boded well.

"Last I heard, we don't make a habit of upending the realm over a rumor or two." Lord Dyon's voice, ever the skeptic.

"I have it on *very* good authority. Word arrived earlier

today by bird from Kavanar—"

"Very good authority? Our direst enemies, those who have constantly battled your people for generations, and you—"

"Piety does not know national borders."

"Well, I promise you those Kavanarian bastards *do*, and they want your land."

Aven cleared his throat from the stone archway that led into the chambers. The room fell silent. His mother stood at his side, looking regal and irritated, and Miara on the other, still in her old riding leathers and newly acquired daggers, which were strapped to her thighs. The two of them together cut a formidable image; he was lucky to have them at his side. He wore peasant clothes—brown leather pants and a plain, dirt-colored linen tunic that had lost its sleeves. A freezing and impractical piece of clothing without his cloak, and perhaps even with it, but he rather liked it. He'd wanted to lose any clothing from Mage Hall. And the lack of sleeves showed off his battle scars—the wounds on each shoulder from when the Masters had tried to enslave him.

Tried, he reminded himself. Tried and failed. If I can get out of that mess, I can figure this out too. Open rebellion was nothing on potential enslavement and murder, right? If he could escape that hellhole alive, avoiding civil war should be a stroll in the garden.

"Glad to hear you missed me, my lords," Aven said.

The group parted as he approached and took his place standing at the table. He forced himself to relax and act comfortable in the tense silence. He tucked his thumbs in his belt and regarded the first voice with a sardonic smile. Lord Alikar. The young, black-haired lord met his easy smile with a glare over an ostentatious bristling of white fox fur around the shoulders of his brown cloak. Alikar was the most junior member of the Assembly, elected for the shortest term, only three years. Born the heir to a wealthy silver mine, Alikar currently presided over the western territory of Gilaren, which shared its border with Kavanar. That was much of the land that Miara and Aven had traveled through, and it occurred to him now that Alikar was also a novice priest of Nefrana, although he hadn't finished his training and still spent most of his time ruling his territory. Aven hadn't thought to connect Alikar's supposed devotion with the number of Devoted squads and bigots they'd encountered. At least, not until now. But seeing Alikar's glare, he couldn't help but wonder. Could the bastard even be welcoming Devoted into his lands?

"Your Highness," Alikar started after a moment, "I've received some news which troubles me greatly. I've heard—"

"It's true." Aven tried to keep his face straight as Alikar stiffened. It was all he could do to keep from grinning in defiance. "But I do believe I can serve our kingdom even more effectively as a result. We face an unprecedented threat."

"But my lord—"

"*What's* true?" Devol growled from the back. "I can

never hear *anything* back here." Devol was not an elected or born noble, but he was a hell of a soldier. Their master of arms always worried he was being left out of things, perhaps because he'd worked his way to a high position through heroism and skill in battle rather than birth. Or perhaps it was because he was simply nosy. And, Aven suspected, it didn't help that he was shorter than nearly everyone in the room and still often ended up stuck in the back.

"I'm a mage, Dev," Aven called.

Murmurs swept the room, but many strove to contain their reactions. Either they were all great diplomats, or they all already knew. Or perhaps both.

Alikar looked to the king. "Nefrana condemns this. We will not abide by this. You must do something."

"Is that so? Aven is the same well-trained strategist and accomplished swordsman he was a fortnight ago. I don't see how this changes anything." Samul folded his arms across his chest.

"This cannot stand. Thel must replace him. If you will not name a new heir, I will call a meeting of the Assembly. This must be stopped."

Samul scowled at him. Dev piped in from the back. "Looks like you've already got an Assembly here, don't you?"

"Lord Sven did not trouble himself to answer my summons," Samul growled. "So, no. We cannot vote formally without him. But an Assembly is not necessary."

"Then I will—"

"Calm yourself. Your rashness is uncalled for." Warden Asten glared at Alikar, leaning forward, her chainmail catching the firelight. "We haven't even heard what Prince Aven's had to say."

"I've heard everything I need to hear. The people of Gilaren will not abide—"

"They *will* abide," Samul thundered. "This kingdom is ruled by *laws*, not the whines of spoiled young kittens."

Aven had not thought it possible for Alikar's face to look any more sour or severe, but he somehow managed it at that insult. "And what about the laws of the gods?"

"There are no laws against a mage as our king," Samul said, voice strained. "Believe what you like, but this land is governed by the rule of law. Akarian law. And—most importantly—by *me*."

"We all must answer to the gods."

The look his father gave Alikar was dark and dangerous. "Do you dare judge me?" he said, his voice quiet as the grave.

Alikar's eyes widened almost imperceptibly, and he froze.

"I am sure that in your priesthood, you must have learned that judgment belongs to Mastikos. Nefrana tells us, do not steal from the gods their right to judge. An eternal hell reaping the fields with a dull scythe—is that not the penalty for those who steal from the gods?"

The king paused. Alikar met his gaze, unflinching. The lord clearly did not know Samul well if he was at all surprised by his king's words.

"Am I wrong? *Educate* me, oh holy one." The king's voice was barely louder than a whisper.

Alikar did not immediately respond, and the silence stretched on. Finally, the young lord spoke. "Your Highness and members of the Assembly, I formally call for a convening of the Assembly of Akaria to meet in the capital, Panar, in two weeks' time."

Aven gritted his teeth. The man had to be a simpleton or a masochist to effectively spit in the king's face. It had come to that already, had it? Aven had known some would reject his magic, but he hadn't thought it would take this form. At least no one had called for him to be banished or executed. Yet.

"Certainly, we must have Lord Sven to have a true vote," Alikar continued. "And as you have nothing to hide, I'm sure you'll want to hold such a significant meeting where the royal archivists and chroniclers can attend. They'll need to record the proceedings for posterity, after all."

Of course. All the Assembly members were here, save one—and Alikar would insist on dragging them to the other side of the kingdom. He was unlikely to win any allies with that move, but perhaps he didn't care. There was no arguing his point, however. The meeting should be properly recorded, and once an Assembly gathering was initiated, it must proceed. The Lanukens should have spent their lives in the capital anyway. Only their attempts to hide Aven's magic had justified staying in Estun so long.

Alikar continued, "Additionally, Anonil and its people

will not support a war against Kavanar under these circumstances, at least not until we have a proper heir."

"What war against Kavanar?" Samul said, spreading his hands wide. "Ah, you propose we should ride to war over this grievous attack on our crown prince? Fine idea, my lord."

Alikar's glare deepened, but he did not reply. Instead, the lord turned and left with a swing of his furred cloak.

Daes settled into his armchair in his private study. Mage servants bustled about, setting the table before him. He'd invited Evana, the knight-princess, to breakfast with him privately this morning. He'd spent the night going over their options, and now he needed to get her take on them. And hopefully win her to do his bidding.

He had no idea how this would go. She was straightforward like he was, which he liked. But he had more experience with simpering politicos and their shallow maneuvers. He knew how to trick their kind into doing what he wanted. Simply asking for help was something he did a lot less often, and with less success.

He leaned back as a young child mage settled a bowl of potatoes onto the scarlet tablecloth. Daes had spent a lot of time in this chair in the last few days. Nearly all of it. Thinking about the events of the last few weeks, he'd verged on wallowing, although he hated to admit it.

Daes's teams had searched high and low after the

prince's escape. Creature mages had tried to follow once they'd realized they were no longer in Mage Hall, but it had been too late. He'd sent search parties out into the surrounding hills and countryside, but they'd turned up nothing. Several still searched, but he was not optimistic. They could be anywhere by now. The creature mage and the prince had dashed out of his hall and pretty much vanished.

His glorious plan had come crumbling down and left him flat on his ass—literally—in front of the king and all of the Masters. Such a public failure filled him with rage and had often woken him at night in a savage sweat, reaching for his sword. Each time he had calmed himself. Only once had he actually taken the sword to anything, and no one had died from his fits of rage. At least not yet. He'd been thinking of acquiring a new bed frame anyway.

So Daes chose to focus on the positive and the fact that he hadn't murdered any valuable slaves or obnoxious peers as a result of this debacle. Especially with the looks Seulka had been giving him. She could try to brush it off on *him* all she wanted, but she was just as culpable, if not more so. She had claimed that star magic was surely entirely forgotten. If there were degrees of failure, hers was certainly worse than his, although less public and dramatic. For all he cared, she could burn if she thought he was going to forget about that.

No. As much as Daes wanted to kill that son of a bitch prince himself, he shoved his feelings into a corner.

Rage only got in the way. He'd long ago learned to slow his actions, to check himself when his blood curdled with anger. The most effective ways to meet his goals hardly ever involved fits of passion, and he wouldn't let his own emotions blind him or stop him from getting what he wanted.

The mage prince would have to pay for this, of course—and the creature mage too. How, exactly, was the question. And he needed to be perfectly calm to execute his revenge.

He had underestimated his enemy. He would not do so again. That others had underestimated the enemy even more than he had did not help anything.

The only positive of the whole debacle was that ultimately, they had wanted a war, and they were still likely to get one. Perhaps even more likely.

And yet—he had hoped they would attack already. Were they marshaling a larger force? What were they waiting for? He swore under his breath as another child arrived with a bowl of eggs.

Of course, at exactly his weakest moment, the knight-princess appeared at the door. Others might overlook her royal status, but Daes knew this was not wise. She was obviously most interested in her role as a Knight of the Devoted Order, but he knew the type: they snubbed their noble birth—until it became useful. Her noble rank would emerge when the unwary least expected it and slap them across the face. Daes instead chose not to ignore it.

She was a vision as always, statuesque in beauty, with a face as elegant and hard as marble. She waited in the doorway for him to speak, but he let the moment pass just a little longer. Some women would think he admired them, and in this case, that was at least partially true. Others would grow anxious in the silence. Either effect was useful to him.

"Princess," he finally greeted, though he decided not to rise. "Please, join me."

She glided forward smoothly. A serving mage pulled out her chair and pushed it under her as she sat. She did not acknowledge the mage even slightly.

"Please, call me Evana."

He smiled warmly. Ah, that was a good sign. Of course, she wanted his help. So this should not be an uphill battle. He hoped.

"Evana. And you, of course, can call me Daes."

She nodded curtly and took a sip of tea. She was all business, and that was a game he knew how to play.

"I've given much thought to your proposition. And our next steps against the Akarians. I appreciate you meeting me privately today."

"Why the secrecy?" she asked.

"Oh, it's not exactly *secrecy*. It's the carefully timed dissemination of information. I will share my plans with the other Masters, just not yet. I'd like to share with you the role I envision for you before I share everything with the others." In truth, he had not yet decided if that day would ever come. If Seulka kept giving him vicious looks, he might have to include revenge on her as *part* of the plan.

"Forgive my foggy knowledge of your history here, but can you remind me—who put you in charge again?" she said with a twinkle in her eye.

He met her gaze flatly with no hint of a smile. "I did."

Evana lifted her chin just slightly. A relaxed interest pricked around her eyes. She was pleased, he thought, although her mouth betrayed no emotion. "I'm listening."

"Help yourself to this food, and I will share my thoughts. Shall we?" She nodded. "All right then. I still believe we can draw the Akarians into war on our lands—"

"Why on your lands? Won't the damage be worse to your property?" she asked. "The farms and villages I passed on the way here were only mildly fortified, although they'd made *some* very minor preparations."

He nodded. "Skirmishes on the border were once frequent, before the Dark Days, and even more common in the centuries before the Akarians united. Having the Akarians on our terrain will certainly do more damage to our people and land. But it will give us much-needed advantages. We will have local supplies, while they'll be easier to cut off from their food supply and reinforcements. Much of Akarian terrain is rugged—hills, mountains, forests—compared to the flat and open land our soldiers are used to. And equipped for, unfortunately. Not to mention the value of drawing the Akarians away from their own fortifications. They'll also have to leave forces behind, while we can mass our forces much more easily with less risk. With the addition of mage forces, I think we may have enough of an advantage to actually win."

She raised an eyebrow. "Mage forces?"

"You saw them training yesterday. The forces grow more every day, in both size and skill. But I'm going to need more. A lot more."

"I thought Nefrana frowned on mages taking up arms."

He smiled and spread his hands as if helpless. Did she really believe that? Nefrana seemed to be against whatever the priests—and perhaps the king—wanted her to be against. The rules seemed to have far less to do with ethics or dogma than politics. But until he knew her better, he would stick to religious reverence, at least while she was around. "Think of the story of the shepherd and the farmer. The shepherd let his flocks wander as Nefrana willed and paid them little mind. The farmer worked long and hard to till the land, never asking for Nefrana's—"

"I know the story." She waved it aside. "Silly, as most parables are. I always felt any decent shepherd wouldn't have ignored his flock."

"True. But the story teaches us that we must use all our resources to defend Nefrana, that we must not leave our fate solely in her hands. Our priests have guided me to use every tool and weapon at my disposal to counter the mage threat. The mages are the greatest weapon I have. Doesn't that change things? If we can stretch our borders across Akaria and perhaps even into Takar, then many more mages will be captured and bound to our will, not running dangerously wild, endangering people's souls. Isn't that worth temporarily arming mages who can be utterly controlled and easily ordered to stop at any time?"

"Perhaps." She looked far from convinced.

"So that brings me to the first point where you are concerned. I want more mages."

She narrowed her eyes. "What does that have to do with me?"

"You know how to identify mages, yes? You have Devoted stones?"

She nodded. "I don't carry them, but my squires do."

"And you have friends or colleagues who may be pursuing their holy mission?" Friends seemed like the wrong word. He was not sure a woman like Evana *had* friends of any kind.

"I know other knights. Of course. What does it matter?"

"And you knights sometimes capture mages and sometimes kill them, do you not?"

"It is up to a knight's preference, possibly the monastery where they trained. Different groups have different standards. I prefer to solve a problem *completely* when I encounter it."

"Ah, but what a waste of valuable resources."

"Your captives seem fairly well treated. I hadn't expected that." She eyed a mage who waited in the corner for any requests from them. "Is that why?"

"Oh, they get their share of beatings. Not everything is worth a specific compulsion. And I am but one Master. I strive to keep the others… prudent, but I don't always succeed. But yes, I consider them valuable property. Do you leave your bow in the street to be stolen? Swords out in the rain to rust?"

She narrowed her eyes again but said nothing.

"One man's problem is another man's opportunity," he said. "What I'm getting at is—I want more mages coming to Mage Hall. I want more slaves as quickly as we can make them. And I *thought* that you and some of your Devoted colleagues could perhaps be counted on for that? Perhaps to capture instead of kill for a few weeks?"

"You're prepared to pay the increased bounties?"

"Of course." He hadn't cleared that with the other Masters, but he didn't care. When the mages showed up, the other Masters would hand over the coin. The three of them celebrated the acquisition of new slaves even more ardently than he did.

"Where do you suggest we *find* so many mages?"

He shrugged and sipped his tea. "I thought perhaps you could figure that out."

The cold expression on her face told him she didn't like that answer.

"But we receive few mages from Hepan. I hear magic is perfectly legal there. Akaria is barely a day's ride. And I've heard of a mage school in southern Detrat, although how you transport a large group of captured mages—or capture them in the first place—is not something I have any particular insight into."

She nodded sternly, although he noted she hadn't exactly agreed to his plan. She wanted to hear more first.

"And then there is still the matter of the mage prince. And the Akarian royal family."

"And your renegade slave."

He nodded, scowling. "Indeed. I did not forget." He stopped for a moment to calm himself. A bit of toast, a taste of tea. Better. Let the wave of rage pass. "I've hired professional assassins this time, sent a few mages to help him. No asking the king. No kidnapping feints or fakes. The goal is to kill him, and the brothers too if possible, rather than simply start a war. The threat of star magic must be completely and utterly wiped out. Estun is a hard target, though—heavily fortified and stuffed to the teeth with loyal Akarian soldiers."

"And if the assassin fails?"

"Estun might be a tough target, but they cannot be safe everywhere. I've initiated a plan to force them out of Estun one way or another." Several plans, actually, but all those details didn't matter here. One plan would suffice for her. "I've bribed a member of their Assembly to call for a vote."

"A member of their Assembly—impressive. Who?"

"The lord of Gilaren. I forget his name. A young whelp, encouraged by enticements of trade deals and discounts and spurred on by the coin in his pocket."

"Gilaren? You must be joking."

He shook his head with a rueful smile. "I know, I thought it would require some kind of underhanded, arm-twisting tactic when the initial offer of money failed, but apparently not."

"Certainly that's the *first* land you hope to seize in this war of yours."

"What war?" He grinned. "No war has started, if you

hadn't noticed, mostly to my chagrin, but it helps me in convincing the Gilaren lord. But yes, of course. I can practically spit on his territory and Anonil from here. There's no way to acquire Akaria without capturing his territory first."

"Or perhaps later, if you have them pacified?"

He raised an eyebrow. "Perhaps. I see you have a strategic mind behind that pretty face."

Where Seulka or another woman might have smiled, Evana glared at him. He didn't understand why, but he preferred her reaction. Maybe he just liked women who weren't so eager to please.

"And that is hardly surprising for a woman of your skill and intelligence," he said quickly, feeling some need to smooth over the situation. Her expression eased. "Of course, I have other activities in motion. I am sending a small team of mages to Estun to cause some trouble and force the Akarian royals out, and perhaps give our assassins some opportunities. A dozen new squads will start training the day after that. If only I had more mages, there's so much I could do with them."

She sighed. "And that is where I suppose I could best help. I will see what can be done, contact a few... friends."

"Were you hoping to charge into battle right away?"

She shrugged. "I suppose I was. But this is a logical plan. Storming into Estun with my bow drawn would be foolish—and most of all, ineffective. It'd be more likely to get *me* killed than the prince. I will help you. Tell me, when will you tell the others? Or *will* you tell the others?

Will your king know of these plans?"

"Does it matter to you?" He left his expression blank, a bit cold. He didn't want to tell her more than he had to, or reveal whom he might be withholding information from. She might use it against him.

"I must understand to whom I can speak of these plans, of course. If secrecy is required, that suits me perfectly. I just want to know what resources I have and how best to utilize them. If the king should not know… it'd be best that I not mention it to him then, eh?"

"And are you regularly in the company of the king?" It was Daes's turn to narrow his eyes.

"No. But we wouldn't want to let a little bad luck spoil your carefully laid plans, now would we?"

He sighed. He supposed she had a point. "Obviously, the other Masters know of my training the mages for war, and you need not hide your plan to increase the number of mages in their service. I will tell them we discussed it. I am less certain when—or if—I will tell them of any of my designs on Estun and assassinating the mage prince in particular. I cannot afford their interference this time. They are too easily frightened, poorly trained in either tactics or strategy or both, and above it all, our king is an idiot. The whole court is more interested in wine and gossip than in their own kingdom's safety. The other Masters may be slightly less drunk, but they'd still prefer to be navel-gazing."

"It is a good thing they have you then," she said with an edge to her voice. He caught her double meaning—she meant both that this was likely true, but also that those he criticized would probably not feel the same way.

"It *is* good they have me," he replied in earnest. "Look at this prince—a star mage, after all these years. They *insisted* the magic was long forgotten."

"And I'm sure you stand to gain nothing here but the protection of your lord and his ladies." She eyed him.

Ah, so she was not above subtlety. That was good, especially when discussion of near treason was involved. There were a select few things that it was really best not to be blunt about. "I certainly stand to gain from this. I make no pretense of this being some kind of altruistic endeavor. Most primarily, all of my power at present comes from these mages I rule—"

"That you and the other Masters rule?" She grinned slyly.

He cleared his throat. "Indeed, yes, of course. As I was saying... I strive to protect my own power here, nothing more."

"Really, truly?" she smiled sweetly. "Nothing more, at all?"

How much should he tell her? How much could he trust her? He hardly knew her. Did he hope for more power through a war with Akaria? He did primarily want to neutralize the threat they posed—but certainly a pleasant side effect was likely to be more mages to rule, more land, more credit for doing good for the kingdom. More deeds to encourage them to forget about the nature of his birth and focus on who he really was. So did he hope to grow in power by all his machinations? Of course. Did he even half hope to find a way to subvert the king, or perhaps weaken him a little? Well, how could he *not* hope for that? The man was weak, foolish, and irresponsible. But it was a long shot, and he rarely thought about it in the light of day, let alone spoke about it to anyone.

"I have found that everyone has layers of reasons behind what they do, Princess," he replied. "You, though, seem to have nothing at all to gain from hunting down this mage prince. Why are you so ardent?"

She frowned, realizing the trick he'd pulled but unable to dodge the direct question. "It is my calling. I do not need a vocation beyond my family. They are willing to support me if they can't marry me off. And yet, I have chosen a profession that is neither easy nor safe. Why else would I choose it other than that I had been called?"

So she *was* a zealot. No faking that. She had seemed rather smart and logical for a zealot, so he had wondered if it was a show. But no. He said nothing for a moment, taking a conveniently timed bite. He had eaten little so far and talked much. He left the burden of talk on her at this calculated moment.

She sniffed. "Well… perhaps there is another layer to it. I traveled to Akaria looking for a husband. I may have a vocation, but I had still hoped to rule something. Somewhere. To civilize a place like Akaria, with mages running wild. But I'd have to go far ashore for that at this point. It may not be worth it, to be so far afield on my own. The Akarian was the last unmarried prince in these great northern kingdoms. And it had actually seemed possible for a moment or two. But then—to realize that he was a *mage*. In hiding. Of all the trickery and deception…" She trailed off, lost in her own thoughts for a moment.

"Deception? He's been deceiving everyone around him, no?"

"Yes. He's not just a mage, but a liar to boot. But if I had married a *mage*… He would have never said anything. The possibility horrifies me."

He nodded. He suspected the matter of the prince's deception slight compared to the dashing of her dreams of conquest, of being a queen and having her own kingdom to rule, like her older siblings. But that was painful to think about, and a little foolish because it had probably been a slim chance for her anyway. Righteous indignation was easier to hide behind, had less sting and more fire. He could understand.

"Well, you shall have your chance to make things right. Small steps, but we will get there."

She gave him a relieved smile as he pulled the topic away rather than drilling further. A small kindness, a peace offering. "I would rather my bow kill the prince than your assassin's blade, I must admit. But I am a woman who puts results ahead of ego."

"I find ego does little but get in the way." Says the man who has fantasies about deposing the king, a voice in the back of his head reminded him. He waved the thought away.

"Indeed."

"I shall send word to the supply master to give you

whatever you need," he said, "should your Devoted lords not be adequately supportive of your holy mission."

She looked pleasantly surprised. "It is settled then. We will scuttle them out and skewer them like this potato." She made short work of impaling the small roasted root vegetable on her knife and lifting it up as if in toast.

"So many to skewer, so little time. But first," he smiled, "we will have this lovely breakfast—together."

Alikar swept down the stone hallway and out of sight. At nearly the same moment, Aven's brother Thel was returning to the king's chamber with Miara at his side. Damn, when had they even left? Had she missed all that? Aven had thought she'd been right behind him. That she could have been pulled away so easily without him noticing was more than a little unnerving after *that* altercation. Had Thel heard Alikar's assertion that he should be heir? His brother had to be expecting it, but he wouldn't like it one bit.

"Well, that was a fine tussle, lots a grumbling, but the boy's just a pup," Devol grumbled. Murmurs of agreement and a few laughs flitted through the group, easing the tension a bit.

"Only slightly less so than our respected prince," Lord Dyon said, an edge to his voice. Aven was barely a year older than Alikar.

"Ah, with comments like that, it's good to be home,"

Aven muttered, clapping Dyon on the shoulder.

Dyon narrowed his eyes at Aven's hand but then shook his head at the empty doorway. "Serves them right for electing him just to get a privileged price on his ore." Unlike Alikar, Dyon's position was his for life. "He distracts us from matters of true importance. When do we ride on Kavanar? This affront cannot be tolerated."

Devol spread his arms wide. "Indeed. Mastikos knows, it's been too long."

"The king tells us you were kidnapped," Dyon said. "Is it true? By agents of Kavanar?"

Miara had come to stand by Aven's side, just behind him, and she shifted uneasily.

"His Majesty didn't see fit to tell us until just now that you're safely returned," Warden Asten added. Her icy blue eyes cast a sidelong glance at the king. She had cropped her blond hair even shorter since last he'd seen her. How long had it been, three months, five? She did not often travel this far west these days. "Welcome back, though. Well met."

Murmurs of agreement followed her words. Aven gave her the same brotherly nod he'd given her a hundred times before when she'd bested him at bowstaff. The two of them had trained together since they were children, until she'd moved up in the ranks to her current position.

Aven cleared his throat. "It's true, but I would not have us ride to war just yet."

"Why not?" demanded Asten.

"Let me explain. I was kidnapped. And I was also

rescued—"

"Hardly. You got free of them on your own," Miara cut in.

"I could not have escaped alone. But no matter. I was held prisoner in a Kavanarian hold for two days. And I discovered a few things about our enemies you will all find interesting."

For a moment he wasn't even sure any of them had heard him. Their eyes had all shifted to Miara, Lord Beneral's gaze especially icy.

"Who's that?" Devol grunted. Aven smothered a laugh.

"My lords, ladies, and wardens, this is Miara Floren, mage of Kavanar. She was instrumental in my rescue."

"Your *escape*," she said.

"Fine, my escape. Miara, may I introduce you to *most* of the fine members of the Akarian Assembly. This is Warden Tana Asten, Lady and Assemblywoman from Shansaren Territory. Wardens are Akaria's elite warriors, and Asten is one of our best." Asten bowed, and Miara returned the gesture. The military elite of Shansaren had chosen Asten to represent them for a lengthy seven-year term.

He didn't know how Asten managed to seem friendly and deathly serious at the same time; he knew no one else with such an air. She had always been that way, even as a young girl. Of course, she had already been an accomplished swordswoman by the time Aven had met her. Aven, on the other hand, had simply been thrust among the warden aspirants and told to shape up. His peers had choices: be good at a sword or do something else. As crown prince, he did not. With peers like her and a competitive streak, he'd mostly held his own.

Aven turned to Dyon to continue his introductions. "This is Lord Jax Dyon, Assemblyman of Liren and trusted steward of military organization and logistics. And Lord Ven Beneral, Assemblyman of Numaren in the south, talented merchant and steward of the White City." The White City was another name for Panar. Beneral worked hard to keep his lovely towered city deserving of its reputation of beauty and plentiful free trade, so Aven tried to use the name as often as possible.

Bows were exchanged. Was she absorbing it all? How could anyone? He would go over it with her later.

"And this is Lady Vitig Toyl, Assemblywoman of Dramsren and expert trader." Toyl was the one that Aven knew least. Like Alikar, she was just starting a shorter, four-year term. But she came across as far more practical and quite a bit wiser than Alikar, as well as two decades his senior. The lady bowed, her pale cloak of fine Dramsren wool contrasting with long brown hair that fell past her shoulders.

Aven pointed out several officers, nobles, and arms masters, more for the sake of acknowledging them than hoping Miara would remember them. "And this is Master of Arms Devol," Aven added at last. Dev mumbled a nicety as he bowed and seemed pleased when she bowed in return. As master of arms, he was not exactly a noble according to some people's estimation, but then again, neither was she.

"We are grateful for the part you played in Prince Aven's return, Miara," King Samul said as Aven finished the introductions. "You are welcome to stay in Akaria as one of our own for as long as you wish."

"Thank you, my lord," Miara said with yet another bow.

"May we all strive to such valiant deeds," Warden Asten said. Asten didn't mean it sarcastically, but Miara frowned ever so slightly. Hopefully he was the only one who'd noticed. "But this attack on Prince Aven is the real outrage. We must determine a swift, brutal response. And we should not be discussing that in front of *anyone* recently arrived from Kavanar." She glanced at Aven. "Except you, of course, my lord."

"Understandable." Miara gave a quick bow. "I will take my leave—"

"Wait." The king held up his palm.

Aven jumped in at the opportunity. "Miara was a slave in Kavanar. She feels far more ill will toward them than loyalty, I assure you."

"Still," Devol started, "do we really need word of this getting back to greedy Kavanarian—"

"I would like to ask her a few questions before she leaves us," Samul said over the starts of other objections. "The mage is aware of the details of Aven's journey, so we can discuss that without concern. Son, please illuminate us on these recent events."

As briefly as he could, Aven described for them the slaves inside Mage Hall, the Masters, the knots, the brand, and all he'd seen in Mage Hall.

"How the hell did we not know of this before?" Lord Dyon's hand had wandered to his sword pommel.

"At the very least, this reveals critical weaknesses in our information-gathering efforts," said Lady Toyl.

"Agreed. We do have spies in Kavanar," the king replied. "But they are carefully placed to alert us specifically to troop movements and military expansion. The few in the royal court rarely learn much and report on the courting of women and the imbibing of wine and not much else. Those seemed sufficient things to monitor, but clearly we missed this."

"I had heard rumors," said Lord Beneral, "but I never thought they could be true. And even *if* the rumors were true, no risk to Akaria had occurred to me." Numaren's borders met Kavanar in the southernmost part of Akaria, along the sea, so Beneral had more opportunity to hear such rumors—and more reason to be concerned. Beyond Alikar's territory of Gilaren, only the Lanuken's own Elaren Territory shared a border with Kavanar, and the mountains were far too dense for even difficult passage. None traveled there by choice, and Estun was as deep into the mountains as most were willing to go.

"Slavery. Those depraved bastards," Warden Asten said. "I wish it surprised me, but their avarice knows no bounds. Gluttonous, corrupt scum, the whole lot of them."

"I am determined to end the practice," Aven said quickly before Asten could further berate their enemies— but also Miara. "We must free these enslaved mages. And I'd like to end those responsible for such evil in the first place while we're at it."

"Then we will respond to this insult with overwhelming force and crush them without hesitation," Lord Dyon said. "And yet... you would not have us ride to war just yet. Why delay?"

"Indeed, I believe Devol is drooling at the smell of blood," Asten said, smiling slightly.

Aven paused for a second, hoping he'd get this right. "Those enslaved mages aren't servants," he said. "They're being trained for war. Kavanar is building an *army* of mages. Have any of you fought against such a force?"

"So these Masters call them evil to enslave them and then exploit their magic for war?" Beneral said, shaking his head in disgust. "Hypocrites."

"We have martial superiority—" Dev started.

"How many mages are in our army, Master Devol?" Aven asked.

"Who says we need 'em?" Devol folded his arms across his chest.

"Our siege equipment can be bolstered relatively easily—" the artillery master piped up.

"Our archers—" started another.

"Miara," Aven said over them, loudly but conversationally, "can mages defend against archers, catapults, infantry?"

"My lord, air mages can fend off archers in a variety of ways," she said as if reporting back reconnaissance. Yes, dispassionate and factual was good. The "my lord" made him wince a little, though. "Wind blows arrows astray.

Fire can incinerate arrows, but it can also be used as an obstacle to push archers back and out of range, although that's not a recommended approach. Energy costly and inefficient, I understand." Asten's eyebrows rose as she spoke, although Toyl and Dyon frowned, more skeptical. Was it Aven's imagination, or was the blood draining from Devol's face? Miara continued on, oblivious to their reactions. "The efficient, recommended technique in the books is smoke or fog to obscure the enemy's view of their targets. And there's always a combination of these, not to mention that an air mage's offensive abilities would cause significantly more trouble than these defensive ones. You can't shoot arrows when you're on fire, in the path of a tornado, and the like."

At this, Devol's mouth dropped open, which brought a smile to Asten's face, but only for a moment. They all sobered as Miara continued.

"Catapults would be more challenging, but if stone is the projectile, a group of earth mages can attempt to take control of the projectile or redirect it. The battle abilities of earth mages are fewer than the other types, but many would likely be available. Aside from earthquakes, they don't have as many practical uses as air or creature mages do."

"Earthquakes?" Toyl blurted, finally showing a bit of concern.

Miara continued, her eyes still trained only on Aven. "As for infantry, well, there are options. A creature mage can cause a number of ailments that would delay or incapacitate troops. They could transform the enemy into whatever they wished, although again, that is expensive and inefficient. Greater damage can be done by transforming oneself or by coaxing local animals to attack, such as wolves, bears, panthers. Even something as small as a raccoon could be used to spoil or poison supplies—" At this moment, Miara happened to glance away from Aven's face at the group and faltered. Their faces wore a mixture of horror, shock, and discomfort. She blushed. "Perhaps this is too much detail. Suffice to say a mage in war is very destructive, depending on type, ability, size of the force, and training."

Samul cleared his throat. "And let me remind you… Kavanar is building an army of them." He paused to let that sink in.

"And we know basically nothing about what it can do," Aven continued, "nor how to defend against it. What Miara has just told us is a hundred times more than we all knew ten minutes ago. We've let overconfidence and piety blind us. We have to develop some way to defend ourselves." Aven tried to keep from scowling, but he was pretty sure he was failing.

"You mean—use magic ourselves? I am not sure I'm comfortable with such tactics," started Lady Toyl.

"Get comfortable with it," Samul boomed. "Whether you would condone the use of magic or not is irrelevant when it is being used *against* us."

He paused, glaring around from face to face. Aven knew this move well—each moment he stared at them, he pushed them back from a challenge. It was not Aven's place to act like that most of the time—at least not yet. But he watched the reactions carefully for who was a problem waiting to explode. Dyon and Beneral were nodding as Dev continued to stroke his beard. Asten didn't meet the king's stare. Toyl scowled back at him, unafraid.

"If it is being used against us," Samul continued, "it is our responsibility as protectors of this land to defend the people from it. That means understanding it at least well enough to defend ourselves and acting accordingly. Whether we *use* magic against them may be something we wish to deliberate at length about. We will not decide that here, tonight. But whether or not we *understand* what magic they can use against us and how to stop them is not up for discussion."

The silence after his words was tenser than Aven had expected. His father put up a rational argument. It only made sense to understand your enemy. None of them had seen what Aven had, though. They had to take him at his word, and that might make this news harder to believe. How could he prove the danger to them?

Samul looked to Miara. "What more can you tell us of Kavanar's abilities?"

"You said something about… earthquakes?" Devol said. "In this damned cave, that's a frightening thing if I ever heard one."

Miara regarded the Master of Arms as if he were declaring the sky blue. "If it's frightening, it only proves Aven's point. Your Great Stone is most prudent, but this is exactly why you should have your own earth mages for defense and watching for attacks."

"Why do you mention the Stone?" asked Toyl. Of course, Aven's parents knew of the Stone's ability to suppress magic, but most did not understand it had any purpose beyond decoration.

Miara stared in surprise for a moment before answering. "Your Great Stone is a magic-suppression tool. It makes working spells more difficult, if not impossible, and thus protects the hold somewhat from magical attacks. The closer you get to it, the stronger the effect. It has a limited range and doesn't reach far outside Estun itself, however."

Murmurs flitted through the crowd.

"How does it work? And where did such a thing come from?" Asten asked.

"And was it here since it was built? Who would have—" started Toyl.

"Where did they find such a thing?" said Beneral.

Samul raised a hand to quiet them. "Please, let's focus on the matter at hand."

"Well, at least the Great Stone will prevent these Kavanarian mages from cooking up an earthquake and killing us all in one fell swoop," Dyon grumbled.

"Not exactly, my lord," Miara said gently. "Enough mages working together could overcome the Stone's power. They probably haven't tried before because transporting enough mages here would not be easy or stealthy."

Dyon scowled. "It just gets better and better, doesn't it? How many would they need?"

"Well, they don't know how large this fortress is or how far underground it burrows. They would need perhaps twenty earth mages for a large dwelling if they can be incapacitated after the spell. Forty, if they need to be able to run. But not knowing the size of the fortress would make the number required to level the entire place impossible to estimate, although with time one or two scouts nearby could figure it out. Also, most earth mages have never worked in unison before, so ideally sixty or more would be better. Not a small number of mages to move without anyone noticing, let alone through a mountain range. But I would point out that this task will grow infinitely easier in the chaos of war. There could be other reasons they have not yet tried to attack this place too. Perhaps you have something the Masters or the Kavanarian monarchy wants?"

"These Masters, how much power do they hold?" asked Warden Asten.

"They are the nobles who rule over the enslaved. And the craftsmen of these fine scars that I've acquired," Aven said, indicating his shoulder with a sarcastic grin. To her credit, Asten didn't gape, but Devol did.

"How do we know we can trust this information?" Dyon said.

Miara scowled but said nothing.

"We have our own Akarian mages," said the queen. "I sent for Elder Wunik when we sent for all of you. He is due to arrive here shortly. Unfortunately, two of our other mage elders could not be reached. Riders should return tomorrow from checking on them."

"How many mages?" Samul said brusquely. His father looked older than Aven remembered. It had only been a few days.

"My lord, my tasks as a spy revolved around eavesdropping and theft. These battle tactics are taught to us from books. Best practices for if we need them later. I did not train with the warriors myself, so I can't report on exact numbers. With a trained air mage's help, we may be able to get a better count. I can say that Mage Hall houses hundreds of mages. Perhaps five hundred would be forced into battle? All are bound to act however the Masters will them to, without question."

Another murmur swept through the group, one Aven did not understand.

"And these Masters answer to the king of Kavanar?" his father asked.

She thought for a moment. "They didn't seem to answer to him very well, honestly. They do, but I am not sure how loyal they are. They may have more power than him in many ways."

Samul frowned, thinking that over. "Perhaps this is why our courtly spies had nothing to report. The impetus comes from elsewhere."

Daes. The Dark Master, of course.

Before Aven could decide if he should mention the man or not, Miara continued, "There are warrior mages, more every day. But I was not allowed to be one. Had too much zest for battle, I was told."

"Too much zest? Isn't that exactly why you should become one?" Devol grumbled.

"Anything that comes naturally to me I have been told is quite evil, Master Devol. I've chosen not to believe that, but your opinion is up to you, of course." That earned more than a few grins, including Dyon's. Beneral's expression was thoughtful.

"Then you were just a spy?"

"Just?" Miara raised an elegant eyebrow, and Devol blustered an apology. "I'm sorry I don't know more. Most of the time, I was—am—a healer."

"Also an important wartime skill," Aven added. Miara looked like she wanted to point out she'd mostly been charged with healing *horses*, so he jumped in before she could undercut her expertise again. "And *that* is exactly why our first response must be to free more mages before we ride to war," Aven said.

Nearly everyone, including Miara, looked at him in surprise.

"Starting with warrior mages," he said. "We will bring them here, and they will tell us of their training and capabilities. Together, we'll figure out what the Masters are planning." Miara's half smile and the glint of amusement in her eyes were more than enough reward for the idea, even if the rest of them didn't go for it.

"I believe—as we've discussed—we should discuss our plans for response without any foreigners or *spies* present," said Dyon. "That is, of course, if your questions are answered, my lord." Samul nodded.

Miara pressed her lips together in restraint. "Please, believe me. I would rather give them a dagger in the shoulder blades than one word of your plans. But it's quite reasonable to be cautious. I would be. I will retire."

"I'll escort our guest," his mother offered, voice gentle. Aven's gut twisted at the idea of the two of them going off without him. What would his mother say—or do, for that matter? He wanted to groan but managed only to frown in concern as the two women left, leaving an empty place behind him at the table.

"Aven, explain your plan," his father said.

He nodded. "This mage army is not a willing force. If we can free them, they will have no loyalty to those that enslaved them. We can offer them safe haven—and hopefully they can offer us aid. With even a handful, I suspect we can eliminate this threat to our land while also righting the wrongs against them."

"But what can Kavanar be planning? How will they attack?" Asten asked.

"I think they want *us* to do the attacking. Drawing our forces into their lands gives them the advantage. We can get more information on all of these questions if we free the right mages. And if they can get out of Kavanar alive."

Lady Toyl cut in. "How can we be so sure of this mage threat? What if it was a trick? Or perhaps it was all a spell, an illusion?"

"I was branded, I was *tortured*. Do you not see these wounds?" He took a deep breath, trying to calm himself before he said something hasty. "Magic doesn't create illusions out of nothing, it influences the natural world. Unless they had armies of very intelligent rabbits they wanted to convince me are mage armies, that's not possible."

"Perhaps this is all just a ruse to distract from *our* discovery of your magic," Toyl countered, unswayed.

"I *told* you of my magic."

"Not until after Alikar had already learned of it and told us."

"Magic is not illegal in Akaria," Lord Dyon cut in. The fact that the usually critical Dyon was willing to defend Aven said something about the gravity of the situation. Or was it desperation?

"I am not trying to distract you," Aven insisted. "I don't know what I can say to convince you of the seriousness of this threat that I haven't already. I don't know who told Alikar, but it was always my plan to share it with you as soon as I arrived. Once I'd seen the threat we faced, I knew I had to act."

"And yet, you were comfortable deceiving us up until now," said Lady Toyl smoothly.

The air began to twitch and bluster around Aven, and out of long habit, he cleared his thoughts and forced the energy back down. But then, perhaps he shouldn't? He no longer needed to. Maybe it would be a good reminder to them all that magic was a real and powerful thing. For now he let the unnatural air currents fade. "I was *far* from comfortable. I've never wanted to be anything but a king to my people. You think I wanted this? You think I wanted to be born with something that could cost me all of it, something I have no control over?" That was giving away far more than he intended, and Aven's voice was more of a growl than he might have liked. Good thing Miara wasn't here to hear him say these things, but all this was a fresh reminder of the resentment, the frustration of so many years.

A quiet fell over the room, tense as a taut bowstring.

"I didn't ask for this magic. But for good or ill, I've got it. I choose to believe it's for a good reason. I choose to believe some good can come of it. I'm going to use it to help Akaria. *If* you'll let me."

Wind whistled outside. No one spoke.

Finally Toyl relented. "Of course, my lord," she said, giving him the slightest bow.

Dyon spoke up. "We must keep unity. Alikar said word came from Kavanar. Who would have information on Aven's magic but those who kidnapped him? They know he escaped. They know their plan failed. This is a blatant attempt to sow discord among us. We must not let them succeed."

Suspicion coiled in Aven's mind at those words. Could this *always* have been their plan? Not to send him back and out him as a mage—but to sow discord? That had to be it. Kidnapping him, killing him, those may have served their secondary concern over star magic, as Daes had revealed. But they hadn't been sure he had it. In fact, when Miara had begun her journey toward Estun, Aven had not yet received the star map from Teron. Their plans revolved less around keeping Aven in particular off the throne and more around weakening Akaria as a whole.

And when Akaria was divided, attacking mage forces would have that much of an easier time, as would traditional forces, for that matter.

Dyon continued, "The last thing they'll expect is our restraint. We can't play right into their hands. They want us to make a hasty move, a mistake."

"Fair points," said Asten. "We can begin mobilizing units on the Takaran side, like mine in Shansaren. Start moving them west, so they'll be ready. This cannot be ignored," Asten said. "They must be punished for this."

"It won't be ignored." His father straightened and folded his arms across his chest. "But we will be more cunning than an immediate blind march on the capital, Evrical." The warden gave a crisp nod of agreement. "Asten, work with Devol and Dyon and any generals we have visiting. Let's plan out some options. And do not share these plans with Alikar at any time."

"My lord?"

"Plan as though Gilaren may be friendly to Kavanar."

Murmurs swept through the group. But Aven nodded. His father was right. Alikar hadn't quite said as much, but the risk was high.

Samul continued, "I want you and your lieutenants updating our plans of attack on Kavanar. I want strategies for the capital as well as Sapana." Asten gave another crisp nod.

"And the mage compound?" Aven added.

"Yes. Mark it on the map, if by some awful chance

it's not there already."

"It's not."

Samul shook his head. "We have no one to blame but ourselves. Ojir, it can't hurt to start working on those siege upgrades. Beneral, let's talk more about those rumors you've heard. I'm interested to see what else we can find out beyond Aven's endeavor to weaken our enemy forces. Which you'll be moving forward with, correct, Aven?"

Aven nodded briskly. "Yes, sire."

"Also, arrange us a… demonstration, let's call it. Let's have the doubters among us see for themselves what magic can do. And I personally would like to understand its capabilities for war better. But first, let us recuperate from our journeys and celebrate our prince's return with a sunset feast in his honor. And Aven—one more word with you, please. You have a visitor."

# 2    Rumors & Agendas

Miara followed the steward and Aven's mother down the stretching hallways. Great arching stone rose more than the height of two men above them. A florid, geometric pattern formed by the arches fascinated her as they walked, and she almost forgot to keep track of their turns. Almost.

She felt safer here than she had in a long time. Safer because she was far from the Masters and because she had a powerful ally here for once in her life.

More than an ally, even.

But it was also a strange place full of unknowns. She, too, was Aven's ally, and to be a good one, she could not have her head in the clouds. Or the fancy arches.

"Fayton, what room do you think?" Aven's mother Elise spoke to the steward. Fayton wore a midnight-blue tunic, the faintest trace of a bear embroidered on the back in just a slightly lighter color. Elise herself wore a gown of bright morning-glory blue that looked simple on the surface, but the cut and flow of it made Miara suspect it was far from a common garment.

The steward led them around a right corner. "I was planning on the far east one back here, my lady. The one with three windows." Were windows so rare here that rooms could be identified by the number they possessed?

Elise smiled very slightly and nodded. All of the queen's movements were calm, restrained, as though it would take much to move her.

They turned right and stopped finally at a far door on their left. Which direction was the mountainside this far in? Had they gone halfway through, or were they facing the other side of the mountain now? She had no idea.

She relinquished her small pack to Fayton at his insistence. She did not have much to settle, but Fayton made a show of helping her settle it anyway. As he went, and she tried not to feel awkward about him touching or moving any of her meager belongings, she wandered around the room. She and Elise had been led into a sitting room with a great stone hearth, bears reared on their haunches carved into the stone of each side. A writing desk appeared stocked with supplies, and a table and chairs awaited meals. The next room revealed a large curtained bed drowning in navy velvet, another large fireplace, and two of the three fabled windows. Beyond the bed, she found another small room and the remaining window. A bathing pool large enough for a person—or two?—took up most of the small room. Some kind of small floor hearth sat under the pool.

"What is this for, Fayton?" she asked, as he seemed

hopeful she would ask him questions.

"Oh, for heating the bath from beneath with coals from the fire. Most comfortable."

"Such luxury," Miara breathed. Too much. How could she accept this when her father and Luha were still trapped in the Masters' clutches? An ache grew in her chest at the thought of them. So many mages remained enslaved. Was she supposed to relax and just not think about all of them? No, she couldn't accept this.

She stepped back out into the regal bedroom. Elise spoke to a servant out of earshot, near the outer door, ordering some food and tea. "I don't deserve this, Fayton. I can't. Don't you have someone important who needs this room?"

Fayton smiled reassuringly. "All the baths in Estun have these hearths. While a great luxury in general, this hold is well appointed in more than its security. Don't let it disturb you."

She wasn't buying it. "So, is this an average room for Estun then?"

"Well, there *are* three windows."

"I don't want any special treatment. I'm no different than you."

"I'm quite sure you are different from me in at least two ways."

"Such as?"

"I am not a mage, and I have no royal heirs in love with me."

She coughed, trying to cover her surprise. They had

barely arrived. How did he know so much? "You are… quite observant."

"I've been told that a few times. I also respect the prince very much."

"How many windows does Aven's room have?" she said. "I mean, the prince's?"

His smile broadened. "One."

"I don't need this," she said, rushing toward him and keeping her voice low. She laid a hand on his arm. "Like I said, you can save this room for someone important."

"I am quite sure *you* are very important, my lady." The ease and confidence in his voice drove her a step back in shock and almost made her believe him.

"I'm no lady."

"But you *will* be, won't you?" he said. She blinked, entirely unsure how to respond to him. His eyes twinkled. "I know our prince very well, I've served him since he was a child. But never mind. You would prefer me to use Miara then?" How had he learned her name so quickly? And… everything else? Perhaps as head steward, that was his job. Miara followed Fayton back out to the main room. He appeared to be done settling her or refreshing her room or whatever he'd been doing. "Is there anything you need me to acquire, my lady… Miara?" he said with a crisp bow.

"Oh—uh, no—I have everything I need."

Elise was settled on a nearby bench, staring into space, when she perked up at that comment. "You can ask for *anything* you need from Fayton, Miara." She paused, searching Miara's face. "It's not an imposition. You're our guest. We have vast stores here; Estun can be self-sufficient for several months—"

"I read as much in my research," Miara replied.

Elise gave her a crooked smile. "You have an uncanny way of reminding me that you were until recently my greatest enemy in the world."

Miara swallowed, eyes wide. She'd asked for that. "Don't forget high treason. I should really have worse accommodations. Perhaps the dungeon?"

Elise snorted. "Anyone actually interested in committing the wrongs you mention would have followed through on them more effectively instead of politely escorting their target back home. Now, please. Give Fayton something to do. He gets bored, and visitors bring all the unusual tasks and breaks from the mundane."

Fayton looked far from offended at this and only grinned.

Miara hesitated a moment longer. "Well, a change of clothes would help. I guess I don't need to wear the same riding leathers every single day."

Fayton looked to Elise with a knowing expression, and the queen nodded. What knowledge were they exchanging? "Perhaps water for a bath too?" Elise offered.

Miara's eyes widened. Oh gods, did she smell? Great. She'd be remembered by all the Akarian Assembly and the queen as that dirty mage slave who smelled.

Well. No. Slave no longer. Who cared if she were dirty or smelly or a mage or a garden snake?

She was free.

"I'll have the water sent up." And with that, Fayton was gone.

Silence settled over the sitting room, and Miara pretended to stroll around and explore and admire the room, but mostly she did not know what to do next. Being stranded alone with Aven's mother so quickly after arriving in Estun was... not what she'd expected. And she had no idea what to do or say next.

"Come, have a seat with me, Miara. I'm sure Aven will join us before the tea even arrives."

With no reason to object and no non-embarrassing excuse to flee screaming in fear, she sat down next to the queen by the fire. Elise's golden curls danced in the firelight. Miara's own hair was probably wayward and falling out of its bun. A thin silver necklace draped across the queen's sculpted collarbones, dangling an emerald that sparkled and taunted Miara with its effortless grace.

Miara glanced down at herself. Her Masters-issued leathers were a brownish-black, a combination of their original dye and the dirt of wear. Her boots were still caked with mud from the roads to Estun. Her most beautiful adornment, in her opinion, was her dagger. She'd never worn dresses or jewelry the likes of what Elise probably had. Why would she have? She'd had no reason to, nor the means to acquire them if she'd desired them.

But would Akarians be happy with a leather-clad, muddy queen with a dagger in her boot? Would they want a queen who wore boots at all?

She had no idea. But she felt worlds apart from Elise

just then. The queen's shoulders and neck were bare and elegant in the dress, the skin of a woman two decades her superior—at least—lined and softened with age but all the more distinguished for it.

Miara couldn't imagine herself looking that regal or elegant at any age. She would always have the scar from the brand on her shoulder. She was unsure if it had fully healed, or if it ever would. She could perhaps heal it, although she wondered if the magic that had created it would change the rules somehow. No matter, she had no desire to heal it, really. Like the scar on her cheek, smoothing it away felt false. She didn't want to erase her past, nor could she.

"He risked everything for you," Elise said, cutting through her thoughts matter-of-factly.

Miara froze, more unsure than ever. It was not a feeling she liked.

"All of this," Elise said, gesturing up and around them.

"I tried to convince him otherwise."

"As did I," Elise said. Her voice was slow, steady. Miara suspected the queen wanted to watch her squirm a little. But for what purpose?

"The risk he took was not lost on me. And seeing this doesn't make it any easier."

"He's quite in love with you, you know."

Miara dodged Elise's gaze by staring into the fire.

"Of course, it seems we were wrong to discourage him, and he was right."

What could Miara possibly say to that? She struggled

but thought of nothing.

"I'd like to know your intentions toward him, if any," Elise said simply.

"My what?"

"Your intentions."

"I have no right to any intent—"

"This is not Kavanar," Elise said, waving away the idea like an annoying insect. "I am not concerned if you have a 'right.' As far as I'm concerned, you do. I have heard my son's words, seen his determination. His feelings for you are strong. What I am concerned with are your feelings toward him."

How could Miara possibly respond to this? She opened her mouth, but no words came out.

"Do you return his sentiments?" Elise said, her voice gentler.

Miara stared at her boots. Why was Elise asking her this? Why was this so hard to discuss? Did she simply want to see Miara's face as she answered the question?

Yes, that must be it. The queen wanted to judge Miara's sincerity for herself.

"Very much so, yes." She tried to keep her breath above a whisper but only barely succeeded.

Elise nodded curtly, the gesture ambiguous. "Forgive me for being so direct. We have very little time. How these people come to know you will be established only once. We must carefully manage the situation if you are to be queen."

"Queen?" My, this woman was frank. Perhaps that

was where Aven got it from. Miara finally met Elise's intense stare.

"You know Aven's wife could be nothing else."

True, but she was not sure how she felt about the situation. Her feelings for Aven were not something she could push away or pretend didn't exist. That hadn't worked very well the first time anyway, had it? Not that she *wanted* to push them away now either. But… she had never imagined herself as anything like a queen. She was a horse healer, by the gods. Still, if Aven asked her to be his companion in this, as in all things, she also couldn't imagine saying no to him.

This was all too much to share with his mother just yet. Perhaps ever. She wasn't even sure how to share it with *Aven*. "You have no… personal objections?" she said instead.

Elise paused. "I know my son," she said eventually. "He is an excellent judge of character. That is one thing I would never doubt in him. I also want him to be happy. What objections would I have? You are no noble, that's true, but you are intelligent, strong, defiant even. You showed me honesty at times when lies would have been much more convenient. And you are no fragile bird in a gilded cage. You know the suffering of the people. You know the impact a ruler's decisions can have."

"Then why did you take so long to answer?"

"So that you didn't think I took this lightly."

A smile crept onto Miara's face. Elise smiled back, a smile of small secrets, the kind between two people recognizing something of themselves in each other. They were both the kind of people that managed what others thought of them, deliberately, with elaborate planning if necessary.

"A capable and reliable partner has always been one of the things Aven most wanted in a wife. And he's wise for that. And I think you will offer more than one unexpected advantage of your own. No, you needn't be concerned about me. What I am concerned about—and you should be too—is everyone else. The king… has not seen or heard as much of you as I have. And there are those who might care less for Aven's personal happiness or the caretaking of this kingdom and quite a bit more for their own agendas and prejudices."

Miara opened her mouth to ask what advantage, and what did she mean by that, and who exactly might she be referring to? But a knock sounded at the door, announcing the arrival of the tea.

"Ah, Camil," Elise called. "Come in. Miara, I'm sure you're famished from your journey. We have apple dumplings, Corovan cheese, and some excellent Pyoramwan tea."

The king's meeting chamber emptied of people all too slowly. Exhaustion hit Aven, hard and sudden, now that the drama was mostly over. For now. He hoped. He didn't yet know what visitor his father referred to, so perhaps more trouble was in store. Also, what were his mother and Miara doing? What room had Fayton assigned her? Not knowing exactly where she was yet again did not sit well with him, especially twice so quickly after arriving in Estun. Had they even been there an hour yet?

The last few stragglers hesitated and were shooed away by two of his father's scribes.

"Do you think she'll try to kill her?" Aven mused.

"Your friend kill the queen? I should—"

"No, no, *Mother*. Mother kill my… friend."

His father grinned at his hesitation. "Your mother has watched you, mostly helplessly, traipse across half the continent with this woman and then risk your very life to save her. I'm not surprised she's interested in a conversation or two."

"I just hope that's all she's interested in."

"Your mother has never had a violent streak. I swear some of the lords wish she had more of one. And your 'friend' is a competent mage. Probably more competent than your mother, don't you think?"

"Don't tell Mother that."

"I'm sure you'll have nothing to worry about even if they do come to blows."

"Probably more like claws or talons, from what I've seen."

"That does sound a bit more your mother's style. At any rate, now that we're alone, there is one bit of news you won't relish." Aven inclined his head in question. "Another suitor arrived for you yesterday."

"I don't need a suitor, I have—"

"I understand that. But your mother and I had thought

you might want to take a little time before you crown your new mage as queen."

Aven frowned. "Well, obviously Mother is queen—"

"You know what I meant."

His blood ran cold. "What's the hesitation?"

"Miara is an outsider. Not to mention technically someone who recently committed high treason."

"That's hardly a fair way to describe what happened."

His father held up a palm. "Let's deal with this suitor first. I simply request you receive her in a polite, diplomatic greeting. You can leave right away, since you've just returned, but the Code calls for—"

"I know what it calls for," Aven growled. He sighed. If his principles were easy to live by, they probably weren't doing him much good. "Where does she hail from?"

As they walked, his father gave him background on the woman, a minor noble from Esengard. She had been deliberately kept in the dark about his return to the castle. Enough turmoil without that. They found her in the library, reclined and reading a book.

Did Miara like to read? At least this one was literate. He stifled an inward groan at the thought. Why was he evaluating her? He had Miara.

The woman rose with slow, regal grace as they approached. His father spoke first. "My son, may I present to you Renala Lorava, Dvora of the southern lands of Esengard."

"King Samul, Prince Aven. I'm flattered to see you so soon upon your return." As she spoke, she swept into a low curtsy. Aven bowed in return. He realized too late that he hadn't reached for her hand to kiss as he usually did. Thankfully, she didn't seem to have expected it. Just as well—too romantic of a greeting anyway. He had to take every opportunity to come across as taken, something he unfortunately had zero practice at conveying.

She straightened. Oaken hair, the color of straw but slightly darker, fell down her back, and a lavender dress hugged her every curve perfectly with carefully orchestrated rows of laces to ensure an ideal fit. How did women get such things on? He should ask Miara.

Actually, did she know? Had she ever worn such a dress? They did not look practical for either caring for horses or kidnapping men. Perhaps her spying had sometimes been in a courtly context, though? Back to the task at hand. It was his turn to say something.

"I'm flattered by your consideration, my lady." Ugh, too amorous. He stifled a wince and hoped she hadn't noticed.

"Have you had a long journey?" She clasped her hands in front, still holding her book.

"Er, yes." Two weeks was not terribly long, but getting kidnapped, tortured, and nearly enslaved twice did add difficulty to a jaunt. He didn't think she was interested in hearing stories of torture just now. Or possibly ever. Good thing he had Miara to tell them to. "It was a bit... hastily undertaken, so that didn't help matters. So please forgive me if I retire shortly."

"Oh, of course," she said, suddenly blushing. A delicate rose spread across her features. Afraid she was imposing already? That was sweet. It was hardly her fault, and there was no perceived slight, but he'd been courted by plenty of women who blindly demanded his attention and time without context, as if finding a mate and producing an heir obviously trumped any other task in importance. And perhaps in some circles that was the case, but not for him. A lady that was more respectful of a prince's other duties was refreshing.

Not that it mattered or changed anything.

She eyed his shoulder. "Forgive my intrusion," she said quietly, "but were you in battle, my lord? You look… injured." Her eyes held a mixture of fear and intrigue. My, she was a timid one, but the interest in her eyes said perhaps there was more to her than that surface fear.

"We do not shy away from battle here," he said, skirting her question. "Perhaps that is part of why you've chosen Akaria to visit?"

Her gaze snapped to meet his in surprise, and her face told the truth of his words. "I—uh—I apologize, my lord."

"What is there to apologize for?" his father said.

"As a lady, I should not express interest in such things."

"Nonsense. Women draw sword here just as the men do." His tone was more fatherly than kingly as he smiled at her.

The way she side-eyed the king levelly told Aven she had indeed already known this. "I had heard, but I thought perhaps it was only a rumor."

Aven shrugged. "We're a practical people. The more of us that can fight, the better, which is especially true in matters of defense. Of course, not everyone is fit for every weapon or every military position, but that's true beyond men and women, young and old."

"Never saw much reason to encourage my wife to cower in fear rather than pick up a bow if I'm the one getting attacked by the sword. And in that case, I'd prefer her aim to be good." Samul smiled. Aven agreed; he had no idea why other kingdoms hobbled themselves so. Perhaps Renala couldn't lift a claymore, but there were plenty of weapons he'd be glad she could wield if assassins chose that moment to strike. Assuming she was on his side, of course.

"Devol, our master at arms, would likely give you a lesson during your visit, if desired, my lady," Aven added.

She gazed off into the bookshelves with a pained expression. "I don't think my brothers would approve."

Samul surprised Aven—and Renala, too, it seemed— with a rough clap on her shoulder. "They are not here, I believe. And I don't know *how* word would get back to them. Don't they plan to marry you away from Esengard anyway? So… perhaps their opinion does not matter so much." Oh, devious man, sowing familial discord. Of course, Aven agreed with him, but still. Aven smiled sideways at the wide saucers of Renala's eyes. Was that at the shoulder clap or his suggestion? A timid mouse, as many suitors had been, but at least an honest one with her own opinions. "Talk with our head steward, Fayton, he can help you arrange it. And now, if you'll excuse my son, I don't want his sense of duty to keep him any longer."

"Of course!" She curtsied deeply again, so much so that he thought she might just sit down on the bench behind her.

At this point, he would have usually made some romantic gesture, or made plans to seek her out later, or offered some poetic turn of phrase. But gladly, no inspiration came to him. Aven simply bowed again, gave her a small but friendly smile, and scampered out.

Jaena missed the blast with her staff. Her body spun sideways, off-balance, and she cursed as she went down. She'd blocked the last dozen, but one had finally gotten through. Damn.

Face in the dirt. Hell. *That* would be the last time. She let herself indulge in the soft vibrations of energy emanating from the soil for just a brief moment. Just to recharge. Not that she needed it. She wasn't tired. She was fine.

She sighed. Her sister would not have fallen. She had rarely made mistakes like these. But then again, Dekana had been a natural at everything. Jaena was not much like her in that respect.

It didn't matter. She had determination and little else. She would be a great fighter or die trying. *Someone* would pay for what had happened to Dekana.

She spread her fingers as though readying to push herself up, only slightly nestling them into the calm reassurance of the soil. The bark-colored, packed earth of the training grounds had more clay than most, leaving it not quite as dark as her skin, but close.

Steps approached. She scrambled to her feet but not fast enough. She adjusted her tawny leather vest and the white tunic underneath, brushing off the dust with her fingers. Much as she loved the earth, she didn't love it on her outfit. Sorin, their teacher, stopped in front of her. Wherever he'd been a few days ago, he'd returned with a fire under his arse. She straightened to her full height and looked down her nose at him. Although he was tall, she was still a good two fingers taller.

"Back at it, Farsai."

He turned on a heel and stalked away. She scowled after him. Ignorant bastard. He liked to throw around epithets, a pathetic attempt at intimidation that only proved what an idiot he was. She wasn't even from Farsa. If he actually listened to a word she said, he would hear no accent. But she wasn't holding her breath for that to happen.

Kae gave her a sheepish shrug and mouthed a silent "Sorry." At least she had him as proof that not all pallid, blond men were like Sorin. She waved off his concern. He was just doing his job. After dozens of practice blasts, she was bound to miss one or two. And how would she get better if he didn't push her? If it were a real battle, those one or two blasts could be deadly.

It was good to have goals. Like revenge. And not missing another volley for the rest of the day. And maybe deflecting one at Sorin's backside.

Kae had far less interest in buffeting her with blasts of energy than she had in deflecting them. At least for her it was a practical skill. Earth mages did not take so easily to combat as air mages like Kae. If they took to it at all. But she would. She had to.

"Again," barked Sorin. He was pacing up and down the rows of practicing mages, observing and "correcting" but mostly just being a nuisance.

She placed one hand on the staff two handbreadths above the other, sunk down into horse stance, and held the weapon straight in a plumb line to the earth, listening for its rhythm, making the connection as quickly and instinctively as possible. This wasn't just any staff, but one spelled to defend against air attacks in particular, or else she couldn't have managed. Fortunately, there was little disadvantage to relying on a weapon beyond the fact that you could lose it.

Supposedly they would also learn how to fight back eventually. Every morning she hoped that was the day, but they hadn't gotten to it yet. If they ever would.

Kae sent another wave of energy, a shock of lightning this time, and this one she managed to capture and channel down into the welcoming earth in spite of her wandering thoughts. Good. It was becoming more automatic.

Sorin had reached the far end of the mages, as far out of earshot as he would get, and Kae seemed to be waiting for him to do so, eying their teacher over his shoulder every few moments. "Have you heard the rumors?" He cupped his hand and kept his voice low, otherwise putting all his body language into readying another blast.

"What?" The next wave hit. The gentler gust of wind sent her a little off-balance to the left, but she worked with it, spinning a little and righting herself quickly. Back in position.

"I'll take that as a no." Kae eyed Sorin's position again, hesitating. "Rumor is a mage escaped." Her eyes widened, and he grinned. "See, I thought you'd like that. Was surprised you wasn't the one telling me." Kae, unlike her, *did* have an accent, some kind of backcountry farm dialect. Refreshing, when those who talked like her mostly had nothing nice to say.

Len, a mage to his left, shot him a dangerous look. "Don't go spreading lies, Kae."

"No lie, if it's true."

"You don't know that."

"How you think they could do such a thing?"

Len shrugged, sending his next volley at his earth mage partner to Jaena's left. "It matters not."

"But—" Kae started, but Sorin turned and was making his way back down the row, one eyebrow raised. Kae shut up.

Escaped? How strange. Everyone knew such a thing was impossible.

Wasn't it?

She shoved a surge of hope back down. It was probably all foolish, childish rumors. Lies. Kids not knowing any better, not understanding how the lure of hope could crush your spirit each time you discovered afresh that you had absolutely no hope of escape. It was all foolish and impossible.

In the tense silence that followed, she struggled to keep her thoughts on Kae's attempts—thankfully all failures—to knock her on her ass. But his words niggled at her, as he'd probably known they would.

Jaena would never get used to being a slave. She didn't know how anyone did, but some seemed to. Or perhaps they just got tired.

Well, she was not tired yet. Especially not after watching the way their capture had crushed her sister, until she could no longer stand it. Until she'd thrown herself from the north tower—or someone had pushed her. Supposedly mage slaves weren't supposed to be able to kill themselves. But Dekana had been physically stronger than most men Jaena knew. Inside, though… Jaena did not believe it had been anything but despair that had killed her sister.

Three years ago, the two of them had been kidnapped and brought here. As daughters of a Hepani diplomat, they hadn't been nobles in Hepan and had been obligated to political marriages on their family's behalf. But Jaena had counted such a fate lucky by most Hepani standards. Her marriage would likely have been more advantageous for her than for her husband. Many nobles tended to choose brides from the diplomatic and merchant class. She'd also harbored a hope that perhaps she could avoid marriage. It happened once in a while.

Poor Hepani women often remained unmarried but also had the least resources to take advantage of such a state. As someone near the middle of the social hierarchy, as the younger sibling, she'd had the most chance at carving out something for herself between the lines of Hepani society. She'd plotted to dodge a husband and become a merchant, open a shop of some kind. Stones, to be honest, she had wanted to sell stones. Precious as emeralds and opals or common as quartz and hematite. In hindsight, her fixation on stones made sense, but she hadn't thought much of it at the time. It hurt to remember the dream, partly because of its innocence. Her most likely destiny, a political marriage, had not seemed so bad. Perhaps an intellectual merchant from southern Akaria who could sweep her off to the White City, or a daring Takaran seafarer who'd be away half the year anyway?

She had accepted that her family's position and her father's determined machinations would limit her, but she had still thought it likely she'd have some hand in her fate. She had still had hope.

She could never have imagined this.

It had all ended abruptly. Her family had been attacked on the road by those damned Devoted, and she'd found herself here. A slave. Sometimes a serving girl, sometimes a blacksmith's assistant. Perhaps a warrior, if she responded to their training. The Masters would see. The Masters would determine. She hadn't even known that she and her sister were mages. She didn't regret learning of her power, but it had not been worth the cost. She'd trade her magic for her freedom in a heartbeat.

Even more, she would trade any and all of it to have

her sister back.

Still. Escape? Was such a thing really possible? If only it had come in time for Dekana. But… Jaena could get revenge much more easily if she were free.

When Sorin reached the far end of the row, she caught Kae's eye. "We should find out if those rumors are true."

"Impossible," grunted Len.

"How?" Kae smiled and lifted his chin in challenge.

"Maybe the mages at the gate. Maybe they saw someone go in or out. Or the healers. Or maybe Menaha has heard something."

He rubbed his chin. "And there's why I tell you this stuff."

"We'll find her at dinner," she decided with a nod, and he nodded grimly in reply.

A messenger darted up and handed Sorin a note. He quickly glanced over it. "I'm called on another mission. Continue practice until the third bell rings, then you may be dismissed." He strode away, a new self-important bounce in his step.

She rolled her eyes. Please. Fortunately for them, Sorin didn't hold the power to compel them like the Masters did. As soon as the bastard was out of sight, they'd be off, and he couldn't do a damn thing about it.

"We need to talk," his mother said once Aven and his father arrived in Miara's rooms.

"So I hear." Aven settled down in an armchair by

the hearth. Oh, by all the gods and ancestors. He had missed such luxuries as cushions. His father moved to lean against the warm carved stone.

Aven glanced with concern at Miara, who pointed furtively at a nearby table. A whole tray of six apple dumplings sat waiting. He leapt to his feet, snatched one, and took a huge bite before returning to them.

Gods. He hadn't been sure he'd ever taste this again.

"I don't know how to go about this delicately," his mother said, "so let's have out with it. Your father and I don't think you should share the news of your relationship publicly just yet." Elise set a cup of tea on his end table. Was there a touch of apology to the gesture, or was he imagining it?

Aven glared from one parent to the other while he chewed on another overlarge bite. "Because of this dvora?"

"Dvora?" Miara asked.

Elise stood and began pacing in front of the hearth, arms folded across her chest. "No, not because of her." She waved her hand irritably, as though shooing away a fly. She turned to Miara. "A suitor arrived yesterday for Aven, a minor noble from Esengard. Dvora is her title, like a lord. Not to worry, though, because Aven is expert in finding fault and repelling potential suitors."

"And also because I'm rather partial to *you* and not her," he added gruffly. Miara smiled back at his consternation.

"Not because of our new visitor," his mother said.

"Why then?" Aven demanded, voice colder now.

"Because right now, Miara is seen by many to be

foreign, first of all," his father said. "The enemy. All they know about her is that she's a mage. From Kavanar, our greatest enemy. Who just began a war with us by kidnapping you."

"By having *me* in particular do the kidnapping, although we've skipped over that part," Miara added.

"I think high treason is easily forgiven for saving the prince's life, don't you think, Mother?" Aven said.

Elise snorted. "I would tend to agree, if your father is amiable too." She inclined her head at her husband, and he gave a rough nod, but not without a slight hesitation.

"There *is* that matter," Samul said. "I will document a formal pardon, even if we don't share it publicly, in case that story becomes more widely known. But she is still not one of us. Yet."

Aven scowled at his father. Miara raised her eyebrows.

"We're not saying you can't be together," his mother added quickly. "I'm just saying we're all going to have to work for it. We need to manage this situation and control how and to whom we reveal what."

"No. Secrets are what got us into this mess." Aven sat forward in his chair, relaxation gone.

"All governments have secrets," his father snapped. "You know this."

"Fine, fine. But this is foolish. We can't treat her like an outsider. We need to involve her in our planning. She has the best information on our enemies we are going to get. She should be working with Dyon and Asten and—"

"It is much too soon for that," his father shot back.

"We don't have time for everyone to play until they make friends. Kavanar is going to act, and they're going to act soon. We need to present a strong and united front, and not—"

"If I have to give you an order to do this, I will." Samul shifted from his more casual pose leaning against the stone to standing, shoulders squared as he faced Aven.

Aven gritted his teeth. "A week."

"A *month*. At least."

"We don't have that kind of—"

"We should see how long we need," his mother cut in smoothly. "You've only just arrived. Miara needs to earn a place in Akarian society that people respect and admire. She needs to define herself to them as someone they know and could imagine being loyal to, not just a Kavanarian spy. That may take more than a month."

He turned a frustrated gaze to Miara, hoping for some support, some clever reason why they definitely shouldn't do this. "How do you feel about this?"

She shrugged, although she looked paler than before. "You are all better judges of the political situation than I am. I can see the logic behind allowing me to establish myself more here as an individual. Also, people might think dark magic is afoot, even if magic can't do that. Or some might worry I've tricked you or manipulated you through some other nonmagical means."

The way his father frowned at Miara as she spoke suggested the king might actually share some of those concerns. Aven stifled a groan.

He hated this idea. Hated it. And with this newly arrived dvora blushing and batting her eyelashes at the same time? Bloody hell. His shoulders were tightening into knots already.

"Fine, one month," he grunted.

"We'll see," the king said.

"But we *need* Miara's knowledge of magic and of Kavanar. It will make a decisive difference in this war. You cannot just relegate her to drinking tea with irrelevant diplomats and advisors."

"I'll discuss it with Warden Asten and Lord Dyon."

See that you do, Aven wanted to snap. But nobody talked to King Samul that way, not even his sons. A different part of him wanted to respond with more deference and say thank you, Father, I'd appreciate that, you're right about all this, as he knew was probably appropriate. But mostly he just wanted to yell. To turn away her knowledge and abilities while forming their plans was pure politics and hubris, the same hubris that had left them so unprepared against the mage threat in the first place. Apparently no one had learned their lesson yet, except maybe him.

Aven sat, eyes locked with his father's for one moment, then another, as he struggled with a response until part of him won out.

"Thank you, Father. Of course. Whatever you think."

The king gave a nod to each of them and left, but Aven wasn't watching. He stared off into the fire.

Shortly after, his mother left them too. Aven moved

from the armchair to beside Miara on the couch. Servants wandered about. They would find no end of chores to complete as long as he stayed in Miara's rooms. Their errands were only an excuse to not leave Aven and Miara alone. Which was just as well, much as he didn't like it.

It would help him stick with his... decision.

She leaned her elbows on her forearms and stared into the fire, which lit her features in a soft, familiar light. He had studied the profile of her face for many an hour, and yet he had no desire to stop any time soon. The jagged scar from the wolf attack on her cheek still felt new and made her no less beautiful. In fact, it lent a certain wildness to her that made his heart beat faster. She had removed her cloak but still wore her leathers.

"Well, that was... interesting. Do you think that meeting went well? What did I miss?" She straightened and scooted closer to him as she spoke. Her thigh came to rest gently against his, and he found himself staring at his knee, a new tension coiling inside him.

"It could have been worse," he said. "Lord Alikar did call for an Assembly meeting to vote on my place as heir. Called for Thel to be king."

She raised her eyebrows. "That was the bit at the beginning, wasn't it? When that sour-faced fellow stormed out. What exactly does that mean?"

"Wait—what did Thel want? I didn't even see him pull you out of the room."

"Oh, he wanted to know if he is a mage."

And he hadn't chosen to ask Mother? Of course, she

had long refused to answer the question, but certainly now things would be different. "And? Is he?"

"Oh, very much so, yes."

The wave of relief that washed over Aven was more intense than he would have expected. At least that was one less thing to worry about.

"You're glad to hear it?"

He nodded. "Back to your question. Alikar's call for an Assembly meeting doesn't mean much by the letter of the law. The king is still the king. He chooses his heir. However, the Assembly can voice their opinion on something, if they desire. And they occasionally do so via a formal vote when it is a serious matter."

"Their… opinion? What happens if their opinion is against you?"

"Nothing specific. They can vote on whether they support the king's choice of heir, but they have no power to make him change anything. But politics is all subtleties. Our united military holds the kingdom together. The territories *fund* the army, as well as similar parts of government. My father *could* ignore them and do whatever he pleased. They could also 'misplace' their next gold shipments or 'forget' to send forces into the battle. Or a lot worse. Of course, he could then later refuse to defend them in their time of need."

She leaned against the couch beside him now, and her shoulder touched his. Hmm. Was putting his arm around her in front of these servants breaking his promise to his mother? If they'd been listening, had she sworn them to secrecy already anyway? No, that'd be unreliable, if not ineffective. He hadn't seen any of them nearby while they'd talked, so perhaps she'd sent them out.

Still, he wanted to do more than let his shoulder brush hers. Hmm.

"What could be worse than 'forgetting' to send troops? That sounds like a pretty low blow."

"They could start an all-out civil war."

She winced. "I hope it doesn't come to that."

"There are six of them. Imagine half vote in support of me and half vote against."

"Are you saying you think civil war is likely?"

"I have no idea."

"Any guesses as to how they will vote?" She bent down to unlace and remove her boots as she spoke, and he watched with too much intensity as her fingers deftly loosened the laces. She didn't seem to notice.

What was her question again? Oh, yes. "I'd wager Dyon would support us. My father, of course has a vote. Warden Asten is exceedingly fair, part of the reason she won her seat as Assembly member, and so I'm sure she will consider all sides. Not sure what she will do. I'm hoping she'll come to the same conclusion as I did with enough information."

Miara nodded. "What of the others?"

"Alikar and Sven are sure to vote against me, both having religious objections in various ways. Beneral—well, he's a mage. He may not be letting anyone know yet, but if he voted against me..."

"He still could," she reminded him.

"Indeed. But we could out him as a mage and he could risk losing his seat, for either that or hypocrisy. But it seems unlike him anyway."

"Who does that leave?"

"Lady Toyl. She's a merchant like Beneral and primarily concerned with stability, I'd say. As many are."

"Hmm, but which way is more stable? Why not keep the heir you've always had, the one the king prefers?"

"The heir who's suddenly developed potentially evil magic powers and out of nowhere declares we're in the middle of a war no one can see?"

She snorted and put a hand on his knee casually. "And what's the alternative—civil war?"

"War if you do, war if you don't, I guess." Trying to act just as casually but feeling far from it, he slid his hand over hers, caressing the surprisingly soft skin, her knuckles, down the lines of her fingers. Gestures he hoped those bustling servants wouldn't notice.

Maybe. He didn't care. They sat in silence for a while, her hand still on his knee as he gently stroked the back of her hand.

She cleared her throat, as if her voice might be rough. "Perhaps if they think one of your brothers can take over, that seems a possible easy path to peace?"

"There is no possible path with Kavanar knocking on the door."

"Yes, but how do we show them that?"

"I don't know. I don't want to wait till they knock

loud enough for everyone to hear them."

"You're trying to tell them. Most of them seemed to be listening."

"We have to show them what magic can do. As my father said, we need some kind of demonstration."

She nodded. "What are you going to do?"

"Well, I was going to ask you the same thing." He smiled.

"Me? Why me?" She pulled her hand away and placed it over her chest as if he were accusing her of something.

He fought the urge to say whatever would get her to place her hand on his knee again. "You're the best we have. I want you to do the demonstration."

"No. You're the Akarian. They won't trust me."

"They'll trust what they see. And me being the Akarian is exactly the problem. I want them to see me for who I've always been, just a little improved. Standing up in front of them and shooting fire from my fingertips isn't exactly going to help that image."

She snorted. "You can't do that yet anyway."

"They don't need to know that, as you so astutely pointed out. But that's another part of the problem with me. I'm not very good."

"Good enough to break the spell to free me. No one in the world knows how to do that, other than you."

He waved it off. "That's just being clever. You're better. You'll show them the real danger they face."

She ran a hand over her face. "I don't want them to see *me* as a danger either." She glanced at the door, likely thinking of his parents.

"They already see you as a danger. Not sure we can change that. And magic *is* dangerous. That's precisely the point."

"But is this how we win them over?" she said gently. "I don't want to… keep this hidden forever."

His chest ached at the worry in her voice. "Well, you're a danger, but on their side? Offering to help? A danger to Kavanar, not Akaria. Maybe we can find some way to emphasize that we're all fighting the same enemy here. They respect strong and capable fighters, remember? Either way, I'm sure your natural charisma and beauty will easily win them over, even as you change them into rats."

She snorted. "One of them is already a rat, it seems."

"Who?"

"Alikar, of course. Let me ask you this. How does that weasel stand to benefit by opposing you?" She frowned in thought, and he mirrored the expression. Good question, exactly the kind a queen should be asking. "He is clearly junior and less respected than the others. They seem unlikely to be cowed and simply accept direction from him, even if he *is* right, and he's not. Is he so blindly devout?"

He shook his head. "I don't think so. Although he has some training as a priest, that always seemed like a ploy to me. Another play at power, another thing to hold over people's heads."

"Could this Assembly meeting be a play for more power then as well? Or money?" she asked.

He scratched his head. Could it? What power could he hope to gain? The Assembly had no power to choose an heir, and even if they did, they wouldn't pick Alikar. Even if both of Aven's brothers and the whole Lanuken family proved unacceptable, there were still dozens of possible candidates. He groaned at even the thought of such jockeying. It must be prevented. But all in all, even if Aven was out of the picture, only Samul could choose an heir. Unless…

"Maybe he *wants* civil war. Maybe in the chaos he thinks he can grab more power, or… something. Seems delusional, but that doesn't mean he's not thinking such a thing."

"Indeed. Well then. Some of them care about trade, stability, maybe the status quo. And some care about power, and in particular—more for themselves." She smiled. "Anything else?"

"If I tell you, will you give me your hand back?"

She let out a short laugh and returned her hand, palm up this time.

He seized it. "They care about military might, of course." He ran his fingers along the lines of her palm, soft as a feather.

"Of course?" Was that a shiver that ran through her? He hoped it was.

"Combined strength is what brought all the territories together. They all know that. It's what has kept peace with Kavanar and Takar for so long. The question is to what degree they care about it. Shansaren Territory is heavily dominated by its military, and as such, strength is Warden Asten's highest priority. Dyon too. The others… it's hard to tell. From their perspective, our territory, Asten's, and Dyon's are all in the north. If we broke over that issue, it might be like splitting the country in two."

She sighed. "Nothing is ever easy, is it? You can't just come back here and say, ho, I'm a mage, and expect them all to nod and carry on?"

"Does it ease your thoughts that there's technically nothing they can do about it?"

"Aside from make your life miserable?"

"Yes, aside from that." He grinned. "And my father's too, don't forget."

She snorted. "Then, no. No, it doesn't. I don't know how we are going to sort out this mess."

"Well, you are quite formidable. I'm sure if you show them the tricks you showed me, they'll bow down in fear."

"Like what, turning them into a mouse?"

"Don't forget their clothes this time, though."

She laughed. "I thought we wanted willing loyalty, not bitter fear?"

"Oh, right. I keep forgetting. Perhaps you can charm them with rainbows and butterflies?"

"I can do butterflies, but you'll have to figure out the rainbows bit."

"Hmm. That may require some additional training from you."

She squeezed his hand at the thought. "I'd be happy to... train you any time, my lord."

He grinned at her, although he flinched inwardly at the title. "If we fail to impress the Assembly—which is quite likely, as not all seasoned soldiers and merchants are easily moved by rainbows—I do still have a few charming smiles up my sleeve."

She pressed her lips together, amused. "Aven, you don't *have* any sleeves right now."

With that, he chuckled. "Perhaps no charming smiles then."

"I'd prefer you save your charming smiles entirely for me." Was there a hint of jealousy to that tone? And… why did he like it?

"Duly noted, my lady. And another point you should not forget. While Alikar can make our lives miserable, we do have options to return the favor to him as well. Many Gilaren businesses owned by the wealthy who support him also depend on coal, ore, timber, and gems from these mountains." He grinned. "Mountains we Lanukens control."

"Not out of charming smiles, clearly. You're fully stocked, I think."

He squeezed her hand and glanced around. Camil was in sight, but off in the next room. Perhaps they had one moment. He leaned closer—

A knock on the door sounded, followed rapidly by the clicking of the knob turning. They both straightened. He released her hand reluctantly. "My lady—water for your bath?" called a servant.

She hesitated for a moment, seemingly unsure of why the servants had opened the door and then not proceeded to come in.

"They want your permission," he whispered.

"Ah, yes—bring it in, please. Thank you." She shrugged helplessly at him as if to say, is this how you do these things? He waved off her concern. But then again, he was used to all this. He had no idea how much of a change this was for her.

"Did you have baths in Mage Hall?" She pursed her lips, eyes laughing. Er, that wasn't how he'd meant that to come out. "I mean, I know you cleaned yourselves somehow, I was just wondering—how." Gods, that was no better.

"Oh, really? Did I smell that poorly on the balcony that first day?"

"I—uh—no. That came out wrong."

She waved it off. "We had communal baths and showers. One large one. A relaxing place—one of the few."

He'd been fighting off imagining her in the bath she would shortly take, but he lost the battle briefly at the mention of *communal.* "Communal, as in shared? Like between men and women?"

She laughed at him. "Yes. Everyone wears towels outside of the changing areas."

He tried to shake off his silly line of questioning. But his brain—or perhaps some other body part—seemed intent on planning out strategies should the two of them ever happen on a communal bath that wasn't in the worst damn place on the continent. "Well, uh, hopefully this will be a reward then. Or something."

"Trust me," she said, leaning slightly into his shoulder.

"Privacy is its own reward." He leaned back against her, wishing for a whole lot more.

Oh, yes, this should be *easy*. Just pretend you don't feel anything. And don't act on any of those feelings you do have. Sure. I can do that.

Like hell he could. Damn Code. Damn his parents. Damn all of it.

"I'll let you get your bath," he said quickly before he could do something stupid. "I should attend to one too. And a shave. Maybe some sleeves. Maybe not?"

"Either look suits you."

"I'll come back after that. We can go to the dinner reception together."

She nodded.

He rose. It felt strange to just wander away with no kiss, no sign of affection whatsoever. Since the day he'd convinced her to admit she'd never really wanted to push him away, he'd felt the connection between them. Like an invisible rope connecting them, a "we" now existed where once there had been only two individuals. Something bigger than both of them. He glanced around again—one woman had headed into the bath area, while another man had just stepped out. Hoping his luck didn't run out soon, he bent down quickly and pressed a soft kiss to her lips. Her fingertips teased down the rough stubble on his jaw. Then he dashed away to the sound of her quiet laughter behind him. At least *kissing* wasn't against the Code's rules, as long as there were other people in the room.

Thank the gods.

3  FARSIGHT

The steward and the queen had produced a closet full of clothes by the time Miara had washed, and a young woman named Camil waited to assist her with them. Miara stared at the garments while Camil stared at her back.

Never had she seen such an impractical, colorful collection of fabric in her life.

"Can I help you, my lady?" Camil's warm, quirky voice was naturally soothing, but Miara felt a bit too exposed by those savvy brown eyes set against olive skin. They saw too much.

"I… I'm used to practical clothes, that's all."

"Oh, I can help you with any of them you like, though. It's all right." Camil approached and peered over Miara's arm as her hands clutched the doors of the armoire too tightly. Camil's eager expression suggested she was more than a little excited to do so.

"I'm… Hmm." She picked up the hem of a gown

of deep sapphire blue. The fabric was impossibly soft, flowing, with golden embroidery around the edges and an elegantly high waist. Fine as the queen herself might wear, and indeed, was that where this had come from?

Fine as something the Mistress would wear as well, and just her preferred color. Miara shuddered.

"Are you all right?" Camil placed her hand gently on Miara's shoulder, of course intending to be comforting but finding just the spot of the brand. Although nearly healed, Miara still flinched away as though the touch hurt.

"Bad memories, that's all." She didn't meet Camil's gaze.

"Not that one then! What about this?" Camil frowned with concern but put on a chipper voice. Ducking into the wardrobe, she reached for the farthest edge of the closet and rummaged around, producing a mossy green tunic with a silvered black ribbon along the collar and trim. "Something practical, I'm sure there's—let's see—" Camil produced leather trousers the color of dark walnut wood, boots, and a black leather belt that was at least as wide as her head—nearly a corset in its own right.

Miara heaved a sigh of relief. "Is this acceptable to wear to dinner?"

Camil nodded vigorously. "Oh, of course. Lady Asten wore a similar green tunic last night after she arrived. Of course, she's a warden." She shrugged.

"What does that mean?"

"Wardens are our elite—"

"Ah, no, I meant, does she dress differently from the other women then? Would the queen wear this?"

Camil shook her head. "No, but Queen Elise hails from Dramsren, more of a hilly, trade-focused region. Beautiful wool and dyes come from there. I think that's where she gets her love of gowns. But you are obviously more of a fighter. Come, this will be quite fetching."

Miara raised her eyebrows. Who did Camil think she would be "fetching" exactly? But... hopefully fetching was good.

She consented to the tunic and trousers and tried to send Camil away repeatedly. What Miara had done to convince anyone that she deserved servants waiting on her, she had no idea. But Camil was as dogged and stubborn as Aven. Perhaps it was a national trait.

Miara sat restlessly, still uneasy that Camil might not actually know if this attire was appropriate for whatever event lay in store. Was she painting herself as nothing like a queen? Would the king think her untrustworthy for dressing like a sword-wielding brigand? Gods, she didn't want to worry about such things. How could she put any effort into considering extravagant silks and slippers and ribbons embroidered with gold when so many were still yoked under the Masters' control? When she had no idea if her father or Luha were even safe?

But she needed help to free them. Support. And these clothes were a tool in a way, just like her daggers. Mystifying and impractical as they might be, if she could understand them, they could also be used to help people in their own indirect way.

Miara also resigned herself to letting Camil braid her

hair—but simply, above the temple, to keep her hair out of her eyes. Her red hair fell in waves in every direction behind her, contrasting with the vibrant, grassy hue of the tunic. It *was* stunning and exquisitely soft. Maybe even fetching. The intricacy of the border must have been created by a master's hand.

Hmm, the dinner would go right through the nightly prayer, she realized. "Do you pray each night?" Miara asked as Camil was finishing the left side braid. Not that Miara was keen to partake, after so many years.

"Me? I say a few words to Anara before sleep. Why?"

"In Kavanar, a bell would bid us all to pray each night."

"Really?" Camil seemed surprised as she surveyed her work. "Must be a Kavanarian custom. Did you enjoy it?"

Miara almost laughed at the idea, but she thought of her father's dedication to the practice. "Some of us did. Acting as one can be a moving experience. But I will not miss it." She'd never thought she'd have the chance to *choose* to pray beside her father. Maybe someday.

Although Aven had said he would join her, Elise arrived instead. "I'm afraid he's been ambushed by well-wishers," she told Miara. "But if you are ready, there's someone who would like to meet you."

Miara's stomach sank. What kind of well-wishers? Romantically inclined well-wishers of noble birth, perhaps?

She cocked her head and followed Elise out, curious as to who would want to meet her when she knew no one. Well, there were all those in the king's chambers during the meeting. Did she have her own ambush in store?

Should she have insisted on waiting for Aven?

Did she really know if she could trust the queen? Perhaps she was leading Miara over a cliff into the sea.

Good thing she'd gone with the tunic. Even if a dark, watery death seemed unlikely, she was much better equipped to run.

"Wunik, so glad to see you," Aven's mother said as they entered a grand hall. Miara felt the oppressive weight of the Great Stone before she saw it, heavy, like air too humid or thick to breathe easily. The glittering and majestic rock took her aback when it came into view. It filled an entire wall of the hall, just as she'd read about but more beautiful than she had imagined. It was as if the rock had been hewn in two, and jagged purple crystal jutted out of the mountain. What had happened to the other half? Miara almost missed Elise hugging the stooped old man in a bright azure-blue cloak. Where did they find the dyes? She'd known no one but the Masters with such a rich palette to choose from.

"Elder Wunik, this is Miara Floren, mage of Kavanar." Miara bowed, and he bowed in reply. "Miara, Elder Wunik is an accomplished air mage and one of my former tutors, such as they were."

"Tutors?" Miara asked. "Is there a school here?"

"Not yet." Wunik's eyes twinkled as he smiled. "Perhaps that can change now. I have been teaching privately for most of my life. These two are my pupils at the moment— Apprentice Mage Derk and Journeyman Mage Siliana."

Miara bowed to his students, and they returned the

gesture. "You don't hide that you're all mages?" Miara asked.

"We're not hiding it in support of Prince Aven," said Wunik.

"But we usually don't get out much," muttered Derk.

"My parents were mages as well as landholders in Dramsren and found me training when I was young," Elise said. "I was lucky in that. Very few do. My parents hadn't had any education."

"I think they just wanted to ask me questions themselves." Wunik grinned.

"Probably true. I was planning to teach myself, discretely of course, until Samul came along. Gave up the practice to marry him." To marry *him*. Not to become queen, or take the crown, or some such thing. An interesting choice of words.

"*Mostly* gave it up, you mean?" Miara pointed out. Was that a terribly impertinent thing to say to a queen? At this point in her life, Miara had spent a lot more time being impertinent to people in positions of power than respectful. How ironic then that she was to become one of them?

Fortunately, Elise smiled graciously and gave a little laugh. "Well, some things you never quite forget, eh? I am hoping Wunik can teach Aven as he taught me."

"He's a good student, he's learned quickly so far," Miara said.

Wunik cocked his head. "You taught him some already?"

She nodded. "He convinced me to do it. That

air-twitching habit he has is not very… discreet. Nearly got us both killed."

Elise chuckled. "Estun gets blamed for being a lot draftier than it really is when he's around."

"He must be quite gifted then, with this damn Stone hanging over his head," Wunik said, glancing in annoyance at the hulking rock. "I feel like I can hardly breathe. But tell me, this star magic—is it true? Not an old wives' tale?"

"That I am standing here is testament to its truth." Miara stood a little straighter at the thought.

Wunik nodded, scratching his salt and pepper beard. "I do not envy Aven right now, or any of the enslaved. But… it is an exciting time. Never in all my days as a mage have we had the chance to leave our hiding, to right the wrongs of the Dark Days, to help the kingdom."

"Well, looks like we're getting our chance," the queen said. "Like it or not. I must check in with our kitchen steward Enrial—I'll be back in a few minutes. Let me show you to your seats."

Miara, Wunik, and his students sat at a side table perpendicular to a head table, where two thrones of silvered black stood between other ornately jeweled ebony seats. It seemed that their table was second in importance to the head table, given its positioning.

"Did you leave anyone behind?" the old man asked as they settled in.

"My father and sister." She swallowed. "I hope we can free them. But the Masters are likely watching them. It may not be possible."

"We can look tonight, after dinner." He laid a reassuring hand on her forearm.

"You must be tired after the long journey. And they might not even be outside." She said it even though of course she wanted to look immediately and skip dinner. But she didn't want to wear out his good faith already.

"Buildings have windows. And as I said, this is exciting to me. I've been alone in my old cabin for far too long."

Derk, the apprentice, cleared his throat. "Excuse me, what was that? Alone *with* the two of us. After all these years, and we're still no more entertainment than a piece of firewood, apparently." Derk sat on the other side of her. Siliana sat beyond him, completely ignoring them all.

"Oh, goat gonads—you're always off for days at a time." Wunik waved him off.

"On quests *you* give me!" Derk shook his head.

"I'm also curious to see the compound you mentioned," Wunik said. "It will help us all start making plans."

"Do you mean Mage Hall?"

"Is that what you call it? Yes. We have much to think through."

"What kind of plans?"

"To free the enslaved, of course. It is our duty to help them." A rush of gratitude and relief surprised her at Wunik's words. The Assembly members had not seemed so sure of any such duty.

Dinner guests drifted in gradually. A flutist and a drummer took up perches in one corner, stirring up a cheerful atmosphere.

"So... I hear you're some kind of spy?" Derk said.

Oh, hell. He sounded intrigued. How could she make spying sound utterly bland and boring? "No. I mean, yes, but—"

"Oh, I didn't mean spying right *now*. Just in general."

"Stealth is one of my skills," she said, dodging. But he did not relent in his intent study of her. She kept her eyes trained on the room. "Most of the time, I was a healer. For animals. Horses." She wished she could say the word with more enthusiasm. Like it was her calling. She could assert that spying was against her will all she wanted, but even the word felt more natural to say. Perhaps it was just the impressions of years of slavery. Perhaps now that she could form her own opinions and shape her own future, the sound of the words leaving her lips would change.

Who was to say she could not be both a spy and a healer? An interesting thought.

He gave her a once-over from head to toe, and she threw him a vicious glare. He was lucky it wasn't a glass of wine. "You don't *look* like a healer to me. Or act like one."

Her shoulders tensed. His eyes locked with hers briefly, and there was something in them—something unusual. Something she was not used to seeing but had begun to recognize. He was flirting, wasn't he? Or at least, he was trying to.

"What do I look like then?"

"Like someone who could kick my ass."

She snorted. "I'm not even armed." Well, apparently she had captured some kind of warrior look in this ensemble, for better or worse.

"Do you need to be to… ?" His eyes twinkled.

Miara couldn't keep the mischievous smile from her face, although she had a suspicion that he'd be much too pleased by it. "No." Actually, maybe he was better at flirting than she'd thought.

A murmur went through the crowd, and the guests stood. Miara and the visiting mages scrambled to follow. A quiet fell, saving her from further conversation. King Samul entered, a woman on his arm who was not the queen and who Miara hadn't seen in the king's chambers either. Who could be important enough to be escorted by the king but not be invited to the king's conferences?

The dvora.

Of course. The suitor the queen had referred to. Her… competition?

The dvora looked every bit a member of the nobility, minor though she might be, and her soft gold hair fell all the way down her back in twisting, elegant curls. A cobalt-blue gown ten times more expensive than anything Miara had ever worn fit her perfectly. Miara glanced down again at her own choice for the evening, the mossy green strikingly different. Around the dvora's throat, silver and sapphires the size of cherries glittered. King Samul led her to a seat at the head table, the second seat away from the throne.

The only seat between her and the throne was likely for Aven. The dvora was being seated *next* to Aven. While Miara sat down here.

She gritted her teeth, struggling to ignore a sudden and unexpected wave of emotion. What even was that feeling—panic, suspicion, jealousy, fear? All of them? Was this whole idea to keep their relationship secret an elaborate ruse to buy time for Aven to rethink his fixation on Miara? Miara groped for a reason why this was not the case but came up with nothing. Indeed, if she were in their shoes, it seemed like a reasonable plan. What could Miara offer the realm that this dvora could not?

This was all a mistake. She would pack her few things and leave tomorrow. He would be better off without her, and she… well, she would have her freedom. Certainly the steward could loan her a horse—

But she knew she would not ask the steward for a horse. Selfishly, she didn't care how little or how much she had to offer the realm. Aven loved her, and she loved him back, and that was rare enough to find in this world. How could she give him up after all they'd been through?

She would not.

She took a steadying breath. She knew nothing about this woman except that she wore the fine mantel of the upper class. The fact that she wore the costume of a queen did not make her a better potential queen than Miara. In fact, the opposite could be true. She was not being rational; it was only fear talking. Another deep breath.

Aven had given her no reason to doubt him. He'd willingly gone into hell and back for her. And if anyone had rescued anyone, *he* had rescued *her*. She tried to put the worry out of her mind.

She studied the crowd as more people paraded in. Aven's brothers, Thel and Dom, entered together. Like Aven, Dom was stocky and muscular but shorter and with the dark hair of the king. Thel was indeed was quite different from Aven, with a lanky frame, a bit of a crooked nose a little too long for his face, and longish blond hair. He did share Aven's disposition, though, as he gave her a friendly wave.

He mustn't be too upset about what she'd told him. While the others had crowded around the table for the meeting, the middle prince had pulled Miara from the room by the arm, though still close enough to watch as some kind of argument broke out.

"I need to—" She had yanked her arm from his grasp.

"It'll just take a second," he said hastily. He lowered his voice. "Quickly. You're the mage, right? The one who's stolen my brother's heart? Can you tell me if I'm a mage too?"

"Your—what?" That wasn't what she'd been expecting.

"Can you tell if I am a mage too?"

"Yes, but—"

"It will be easier for him if I just know."

"*What* will be easier?"

Thel glanced nervously at the chamber. "Some of them are sure to call for me to take his place as heir. But how do they know I'm not a mage too? I'd rather know before they do."

She narrowed her eyes at him. What would the answer mean to him? Could this be a trick?

"Look, I don't *want* to be king. I'm nothing like Aven. I would hate to deal with these kinds of machinations day in and day out. I much prefer books to men."

"Why don't you ask your mother?"

He made a face. "I asked years ago. She won't tell me. Said it's better for me not to know, if it's not obvious like it is with Aven. Well, look how that turned out. Can you tell me or not?"

"Fine," she said, giving him a sharp nod. She reached out, and there it was—the taste of earth, nitrous and calm, deep and still.

She glanced back at him but then kept her eyes on the crowd, watching for any signs that they might be overheard. "Aven told me you're an academic. You're drawn to books. But you don't just like the books, do you? You like the libraries, the deep libraries of Estun. The underground, the darkness feeds you. The mountain is like your lifeblood. Locks open for you that were stuck or closed to others. Your hearths stay warmer than they should in the night and need less tending. You never feel cold here anyway. Others think the mountain is dead, but you know better." She turned to meet his wide eyes, as though she'd stolen thoughts from his head. She didn't need to, though. "I think you have your answer," she said. "You've always known."

In the dinner procession, one of the tall, dark-skinned lords from the king's chambers caught her eye and brought her out of her reverie. Aven had introduced him as Lord Beneral, but she'd thought she'd seen his face before.

Wasn't he one of the mages who'd accompanied the queen to confront Miara while she still held Aven captive? Did he know their secret? Or, perhaps *she* was the one who knew *his* secret.

She felt eyes watching her again—this time, Aven's, as he entered arm and arm with his mother. He'd shaved and wore a midnight-colored doublet, a black cloak with a mantle of black and silvered fur around his shoulders, and a simple silver ring for a crown.

By the gods, she was staring. Was she revealing something by staring? No, no—everyone was staring simply because they were being attentive, although perhaps not as wide-eyed as she.

*This* was the man who wanted her? It was one thing to kiss the tousled, battle-torn warrior she'd come to know over the last few weeks. *This* man seemed like quite another thing altogether.

His gray-green eyes lit up when they caught hers. Did his eyebrows rise slightly as his gaze slid across her, or was that her imagination? If they had, was that a flicker of approval or concern? He flashed her a grin. She bowed her head in what seemed like an appropriate acknowledgment.

"That the prince?" Derk asked. "The one all this ruckus is about?"

"Yes," she replied. "That's the one." Damn, her voice was husky. Get it together, Miara. At least he hadn't escorted the dvora himself. Perhaps she could convince herself that meant something.

"So you say you're a healer. Creature mage then?" Derk asked her.

She nodded, glancing at him as briefly as possible before returning her eyes to Aven. He'd sat down by the dvora and was no longer returning her gaze. Finally, everyone was seated. Every noble on the dais wore some shade of blue, from a bright vibrant hue to Aven's dark midnight shade. Even the Dvora. Miara frowned. Through her deft choice in wardrobe, the Esengard noble easily blended in as one of them. She looked as if she belonged there, in that seat. The gown was an artful, clever selection and a move that hadn't even occurred to Miara. Damn.

She watched him covertly while they ate and tried to think of other things. She *was* rather good at watching people without letting on. Perhaps she had some skills suited to court life after all.

And come to think of it… she needed to figure out something for that damned demonstration. "Wunik, do you think you can help me with a magic lesson for the king and his Assembly?"

"I'll help you," Derk's overeager voice chimed in. Beyond him, Siliana snorted.

Miara opened her mouth to reject the offer, but Wunik spoke first. "I think he'd be a great help to you. Show these men what a young, strapping boy can do."

"Boy! Please—"

"You're more experienced, sir."

"I'd also rather save my energy for the real work of finding and freeing mages, if you don't mind," Wunik muttered.

Derk's sidelong glare said he had heard that slight but chose to ignore it. "What do you need to do?"

"Well, I'll need a range of mages to show off certain abilities, although we don't seem to have any earth mages at all. Ironic, with everyone living in this damn cave."

"It *is* oppressive, isn't it?" Siliana finally chimed in for a moment, and everyone nodded.

"And I could use advice on what we should show them."

"We should show them healing." Siliana leaned around Derk.

"Hey, I thought you were ignoring all of us," Derk said.

Siliana ignored him. "All Akarians are warriors, deep down, or they care about one. And part of that is getting thumped. Struck. Stabbed. Sometimes, killed. We show them how much we can do on that front, it should be a powerful motivator."

Miara nodded. "That's good. And that means we're going to need injuries to heal, won't we?"

"Lucky us." Siliana smiled defiantly. "We can take it."

"I'd suggest you don't use any spell specifically to injure," Wunik mused.

"That's not our strength anyway, right?" Derk leaned back farther as it seemed like Siliana was not leaving the conversation anytime soon.

"Maybe Aven can help us find someone to wield a traditional weapon for our injuries." Miara bit her lip, thinking. "Or… we can wield it ourselves."

"Not sure I'm up for that," Siliana said, "but you're welcome to."

Miara only half listened to the other woman as she chewed over an idea. How many of those Assembly members were seasoned veterans? How many of them would have the fortitude to stab themselves and then heal themselves again? If they even could. If she had to look dangerous, perhaps she could make a different kind of good impression on them. A fierce one. Miara glanced at Aven and the dvora, who were politely talking and not looking in her direction. Neither of them looked particularly rapt. The ability, both mental and physical, to wound herself just to show she could heal the wound… Well, *that* was one thing Miara offered that the damn dvora couldn't. At least, she hoped. Guts. Bravery. Possibly a certain kind of stupidity. She shrugged to herself.

"What about air? What should we do with air?"

Derk and Wunik threw ideas out, from the too mild to the too destructive, and the creature mages provided critique. Setting the stables on fire was probably too much, and they had little magic to rebuild buildings anyway. Snuffing out a candle was far too practical and mundane. Turning a bit of beach into glass—where did they think they were, the Gulf of Panar?

Still, Miara was glad to plan with them. It gave her something to take her mind off the fact that Aven talked only to the dvora for the entire meal.

Once or twice, he would feel her gaze and toss her a smile. She would nod back, and she made an effort to look very engaged in the conversation with Derk and Wunik and not at all miserable.

Stop worrying about this. Nothing could be done to change the situation in the short term anyway, except maybe employing one of those dresses that reminded her of the Mistress and seeing what effect it might have. Damn that woman, why should the Mistress ruin an entire category of clothing for the rest of Miara's life anyway? But no. Miara was not going to earn the respect and acceptance of these people based on what she looked like. This dvora had a head start on her anyway in that arena, and since when did looks alone win loyalty?

She would win them over with what she *did*. And if that involved slicing herself open just so she could heal up the wound, so be it.

Eventually, they'd detailed much of their plans, and the conversation drifted to other topics, such as how magical skills were taught in Mage Hall. Miara had expected that comparing notes with them would reveal very different spells and strategies, but in fact they used mostly the same techniques. After a few generations of practicing in isolation, she would have thought the spells would have diverged and evolved more, but apparently not.

Wine-poached pears appeared to signify that the meal was nearly over. The tangy, sweet, cinnamony smell overtook the room. Oh, by the gods, what a beautiful dish. She had marveled at how well appointed Estun was, and how comfortable, and clean… A lot of these things felt like luxuries, like things she didn't deserve, to the point of discomfort. She doubted she would ever feel comfortable with a servant waiting on her… But *this*. This she could get used to. This was bliss. She took a huge bite.

"Still hungry, huh?"

Mouth too full, she glanced up and saw Aven standing before them. Oh, wasn't *that* great timing.

"After all this? How are you all faring this evening?"

Wunik saved her from having to speak. "Most excellent, my lord. I'm just draining your mage here of what knowledge I can glean of Kavanarian advances in magic. I think she's started taking overzealous bites to save herself from my incessant questions."

Your mage? What did Wunik know about them? The slightest shift in Derk's posture told her he had noticed the turn of phrase too.

Aven leaned forward, the knuckles of his fists on the table. "This dinner is going to go on for *hours*. Are you two ready to retire soon?"

"Now would be excellent. I thought you'd never ask." Wunik began folding his napkin as if he couldn't stand to wait a moment longer.

"What about us?" Derk said with an indignant frown.

"I'm sure you're both quite tired and wish to get some rest after our journey. You can join us tomorrow," said Wunik in the voice of a teacher who was not about to bargain. Derk grumbled and took a bite, turning away to Siliana, who only seemed to care because now she had to deal with Derk alone.

Aven and Wunik were staring at her, she realized. Miara nodded vigorously and tried to wash the rest of the pear down with a swallow of wine.

"You two finish up and head just outside the hall, and I'll meet you out there?" Aven looked relieved. Why should he look relieved?

Wunik nodded. She mimicked him. Aven swept back to the head table with a majestic flourish of his cloak. It *was* damn cold in here. She needed to add a cloak or something tomorrow. Perhaps where they were going would be warmer.

She caught herself staring after him and tore her eyes away. How strange to see someone she felt she knew so well—or at least was beginning to—in such a new light. He had always been chivalrous, polite, and rather dashing. But nothing like a crown and the trappings of royalty to reinforce that this was a man who would someday be a king. She had thought she'd seen it in that commanding voice and strong jaw, but it had been only a glimpse of the reality. His eventual power was not something she'd fully understood. She knew Aven the man, but she was catching many more glimpses now of Aven the prince. Aven the king.

She bit off another dreamily delicious hunk of pear and chewed thoughtfully.

Even before they'd hunted down any dinner, Jaena dragged Kae around from the bathhouse to the weapons hall, hoping to find Menaha. As if to mock their grumbling bellies, they finally found her *in* the dining hall. It was full-on dark by then. They'd endured the compulsory evening prayers just outside, and by now they were starving. They heaped cold bacon, cheese, and turnips onto a trencher and joined her. Another senior warrior mage Jaena did not know ate with her.

"I didn't expect to run into you two here." Menaha's smile was sweet, but she clearly knew they wanted something. "How are your lessons going?"

Kae rattled on excitedly for a few minutes. Menaha was an air mage like him, so he could explain the various offensive techniques he had mastered. It was not nearly so exciting to explain that she'd mastered not getting knocked on her ass. But no matter. The other woman finished eating, said goodbye, and left them as he detailed every bit of his recent training. Kae rather adored Menaha in his own way, and she nodded and smiled and gave him a few tips.

When the other mage left, though, he slowed his tale and gave Jaena a long look. Ah, so he hadn't forgotten the purpose of their visit amidst his rambling. He'd simply seized the opportunity to bore the other mage to tears. Now he wanted her to take the lead.

Jaena cleared her throat. "Menaha, we heard a rumor."

The older woman raised an eyebrow and leaned back in her seat. "Is that so? Care to share?"

"Are you the gossiping type?" Jaena asked. She hoped the leading tone to her voice would convey that she meant more than what she was saying.

"I am. At times."

Jaena nodded to Kae, as she'd felt him staring at her, hoping to chime in. "We heard some mages escaped," he said, quick and low. He glanced around, looking highly suspicious. Hell, no one would ever suspect him of being a spy. Or would suggest such a thing either. "Or, one mage, at least."

Menaha raised both eyebrows now. "That *is* quite the rumor."

"Do you know if it's true?" said Jaena quickly. "Or where we could find out?"

Menaha surveyed the room around them much more naturally than Kae, but only chatty mages sat on all sides, busy with their own conversations. Then she leaned forward, both elbows on the table beneath folded arms, and spoke in a low voice. "I know of a mage who has disappeared."

Jaena glanced at Kae, then back at Menaha. The hope in her chest threatened to swell and envelop her—did she dare let it? "Who?"

"The mage Miara."

"The healer?"

"And the spy. When she returned from her last mission, I saw her in the bathhouse."

"And?"

"The brand on her shoulder looked like it was healing."

"Healing!" Kae exclaimed. The two women silenced him with simultaneous glares.

Menaha nodded. "I haven't seen her since. I went to her rooms, and guards stand at the doors. Her father and sister have not returned to their jobs, nor has she. I do believe at least Pytor—her father—is still in the apartment but under guard for some reason."

"How?" Jaena breathed. "How is it possible?"

"I don't know. I wish I had asked her more. But it must have had something to do with her last mission. She had not been working in the stables. She'd just returned and was off duty for a few days."

Jaena nodded, thoughtful. That wouldn't really help her; few likely knew the nature of the mission. Dekana had never wanted to share the details, and Jaena hadn't been sure she'd been allowed to. Those who did know the details of Miara's mission, like the Masters, would not want to tell her.

"Let me know what you find out," Menaha said with a smile. Then she rose. "Good to hear about your studies, Kae. Keep up the hard work." And then she turned and headed out.

Jaena almost called after her, longing to think of one more question to help them unearth the truth. But barely after she'd left, two guards strolled down the aisle beside them, surveying the mages as they ate.

Odd. The guards did not normally stalk around the eating areas like this. They were usually dozing outside. Perhaps their approach was what had moved Menaha to action.

She studied the guards more closely. "New daggers—do you see?" She pointed at the nearest guard as he ambled by. Kae glanced up, trying to look casual and failing. He nodded, subtle as an excited puppy. "Something is going on," she whispered.

"Yeah. But how do we get in on it?"

Miara and Wunik waited outside. The stone foyer encased them in intricate, delicate geometric carvings as the halls spread out in three directions from where they stood. Elegant archways soared up to ceiling seals that held all manner of orderly, symmetrical patterns and designs. Wunik just fidgeted and watched the door.

Aven finally appeared around a corner, striding toward them alone. She heaved a sigh of relief. Had she been holding her breath?

He trotted up to them and took her by the hand, smiling and raising it to his lips with a kiss.

"Aven—" she started, glancing at Wunik.

"It's all right, he knows," Aven said.

"What? How?" she said.

"My mother consulted him about a way to free you."

"I wasn't very helpful," Wunik added. The old man grinned.

"Your mother—when?"

"You were still knocked out at the nomad camp," said Aven.

Gods, she had thought he was a fool for not running, but she'd had no idea how far his foolery—devotion?— went. His mother probably hated her. She'd tried to free her son, but instead, he'd gone off on some noble mission to free a woman who could do him nothing but harm. A miracle the queen had even been civil.

He grunted in irritation and relinquished her hand with a squeeze. "This way." Aven led them up the stairs, Wunik trailing.

"Where are we going?" she asked.

"The balcony." Where it all had started. Where they'd first met. "I should like to see you there without a dagger involved." He gave her a grin.

She snorted. "I thought maybe it was the dagger you were attracted to."

"Hmm. We should test both ways and find out. We also need starlight, if we're going to free anyone."

"Now? Already?"

"Why wait?" Aven said. "Night's fallen."

"You don't want to rest first?"

Aven waved off the idea. "I know you are worried about them."

She ducked her chin, feeling like he'd seen right through her. She hadn't said as much, but it was true.

"We'll start with your family, of course, if we can find them," Wunik added. She looked from Aven to Wunik and back again. They were both deadly serious about this. Well, just as well. They were the air mages. She was just along to point directions. "Let me get my tools. Is it just up this way? All right, I'll meet you two there. And perhaps some heavy cloaks?"

Something about his tone of voice said that he didn't

really need the tools. From the expression on Aven's face, he both wanted to keep Wunik with them and send the man away.

A spiral stair greeted them, and after circling up many flights, Aven strode down a dark hall lined with torches until they reached a heavy wooden door.

"I hadn't realized this door was wood. Would have been easier to get inside than I had expected," she said as he heaved up the crossbar.

"Well, it is a heavy crossbar. But that's a good point. Any creature mage could get to this balcony easily. This door should at the very least be guarded, if not made of iron and better locked. Wait—your plan was to come *inside*?"

She shrugged. "I didn't say it was a *good* plan. I had no other ideas. Estun is pretty impenetrable, and you were my first kidnapping, after all. "

"And your last, I hope," he said, the glint in his eye casting a double meaning to the words. "I've seen the effect you have on your captives. Driving people to risk their lives, fits of madness and devotion."

"Don't worry, not everyone is as crazy as you."

He heaved the door open, and she sauntered out. She hardly remembered the tiny balcony, she'd been so focused on him at the time. It was barely beyond sunset, but already some stars were visible.

He left the door open behind them. Although he hadn't explicitly stated it, she had the impression that they weren't really supposed to be alone together. That made a certain sense, since all sorts of allegations could be made when it was just one voice against another.

And yet—now they were alone. He stood farther from her than usual. Because he was supposed to, or because of all his talk with attractive and elegant suitors? Perhaps he was seeing the error of his ways already.

"How's that Code of yours doing?" she said. Maybe she could invite him to explain why he was standing farther from her than he had since… possibly before she had kidnapped him.

He smiled sheepishly. "Rigid and uncompromising as always."

She cocked an eyebrow. "Rigid, eh?"

He snorted and shifted his weight. Well, this wasn't how she'd expected to spend actual alone time here with him.

"Did you find much entertainment in your dinner companion?" Did her words have an edge to them, or did she imagine it?

He blinked. "What?"

She didn't want to repeat that. Now it seemed petty, maybe a little weak. "You're—we—" Where was she going with this? "I wish I could have sat by you at dinner." There, he liked the straightforward route, and so did she, although it could be tough to spit out.

Understanding came over his face, and he strode to her now finally, pulling her into his arms. "Oh, Miara, it's just for now. Don't let it—" But he stopped. His frown said he disliked it too.

"It's fine. I understand. Really, I do."

"No, I'm so sorry about all this. My father can be slow

to trust people. It's bullheaded."

"Not a bad trait in a king, really."

"Trust me, you have nothing to worry about from Renala. It won't be long, and you'll be sitting right with me, I promise." Relief did wash over her at that. He glanced at the doorway.

"Are we not supposed to be out here like this? Are you not supposed to be alone with women?"

"Part of the Code." He shrugged. "It seemed foolish to abide by it on the road after all we'd been through. But here, people care about it. For a royal heir, being alone with women can create tough situations, ones that can be used against you. I mean, obviously that changes when you marry them, of course."

*Them.* She supposed it would have been odd to be discussing marriage between them in particular at a moment like this, but... the topic hung in the air. And the lovely, golden-haired dvora hung in her mind.

"But I *want* to marry you," he said, suddenly seeming to realize that that might be unclear. "So, it's—I don't know—"

She glanced at the doorway. No sound from the stairs yet. Pushing herself up on tiptoe, she pressed a soft kiss against his lips, and he rumbled deep in his throat as he leaned into it. Into her.

Sure, he wanted her. At least he *thought* he did, for the moment, and the caress of his tongue against hers was convincing. He claimed he didn't want to hide their love, but wasn't this arrangement far more convenient for him as well? No awkward questions, no extra pressure on top of an already dire situation. What if, on some level, he sensed all she lacked as a potential monarch, and that was the true reason he'd agreed to all this? A terrible thought, but she could not deny the possibility. Perhaps he had regrets, or he knew deep down she was a poor choice and hoped this month would test her, would show her true mettle. Would allow him to distance himself if she failed, as she inevitably would.

And all this could be simple infatuation, a temporary obsession forged by the intensity of their journey together. When he started to notice each way she came up short, all he required that she did not have, would kisses such as these fade slowly into moonlit memory?

She could only hope he wouldn't. And kiss him while she could, damn it.

In spite of the open door, Wunik knocked moments later. She quickly wiped her mouth with the back of her sleeve and caught herself straightening her tunic. Wunik marched in, arms full of tools and cloaks, his eyes wisely trained up at the sky and pretending like he had no idea what had been going on. Had he had a wife who'd passed? He did not seem unaware of the ways of lovers.

He handed her a cloak. Funny, the cold hadn't been bothering her until Aven had hastily stepped away. Things had been quite warm a moment ago.

Wunik sat on a bench and took a wooden bowl from the bag he'd brought with him. So he did indeed have tools. He also took out a skin of water and filled the bowl. "Watch carefully, Aven. You'll try this next," he said, beckoning them toward where he sat.

"Water, Wunik? That's different. My colleagues just used their arms or the open air to frame the spell."

"Just a little something I do, not a normal Akarian practice. Most of the admittedly few mages I know who can do this use the air too. But I find something about the physical conduit seems to require less energy."

Interesting. Aven joined Wunik on the bench. Miara felt too anxious to sit. And the air froze her to the bone, in spite of the heavy, black, fur-lined cloak. She pulled it tighter around her and paced back and forth instead as Wunik described the farseeing spell.

"The learning will take time and much practice. You won't get it right away, but don't worry about that. Useful, intense spells such as these don't come without practice." Wunik plucked a red rose petal from a nearby bush and dropped it into the water.

"Do you need that?" Miara asked.

"What? Oh, the petal, no. Just an offering to Anara. Nothing magical about that part."

More interesting bits all the time from this clever mage. A pious mage? The only religious mages she had ever known were the self-hating sheep of Brother Lithan's circle. Even Brother Sefim focused more on the Balance and walking the Way than he did on the deities themselves. He *was* of course still a priest of Nefrana, but he never spoke about the goddess. If she and Aven could free him, what changes might he make? She had never met any priests of Anara or Mastikos—did they denounce mages too?

Wunik differed from the mages she had known. Was this what a freemage was like? Excited for adventure, bored but still happy, someone who had known love? She had thought that all mages were by necessity depressed, stifled, exploited. But every time Wunik opened his mouth, he showed her another side of who her people could be.

Who she could be.

Interesting. Perhaps there was still time for her father to grow into an old man like this elder, instead of... something less.

His use of water also intrigued her. No mage type held power over water, a proven oddity of nature. Given that mages could influence earth, sky, and living creatures, it followed that some mages should be able to sway the seas, oceans, rivers. But no one had yet witnessed such a thing. Even magic could be mysterious at times, she supposed.

Wunik started and stopped a few times, demonstrating how the light pooled between his hands. Of all the air spells she had seen, farsight was still the most awe-inspiring. Creating a window into another place in the world... Strange and powerful, indeed.

Still, she wished Wunik would hurry up. It had been two days, almost three now, since she'd kissed her father and Luha goodbye. How had the Masters responded to her escape? Were they safe?

The Dark Master's intense eyes flashed through her mind. The other Masters would accomplish nothing without him, and they hardly mattered. But the Dark

Master would not let them get away with this without a fight. And as long as her father and Luha were his slaves, that gave him a great deal of power.

"All right, Miara, point the way for us," Wunik said. "This won't be the easiest by twilight, but it's not getting any brighter out."

She guided him along the path she had taken with Aven. "There is probably a straighter route over the mountains, but I don't know it. I haven't walked that way."

"Well, fortunately this takes less energy than walking," he said with a grin.

The forest and hills slid past. They found the border to Kavanar and crossed it. Soon they saw the golden plains, the wheat and barley fields.

Finally, Mage Hall loomed before them. Seeing it for the first time since they'd escaped, her heartbeat quickened a little. What had she expected to feel? Tension knotted her shoulders.

"There—that building." The dormitories were full of people at this hour. But the windows to her family's rooms were dark.

Wunik veered closer. "Shuttered."

"Can you check around the side of the building? The door?"

He nodded, and the image slid to the other side of the building.

"Guards?" Aven said.

"Those are not normally there," she said. "It's not like we can run away—" But she stopped. That was no longer true. They were responding accordingly. "We weren't usually guarded like that. At the gates, yes, but that was as much against outsiders as to keep us in. Let's check the gates and see if security's increased. But—there might be one more thing. There, check that building. That's the bathhouse, and the food hall is close by. We might see one of them going to or from there."

The ground slid beneath them, but they saw no one on the way to the bathhouse. It seemed eerily empty.

"Is there a curfew?" Aven asked.

"No… at least there wasn't when we escaped." Then her eyes caught on someone leaving the dining hall. "There. I see Menaha, that way." They followed her gesture around the bathhouse, toward the food hall, but Menaha was gone. "No, wait, that way. Damn, she's gone inside. Hmm." She groaned and groped around in the surrounding area with her mind. If she could find a creature nearby, perhaps she could follow Menaha into the building that way. That would be a lucky chance, and very draining, if she could keep her mind connected to the cat at all over such a great distance and no sight inside the building. Still, she found a small gray cat and whispered her greeting. "But maybe—over there, who is that?"

A silver tabby darted out in front of Jaena as Menaha turned south and headed into her building. Jaena had been hoping to reach Menaha to ask more questions, and she normally ignored strays.

But there was something unnatural about it. It studied her too intently.

She stopped. The cat regarded her evenly. Jaena felt a tickling in her shoulder brand and scratched at it absently.

Reaching out, she felt a presence. Oh. Not just a cat, but a mage too. As an earth mage, Jaena could not feel the size or location of life forms very distinctly, but she could sense the increased energy that meant a mage was close at hand somewhere around the cat. The earth underneath them sang and shook ever so slightly for the joy of it, not that anyone but an earth mage would notice such vibrations.

*Greetings, mage,* came a familiar voice.

*Greetings,* she replied. Where did she know that voice from? She could not send thoughts like a creature mage could, but she could serve them up clearly on a figurative mental platter. Her brand continued to twitch. Why would it bother her for looking at a cat or hearing a mage's message, of all things? An icy knot formed in her shoulder, something she'd never felt before. Now it was getting creative? Stupid, stupid thing. She tried to ignore it.

*Jaena, is that you? It's Miara.*

*By the gods, Miara. We were just talking about you. Did you really—* Jaena had not known Miara well, but she had been a spy like Dekana. They had met a few times before.

*Yes. I did.*

*Gods.*

*I'm looking for news on my father and sister. Are they all right? Do you know? He's a gardener named Pytor. Luha's a stable hand.*

Beads of sweat had formed on Jaena's forehead, and the night suddenly felt far too warm for so late in the harvest. What in all seven hells was wrong with her? The cat had wandered off, but Jaena could still feel Miara's presence. *Menaha mentioned him. She says they haven't returned to work for two days. They appear to be locked in their rooms, under guard. The guards have new daggers.* She wasn't sure why she included that final detail, but it seemed like it might be helpful.

*How did you know I escaped?*

*Rumors. We asked Menaha if she knew anything, and she said she saw your brand healing. That you'd recently come back from a mission, but that she hadn't seen you for two days. And that your family was locked in their rooms.*

*But they are safe?* Miara's voice sounded relieved and worried at the same time.

Of course that's what she would want to know, but Jaena could not know for sure. *I could try to find out?* The strange wave of heat had fallen away, and she felt cold again. Icy, even. She wiped the sweat off her forehead with the back of her hand. Was she coming down with something? This was no time to get sick. *Please—if you can tell me how you got free, if there's some way I can help you—* The sudden intensity of emotion behind her thoughts made them fall to pieces, and she pulled herself together. A lack of clarity in communication was the sign of an amateur, and she'd be damned if she looked like an amateur at a moment like this. Even with only three years of training, even coming to Mage Hall late in life, she was better than that. She would be the best. She *had* to be. How else could she get back at them for what they had done? She would not mess up her one chance at getting free by acting like she was less skilled than she truly was.

*I never got to say... I'm so sorry about your sister.*

Jaena gritted her teeth at inadvertently sharing her grief, although an ache exploded in her chest. Not. Now. She was better than this. *I'm sure I can find your father. Where are your rooms?*

A pause. Her heart skipped a beat. Had she scared them off already? Gods, no—she was better than this—she had to know how it was possible—she had to get—

*Air mages,* Miara said. *One moment—hold on.*

Air mages? What did that mean?

*Air mages are how it's possible. Had to speak with my... friends. Two air mages here with me. It's air magic that forms the control spell of the brand, and air mages with the right knowledge can break the spell.*

*And you have two with you? Can you—*

*It is already done, actually. My... friend got a little overeager.*

Something was off about the word "friend," but Jaena had no time to worry about that now. She looked down at her shoulder, hoping to see some change, but it felt much the same.

*That was the heat, the ice, the itching. It didn't feel any*

*different for me at first either. I didn't know it had happened.*
*Test it and you'll see—but discreetly. You'll notice when it*
*doesn't stop you, not before.*

Now Jaena's heart really did skip a beat. She could
hardly believe it—she hadn't even had to ask. She would
have begged. She would have done just about anything.
And yet it was already done. What could she do to test
it that wouldn't get her noticed?

*As a freemage, you can do whatever you like now. But I*
*do have a favor to ask of you.*

*Anything,* Jaena replied. She regretted responding so
quickly. But then, what price was not worth paying for
her freedom?

*If rumors are spreading, changes will come to Mage Hall.*
*They will start making it harder to escape. Each mage that*
*gets free will make it harder for the next one. If you stay for*
*a day or two more, we can liberate others. Then you can all*
*get out at once. More can escape that way.*

*I can do that. Of course.* What was one more day?
Although the idea of staying willingly was so ludicrous
as to seem impossible, it was the least she could do to
try to help a few others escape. *But isn't there something*
*more I can do?*

Another pause. Jaena waited. She glanced around.
She had been standing still since the cat left her for who
knew how long. Would someone think it odd? No guards
were close enough to take notice. Hopefully she had a
moment or two more. She started to walk, as slowly as
she could imagine possible, to look a little more natural.

*Look for ways to hurt them, if you can do it without risking your freedom. Make it easier for others to escape. Information we could use against them in the future is useful, anything on current preparations, supply levels, even the number of mages training with you. But don't tell anyone about this. The rumors do not help. They will get back to the Masters, and they'll use the information against us. But if you do have someone close to you—*

*I have a few friends here. Not many.* Not without Dekana.

A pause. She wondered if Miara could feel the swelling of grief, for the creature mage continued just as the tide of emotion ebbed. *Menaha, at least. Choose anyone else you need to. We can free mages only by the starlight. Get them to come outside at night, and we'll find them and do what we can.*

*Outside, at night? You're right. If the Masters know of that, it will be easy to stop.*

*Indeed. So don't tell.*

*How long should I wait?*

Another pause. *Two days' time. Leave after sunset—not tomorrow, but the day after. We should be able to free a few more between now and then. And if you hear any news of my father—*

*I will seek it out after my workday is finished tomorrow,* said Jaena.

*Head toward the Akarian border. The city of Anonil. There is an inn with an apple and an arrow on the sign. We will get someone there to meet you.*

*Thank you,* she whispered with more gratitude than she could remember having ever had for anything in her life.

*May the Balance protect you.* And with that, the presence was gone. Jaena turned on her heel, headed toward Kae's rooms. The earlier in the night she got there, the better. Time to concoct a story to get him to meet her after dark, something that wouldn't make him think her in love with him, without telling him anything about what had just happened. Oh, that should be easy. That man loved rumors almost as much as fruit pies. Maybe more. Still, he was one of her only friends. And she wouldn't be out here in the darkness getting lucky if it wasn't for him.

Then she would find Menaha. Then sleep. Two days couldn't pass quickly enough.

# 4    THE TASTE OF FREEDOM

Miara had just gotten into the bath when Camil timidly announced, "Prince Aven is here to see you, my lady. Shall I ask him to return later?"

"No! Uh—we can speak through the door like this."

"Yes, my lady."

"Miara! Did it work?"

She laughed. He'd passed out on Wunik's shoulder without even seeing the fruits of his labor. "Yes, Aven," she called through the door. "It worked. We must send someone to meet her at the Apple and Arrow in Anonil. Do you remember it?"

"How could I forget?" They had stayed one delicious night there on their return. He hadn't overexaggerated his fondness for apple dumplings. "I'll have a scout sent there."

"You need to learn not to drain yourself to incapacitation like that."

"Ah, well, I had to sleep. What difference does it

make, eh?"

Well, perhaps we could have slept *together*, she thought. Or at least stolen a kiss good night. Or... something.

She'd woken up reaching across the blankets for him. She'd missed him, as silly as that seemed after such a short separation. Surprising that after only a few days, she expected his presence in the morning. Longed for it. And this morning, he hadn't been there.

Jaena's freedom was worth it, she chided herself for the hundredth time. Aven has his priorities in the proper order. "With an air mage to assist you—two, in fact, with Derk—you don't need to be incapacitated in the future. It's unnecessarily risky. You could have taken... longer than one night to wake up." You *could* have not woken up at all, she wanted to add. But Wunik would teach him that. Aven usually passed out long before then, and both she and the elder were there to monitor their young student for now as he learned.

"I know, I know. I'm overeager. I never claimed otherwise." She snorted to herself. He might be overeager as a mage and rescuer, but he didn't seem to be overeager about *everything*, as her empty bed this morning had attested.

"Complacent and lazy, you are not," she said instead.

"How are the clothes they've gotten you?"

"They're... fine. Very fine, indeed."

"But you don't like them." Damn, how did he know? Her search for a word betrayed her.

"I didn't say that."

"What's wrong with them?"

She hesitated. "You are all giving me so much. I cannot complain over something so silly as clothes."

"Silly? Hmm."

"She thinks they aren't practical, my lord," Camil interjected.

"Camil!" Miara put her hand over her face and rubbed her eyes.

"Thank you, Camil. Can you find—or make—some things more practical but still of the proper caliber?"

"The only one I've ever known who wore dresses like that was… the Mistress." She hated to even go so far as to say her name in this safe place, but the dresses hanging in the closet made her think only of the hateful woman. "But I'm not going to let her ruin them all for me forever. I could just use more… variety."

"That's good to hear," Aven said. "Of course she shouldn't ruin anything for you forever."

"I had thought to imitate Warden Asten, my lord. Would that be fitting?" Camil said.

"Perfect."

"If I may, I'll take your leave to speak with Steward Fayton immediately."

"Thank you, Camil. I don't want our guest to be uncomfortable any longer than necessary."

She winced. "I am far from uncomfortable!" she shouted. "I can wear them just fine! I'll wear burlap sacks and be damn happy about it!"

"Your breakfast is on its way, my lady, and there are two attendants in the seating room should you need assistance dressing."

"I'll wait for her out here," Aven said, more to Camil than to Miara.

Was this a chance to steal a moment or two to themselves? Certainly not with her stuck here with suds on her knees in the bath. She rinsed the rest of the soap off hastily, stood, and climbed from the bathing pool. She dried herself imperfectly and threw the towel around her.

She searched the bathroom for more towels or some sort of robe. She found a shift hanging on a hook but couldn't remember if it was the one she'd worn the night before or a fresh one. Well, no matter. The dirt of one night was nothing to being out on the road or how long she wore things at Mage Hall, but people seemed to have higher standards here. She would put on something else shortly.

"Yes, uh, you can leave it there. That's fine," she heard Aven saying with a cough to clear his throat.

The door clicked shut again just as Miara opened hers. The thin shift was not something she would have worn in front of anyone else, but it was appropriate enough to wear before Camil returned to dress her. She winced at the thought. She could dress herself, thank you very much. But if it was an excuse to share some small intimacy with Aven… it was worth it.

A tray of tea, cheese, and dumplings sat before the fireplace in the outer room. Aven's eyes locked with hers with a smoldering intensity. She answered only with a small smile.

"You're cruel, you know that?" He smiled back.

She nodded as she came closer and leaned against the doorframe between the two rooms, letting the shift reveal what it pleased. "You like it, though."

He snorted but did not deny it.

"Did I mention I told the mage to wait?" she said.

"Wait?" he said, coming closer himself.

"The one you freed. I told her not to leave yet."

"Why by the gods did you tell her that?" He glanced around the outer room and, apparently seeing no one, stepped closer and pulled her into his arms. She returned the embrace, at least for a moment. Who knew how long they had till Camil or one of the others came back? Would they *really* be able to hide this from their attendants anyway? Aven visiting her rooms at all would certainly invite suspicion. He tucked his head against her neck and her hair and breathed deep, taking her in. Ah, now this was the overeagerness she'd spent the first few hours of last night longing for. Or at least something close to it. His scent caught her nose—musk and wood smoke.

"Well, you were already out and sleeping like a baby on Wunik's shoulder, so I couldn't exactly consult you. Escaping will get harder for each mage that tries. If you can rely on others for the energy, perhaps we can free more than one a night. I thought several could try to make a run for it at once."

He nodded, his face still buried in the hair of her shoulder. "When did you tell her to leave?" His hands ran down her back, circling around her hips. They should stop. Perhaps a moment longer.

"Tomorrow night. Should give us at least tonight and perhaps part of tomorrow. Think you can cooperate to perhaps free two or three? Maybe teach someone else how to do it?"

He pulled away, smiling sheepishly. "Well, when you put it that way, I can."

"It's fine. One more mage is free today that wasn't yesterday. Tonight, we aim for more."

He nodded. "I have to tend to administrative things this morning—duties that a certain kidnapper kept me from are now far overdue. But you can explore Estun. There's nothing off-limits to you here."

"Nothing?"

"Nothing. You'll be queen here someday, Miara. I promise you. You can do anything you like."

She swallowed. She was not as sure about that as he was, but she was certainly willing to go down that road and see where it ended. "Huh. Anything…" Anything at all. She'd never had a day where she could do absolutely anything, at least not since she was very small. What in the world would she do?

"Hopefully I can find you at noon, and we can eat together. I'll send word with Fayton if I can't." He released her and stepped away. They had gambled for long enough, it was true.

"Is it wise to spend so much time with an insignificant guest like me? People will start to talk. What about your other visitors? Don't you need to attend to them too?"

"I'm simply showing my gratitude to my rescuer. Let

them talk."

"I don't know if your father would prefer to hear you say that."

He frowned. "Most likely not. He'd probably prefer I wasn't here now either, though."

She looked away, off into the fire. "We should talk to him about this idea of his again. It's—" She groped for better objections than she'd been able to come up with on the spot. "It's not fair to lead on suitors, if they have no chance. And wouldn't it help people to trust me if they knew I'd already earned your trust?"

His frown deepened. "Unfortunately, I'm not sure how perfectly they trust *me* at the moment either. They are right that our news might be... a lot to handle at once. Probably too much."

"So you agree with them?"

"No," he said quickly. "Well, maybe. Some of it. It's not what I would do if I were king. But if you hadn't noticed, I have a tendency to put principle over practicality at times. And I'm not terribly experienced at this whole 'ruling a kingdom' thing."

"You seem like you have good enough instincts to me." Her turn to frown. "Just because your father has spent more years on the throne doesn't mean he always knows better than you."

He shrugged. "But it *does* mean he gets to order me around. Mostly. But, hey, I'm just talking about lunch, not plowing the fields on the banquet tables." She snorted at that image, although a momentary thrill at the idea shot through her. He grinned back. "As fun as that might be." His eyes ran over her again. The risk of the shift had been worth it. "I don't think he can object to a simple lunch. But I can invite the dvora, if you wish. Or Warden Asten. Or Devol. I think you'll like them all."

Miara doubted that, but she kept it to herself. "If we wish to keep this secret, then the more the merrier." As if to spite herself, her voice came out dour and utterly unenthusiastic, and he let out a bark of laughter. He stepped forward, as if he meant to embrace her again.

*Click.* The now familiar turn of the doorknob almost made her groan—almost.

Camil bustled in, several outfits in hand, humming to herself, and oblivious to them.

Miara glanced at Aven with laughing eyes, and he returned her amused expression. She stepped back so they were no longer clearly able to see each other. Might as well make an effort, if this secret was to be kept. For now.

"We'll speak later," he said on the other side of the door, his voice sweet and warm even as his words were formal. "You're free, Miara. Enjoy it." And with a dozen heavy thuds of boots on the floor, he was gone.

Camil plied her with new choices that the young lady seemed sincerely excited about.

"Where are these all coming from?" Miara asked, amused by Camil's enthusiasm.

"Well, I had the foresight to tell some of the seamstresses to start on a few things yesterday. Tunics are rather quick to make, you know."

"No, I've never sewn a thing in my life."

"Is that so? Well, yes, they're fairly simple. And also Warden Asten was willing to part with a few pieces."

Well, that was mortifying. Miara winced. "So... you begged these from the warden?"

"Oh, no, I purchased them from her for a generous price. And then she can get her own new pieces. Delight for everybody, don't you think?"

Miara had no idea if that was delightful or horrifying. Asten seemed widely respected, however, so if she had to literally wear the dress of another, it might as well be the warden's. Miara let Camil choose the eventual outfit and was rewarded with a stormy blue-gray leather dress, the bodice fitting snugly over a white chemise. Yes, good colors, Akarian colors. Camil again insisted on having her way with Miara's hair, and as she sat, Miara considered what she should do with a morning all to herself.

How to prove herself to these people, become one of them? She couldn't even imagine ruling them, but perhaps if she felt like one of them, the idea would become clearer. Aven and Elise certainly didn't seem to have any trouble with the notion. This was also a rare opportunity to make her own choices for once. And then there were *her* people—her father, Luha, the others. What else could she be doing to help them?

She smiled to herself. She knew exactly where to start.

Before she headed out on her own, she had one request for Camil. "Can you get me some... pots?"

"Pots, my lady?" Her delicate bronze features didn't

try to hide their frown of confusion.

"Um, yes. Pots for plants. Of soil."

"Plants?"

"No. No plants. Just pots. With soil in them, but without plants." Miara didn't know how to better explain. Camil shrugged and nodded. "Dead plants are fine," Miara added, trying to be helpful but starting to realize by the look Camil gave her that that might have sounded a little strange. No matter. Camil would understand when Miara was through with them.

She took a hesitant step out of the room. She could feel Camil's eyes on her back, ready to come to her aid. But this was something Miara needed to do alone. She had no idea which direction she was going. And she liked it. The only way to learn her way around here would be to jump in. Before Camil could speak up, she turned abruptly, choosing a direction at random, and headed down the hallway.

She would find her way around this place. She'd become one of them. She'd make a home here. It had to start somewhere.

For the first time in three years, Jaena was awoken by something other than a burning in her shoulder. She slept heavily, and while others arose to the bells and chimes that were supposed to wake them, she tended to need the brand's painful reminder to actually open her eyes.

Assorted pains stabbing her shoulder was the worst way to wake up that she could imagine.

And today, they were gone.

Instead, one of the other girls that shared their arbitrarily assigned rooms left and slammed the door behind her.

Jaena sat up. Everyone else was already gone, off about their duties. She was glad to miss them—they were not women she would have *chosen* to live with—and so it was a relief to have some peace, just as the lack of pain was a relief.

But would it be harder to keep this secret than she had thought?

She scrambled to pull on a clean white tunic and her usual leather vest, one of the few things she retained from Hepan that she actually used everyday. She splashed water over her face. Neat, thin braids tumbled about her face as she unwrapped her hair, and then she headed for the stairs. As she spiraled down, she wove the tiny braids into two larger ones to keep them out of her face. Thank Anara they weren't harder to deal with in the morning, because she had no time. Of course, they'd taken Dekana hours to put in. And Jaena had no idea who she would find to ever do them again when she needed to take them out. Or if she would find anyone at all. A familiar despair settled over her.

Even though Jaena was free, nothing could bring her sister back.

Her footsteps echoed bleakly in the empty stairwell

as she hurried down. Shafts of morning sunlight pierced her, making her squint, too attentive, too cheerful. How would she explain her lateness? Where was she even assigned today? She didn't know yet. She would have to go to the Master's Hall to find out. Great.

Outside, a few still funneled into the various buildings, so she was not the very last person. But she'd been close to horrendously late. What if her annoying roommate *hadn't* slammed the door on her? How was she going to keep this up?

It would be fine. It wasn't long. She could get through a day without them discovering it, surely.

She trotted toward the stairs where one of the Fat Master's favorite mages handed out assignments. Before Mage Hall, Jaena had been fond of exercise in the morning. Sometimes a run, sometimes dance or meditation. Her father had prized grace in his daughters, and running didn't impart much of that. Still, it was good to get the blood pumping. Now outside that world of diplomacy, it was nice to be something more than a graceful, tactful flower. She could be strong. She could be tough. And she was.

Most earth mages were. Perhaps she had always been.

The taskmistress greeted her with a suspicious glare.

"I, uh—threw up," Jaena blurted. She'd seen it happen once. Physical illness could keep you from following the brand's orders, even if you wanted to.

Right?

"Here. You're needed in the smithy." The woman, who

was also on the rotund side, like the Fat Master himself, held out a knapsack. "They want help with cooling. Then you're on delivery duty. Casting horseshoes today, shoeing them tomorrow."

Jaena groaned, but she grudgingly took the empty knapsack. Slinging it over her shoulder, she headed toward the smithy. Earth mages had the most boring jobs. Kae got to blast people on their duffs all day. And her? She was stuck cooling slivers of metal.

Over and over and over again.

But not for long, she reminded herself, and that put a bounce in her step. This would likely be the last time she had to cool horseshoes. At least, if everything went off without a problem.

She greeted the master blacksmith with a nod. A dozen smiths slaved away in the heat, but they regularly worked together and always without a word. He preferred not to stop clanging for niceties. She had to agree. She dropped the knapsack and headed to sit by the coals. They weren't blazing hot, and each day grew colder and colder. But they didn't *need* to be blazing hot, because they had only been to get the smith started. Now he had her instead.

She paid little heed to his work but managed to heat the steel, funneling energy from the earth beneath her feet. Sometimes she took off her boots for a better connection for intense work, but today's work barely required her attention, let alone her whole energy. But it *did* make the smith's job far easier, and she was glad for that, so it could have been worse.

Most efficient was when the earth mage *was* the smith. And sometimes that was the case. But occasionally air mages took to it too, like this fellow, drawn to where earth met air in the fire and heat. They were still competent mage-smiths who could keep their fires going with amazing heat and regularity.

Jaena was just glad that they hadn't tried to make her into one of them. To be a warrior was far better than a smith, at least to her. She would be more independent, more able to defend herself. Maybe more able to get some kind of revenge on behalf of her sister.

This is almost over, she thought. Nothing to get worked up about right now.

The shoes for the horses piled up in a sack near the hearth. She alternated between keeping a steady heat in the shoe as it curved around the horn of the anvil and cooling the shoes as rapidly as she could. Then the smith would drop them into the sack to take to the stables. One after another clanked into the pile, until she doubted she would be able to carry the thing soon. She'd take a break and head over to the stables shortly. Just one or two more.

A scream sliced through the regular clanging of the smiths working, and Jaena's heart leapt into double time.

"Anara protect us," she whispered, mostly to herself. No one could hear her, because the screams continued.

Her smith stilled, staring down at the anvil, his dark eyes bleak and empty. The Masters were making another slave.

There's hope, she wanted to tell him. Someone's discovered a way out of this. But she really had no idea who or how or why. And this was neither the time nor the place to explain. If only she were a creature mage and could plant the words in his head without *them* hearing.

She stood, forcing herself to act steady, to appear strong. She pointed at the knapsack, and he nodded. She hefted it to her shoulder and strode out of the smithy, trying to pretend she wasn't running away. Trying to look like the screams made no difference to her.

All too quickly, she reached the stables, emptied the shoes into their nearly empty bin, and was on her way back. She tried to think of something that could delay her. But any variation from the norm could be a reason to suspect something was up. A way for them to take that brand to her too. Again.

If she had thought being enslaved once intolerable, she imagined a second time might drive her mad. Dekana hadn't been able to tolerate even once. But she'd had it worse. If Jaena ever finished her training, she'd likely find out for herself.

So she needed to make sure she didn't finish her damn training. She did not hesitate to head back. She would do everything as perfectly as they said, *better* than she had as a slave if she had to. Until darkness fell tomorrow—then she would be gone.

She was nearly back to the smithy. She would have to walk past the branding area—going the long way around could draw attention, and it wasn't worth them noticing her. But, gods—she didn't want to see. Fortunately, the screams had stopped. For now.

"No, I'm coming with you." The Tall Master's voice close by grated across her nerves, and she staggered back a step involuntarily. "I'm the one who tackled the prince last week, so I'm not trusting this to you. First that, now this one. You have to actually *hold* them if you don't want them to get the jump on you. Idiots."

As she rounded the corner and stepped inside the smithy, the first of six guards trotted forth and slammed into her, sending her stumbling to the ground. The five others guards jogged past her sprawled form on the smithy floor without reaction. The Tall Master followed along behind them. Perhaps she *should* have gone around the long way.

Jaena sat up and stopped short. Blood dripped from the table where the slaves were branded and smeared across the floor. A lot of blood. What had happened here? Sure, one could bleed a little from the brand, but it was mostly a burn. Whoever had been brought here must have been beaten—because they'd tried to run?—or already injured.

She had stared for too long. She glanced around to see if anyone had noticed her. No one stood nearby. Anyone else in the smithy huddled close to their hearths, as far out of sight and mind of the Tall Master as they could reach.

Her eyes caught on a pole of iron on the floor near the hearth. The brand they used to make slaves had been knocked aside in the fray, now resting in the blood splatter. The unimportant-looking object steamed and radiated a violent heat, both physical and magical.

And here it sat, not three feet from her.

She scooted a measure closer to it. What was she doing? She needed to head back to her smith, keep her head down, and wait until tomorrow night. And then she'd be out of here. She'd be free.

She slid toward it again. As a slave, she would have been compelled not to touch the brand. She hadn't truly tested her new freedom yet, not deliberately anyway.

Her hand shook as she reached for the brand. Her fingers wrapped around the long handle. Nothing happened, no burn in her shoulder. She could feel the hot steel, but something more resided in the end, a twisted, sulfurous energy, more like air magic. More like a maggot made of fire. More like pure evil imbued in metal. Strange.

Even if she escaped, this device would be able to enslave her again if they caught her. And while she fled, the enslavement would all continue.

*Think of some way to hurt them.*

This was her chance—her chance at revenge. She had thought she would have to wait a long time for revenge against them. And yet. She stared at the bleak metal. What loss was Jaena to the Masters? A young apprentice who would maybe someday be a warrior but for now was mostly good for speeding the production of horseshoes? How could she even compare the two?

Before she could think better of it, she took the knapsack off her shoulder, opened it, and stuffed the brand inside, cooling it with a spell as much as she was able. The evil bit was not something she could influence, and it hissed as it hit the burlap canvas, but the metal handle cooled. A whiff of smoke caught her nose, but it would be hardly noticeable in a smithy.

She scrambled to her feet, trying to look calm as one of the smiths moved into view. Smoothing her tunic, her eyes caught on a guard not six feet from her, waiting just outside the door. Of course, he watched for intruders, not mages already inside. She swallowed and strolled as casually as she could back out of the smithy, hoping he couldn't see her shaking. I'm fine. I'm cool. I'm collected. Nothing to see here. Just carrying more shoes to the stable. My, that smith is fast.

Turning the corner, she gasped. She'd been holding her breath. So much for looking casual, but it had apparently been enough to fool that guard. A crowd of young mages headed toward their classrooms, and she melded into their group.

Now that the deed was done, her mind began to race. The Tall Master would realize the brand was gone any second. She had very little time. Where could she hide it? Would they be able to use magic to detect it somehow, or could she hide it in a more normal way? Should she toss it and get away from it so they wouldn't suspect her? Now that she had it, what in the seven hells was she going to do with it?

What had she been thinking? But then, she thought of Dekana, and she kept walking with a slightly faster step.

"Master of Arms Devol?" She approached the short, bearded man inspecting the practice swords on the right side of the Proving Grounds, hoping she remembered his name correctly. The great, indoor cavern was lit only by three jaunty fires that raged in central braziers, leaving the Grounds dark and the morning sun hidden from view.

He nodded curtly, glancing up at her, then back down at the sword in his hands. He must have deemed it acceptable because he put it back on the rack. "Ah, Miara, was it? You Prince Aven's guest?" he said. His voice was deep, gravelly.

"I am."

He held out a hand to shake hers, and she returned it heartily. His skin was appropriately rough for a soldier. "Tell me, my good woman, what brings you to my Proving Grounds?"

"I would like to learn the sword. Can you tell me who can teach me?"

"You said you wanted to be a warrior. Not wasting any time, I see." She nodded. "Why didn't you ask your friend the prince?"

She hesitated, then decided on honesty. "I had thought... hoped, perhaps... to surprise him."

He barked out a laugh of surprise that settled into a smile. His scruffy red beard and chin jutted to indicate the sword rack. "Choose your weapon."

A test? She hoped to learn and hadn't claimed any prerequisite knowledge. Still. She needed to prove herself to all of them—one step at a time.

She studied the array of blades. "These are too large," she said, pointing at the heaviest claymores on the right side. She had seen Menaha do a lot of damage with such weapons, and someone like Aven might wield them well, but that was not playing to her strengths. She hefted a lighter sword on the left side, about the length of her thigh, and examined it.

He seemed to think she'd made a selection. He picked up a shield beside him and held it out. "And this," he said gruffly. Or maybe his voice was just always made of rocks.

She glanced at the shield, then the rack again. "No—this," she said, choosing a second sword much like the first, but with prongs around the hilt.

Now his smile broke into a grin. "Oh, I like it. I'll do ya one better," he said and leaned back to the other side of the rack, returning with a small ax. "This you can still do your slashin', but you can also catch, deflect, hook them in the knee. More utility, if you ask me. Although some people prefer the slashin', and the blockin' is a bit different."

She couldn't help but grin at the zest in his voice. "Is this my first lesson?"

"It is now. C'mon over this way now." He gestured to the other side of the grounds. The area was so dark she couldn't see where they were headed. "I'll teach you them all, if you keep showin' up." He talked as they walked.

"Are you—are you going to be practicing?" a timid voice said from the seats.

She and Devol stopped and turned to see the dvora, fidgeting anxiously in a dress of dull, golden silk. Her cheeks were flushed with—was that embarrassment?

"I'm just learning," Miara said lamely, wishing she could have said something more bold, more profound.

"Her first lesson," Devol grunted.

"Might I—could I—" The dvora seemed to want to ask for something but was unsure how to go about it. "Can I watch?" Miara was sure that was not what she had been originally going for. But then again, it was none of her business.

Devol seemed to be waiting for Miara to answer. "Of course," she said. Damn, just what she needed. An audience, and a rival, no less. But what else could she say?

They continued a few dozen feet, and the dvora followed them to a seat nearby. Thel entered the grounds and joined Renala. Great. Didn't they have anywhere to practice that didn't invite an audience? Actually, with what she knew about Akaria, that made a sort of sense. And perhaps if people knew she was determined to fight, that might be a good thing.

Not until Miara had neared the end of the grounds did she see what they were headed for. Effigies made of straw, stuffing, and wood awaited them, looking a little slouched, beaten, and worse for the wear: practice dummies.

Lord Dyon stopped short on the threshold, his arms full of documents, and stared. Aven met his gaze. "What is it?"

"It's just good to see you back, that's all. Wasn't sure that was going to happen," Dyon said.

Aven suppressed a smile, and they set to work. And to think he'd thought Dyon a maddening curmudgeon. How things had changed, perhaps for both of them. Unpacking a dozen documents, Dyon squinted at the first name on the list of warden aspirants and read it carefully. "Zedagen, Arnov. Of Anonil, Territory Gilaren."

Aven ran down his list of questions about the candidate, including a few new ones that raised Dyon's brow. The old buzzard didn't criticize, though, so he must have approved. After being nominated by their territories, aspirants were tested by a slew of generals, Dyon, Dev, and others, and the results handed off to Aven and his father for the final selections.

After he'd graduated from warden training himself, he'd taken on most of the responsibility for these reviews. He'd never worried too hard about them, as the wardens simply wanted the best. Some candidates came in with superior skills in a variety of things. He might have to make a tough choice between one who excelled at archery but failed at everything else and another who was above average in many things, but he had never thought too deeply beyond the measures of the tests concocted by the generals and military training men.

"Rogonen, Adia. Of Panar, Territory Numaren."

And now, he had to wonder. Everything seemed different now. He had not yet seen war, but they were in one, like it or not. He'd caught the smell of it in the burned flesh of his shoulder. Was there something more he should have been searching for? Something deeper? What if these people were the ones to make the difference in the end, in a conflict with Kavanar?

"Westfar, Pel. Of Senata, Territory Shansaren."

His context was now completely different. Sure, these aspirants knew weapons. They excelled at speed and strength. Many were well trained, and those who weren't had exceptional natural talent. But had he paid enough attention to if they were smart? Adaptable?

What would they do if they encountered a fireball aimed at their head? Which test could show him that?

"Jonquin, Sania. Of Panar, Territory Numaren."

After they'd gotten through reviewing the aspirants, plenty of other work awaited. Generals in Shansaren requested funds for new armor. The archery units sought review of their new candidates for leaders, as one of their great mentors had retired, leaving a line of promotions to sort out in her wake. One cavalry unit had updates on horses retired and acquired and proposals for the spring. It hadn't been long, but the work had been set aside before his little "trip" because of all the gatherings with the Takaran delegates. And now it absolutely had to be done.

Akaria had its own military class, with soldiers employed and supported directly by the king. The arrangement was one of the things that made Akaria stronger than its neighbors. It was easy for the surrounding kingdoms to recognize the benefits of a dedicated martial force—and a lot harder to build one. Aven's ancestors had convinced enough members of the richest and most powerful families to actually send the gold to pay, support, train, and feed enough men and women to make a significant standing army, and that was the real achievement they all clung to. In spite of the fairly obvious recipe for martial superiority, their neighbors had not done the same.

Then again, if everyone turned on him and his father because he'd been born a mage, Akaria could end up in exactly the same weakened situation—or worse. He had to believe that the territories would put more importance on Akaria's strength and safety than they did on Aven being born able to blow some leaves around in the wind without any hands. He was the same man they'd always known. He did the same things he'd always done. Well, mostly. He loved Akaria more than almost anything. He had to hope that meant something.

But, well—it remained to be seen. At least no one had tried to exile him yet.

A knock on the door. Aven glanced at Dyon. "It's enough," the lord relented. "At least the young ones will get their promotion news."

"We can do more tomorrow," Aven said. Then he nodded to the soldier at the entry to open the door while Dyon organized his various vellums, parchments, and papers and piled them up to go.

Teron poked his head in the doorway.

"By my ancestors, you're still here?" Aven said, and Teron grinned in reply. "Come, come. I'm kidding. I'd heard. But you weren't at dinner yesterday?"

Teron came in and gave a small bow, and Jerrin hovered behind him. Aven waved both men in, and they sat down before the desk Aven worked at. It wasn't really *his* desk, as much it was a center of military affairs. But Aven ended up using it most, as that was one of the duties his father had assigned him. It could have been assigned to Thel or more likely Dom, or any other lord, lady, or warden. But his father had given it to him to prepare him.

"The map—" Aven started, unsure of where to begin. Then he stopped and picked up the book Teron had given him. "Did you know what this was?"

Teron shrugged noncommittally, but smiled.

"What about this?" He opened the book and unfolded the star map.

Teron shrugged again.

"You told my mother you were looking forward to talking to me about it." Aven narrowed his eyes at him as Teron's smile broadened. "So—let's talk."

"I had a feeling it might come in handy to someone. I hoped you were that someone," Teron said, still evasive.

"You said as much when you gave it to me."

Sensing Aven's slight annoyance, Jerrin put his hand on Teron's arm. "It's time, Son."

"Son?" Aven looked from one to the other. How—and why?—had they avoided disclosing *that* little tidbit?

Still—Teron hesitated. He looked to his lap and didn't meet Aven's eyes.

"Well, it did come in handy," Aven said softly. "It

saved my life and kept me from joining the ranks of Kavanar's slaves."

Teron looked up in surprise.

"I owe you a *great* debt. More than I can ever repay. But I can try. What can I do?"

"Is the map—" Teron started, then hesitated, then seemed to throw caution to the wind. "I didn't know what the map was. I *did* have a feeling. I thought maybe the map was air magic. It looked like it might be one of Zaera's ancient maps, or a copy of one."

"Zaera?"

"A mage of the Dark Days, one of those who commandeered the mind of the king," Jerrin said gravely. "A great villain, some say. Others disagree."

"I had researched her past, looking for clues—" Teron started.

"And what reason did you have to research *her* past?" Aven said, hoping they would finally spit it out.

Teron looked at Jerrin, clearly afraid. Jerrin jerked a finger toward Aven as if to say, out with it. Teron hung his head.

"Which one of you is a mage? Or is it both of you? Or your whole delegation?"

Jerrin shook his head, but looked relieved Aven had figured it out. "My son—and my wife."

Jerrin had come to Akaria without any wife. Many Devoted dwelt in Takar, and the elder Devoted even made their home in the temple there. Was the woman even still alive? Was this why they were afraid?

"And where is she?"

"We don't know," Teron whispered. "I've tried, but I can't... Magic is a death sentence in Takar. I don't know any spells... I've tried anyway, but..."

"We think she is in Kavanar." Jerrin's jaw was clenched, tense. "That, or dead."

Well, they were in luck. But they didn't know it yet. "Why did you come here? Was it really only as part of the delegation?" Aven said.

"We hoped to find a way to stay," Jerrin said quickly. "But Takar watches us even from afar. And there is no reason—"

"I owe you both my life—and far more than that. I will gladly grant you residence in Akaria as full citizens or permanent delegates if you wish." Their surprised stares were more reward than any cheers he could have hoped for.

Finally, Jerrin recovered first and snorted. "Well—you were right that burying your nose in all those books finally came in handy." He clapped Teron on the back, which seemed to finally snap him out of his stunned state.

"But... why the fight?" Aven said to Jerrin, since he seemed to be far more communicative at this moment. The fight in the Proving Grounds on that fateful day seemed like a lifetime ago. "Was it really that you simply wanted to spar?"

"I thought you were a mage, but I was afraid I was wrong. I have never been trained—" Teron sputtered.

"Well, that makes two of us."

"I thought I might be able to see some evidence if I

stirred up some benign trouble," Jerrin finished.

Aven smiled ruefully. "Well, you were right. It worked. Unfortunately, the trouble stirred up was not entirely benign, as that Devoted Knight was watching as well."

Teron scowled. "We heard. She told us before she left. Narrow-minded fools, all of them. I needed to give *someone* the book I'd found in your library. Someone with more ability than I to figure out what it meant. I needed to know if it could help us find Mother." Teron's voice faltered, and he put his head in his hands to try to recover his composure.

Aven took a deep breath. These men weren't diplomats, more like refugees. He would never have guessed. What if he had never met Miara? What if he had refused to even fight Jerrin that day? How long till he would have sent them packing back toward a death sentence?

He caught the eye of the guard again at the door. "Send for Fayton, please." With a crisp nod, he stepped out to send for the steward.

"This evening, I am convening a group of freemages of Akaria. It would be my pleasure to have you in attendance, if you are not previously engaged." He smiled. The unnecessarily honeyed words of diplomacy were a touch of humor. He hoped they would calm Teron. But he also hoped it would be an important occasion.

Mages of Akaria had not gathered together openly in generations. Well, this gathering would not be entirely open. He was only telling those he knew he could trust. But still. Many of them would be revealing that they were mages to those in attendance, and all of them were taking a risk.

Teron looked to his father.

"Teron will join you," Jerrin said, voice grave again. "And I would, if you'll have me, although I'm not a mage."

Aven gave a crisp nod. "Yes, come. Excellent. Now, the remaining matter is—do you wish to stay in Akaria?"

"Of *course* we do—" Teron started.

"As permanent diplomats or citizens?"

Jerrin eyed Teron. "We will have no support system here, no occupation. Only what we've saved. They do not need us as handshakers and brandy drinkers."

Aven wondered how they had convinced anyone in Takar that *they* had needed the duo as handshakers or brandy drinkers. But he was glad they had.

"Can you separate from them politically? Will they take offense?"

Jerrin shook his head. "We were chosen for the Akarian delegation very specifically. Old, crusty warriors like me are not well respected among Takarans. Our people honor peace, we seek enlightenment. I like beating things with a mace. They thought you might like me."

Aven smiled. "Well, then they are correct. But not for the reasons they thought, eh?" His smile widened. "And I *knew* you were holding out on me, saying you had no preference. It's maces next time, old man." Jerrin snorted. Aven spoke as he straightened the papers on the desk. "I can certainly help you find a way to make a living. I wouldn't be doing much to repay my debt if I left you to die in squalor, now would I?" That would probably also be against the Code, if not the Way as well. "There's the army, the mines and refineries, the upkeep of this hold at the bare minimum. Hell, there's even a mage that has two apprentices he supports. We'll find you something."

Jerrin nodded. "It would be nice not to take advantage of your hospitality any longer. It's been too long. I am truly sorry for that."

"We had no other option." Teron straightened.

Aven waved it off. "It's settled. See you this evening?" He stood. They took the hint and stood as well, and they all strode to the door together. "I'll speak with my head steward Fayton—he'll be in touch."

"Thank you, my lord," Teron said, bowing deeper than Aven could remember.

"No," Aven said. "Thank *you*, my friend."

The two men left. Aven turned to hurry and finish his work. He needed to find Miara and make sure her morning had gone all right. He needed to eat. He needed to review these mine statements and inventory lists. He needed to look at the updated maps of Anonil and Panar. He needed to think of a way to find Teron's mother, a needle in the haystack of Mage Hall.

He needed to get all this work out of the way so he could focus on the real issue—were they truly ready for this war with Kavanar? Even if he could get them all to quit squabbling and support him, he was not so sure.

Jaena ducked inside the stables when she arrived, looking for a nook to hide her quarry. Where could she hide this damned thing that none of them would expect? Mage Hall was not very big. How long would it take them to simply canvas the area, look at every corner and cobweb?

She glanced around. The stables were relatively quiet now, only one mage bringing a horse back into its stall at the moment. The rest of the stalls were empty—out in the fields or at work some other way. Burying the brand under horseshit sounded like a fair treatment of the wretched thing. It was a start.

She pretended to wander to the other side of the stables, looking for the wagons that went to and from the farm towns to buy goods. But of course, they were all gone. They would have left an hour or two before, first thing in the morning, and wouldn't be back before lunch. She could have perhaps stowed away in the bed of one of them. But no chance now. The stables, too, were cursedly clean, with nary a bit of equine excrement for her to hide this damn thing under.

Who else went in and out of the gate? Legitimately?

She scratched her scalp absently. The shepherds came and went, although usually at the start of the day too. Serving girls took food at lunchtime out to the workers in the few fields farmed by Mage Hall, shepherds in the hills, and a few others.

Sometimes they even brought out food in their knapsacks.

Back in the stables, she searched for the spot where the stable hands relaxed. Where did they wait or take breaks? Had Miara worked here when she was not yet free? Certainly there had to be *some* food that wasn't for horses around here.

She found nothing. Apparently, when they wanted to relax, they left.

She'd been there too long anyway. She headed back into the flow of people. She would just have to go straight to the source. The meal hall was on the way to the nearest gate. Serving girls would come from that way anyway.

Was she leaving? Now? Was she really doing this?

It was too late to question any of it. But if she succeeded, if the Masters could no longer make new mage slaves, that would be worth a more difficult escape for other mages in the future. Wouldn't it? And at least their ranks would no longer be growing.

Besides, the Masters deserved this and far worse.

And Dekana had deserved far better.

She ducked inside the food hall. She glanced back at the knapsack. Faint smoke drifted up, curling into the air. *Well* then, she had better hurry. She doubled her pace.

Serving girls ferried bowls and baskets from back in the kitchen toward the table of lunch offerings. A hefty basket of bread sat nearby, alone and unattended, probably while its owner went to get another.

She scooped up the basket like it was her job and headed back out, chin in the air.

Everything is fine. Everything is normal. Just taking food to the farmers in the fields. This is what I do every day, of course.

Her heart was pounding. She stopped for a moment beside a bush and crammed a few loaves of bread into the knapsack. And to check if the damn thing was going to burn a hole through the bottom. It had cooled, but only slightly, so she forced another cooling spell into the metal.

She tightened the knapsack as much as she could and knotted the drawstring once, twice, three times. If someone wanted to check this thing, it was going to take them forever to undo her efforts. It had to be a pain—not worth checking.

Then she hovered there for several long minutes, looking for signs of other girls headed into the fields. She spotted a group of three strolling pleasantly and chatting, one with a basket of cakes, one with a sack, another with numerous waterskins draped over her shoulders.

Jaena fell into a casual stroll a dozen paces behind them. Sure enough, they headed for the gate and gave the gate mage a friendly, familiar nod. A pumpkin walnut cake was offered and accepted. Everything was calm, casual. Although cold, they were just out for a stroll on a brisk autumn day.

When it came Jaena's turn, she too gave the same nod to the gate mage and pointed at her basket. He waved her off, happily munching away. Pumpkin walnut did sound good right about now. What would she do for food once she got out of here? Time for figuring that out later, and at least now she had this bread. She strolled out the gate. This is my job. Shepherds and farmers need their lunches. An important task. Nothing much to worry about except getting these breads to the fields.

And just like that she was out. She was... *free.*

She fought the urge to bolt. She imagined herself throwing the basket aside, bread spilling all over the road as she sprinted away. But that would just get her caught.

Instead, she marshaled all her self-control to continue behind the three girls down the road and onto a side path, turning toward the hills. Ah, good. These girls were headed for the shepherds. Nothing too close.

At the first stand of trees, Jaena slipped away, melting into the shadows and quickening her pace. She checked the sun. She needed to head east as quickly as possible, as unnoticed as possible.

May Miara forgive her for not following the plan.

Behind her in Mage Hall, a low bell rang that she had never heard before, heavy and sullen as it echoed off the hills. Someone, somewhere inside, was raising the alarm. Now they would start looking for her.

May future freed mages forgive her if the Masters never opened the doors of Mage Hall again.

# 5     HIDDEN

Jaena hiked as casually as she could along the edge of the East-West Road toward Anonil, but gradually the bells from Mage Hall escalated from one low, sullen ring to many. She started off with the theory that normal people would be strolling down the road at this time of day, and it was best to blend in. No reason to act conspicuous. Renegade mages would flee through field and hedge and forest, like they had something to hide. She didn't think the grain fields would hide her dark profile very well, especially those that were cut low now that the harvest had begun.

The brand poked her roughly in the back with each step as if seeking to slow her down or exact its own revenge. Not a chance, she thought. I'll fling you into a lake where you can't be found. I'll bury you in the deepest canyon I can find. Something. I don't know what I'm going to do, but as soon as I get away from this place, I'll be burying you in the most obscure and terrible place I can think of.

As the bells in the distance increased, she began looking for somewhere off the road in case she needed a different, less obvious path. A few hundred feet ahead, a path snaked through uncut fields toward a village. The path led over a small stream—barely more than a trickle, nothing like the great rivers of her homeland. A small bridge crossed it.

What was that sound behind her? How far back were they? Were those horses—the horses of a farmer's wagon or a Devoted Knight?

She darted off the edge of the road and raced toward the path. As she turned down the path, she heard barking in the distance. Dogs too? She groaned. But that was where the stream would come in handy. She hoped. If she could get beyond the stream and beyond the town, there should be many scents for the dogs to sort through—and many people for the Devoted to question. Perhaps that could at least slow them down. And in the town there might be something she could steal to hide herself better, or perhaps even a horse.

She ran as fast as she could, bent into an awkward crouch to keep hidden amid the waving grains. At the bridge, she dashed off the path and through the water, doing her best to leave tracks up the other bank and into the field.

In her haste, she didn't notice the stray rock at the field's edge until it was too late. Her foot met it sideways, bent wildly, and sent her reeling. Sharp pain twisted within her ankle and shot up her calf, and she muffled a cry. She fell, her body landing with a splat in the mud and her face narrowly missing being fully submerged in the water.

She lurched upright and tried tentatively to put pressure on her foot. Pain arced up her calf.

Damn. Change of plans, then. She looked around frantically. She had to buy herself some time.

On the far side of the stream, under the bridge, she began to work. With her magic, she burrowed a small cave under the base of the bridge, a good four feet deep and wide, and limped inside, curling up in a ball. She cast the damn pack aside after it dug into her back, then rubbed her ankle as she gradually layered the wet mud back up in a high wall all around her, leading up to the base of the bridge above. Unless they were familiar with this bridge, they wouldn't notice the newly expanded mud column supporting the far beam.

She rubbed her ankle and shut her eyes. Would they follow her this way? Did they know her scent?

Would this damned trick work? Let the earth *please* save her, just this once.

The hoofbeats came closer. She was not fully encased in the soil and could see up between the slats of the bridge planks. She'd just have to hope they didn't think to look down.

"The hounds say this way!"

Finally she could hear not only hooves, but the huffing of horses and panting of dogs. Shouting—and then sniffing—seemed to get louder and louder.

"Er—across the bridge—"

A horse thundered over the bridge above her, bits of dust and debris raining down.

"Wait—no, the trail leads into the field. But—hrm."

"What do those damn dogs think they're doing, going in circles like that?"

A hideous growl sounded, barely a few feet away. Another. She didn't want to think about what they would do if they found her. Would the dogs think to dig? Give her away?

The tips of claws clipping along the wood planks told her one was approaching. When he reached above her, he whined. Thick, black paws scratched at the floorboards. Damn it, why did these men deserve all this power, and she so little? Where were *her* dogs to fight these bastards off? If she ever made it to Akaria, she would never let herself be caught so helpless again.

Hmm… Come to think of it, though—was there something more she could be doing to defend herself? She had no staff, but maybe she could create something. She reached her mind out and felt her way down the wet earthiness of the stream's edge. Couldn't try anything too close and give away her presence.

"Nefrana's tears, now he's digging in the bridge pillar. Why'd you make us bring these fool creatures?"

"Shut up, they smell something. What's your crystal say?"

What crystal? Did they have a way to detect her presence somehow? Perhaps that was how she had been detected and captured in the first place. But that was before she'd had any training. She pushed it out of her mind and tried to focus her thoughts on the experiment she'd begun to form far down the riverbank.

"Well, it's all aflutter, but could just be a spell on the bridge makin' it act up. Hard to say the source. But there's no mage around here. C'mon. Let's dig into that field. You two—ask around that town. Tell 'em to be on the lookout for a renegade mage. Should be considered very dangerous and may be killed on sight. That should make 'em quake in their boots at the thought of such nastiness creepin' around their filthy hovels."

"Aye."

"Yes, sir."

"Wait, by the gods—"

"What in the donkey's balls is *that*?"

What did they see? Had it worked? She'd done her best to mound up the mud downstream in the form of a small but hopefully vicious-looking dog. Could she make it move?

The thing more slithered and slid than moved like a dog, but the earth complied with her pleas, moving itself like a living creature, splatting and splattering down the bank, away from Jaena's hiding spot.

"Take the dogs. Get—whatever that is. Go."

"No chance—I'm heading back!"

She finally dared to breathe as she heard the last one take off—either toward the town or her earthen effigy or away in apparent terror.

Huh. It had worked. She would have to remember that trick.

She might be nearly incapacitated, but she had eluded them for now. When night fell, she could climb out of this cave and get on her way again. Until then, she could only wait.

What else could be created from the soil? What else might such creations do? If only she'd had more time to learn the ways of combat for an earth mage. If only they hadn't spent *so* much time forcing her to practice defending herself from Kae.

No matter. She was on her own now, and she'd do just fine figuring it out by herself.

"Can you also ask Enrial to send up some lunch to the small library? And clear it out of... anyone relaxing in there?"

Fayton gave him a crisp nod. "I'll see to the Takarans, my lord."

"What would I do without you, Fayton? I've kept you quite busy lately. It must have been nice to have me gone for a while."

"At least you present a challenge at times." Fayton's eyes twinkled.

Aven hoped that was a compliment. "Have you seen Miara?"

"In the Proving Grounds earlier, my lord. But she's returned to her rooms now."

"Thank you." Aven loped up the stairs to Miara's

rooms. What had she been doing there? The doors to her rooms stood open as he approached up the hallway. A sound caught his ears, and he stopped short.

Humming. Or... singing?

Indeed, inside her rooms, he could hear Miara's voice but in a timbre he'd never imagined. The notes were not yet joyful and free, but they hinted at such lofty heights, flirting with abandon, but not quite reaching it.

He stood for a moment, only listening. Strange how a voice could convey so much emotion. Strange how such a simple sound could stir him so, both mind and body.

She was happy. But it was more than that, wasn't it? She was happy here in Akaria with him. Or at the very least, because of him.

He stepped closer as quietly as he could and rounded the corner, hoping to lean on the doorframe and admire her before she noticed him. His mouth fell open at the scene.

Her room was flushed with life, quite literally. Climbing roses, their petals red as blood, snaked around the bedposts in the bedroom and climbed the walls of the sitting room toward the sky. Lush, green leaves fluttered in a drafty wind, and he wondered idly if he was the cause. Pots had appeared—were those the decorative ones from near the main gate? The plants grew as though they had lived a hundred years this way. Another pot by the bed overflowed with herbs and silver flowers. Another held an array of purple blooms he couldn't hope to identify. The hearth was the only area *not* overtaken by the wild, and the fire blazed with its own joyful intensity.

She must have heard him catch his breath because she turned, faltering. "Don't stop on my account," he said. She blushed. He understood, he couldn't sing in front of other people either. Or carry a note half as good as that. "Look at all this. You've been busy."

She smiled. "You're right, the mountain *is* stifling. Beautiful in its own way, but you did not exaggerate."

He stepped into the room. The air was fresh with the wet smell of plants and the fragrance of flowers. "No need to explain it to me." He strode toward her, wanting to be closer. Not as close as he might want, but... closer.

She met him halfway, and they stopped inches from each other. He lifted a hand and ran it tentatively along her cheek. Her hand slipped over his, and she leaned her face against his palm. "This place is stifling in another way too. There are so many people here. I miss... the road." Of course, he knew she meant more than the road.

"I miss it too," he said. "The upcoming Assembly meeting means we'll have to leave for Panar soon. You can see the White City. Unless you already have?"

"No. You were my only mission into Akaria." She pulled away slightly and pressed a kiss into his palm. Shivers ran through him, and it took every shred of his discipline to keep himself still and unmoving. All possible responses included things they shouldn't yet be doing.

Camil's soft humming from the bath chamber resumed, closer now. Miara released his hand, and Aven took a quick step back as Camil fluttered into view. She carried a basket of linens, hummed more, and utterly ignored them.

They stood awkwardly, not even successfully pretending that they had been doing something else, while Camil passed. Luckily, she paid them no mind.

Miara relaxed as the humming faded down the hallway. "Did you come to eat? Should I call her back?"

"I had… something in mind." He smiled wryly.

She let out a bark of laughter and folded her arms across her chest. "If you had *that* in mind, you better have brought a chain for that damn door. Or something stronger. Every time I lock it, they come back in anyway. Horses to ride us away from here could also come in handy."

His smile broadened into a grin. "I had something in mind… for lunch."

She snorted. "You are an eternal romantic." He was about to insist that he *was* indeed an eternal romantic, but her grin had faded. "Lunch with guests?"

"I thought you and Wunik and I could look over the… map." He left out calling it the star map at the last second, wondering if anyone could be in the hallway listening. And someone still tottered about somewhere in the bedchamber. "Maybe he can translate more of it. Then later tonight, I want to gather up as many mages as we can and figure out what to do next. But I want to get his take on the map first."

She visibly relaxed. "That does sound like a good idea. Let's go." They headed out of the room and down the hall. "Do people keep pets here?" she asked as they went.

"The roses aren't enough for you, eh?"

She smiled. "I'm just getting warmed up."

"I'll need you to redo my room next."

"Perhaps we should start by you actually showing me your room."

"Oh. Yes, indeed. Tonight, perhaps?"

"If your lordship desires it," she said with a surprisingly seductive edge to her voice. He failed to stifle a delighted laugh. "And manages not to pass out."

"You could be quite the courtesan if this whole thing with me falls through."

She snorted.

"You doubt my taste?"

"I'm not... the graceful, glittering type."

"Well, you're my type, that's all I know. Akarians love tough women, you know." Her smile was broader now. That had been the right thing to say. "I'm sure you can get a cat, dog, crow, owl, snake, beetle, squirrel, perhaps a mongoose from Takar—" His list was rewarded with a giggle. "My brother Dom has a pup. Well, a full-grown dog now. We can ask him, if you like. People do keep some pets, and if they don't, I can't say it's because there's a good reason not to. Not that this is the easiest place to take a dog outside, although I suppose that might be easier for you than most."

They turned a corner. She opened her mouth to say something else but stopped. Both their eyes caught on Derk, one of Wunik's apprentices.

"Ho! Miara, Prince Aven." Derk trotted over to them.

"Old Wunik's banished us from his company again. Siliana and I are going for a ride. Would you care to join us?"

He phrased his words as though addressing both of them, but he gazed only at Miara. Aven narrowed his eyes at the mage.

"A ride does sound wonderful—" Miara started. Aven's glare snapped toward her—did she *really* prefer a ride with this dolt to lunch with him? Her voice sounded sincere.

"So dark down here, like a dungeon, by the gods." Derk finally condescended to acknowledge Aven for a brief moment. "I don't know how you stand it, really. I'm going mad."

"—but unfortunately, mundane duties keep us," Miara finished.

*Us.* You hear that, you cocky bastard? She said *us*, and she meant me and her, not *you.*

What had gotten into him? Of course, the fact that he couldn't assert any relationship between them with a clasped hand or arm around her waist didn't help.

"Ah, well, I am sure there will be more opportunities to take a ride in the saddle." Derk gave her a wink. Aven barely stifled the need to throw him down the nearby stairs. If anyone were taking *any* saddle rides, it would *not* be this ignorant lout. "And perhaps if we ride too long, one of us will be in need of your services, my sweet healer, and we'll come looking."

Miara did not return his warmth now. Her lips were pursed and brows drawn, cold as stone, but the mage didn't seem to notice. Or perhaps he just didn't care.

Or was it that not everyone could read Miara as well as Aven could? "Siliana is quite accomplished," she said. "A journeyman, isn't she? Doesn't that mean she's more experienced than you?"

Derk frowned in response.

"I'm sure she'll have no need of me. And if you're nice to her, then perhaps you won't have a problem." Because you won't be getting any healing from me, her words implied.

Derk shrugged. "Next time, my friends." And he sauntered off down the hallway.

Aven rolled his eyes as they strode away. Gods, he knew that type. Wouldn't take no for an answer. No matter what someone said, he'd ignore it and try to get his way. Such men made him glad he knew his way around a sword. Or mace or polearm or warhammer, if necessary.

Both of them shaking their heads, they continued toward the library. At least Miara had been straight with him. That kind only used politeness against you. But had she really wanted to go on a ride with him?

He didn't have time to decide or sort through the implications before they reached the library. Wunik waited, hovering impatiently around the center of the room.

"Thank the gods you're here. I'd nearly decided to devour this without you. I only have so much restraint, you know." Wunik spread his hands wide over a low table that held many diverse, tiny plates. Dumplings of every kind: meat, cheese, jam, potato, and onion. Breads, cakes, butters, a steaming roast. Urns of roasted carrots and pears poached in something sweet. Olives, dried fruits, dates. Wunik turned a raised eyebrow and a grin on Aven. "You mean to spoil me rotten, I think."

Aven smiled back. "Or tempt you to not go back into hiding. Or possibly my mother hopes to fatten us all so that we are too rotund to ever leave." They tucked into a few of the delicacies. Libraries were not made for eating, and so he sat on the floor, legs crisscrossed in front of the low table. And with only a minute or two of hesitation, Miara followed and knelt at one end, by the array of dumplings.

"I'm sorry we couldn't do more for your family last night, Miara." Wunik settled himself as well.

Her face had lit up at the inspection of the treasures on the table, but now it fell ever so slightly. Would Wunik even be able to tell, or was it just something that Aven could see? "It's… all right. We did our best."

"Still. We'll try again tonight with the starlight."

"Of course. We saw Derk on the way here." Miara popped a dumpling in her mouth. Eager to change the subject? "He wanted us to go with them out for a ride. You didn't want them here?"

Wunik frowned. "No. I didn't. Not until I've seen this map. Derk is young. Ambitious. Siliana is too, honestly, and I'm glad of it at times. But she's older, wiser. She's seen more of the world. This map… It could be very dangerous."

"We didn't tell him we were coming here," she said. "I didn't say where we were going, just that we were occupied with 'mundane duties.' "

Wunik nodded. "Just as well. I won't discuss this with them either."

Aven hunted down a napkin and cleaned the food off his fingers. "Well, let's get to it then." He cleared a place on a higher table next to Wunik's armchair. This table was desk-height and well lit by the nearby hearth and candelabras and yet wasn't *too* close to any of those sources of flame. He probably ought to make a mundane copy of the thing soon. Although, perhaps he should understand it better before he divulged its secrets into plain ink and vellum.

Aven took the star map from a pocket and unfolded it carefully. "This—do you recognize this?"

"Is this it? The map of the stars? The one they spoke of?"

"Yes." Aven blinked, simply admiring it for a moment. Such a strange and subtle gift from the past.

"Sweet goddesses. This is what you used?"

"Indeed. Here is Casel. I already knew the stars and some of these meanings, but they are written here in the old language. But others I can't translate. And many of the characters are missing—they appear only in starlight."

"Yes, I see. There are actually two forms of Serabain here. An ancient version and a more modern one. Modern for an ancient language, that is. I doubt I can read the oldest, even if the missing pieces were here. You see this character? That one? Telltale signs of the older tongue. We'd need quite an expert in ancient languages to read these. But there is plenty to look at otherwise. Here she is—freedom. And joy. Intellect. Passion. Courage.

Ferocity. And—" Suddenly the old man stopped short.

"What is it?" Miara got up and joined them, leaning over the back of Wunik's chair.

"This *is* one of Zaera's maps. Or it contains the same information."

"What do you mean?" Aven studied Wunik's frown.

"This is very dangerous indeed, my friends," he breathed.

"What does it *say*, Wunik?" Miara stepped closer.

"Here. This one." He pointed at a star Aven hadn't been able to translate on the opposite side of the map of Casel. "I know the language well enough to guess what the letters would be. We can check it in starlight, perhaps, although we must do it discreetly."

"Why?"

"This one says 'slavery.' "

Miara took an involuntary step back. By the gods.

"What do you mean, slavery?" Aven asked.

"Just as you used star magic to free Miara, they used it to enslave in the first place." Wunik's voice seemed far away, underwater, under glass, as if she'd fallen out of the conversation and was simply watching Aven and Wunik from somewhere else. If this map could do what she thought it could... "This map contains clues to both. It means someone could use this map to control the minds of others, if they knew the right spell. This map tells us which stars control which energies, although not the appropriate spells. Starlight could reveal that."

"But how could one enslave another with just a star?" Aven said slowly. The question brought Miara back to reality, and she stepped closer to them again. Any steps down this road must be stopped.

"How did you free them with just a star? But more importantly, do you *really* want to know the answer to that question?" Wunik squinted hard at Aven, indicating his opinion on the matter.

"Well… no."

"You're damn right, you don't. It's dangerous enough to have the knowledge, but for a king to have the knowledge—"

"A prince—"

"A crown prince who will someday be king, if we get our way. You want a kingdom ruled by laws? You want people who follow you happily and willingly? You cannot be tempted with this evil. You cannot have your political enemies know this evil even exists, to accuse you of it."

But Aven was not easily deterred. "But to free Miara, I imitated a healing spell. Systems seek to return to their natural state. How… What would possibly be the opposite of that?"

She grimaced. "You *can* do a spell of injury. But it's repulsive."

Wunik nodded in agreement. "Few mages even speak of such things, let alone teach them. Hideous."

"I don't understand," said Aven.

"It is possible for a creature mage to learn to rend flesh

apart the same way they learn to mend it back together," Wunik explained.

"Like maggots? Or something?" Aven looked thoughtful. Why had he said that?

"Or a knife. But I can't imagine working such a spell."

"Why did you ask that?" Miara cut in. "About maggots."

"The brand—that was how the energy felt to me. Fire too, but a lot like maggots. Did it feel like that to you?"

Miara frowned. "It was twenty years go. I don't really remember it."

"A spell of injury would be physically painful to the caster, nauseating, and deeply against the Balance. It might even induce madness, although we're not quite sure; it may simply be that mages who have chosen to cast such an awful spell were already mad. Also, we know a *lot* more energy-efficient ways to hurt someone, if that's your goal. In a way, that is a blessing. The spell is rarely taught because for a creature mage, it's much easier to charm an animal or grow your own claws than to rend another human's flesh with your magic. But it *is* possible."

"The Dark Days *were* deeply wrong, though, weren't they?" said Aven.

"Well, there's wrong and then there's wrong," muttered Wunik.

"What is that supposed to mean?" Miara said.

"We all generally agree that to kill a man is wrong." Wunik straightened from looking at the table and leaned back in his chair. "But what about when that man is holding a knife to a child's throat? Suddenly things get a lot more complicated."

"Then is it more wrong to kill him or *not* to kill him?" she muttered.

Aven squinted at the map, almost glaring at it. "What are we going to do with this?"

Was he dodging her? "You didn't answer my question."

She must have surprised him with her insistence. He straightened with a blink and regarded her levelly. "I would kill him, and I wouldn't think twice about it. You always defend a child."

"Because of your Code?" she asked.

"But what if the child—" Wunik started.

Aven eyed him sidelong into silence, and the old man stopped, laughing a little at their seriousness. "A child has more of a chance to change," Aven said in a hard voice. "The man has *had* more of a chance to become wise. There is always a way to turn a situation this way or that. You act as well as you can with as much information as you can get, and you don't look back and worry on it."

Miara found herself smiling at that.

"But yes, the Code says that too." Why did he seem to admit that grudgingly? Frustrated with his Code these days?

"Why did you say that just now, though? About more than one type of wrong," Aven asked Wunik.

"I have heard many stories of the Dark Days, some of them quite questionable tales. I thought this sort of thing was one of them." He gestured at the map. "But some of the stories give the mages who created the tools for the Masters good reasons for doing so."

"That's hard to believe," Miara cut in. But then again… what mage would *want* to do this? Perhaps they had been under duress? If someone ordered her to make a brand or they would kill Aven… she would probably do it. The first action could—hopefully—be reversed, while a death couldn't. Gods, what a thought.

"So back to… what are we going to do with this?" Aven said.

Wunik jumped in. "I'll tell you, I don't want Derk looking at this, to be frank. This knowledge must be carefully guarded, if we distribute it at all. It might be better to put it back in that book and back on the high shelf where it had been hiding for so many years. You know the spell now. You know the star you need. You teach it to me. Perhaps we don't even need the map."

"We could destroy it," she said slowly. "No one should have the power to enslave another."

"True," Aven said. "But destroying this map won't guarantee we've destroyed the power to enslave. There could be other maps, other brands, other people who have this knowledge. We don't know if this is the only way to enslave someone—perhaps there is another way. We can't even translate all of these. If we can find someone versed in ancient languages—"

"Holy languages, in particular," Wunik cut in, eying the map again.

"—then we will at least know what we are dealing with."

Miara nodded. "As much as I want to stop it all… it's

best to know your enemy well. Any information about them is valuable."

They all nodded. Wunik leaned forward and plucked a dried cherry from a delicate bowl. "I don't see much else here I can translate. We need to find someone who knows ancient Serabain dialects. We can see what we see in the starlight. But doing that while avoiding my apprentices in this cave of a hold will not be easy."

"And possibly not worth the risk," Miara added.

"All right. Let's not share it with the gathering tonight. I'll keep it with me until we can figure out somewhere to lock it up or hide it." Aven tucked it in his leather jerkin and the gray tunic beneath. "You mentioned Derk… Anyone else we should be very careful to keep it away from that either of you can think of?"

"Alikar, obviously," Miara said. "I know he was against you, but he also had the scent of magic on him. Sorry I didn't mention it earlier. Someone around him is a mage, even if he doesn't know it."

"And someone sent him that letter from Kavanar," Aven agreed.

"*None* of your lords should see this," Wunik said. "Or even know of it. You should not tempt them with the knowledge that this evil exists. Many a man or woman would long to use it to take the throne. If it could happen to the old king of Kavanar, it could happen to you or your father. Or they could accuse you of using it, even if you haven't. You don't want anyone to have even the option of being like those Kavanarian bastards. We don't need to tempt people."

Aven scowled and popped an olive in his mouth. "Indeed."

"Now, are you ready for some lessons?"

"You don't need me, do you?" she asked. In some ways she wanted to stay and watch. Aven's exuberance in every small discovery was rejuvenating to say the least. But she also longed for more of her newfound freedom. She could find Dom and ask about his pup, or she could simply sit in her room and do nothing.

The choice was hers. It was delightful. And also a little frightening.

"Not if you have other things to attend to," said Aven.

"Just enjoying this new thing called 'being able to do whatever the hell I want.' Come and get me for the mage gathering? Or dinner before?"

They nodded and set to work, and she wandered out into the hallway, leaving them to their practice. A few feet later, she stopped. Decision time. Out of all her dozens of options, she needed to choose one. Or at the very least, she needed to choose a direction to start walking while she considered her options.

The library door opened behind her, and Aven's boots came thudding out. "Your rooms are down there. Proving Grounds, kitchens, that way. Terrace to the left down that hall, another small library to the right of that one. You'll learn it eventually, I've had years."

"I know," she said with a smile. "I keep track of these things when I can."

"I should have guessed." He smiled back and hesitated for a moment as if unsure if he should go back inside. She had a feeling these directions were just an excuse to follow for a moment anyway. She glanced around. The hallways were empty and silent at the moment, as if nothing lived for miles around, as if they were quite alone.

"Thank you, though," she said. She stepped toward him and took his face in her hands, that shaggy brown hair brushing her fingers. She missed the feel of the stubble on his jaw, though she did not mind the addition of the musky smell of Estun's soap. She leaned forward and pressed a long kiss to his lips. He reached for her, reached for more, but she pulled away. "Later," she whispered. "Right? Later?" He gave her a chagrined, crooked smile.

There. Perhaps *that* would help him remember not to pass out tonight. Of course, she still had no idea how they would get a few moments alone even if he *did* manage to stay conscious. Or if sleeping beside him all night was an entirely ridiculous and impossible goal, at least for now. But she would cross that bridge when she came to it.

She turned away, striding down the hallway toward the Proving Grounds with a spring in her step. Maybe instead she would find Devol. Or go to the other library and read a book.

The choice was hers.

Twilight had fallen, and the air had started to cool

when Jaena began to dig her way out. Since she couldn't see who might be nearby, she started out gradually, slowly moving the earth back to where it had been before she'd built this fortress of dirt around her. Then she paused and waited for some exclamation, some expression of concern. But nothing came. She'd cleared about half the dirt, nearly enough for her to crawl out, when footsteps approached.

Should she tunnel herself back in? It was probably too late for that. She could simply stay still and quiet. The sky was darkening. No one would spot her here under the bridge.

Her senses caught a tendril of earth magic. How strange. Was there a mage here? A potential ally? How had the Devoted looking for her not captured *that* mage then?

The footsteps grew louder. Heavy, hulking, a large man's boots. They went over the bridge and stopped just above her. If this was a mage, a potential ally, should she get out? Should she show herself?

The boots strode across to the other side of the bridge and down the path. She scampered out of the hole, clearing the last of the dirt in silence. At the very least, she'd like to get a look at this one who carried earth magic as he headed toward the main road. She took a few steps, straightening herself and brushing pointlessly at the half of her covered in dried mud from her fall on the bank. She started to coax the mud from her clothes with a spell when she felt eyes on her.

She glanced up and froze. On the opposite side of the

bank, the boots had not continued on toward the main road, but they had instead turned around and come down to the stream. And they were facing her.

For a split second, she wanted to bolt—run—she hadn't expected to actually come face to face with anyone. But it was too late for that, wasn't it?

Her eyes locked with the man in the heavy boots. Heavily muscled and broad shouldered, covered with soot and ash, he wore a tawny leather apron over a commoner's work clothes. For once, a man that was taller than she was. A blacksmith?

Had he seen her limp? His brown eyes flicked down to her ankle, then back to her face. He had the rosy, pale complexion of Kavanar and black hair braided at the back of his neck. The black locks were broken up by several streaks of white that caught in the rising moonlight and swept from over his left eye back into the braid.

He studied her. "You're hurt," he said simply. "Do you need help?"

She only stared for a moment, struggling to calculate how to respond. She must have stared too long because he asked the same thing again in another language. Did he think she might be Takaran? Silly. Takarans were not as dark as she. He tried a third. Was that Farsai? Not that she knew it. What kind of blacksmith knew three languages?

"Sorry, you startled me," she managed quickly. "No, no, it's all right. I'm—just passing through." She wanted to wince at her words but managed to stifle it. That sounded ridiculous. Clearly she had not inherited her father's talent for smooth talking. Aye, just passing through, hiding under a bridge covered in mud and not anywhere near the path, but I'm just a traveler passing through. She took a step back toward the path but only succeeded in emphasizing her horrid limp. She failed to hide her wince and closed her eyes to the pain for a moment. She'd either momentarily forgotten the agony, or it was getting worse.

"Your leg—let me help," he said, starting forward. Only the stream he needed to cross made him hesitate. It was not even an arm's length across but must run heavier in the spring for the bridge to be there. She gave him a wary look, hopping a few shambling steps away from the stream. What if he had heard they were looking for a mage? Could this be a trick?

He regarded her steadily for a moment, eyes locked with hers, but calm. Indeed, there was an unusual openness to his eyes, as if he hoped she could see his worth in his gaze. Not so guarded, not so squinting, nor so narrowed as most strangers' were. At least, not at the moment.

"Where are you headed?"

Donkey balls, she hadn't made up a story to cover her tracks. All day sitting in a damned hole, and she'd spent it plotting spells and traps and no backstory at all. What had she been thinking?

"I'm sorry, I forget myself. I don't talk to many lovely women."

She glanced down at her mud-covered leather tunic and formerly white tunic. At least the leggings had already been brown. She gave him a dubious look.

He was undeterred by her expression and took a quick leap across the small stream. He held out a hand. An optimist. She grudgingly shook it and managed a weak smile, mostly out of relief. "Mostly farmers come to visit my smithy. We're all dirt covered here. I'm Tharomar."

He seemed to trust her readily. *Too* readily, really. She could be a bandit, or a trickster. Have companions hiding in the grain, waiting to pounce. A woman looking to seduce him and then thoroughly rob him blind. Although she *did* mean him no harm, he had no real way of knowing that. Then again, his bicep was probably the width of her head. He probably had little to fear from anyone, if he knew anything much about the arts of defending himself.

"I was walking to Anonil, on the border," she managed. Hey, that was the truth. Now for the lie. Perhaps she could pretend to be a merchant. That had always been the plan, the hope. "Meeting my brother there to pick up some items—goods—to trade back at home."

Tharomar nodded gravely, pressing his lips together as his brow creased handsomely. "Well, my fine lady, I do make a fair number of excellent items in my smithy for passing traders to peruse. I hate to be the bearer of bad news, but I don't know as you'll be making it much farther tonight with that ankle. There's no inn in this village, such as it is, but I'm sure you could board with someone. It's nearly sunset anyway, and you'll not do much better finding inns to the east. Especially at the pace you'll be going. You should probably rest. Are you sure

I can't help? You could rest it, check my trade goods in the morning, and be on your way. How did you hurt it?"

She hesitated. *Oh, just falling down a hill while not paying attention and probably costing me my life eventually, that's all! Those Devoted bastards are scary, though. Can you blame me?* She said nothing.

"Are you *sure* I can't get you some wine to dull the pain, at least?" he said with a crooked smile. *Damn, he was handsome for a smith.*

A smile betrayed her true feelings on her lips.

"Beer? You don't look like the type. I have an excellent mead. Could I tempt you with that? Oh, I know. Brandy?"

She snorted. "Are you trying to get me drunk?" She laughed because she meant it and also to warn him that she was not entirely naïve. "Is this a good method for parting trade customers from their coin?" *Not that she had any.*

He sobered quickly. "Oh, no, no—not at all. I just get injured myself often enough. Something to ease pain is a necessity in my craft."

"You said you're a smith?"

"Yes. Come, there's no healer in this town, but I've got a few salves. They won't speed the healing, but they'll dull the ache. I swear on Nefrana's blooms in the spring, I mean nothing but to help you." He scratched the stubble on his chin and gave her a soft, friendly smile as he waited for her reply.

She hesitated. *What was a smith doing out here on the path anyway, that he could just abandon it and turn* around and head home again? "I'd hate to keep you from whatever errand had you on this path," she said warily, taking another step away from him.

"Oh, I was just going to check on my neighbor Nemin. Supposed to carry a package for me into the city tomorrow. But he'll be by in the morning anyway. Was nothing important."

Could she afford to shelter here? What if the Devoted searched the buildings? Then again, could she afford to limp along in the darkness, especially if she couldn't even easily run and hide now? Could she afford to be out in the open if she was such a slow target? Perhaps by morning the ankle would be improved.

"Besides, did you hear those riders coming through?" he added. "They said there's a renegade *mage* escaped around here. Told us to be careful and to kill him right away if we saw him. You don't want to be caught out here alone in the dark with that ankle and some crazed mage on the loose, do you?"

She swallowed. "I—uh… No. I don't." Smooth, Jaena, real smooth. Still, Tharomar was either *very* trusting, very dense, or pretending not to notice her awkwardness. If he took note of it, he showed no sign. Perhaps she was just so prevailingly awkward that this stuttering seemed typical. "All right," she said, breezily now. "When you put it that way, it would be best to stay somewhere. At least until the morning."

He swept up to her with surprising grace for his size and threw one of her arms over his shoulder. Well. He was holding nothing back when it came to helping her. The length of his body pressed against hers as he drew some of her weight and led her carefully up the riverbank and onto the path. He smelled of hard work, sweat, the earthy substances from within the smithy—not something she'd want to scent her home with, but not unpleasant either. This close she could see the rough linen tunic he wore beneath the leather. A pendant of a golden shaft of wheat swayed gently across the skin of his chest—a symbol of Nefrana. Kind as he was, she needed to remember she was not safe here.

"Right. My home is just down that way," he said, pointing. They began limping forward.

"So you're the blacksmith for these surrounding farms?"

"Indeed. Smithy is right over there."

Even at the sight of the smithy, hunched and billowing smoke near a small home, she could feel the energy radiating from it. Why did his smithy have so much magic swirling around it? Why did *he* have these bits of earth magic swirling about him? He seemed completely unaware that she was a mage. He was clearly afraid of this renegade who could certainly only be out to do him harm. A typical Kavanarian point of view. Where was the magic coming from? Could it just be the concentration of metal and earth in the smithy? Natural energies? No. As they moved closer, she could feel even more clearly that it went beyond raw, natural energy. There were spells, although none she readily recognized. Strange.

He led her to his home, a small wattle and daub

cottage. More spells stirred, foreign and indeterminate. He helped her remove her pack. Gripping his arm, she eased gingerly into the seat by the fireplace. The warmth of the cottage alone felt better already. He knelt on one knee to stoke the low-burning coals and readily revived the flame with a log and a few flicks. His sleeveless tunic revealed rippling arms and shoulders, his strength handsome and well earned by honest labor. He would make a fine warrior. But perhaps blacksmiths were even more important than warriors to armies. What was a warrior without a blade or shield?

"So what'll it be?" he said.

She lifted an eyebrow.

"Beer, mead, brandy?" He grinned. "I suppose I also have tea, although that won't take the edge off." He had an angular jaw and intelligent, fiery eyes. Too intelligent for a smith in this small of a town. And how many smiths in these sorts of places knew three languages? Or more, even?

"What do you recommend? You're the injury expert."

Instead of replying, he moved forward to examine her ankle. Since he was still down on one knee, her foot was close at hand. She must have twitched and revealed her fear, because he stopped quickly. "May I?" he said, very gently, as if inviting her to stop him.

She finally nodded. He took her boot gingerly, and only now did she notice her foot had begun to swell. Oh, gods, this was all a mistake. Why had she ever taken that damn brand? She could have escaped in the darkness of night, and no one would have known any better.

No. The triumph of taking away their most powerful weapon was *not* something she was going to regret. She would find a way out of this. She had to. She would be free of that niggling voice burrowing into her shoulder, and she would make sure they never did to another what they had done to her. What they had done to her sister. But she couldn't focus on that now—she couldn't explain tears at this moment to this smith, this Tharomar. Instead, she focused on her freedom.

She savored it for a moment, cherishing it in case she lost it, in case they recaptured her.

Silence in her mind.

Beautiful.

His fingers drew her back to reality as they unlaced her boot, surprisingly gentle and dexterous. Almost… intimate. Was that heat in her cheeks a blush? She had always assumed peasant smiths like him would be rough brutes. Most mage smiths she knew were, and they were far more bookish than the average smith. How many smiths were so quick to go from pounding metal to untying intricate laces?

Perhaps he wanted to unlace more than just her boot. Perhaps she wanted him to as well.

He glanced up at her, only concern in his eyes. She felt abruptly disappointed. You do not have time for this, she told herself. Get it together.

His fingers gently pulled her legging up her calf a hand's width, revealing a swollen ankle that was already turning colors. She swore.

"You did a number on it, all right. Mead, perhaps? I think it's the strongest I've got."

"Mead it is. And any salve you have would be much appreciated. I can repay you in the form of work, or I can return with coin from my brother's sales, if you wish," she lied.

He nodded. "I'm sure we can find some mutually beneficial arrangement. Or I have heard the gods bless those who help strangers in need. So I'm sure the balance will come due, one way or another." He grinned at her.

She returned his smile, but her own faded as soon as he turned away. She was not so sure about any of that. She stared at her ankle, feeling disgusted with herself. How long would it take to heal? How long till they came back through the town, searching for her? She had likely failed before she'd even really begun. And she had no way to contact Miara or Menaha or any of the others. Or to get help.

Damn the Masters. And the Devoted. And all of them, damn them straight to hell.

He stood and went to a nearby cupboard. Only then did she notice the interior of his home beyond him, the seat, and the fire. A cupboard, a small table with another chair, a wide bed on the far wall. Just one room. The bed looked inviting. Easily wide enough for two. But there were no signs of a woman in the cottage, unless she was perhaps even more brusque and burly than Tharomar. Thick, heavy tomes lined one of the shelves of the cupboard, but she could not see them well enough to guess their purpose.

"Here you go," he said, turning and handing her an earthenware mug. He set a kettle of more mead over the fire to warm.

The fired clay and mud of the mug was almost as rejuvenating as the mead. She held the drink in both hands and took a deep, slow drink.

"And now this," he added, returning to one knee by her ankle. He held up a small jar for her inspection. The label read: MOUNTAIN DAISY.

She considered quizzing him on what was in it or what a mountain daisy was, but really she had nothing to judge it by. Mages had healed her in Mage Hall, and before that, her mother had hired apothecaries. She knew nothing about what people used for injuries like this or what would be effective. She simply nodded, feigning confidence and understanding.

He took a glob and smoothed the slightly cold cream across her skin. Indeed, a flowery scent caught her nose. She was intensely aware of each movement of each finger and the exquisitely lovely sensation on her skin above the pain. How strange that she reacted so much to his touch.

Or was it his kindness she was reacting to? All the world hunted her. But not him, it seemed. At least, not yet. She glanced at the pendant but tore her eyes away. He had no way of knowing that she was a mage, it seemed. Here, for the moment, she was mostly safe.

"I'll be back in a few minutes," he said, wiping off his hands and closing the jar. He pushed over a small stool and helped her rest her foot on top of it. "Keeping it up should help. I've got to make sure the hearth has cooled in the smithy, perhaps rinse off so you don't suffocate from my stench in this tiny hut. And prayer, of course. You enjoy that mead. I'm sure the goddess won't mind if you pray from a chair. I'll be back." He grinned, and she nodded, taking a drink.

She felt the sudden urge to tell him no, to leave the scent of the earth darkening his skin. How bizarre. Why should she even care about such a thing? She must be tired. Or there was something very, very unusual about this Tharomar.

Once he was gone, she tried to search the room as best she could, hobbling and hopping on one leg. She found nothing suspicious. He had an immense book collection, mostly religious texts. Three shelves held leather-bound tomes of various types, some in other languages. How strange. The only ones she recognized were *The Book of the Vigilant* and *Kyaeer's Verses*, not that she really knew much about either beyond that they often belonged to acolytes of Nefrana. A small ceramic pot contained a dozen more golden wheat pendants on chains like the one he wore around his neck. Why so many, she wondered? A strange vibration came from the pendants, not exactly magical and not something she understood. All of this made some of her uneasiness return. Tharomar did not seem like he could be a Devoted Knight, but he was clearly very concerned with matters of the soul. This safety was only temporary.

Unless he was off getting the Devoted Knights right now. She swallowed and hoped that was not the case. Limping lamely toward Anonil all night did not seem like a better plan, but it did not ease her mind to simply *hope* he wasn't betraying her. Perhaps she could at least find a knife or something to defend herself if need be.

The home was otherwise well stocked. Should she swipe something to put in her very empty pack? Well, she still had the few loaves of bread and those three knots to get through. The idea of taking something twisted her stomach, though, and she abandoned it. He had been nothing but kind to her, and theft from him, especially so quickly, was also probably a sure way to end that. Perhaps she could simply ask him for a few things or offer to repay him for a few ordinary things with trade? That seemed best. And who knew how long she might rely on his hospitality. It was best not to test it prematurely.

Her search for a weapon of some sort did not turn up much. No serious weapons were hung anywhere, or even anything that could be particularly dangerous, unless some of those salves and herbs were poisonous, which she was entirely unable to recognize. If he was armed, he kept implements of war in the smithy, it seemed. He was probably the most dangerous thing in the cottage, from her perspective. She settled for a butter knife that she tucked underneath but not inside the pack. Perhaps if he found it he would simply wonder how he'd managed to drop it there.

She poured more mead and returned to her seat.

Now she surveyed the home again for places to hide. If the Devoted came back before he returned, or in some unforeseen circumstance, she would need options. Sadly, she could not think up many options and only concluded that she could definitely hide somewhat under the bed, unless someone looked directly under it at her. Otherwise, the home was sparse enough that there wasn't much else. The cupboards were stocked full, and the table provided no opportunities to hide.

She continued to drink the mead and began noticing more spells the longer she sat. The hearth that had burned so steadily, so low, and reignited so easily—it was no coincidence. The slabs of stone were imbued with energy, not exactly spelled but simply charged with a mage's powers. Why? How? And who was the mage creating them all?

Could Tharomar be the mage? And if so, how could no one have noticed it?

It must be him. She had never known she'd had powers before they'd captured her. He must simply not know. How unfortunate that he be so pious then. Unless he had a wife or partner. *Someone* had to be casting these spells. And if he did have a spouse, he really should not bring home young women and leave them alone in his cottage like this.

She reached out toward the smithy. The swirling mass of energy thrummed with power. The spells were not intent on doing any specific things, but instead, the mage owned the metal, the stone, the hearth more fully. The rock and iron around the smithy sang with joyful power, his in more ways than one.

Another mage who didn't like mages. And didn't know he was one.

Great. Just great.

Eventually, she heard footsteps returning. Indeed, it was no wife. Tharomar again. Clean and thrumming with fresh, strange energy. Where had he acquired that from?

He had also brought her a pie.

"What the—" she started.

"You need to eat, don't you?"

She nodded and accepted the dish. She discovered with delight a meat pie drowning in a steaming stew of soft carrots, turnips, and gravy.

"By the gods. Where did you get this?"

"Morigna, on the other side of the smithy. I brought you a change of clothes too. Thought you might want to get out of that muddy mess."

She slowed in her chewing, and only partly because he'd acknowledged she must look like she'd just rolled out of a pigsty. How was she going to repay him for all this? Oh, and who cared what he thought of what she looked like anyway.

"We barter for everything around here. Don't worry about it." He met her gaze levelly as if trying to reinforce his sincerity. He had read her too easily. It was unnerving. Up until now, the fact that he hadn't read her well had only worked in her favor. She didn't particularly want that to change. "Want me to step out while you change? This place isn't designed much for privacy." He gave her an apologetic smile. "Water there—to wash with, if you like."

She nodded, and he stepped out again wordlessly. She washed as quickly as she could and slipped into the new clothes he'd found. Thank Anara, not a dress. The tired grayish-brown trousers and tawny tunic were worn. Patches of cheerful red and orange covered a knee, an elbow, and a handful of other spots. Well, all the better. She didn't need the guilt of leaving no coin and disappearing with an outfit the farmers had worked hard to get. Unless… these things were still not the worst they had. No matter, nothing she could do about that now. She would keep a mental tally of all she'd received from them and try to send payment once she was safe in Akaria. *If* she ever made it safe to Akaria.

She coaxed the mud out of her previous clothes gently, leaving a dusting on the floor that she hoped he wouldn't notice. Folding the now clean clothes, she tucked the tidy pile behind the knapsack. Untying it wasn't worth the risk of exposing the brand. Hopefully he wouldn't notice the clothes were now clean and that she hadn't really needed a change of clothes after all.

"Tharomar?" she called. His name felt strange and awkward on her tongue.

He returned with a smile, and she returned to her chair, glad she didn't have to limp over and get him. As she ate the rest of the pie, he busied himself around the cottage. She studied her mead and the flames. She tried not to think. It helped, and the ankle did feel better. She felt… less terrified that her whole plan had gone off the rails and she had completely lost control of the situation. Perhaps it was just the mead. She unwound her braid of braids and let them fall around her face. She relaxed, her eyelids drooped. She listened to the crackle of the fire. The sound of him crushing something in a pestle behind her perked her anxieties once again. What was he up to? After some time, he stopped his machinations in his nearby cupboard and jutted a chin at the bed.

"You can sleep there, if you like. Or Morigna can make room by her fire, but she does have a young babe. I can sleep on these rugs. I fall asleep there half the time anyway." He smiled.

"I… I do think I could use the rest," she said sleepily. Well, that wasn't much of an answer.

He seemed to understand without additional clarity on her part. Again he took her arm over his shoulder and helped her hobble-hop over to the bed. Did he release her with hesitation, or was that her imagination? His warmth left her side, leaving her cold. She eased herself down on the far side of the straw mattress, nearest the wall, as he covered her with a scratchy, gray wool blanket. He moved away again, back to his cupboard, then to the table, then the cupboard. She relaxed a bit more. She wound the scarf she'd found in the new set of clothes around her hair, both for warmth and to protect the braids.

How could she possibly be so relaxed when she had the stolen brand to make a mage a slave in a bag five feet from her bed, and all the Devoted and guards of Mage Hall looking for her?

What had been in that salve? Or was it the mead? Or the meat pie? Or those dashing brown eyes? Or maybe those spells today had just been more tiring than she'd thought.

He came back to check on her periodically. Once, when she was nearly asleep, he stayed for one moment, two. She could feel him watching her. He pulled the blanket up slightly over her shoulder. Her brand was but inches from his fingers. What would he think of it? Would he be repulsed to see it?

She opened her eyes a little. A small, concerned smile graced his face, nothing more. No hint of malice or even surprise.

"Why are you helping me?" she said, letting fear color her voice.

He blinked. There, *now* he was a touch surprised? He quickly hid his surprise away, making her uneasy once again. He was hiding something. Whatever it was, it was unlikely to be good. Still, she couldn't convince herself of any malevolent motives while he stared into her eyes.

"Because," he said, shrugging, "someone helped me once, and it made a world of difference. Besides, it's the Way. How you deserve to be treated." Was he flirting, or was she imagining things? Or was it the mead? "It is how I would want to be treated. And have been, in my time of need. Don't worry. It'll come back to me in the end."

They were both silent for a moment. He patted her forearm reassuringly.

"Tharomar?"

"Yes?"

"You are… different."

"I have heard that a few times."

The mead was lulling her toward sleep.

"Tharomar?"

"Yes? I'm still here." Her eyes were closed.

"Sleep beside me. It's all right. No point in sleeping on the floor."

"Are you sure?"

"Yes." It was a small way to repay his kindness and make her stay less of an imposition on his life.

"Nothing untoward will come of it, I promise you." She barely heard him nestle into the straw mattress beside her before she drifted off to sleep.

# 6 GATHERINGS

Aven's balcony had been transformed. Additional benches and chairs dotted the garden, now filling with people. Torches had been hung in sconces he hadn't realized were there, and three blazing braziers made some attempt to provide warmth and light. Aven still wore his heaviest cloak, though, and had exchanged his leather jerkin for a black gambeson.

Aven scanned those who had gathered. No one had turned down his invitation, unless he counted Beneral, who was not yet ready to reveal his magic so openly. Everyone else had come. How many people outside their group knew that this was happening? He hadn't asked any of them to keep the event a secret, knowing that might have encouraged gossip. But he didn't exactly want the whole kingdom to know, let alone Kavanar. There was probably little hope of preventing that, though.

"Thank you for coming, everyone." He held out his

hands wide as the group quieted. "I spoke with most of you personally. But in case you haven't heard, I've been causing a bit of a ruckus." A ripple of laughter flitted through the crowd. "We as a kingdom pride ourselves on our military strength. But we've let ourselves neglect one area: magic. We must be better trained and equipped to defend against whatever mage army Kavanar chooses to throw at us. And I've heard a few of you might be able to help with this problem."

"Are we going to war?" someone asked.

"Possibly. It is as yet unclear."

"What can we do to help?" said another.

"The king is considering exactly how he wants to handle this," Aven said. "There are a lot of things we don't know. The first step I've been tasked with is to free more mages, with help from Miara and Wunik. To aid that effort, we need air mages. For those prepared to defend Akaria from the mage troops Kavanar is building, we need to organize ourselves into units that can work with the rest of the army. We need to plan our defense strategies for each city and as units. We can't wait until the lords are ready, because that might never happen. In particular, earth mages that we can train to defend Estun itself would be a good start."

"There's also simple training to defend yourselves," Miara added. "How many of you have any instruction?" Wunik and his apprentices, as well as his mother, raised their hands. Most others did not. "Those of us with some magic lessons to draw on should begin teaching the others."

Elise spoke up now. "Miara and I can work with creature mages. Wunik and Aven are air mages—you'll want to start on star magic first?"

Aven nodded.

"I can show them some other stuff too," Derk grumbled.

"Do we have any earth mages that are trained?" Elise asked, ignoring him.

Wunik shook his head. "I may be able to help with some basics, but generally no. I've found earth magic isn't very fond of me."

Miara swore under her breath. "Figures."

"Well, we'll just have to figure it out," said Thel. "Maybe we can find a book to reference."

"The riders we sent to check on the other elders should be back, or they will be by tomorrow. Elder Staven is an earth mage. If he's all right, then we may have help. If not, well…" Elise trailed off.

"Also Jaena, the mage we already freed—she is an earth mage, assuming she can escape and make it to Anonil," said Miara.

"You freed one already?" Teron asked, his eyes alight.

Aven nodded. "And we'll be freeing another shortly."

"I asked Jaena to wait until sundown tomorrow to flee," said Miara. "That way several mages can flee at once and give us more of a chance to free a few before the Masters catch onto what we're doing."

"We are targeting warrior mages to gain information on what Kavanar plans to do," Aven said. "Also sounds like we'll need to look for earth mages in particular. Is there anything else we should be looking for?"

"Healers," said Siliana. "Our numbers being much smaller, we're unlikely to match their combat ability anytime soon, especially against mages with decades of practice. If we have our share of healers, that can only help."

"Great, yes. Any other ideas?" asked Aven.

"Any mage slave who works directly with the Masters," said Miara, "could have valuable information on what they're planning, no matter what type of mage they are."

Aven nodded. "We'll be most constrained by who we can find. They have to be out at night and unguarded, which isn't common. All right. Let's break into groups. Air mages over here with me. Creature mages with Miara. Any earth mages?" A few hands raised. "Ah, well—Thel, you take them."

"Me?" Ah, Thel. Someone should explain to him that younger brothers of crown princes were supposed to be always angling for the throne, not ducking the slightest attention or responsibility.

"Yes, you. Compare experiences and anything you've figured out so far. Or go hunting for reference material." Thel should like any excuse to go back to a library, and indeed he raised an eyebrow, looking intrigued now.

"Once we are organized, Wunik or I should be able to help out," Miara added in their direction. Thel nodded, a bit relieved, and the groups moved apart, finding new places to gather separately.

What would Dom be up to tonight? Aven had tried to look for him, but hadn't found him in the few hours he'd had to search. If Dom was a mage, he might as well admit it and join the lot of them. If he wasn't, that was going to definitely cause trouble. Aven needed to ask Miara if she had thought to check.

As if reading his thoughts, she stepped away from her group and approached.

"Are you going to look now?" For once, he could see the deep sorrow and concern in her eyes. She hid her worry well, didn't she?

"Soon." He nodded. He wanted to put an arm around her, to comfort her, but kept it clenched at his side.

"Will you look for them?"

"Of course," he replied. "After your father and sister, we will look for another mage's mother too. He's not sure if she's there, though." Aven wasn't at all optimistic about spotting Teron's mother. Even if she was enslaved, she was unlikely to be outside. "Hey, you didn't happen to notice if my other brother Dom had any mage abilities, did you? I haven't been able to find him to approach him about it."

"No, I didn't think to check, but I will if I see him. Because Alikar might want him to be the heir then?"

"Yes, and because he might actually take him up on it, unlike Thel."

She narrowed her eyes. "Do you and he not get along?"

"Oh, no. We get along as well as any brothers do. But he was always more amiable to the idea of leadership than Thel was. Oh, also—my father wants the demonstration to be in two days, in the morning. We should work out the details."

"Yes. I talked to Wunik and company about it, and I think we have a good plan. Need to figure out where, though."

"Great, we can work on it tomorrow. Anyway, we should probably get back to our groups."

She gave him a smile and a crisp nod. They plodded solemnly back to their separate groups. He should have organized them differently. He wanted her by his side. But no. She and Wunik had the most to teach here. Putting them together made little sense, except to his heart.

Wunik had begun by taking stock of their group. Far more air mages sat in their circle than any other type—the two of them, Beneral's apprentice, Derk. Five total, if they counted the absent Lord Beneral. Beneral was not yet comfortable revealing his status, but he hadn't denied he would help eventually either. Unlike the completely novice earth mages, most of the air mages had either independent experimentation or actual instruction under their belts, or both. Hopefully they could use this to their advantage, somehow.

Drawing out the bowl and water, Wunik explained farsight again, and Aven tried to listen carefully, as he'd far from mastered it. He found himself at times studying the group instead, though. Teron sat as close as possible to the elder, as if he feared he'd lose the chance to listen with the next words that passed. Derk stared off into space, having clearly heard this explanation more than a few times before.

Really, this was a rare chance to survey his forces, so

perhaps it was okay if he didn't master farsight in this exact moment. He needed to understand what he had to work with. The Dark Master had what, five hundred mages? It could be more by the time Akaria actually faced them. Kavanar's forces would be skilled and unwavering in their determination to complete their mission. At the same time, they were not truly willing. If Miara could find cracks in her compulsions, others likely could too.

Aven watched each mage in turn as they settled into their groups. Nearly all looked nervous, tentative, unsure. Nothing like soldiers. Nothing like powerful mages. Nothing like something to be afraid of, and definitely not like people who were evil conspirators out to corrupt souls.

Many of them had never admitted they were mages publicly, let alone been in a room with so many mages at once. Perhaps they were simply nervous because this would be a great place for someone like Alikar to massacre everyone and end this before it started.

Which was why there were six guards at the door and surrounding hall.

Aven took a deep breath. They were untrained, naïve, green. But they had taken the first steps. It would come to them.

A huge part of getting a force to fight together was throwing them in the same room and lobbing some danger at them. They would figure it out, hopefully before too big a danger landed in their laps and exploded in their faces.

"I always found that earth mages had far better success with garden augmentation." Elise tapped her chin thoughtfully. She and Siliana were deep into the details of magically aided cultivation. Aven's mother clearly missed talking about magic. Too bad Miara hadn't realized this sooner and found a way to make some use of it. But better late than never.

"Oh, well, yes. The soil is important, but so are the creatures *in* the soil," said Siliana. "The tiny little creepy crawlers, the worms, even the bits of the dirt that are alive—you can encourage all that. And of course, discouraging the pests is a key concern."

Miara found herself trying to tune them out. All the talk of gardening formed an ache in her chest that grew and grew. Her father would have had a lot to say in this conversation. A lot more than she did. All Miara had to offer would be tips on horse manure, and she didn't feel like making that point at the moment. Being associated with excrement wasn't *quite* the impression she was going for.

Her father would have laughed at that. He would have put her at ease with these two women. He deserved to be here. She clenched her fists, thinking of their locked doors and guards the night before. She hoped tonight that Jaena would have some information or that they found a way to get to her family.

And if they didn't? Gods, let them not be paying for

Miara's freedom. Luha was young, vulnerable—Miara shoved the thoughts aside. No point in racking herself with worry over something if it hadn't even happened. She was doing everything she could.

Irritable now, she was close to interrupting Elise and Siliana and directing them back to the fact that a *war* was looming, not a famine, when the door to the balcony opened. Aven's brother Dom peered inside, then entered and shut the door. Miara stood and approached him.

He gave a chagrined smile at her approach. "Damn, it's warmer out *here* than inside that damn cave with all these fires raging."

"Can I help you?" Perhaps it was presumptuous to block him from entering a room in what was effectively his own home and she was only a guest. But after what Aven had said, she'd prefer to be sure he was an ally before she let him roam around. If he were a mage, it wouldn't matter. If he weren't... his reason for arriving could be darker.

"It seems there's a party, and I'm not invited."

She narrowed her eyes at him. Why was he really here? "I'm sure you could be invited, if you like." Aven had indicated as much, but she let it remain ambiguous. Her words were friendly on the surface but had an edge to them.

"How exactly does one get an invitation?" Dom folded his arms across his chest. The coldness of his words made her wonder if he'd been chatting with Alikar when Aven had been looking for him.

"One only has to be a mage, or a friend of mages. Are you?"

Dom froze. Ah, he had actually not realized that was the point of this meeting. Interesting. He glanced around, eying who attended. "But Thel is here." He seemed—jealous? How much rivalry did these brothers have? Was he the one always getting left out of things? Dom put up a gruff front, so it was easy to forget that he must be the youngest, the baby of the group.

"Yes, he is."

Now it was his turn to narrow his eyes at her. "Are you… stopping me from entering?"

She smiled sweetly. "What, me? Could *I* actually keep you from entering?"

"As a matter of fact, you do look like you'd at least put up a good fight. I doubt I'd leave without bruises. Am I getting bruises today?"

"I have no idea what you could mean."

He sighed, seeming defeated. "Okay, fine. I'll leave." He turned to leave.

"Cuts and scratches are more likely." She propped a hand on her hip. "But I never said you *had* to leave."

Partially turned away, he eyed her over his shoulder. "Then what do I have to do?"

"Well, you have to be a mage. Are you?" Or a friend of mages, she had said. She'd conveniently forget that piece if he already had.

He cocked an eyebrow. "I don't know. Can you tell me?"

"Of course." She frowned. "But I'm sure your mother—"

"She didn't want to tell us. And to tell you the truth, I didn't want to know either. It's not like it's done Aven any good."

"Well, I have it on good authority that you're probably going to be formally asked if you're a mage fairly soon, considering Thel is sitting over there."

He clenched a fist, turning back to face her now. "Damn Alikar and his schemes."

"And his bigotry. I wouldn't blame you for not wanting to know."

He grumbled. "Can I just go sit with Thel and be done with it?"

She grinned at him sweetly again. "No. That's earth mages only."

"Fine," he growled. "Tell me then. But I'm *not* going to be happy about it."

She shrugged. "You can just go back to your room. Isn't there a dvora somewhere looking for a mate? Perhaps you could help with *that*."

His chuckle finally broke his disgruntled exterior. "Indeed. Although I think Thel may already be... helping on that front." He stopped and laughed again. "I can see why he likes you."

"Who? Thel?"

He rolled his eyes. "Not too perceptive, though. Don't be coy."

Her eyes widened slightly. She hadn't realized that Dom knew. How much of a secret could they keep if so many already knew or were figuring it out? Or maybe he didn't, and he only suspected. She wouldn't confirm or deny it.

"Just tell me if I'm a mage so I can go start hunting for a cave in the mountains to be exiled to when this all blows up in our faces. I want a real nice one, and I better get a jump on it if all these bastards are gonna need one too."

"Fine." She reached out for the scent of magic underneath him. Life energy teased her senses, his heart beating, his blood alive as it raced through the veins, but she pushed past it toward the soul underneath.

The scent of fur swept through her mind—snowy wolf, wet bear, the clean scent of the wind beneath the hawk in flight. These scents were not still or softly vibrating like the earth, or twisting like the air, but rushing with the energy of life. The speed dizzied her, the power surging forward like a stampede off a cliff.

Yanking herself free before she tumbled over the edge, she staggered a step back in spite of herself. When had she closed her eyes? The draw of magic like her own could be more intoxicating than the others. His magic, like Aven's, was rare—so wild, so strong. Had he found ways to work around the Stone too, but as a creature mage, not realizing that he was doing it? Did he heal faster? At the very least, his dogs probably listened to him better than they would most. Perhaps having a companion around helped him survive the constant mental weight of the Great Stone.

"What is it?" Dom said, a note of concern in his voice.

Miara stole a glance at Elise. Underestimating the queen's power was easy under that elegant exterior. King

Samul, too, must have wasted a great deal by not fostering his own abilities. How else could all three sons be mages, and all three with plenty of raw ability, even while taking root in the shadow of that damned Stone?

"Tell me," Dom growled. "You know. Why aren't you *saying* anything?"

"Sorry. You are indeed a mage. A creature mage, like your mother." Dom looked down at the floor for a moment. She couldn't read him. "Are you all right?"

"Yes. I—I'm good. Tell you the truth, I didn't think there was much of a chance for me. Since my father isn't a mage, what are the chances we could *all* be? I thought for sure we couldn't be so lucky."

"Lucky? You were just pointing out that it had done Aven no good."

"I have no interest in warring with my brother." He scowled at the thought. "I would have no problem being king, but I do have a problem with Aven *not* being king. He's worked all his life for this. I can't believe—it doesn't matter. I also have absolutely *no* interest in being someone's pawn, which is what I would likely be to men like Alikar."

"You are wise to recognize all those things."

He ducked his head as if embarrassed by the compliment. "So yes. I'm lucky that we're all mages. You want a Lanuken on the throne, you get a mage, I guess. What are the chances for all of us, without Father?"

He asked the question rhetorically, but Miara raised her eyebrow and smiled slyly in response. "Indeed. What *are* the chances." He frowned at her with a tilt of his head.

He caught her implication, and she'd leave it at that. "Do you want to join us then? Your mother, Siliana, and I were reviewing our options in the creature mage group. Well, honestly they'd gone off topic into gardening, but I didn't have the heart to stop them and remind them we have a war to plan. I'm sure you could also go about your evening and pretend none of this is happening."

"Alikar is stalking the halls already. I had to dodge him twice to get here."

She frowned. "Not because—"

"Yes, because. He wants me to be king. And if I have to choose between the two, I definitely want to be *here*." He strode past her.

Miara reached out to Aven. *Dom came here on his own. He's a creature mage. You wanted to know, sorry to interrupt.*

An enormous sigh of relief flowed from Aven. *Thank you.*

As Dom approached, Elise's eyes lit up, though she strove to conceal the expression. Her face held no hint of surprise.

Of course she'd known all along. If one of the princes had not been a mage, they would have had a hugely different situation on their hands. It would have been reckless for her *not* to know. And on top of that, certainly Elise must have wondered when they were children as well. If Miara ever had children, she'd certainly be excited to see what type of mage they turned out to be—

She stopped still for a moment and blinked. Where had that thought come from? She had *never* thought about having children with any kind of anticipation before.

No time to unpack that idea at the moment. Back to Elise. Realizing how the queen had sought to know the lay of the land ahead of time, Miara realized it had been foolish for *her* to not have already sought the information out. She was being idealistic, naïve even, to think she should abide by some kind of polite privacy in this situation. Their enemies wouldn't. If Alikar had a mage on his staff—and he would, if he were clever—then he could easily find out as well.

Understanding the complete situation was just part of protecting herself. No, not just herself. Protecting Aven too. And all of them. Next time she would have to check sooner and gather information faster. Politeness and privacy were silly things to put over their own safety, especially since the subject of her investigation wouldn't even know she'd been snooping about them. She had so many things to learn here. She'd slipped up because she had so many things to investigate it was hard to track them all.

Leaving the creature mages to their discussion, she crept over to where images flew through the air beneath Wunik's hands. The forests, the rivers, Anonil, now the fields of wheat. Then Mage Hall loomed beneath them.

"You're just in time, Miara," said Wunik without looking up.

A bronze-skinned man who looked like he could be from Takar, or possibly Detrat, gasped at the sight. And indeed, it looked especially looming as darkness fell around the black, hulking shadows of the buildings.

Wunik skillfully slid the view straight back to the dorms where she had spent so many years with her father and Luha. Again the windows were shuttered, and again guards stood outside the door. But there was something different, something she couldn't quite put her hands on. Had there been two guards yesterday or four as there were today?

And worse, there was no one about.

Miara stepped closer. "Something's different," she said.

Wunik nodded, not moving his eyes from the image. "More guards. Are those windows boarded shut?"

"I think so." Her family's windows. Wunik pushed the view back so they could see more of the compound. "There's no one anywhere."

"Could they have caught Jaena so quickly?" Aven said.

"She was planning to wait until tomorrow to try to leave." Gods, what if she had been freed only to be recaptured and re-enslaved without leaving?

"Did she tell you she was going to talk to anyone in particular? Anyone we should try to find, who will be looking for us?"

"Uh, yes, Menaha. Another friend of hers she thought of. I don't see any of them at first glance. Menaha's rooms should be in that building over there." Wunik deftly swung the view to the other side of the large grassy center of the Mage Hall compound.

"There—look." Aven pointed to a window near the top of the building. The shutters were open, and two people were not quite leaning out, but close.

"Go closer," Miara breathed. Wunik complied. "It's them!"

"We've got to free someone while we can," Aven said. "Which one should I start with?"

"The older one, Menaha. Don't go killing yourself now." She was only partly joking.

"I'll help," said Derk, surprising her. "No need to get shit-faced."

Well. She'd never heard it put quite like *that*.

"You explain what to do, and I'll feed," Derk added.

Wunik nodded. "Let's get started."

As Aven explained how he reached out to the star and poured the energy toward the brands on their shoulders, Miara's stomach twisted a little. It was not much of a stretch to realize that a map that freed slaves could also reverse the process. As much as more help in freeing them was immensely valuable… what danger did they risk by planting thoughts of slavery in the minds of even a few powerful air mages? She sighed. It was a risk they had to take.

Miara blocked them out and reached out to Menaha instead.

*Menaha—it's me.*

*Oh! Thank the gods, Miara.*

*What's going on?*

*Oh, stars in heaven, do I have news for you.*

*My father? Luha?*

*I haven't been able to get to them, but as far as I can determine, they're perfectly fine and just locked in their rooms. I was able to walk by and hear the sounds of the hearth fires. I don't see why they'd guard the rooms if they weren't in there and alive. Sorry I couldn't find out more.*

*It's all right. What news then?*

*Something serious has happened. We can't figure just what, but it was around midday. They locked everything down for a few minutes. The deep warning bells rang. They shut the gates and sent those in the fields back inside. They even took horses out and brought the farther shepherds back in and left the flocks abandoned. Insanity. They haven't even let us out of these buildings yet for dinner. I'm not sure when or if they're going to. Every so often you can see the Tall Master going from building to building. He's looking for something, I think.*

The Tall Master. Strange indeed. What could he be searching for? They rarely saw him doing anything but torturing people in the smithy. Could Jaena have escaped early? Would that have led them to lock everything down? They hadn't done that when Miara escaped.

Perhaps the Masters thought one was an anomaly, but two was a pattern.

"It's done," Aven said softly. "She's free." Miara tore her eyes and mind away from Mage Hall for a moment. His face had paled, and he slumped against the bench's back. At least he was conscious. He glanced at Derk. "Got strength for two?"

Derk glared at him. "I've got the strength for ten. Go."

What was that all about?

Miara turned back to the mages. *Menaha. You should feel different—the spell is broken. You should be free.*

Menaha's eyes widened. *Kae?* Her voice was not

hopeful. She dreaded hearing they could only free one. Miara hadn't even realized the boy stood next to her. Boy or sort of a man, perhaps sixteen or eighteen, with an earnest, innocent face that might have concealed some of his actual age. Was this the friend Jaena had spoken of?

*They're working on it.*

Menaha heaved a mental sigh of relief. Just then, a terrible slam drew all their eyes. The Tall Master stormed from Menaha's building, grumbling obscenities at the guards he had in tow. He marched toward another building and toppled a statue of Nefrana with a kick on the way.

*Damn hypocrites.* Miara wasn't sure if Menaha had intended to share that thought with her or not. But, yes.

Miara reached out to the young man's mind. *Kae?*

His eyes and ears perked up, far less subtle than Menaha. *Yes?*

*They are working on breaking the spell in your bond right now. It will take a few minutes. Then the two of you should get out of this window, lie low. Do you know anything of what has come of Jaena? Where is she?*

*She was going to wait until tomorrow to escape. I saw her heading to work a trifle late, but she was still here this morning just before the bells began to ring.*

*Where had she gone to work?*

*I saw her heading to the smithy. She sometimes assists the blacksmiths.*

Miara rubbed her chin. What could have happened? Or did it have nothing to do with them, and Jaena was simply asleep inside somewhere?

"It's done," Derk's voice cut in.

Miara reeled herself back to reality and saw Aven with his elbows on his knees and head in his hands—groaning, rubbing his face, but conscious. Excellent. She went back to Kae and Menaha.

Miara spoke first to Menaha, then repeated her message for Kae. *Well. The plan was to wait till tomorrow at sundown. If they keep you locked up, though, you may need to take whatever chance you can get. See if you can find out what happened to Jaena and if she's still there. But the most important thing is that you get free. They are reacting harshly, and it will only become harder with time. You don't happen to be a creature mage?*

*Air.* Both of them responded the same.

Miara sighed. Air magic wouldn't help them escape, but the growing number of air mages on their side was certainly not a bad thing. If they could make it out. *All right. Head to Anonil, to the Apple and Arrow. We've sent someone there to watch for you.* She repeated the instructions to each of them.

To Menaha alone, she added, *If you can find Brother Sefim, can you tell him to attempt something like this tomorrow night? We can only free people at night.*

*That is a problem then. We'll have to hope this curfew doesn't last, as the temple doesn't have shuttered windows. But yes, I'll try to find him and tell him.* Menaha nodded her understanding.

*Thank you. May the Balance protect you.*

*No, thank you, Miara.* Menaha's words were heartfelt.

*Even if I don't make it out, a few moments of relief after all these years means so much to me.*

*Don't talk like that. We need you, Menaha. We need to understand what they are planning. Let's make it not just a few moments, but years of relief. Of freedom. I'm sure this is temporary while he searches for… whatever he's searching for. They have to feed you sometime, right?*

Menaha nodded, but Miara knew the older woman was not so sure. Menaha was just being realistic. In that environment, especially if it worsened, escape would be hard.

*Good luck,* she told Kae. They would need all they could get.

Miara snapped back to reality. Aven caught her eyes with just the corners of his mouth curving in a smile. His skin was even paler now, and his head rested against the back of the bench heavily. Wunik looked like he would tip over if he got up.

"Well, two in one night," he said softly.

"That's double, and all we are going to find anyway, I think." Wunik was scouring the area around Mage Hall, but only guards were coming into view. "Quite an improvement, eh?"

"Yes."

Wunik glanced at Aven, seeming to remember him. "Oh! You made it through awake. Good job to both of you." Derk had a you-better-say-that expression on his face, but he did smile. Maybe he just didn't receive quite enough recognition from his teacher, hence that huge chip on his shoulder. "Aven, should we wrap up? I think we've done a great deal tonight."

Aven looked like he wanted to nod but was too tired to do so. *Want me to get their attention for you?* she whispered to him.

*That'd be a help. I'm not sure I can move my arms.* Fortunately, he seemed more amused by this than alarmed.

Miara stood and strode back to the door where the nearest brazier would easily light her for all to see. "Everyone? Aven would like to say something before we retire for the evening."

Slowly, the other groups of mages rose and gathered around the air mages. Wunik continued to scour Mage Hall, but no one came into sight.

"Is that—where they kept you?" Thel pointed at the window of light.

"Yes. And a whole lot of others too," Aven replied. "How did things go, everyone?"

"Teron and I are planning to scour the libraries tomorrow, since I hear that worked out well once before," Thel reported.

"And I'll be meeting tomorrow with our newest creature mage to give him a few pointers. Since I have nothing else to do." Siliana shot Wunik an annoyed look, before beaming a smile at Dom. Oh, that annoyance was a cover, wasn't it.

"Great. We freed two more warrior mages. We'll meet here again tomorrow night to try again, if any of you care to join. The more we can figure out before we head to Panar, the better. Feel free to keep working, but I am retiring for the night."

Nods all around. Miara realized too late she had ended up rather far from Aven, and that perhaps this would be the appropriate time to simply head back to her room alone. If there was nothing between them, then that's what she would do.

She couldn't bring herself to do it, though. She drifted back toward him, feigning interest in fresh sights of Mage Hall even though seeing it only gave her pangs of nausea and dinged her hope.

"See anything?" Miara said. She knelt next to the water bowl, in front of Aven's feet and to Wunik's right.

"No," Wunik replied. "We may quickly be unable to make an impact if they keep this up. Let's hope this is only a temporary measure."

*I want to help you back to your room,* she said to Aven without looking at him. *Or make sure you make it there safe. I didn't like letting Fayton handle it last night.*

She caught his smile out of the corner of her eye. *You have a talent for good excuses, my love. You know Fayton is perfectly trustworthy. Interesting how talking this way makes… ulterior motives more obvious.*

She snickered to herself, then hoped no one noticed. *I miss sleeping beside you too, of course.*

*I do too. If we could think up a reason…*

That buoyed her hope, and she strained to think of something while Wunik scanned the same area of Mage Hall again. They saw no mages, and she thought of nothing plausible. Short of him suffering from some kind of fever or illness, she had no special skills that would require her to attend him in a non-romantic manner. And there were other healers, like his own mother and doubtless non-magical royal healers, who could also do the job and were already married or men. Although, come to think of it, she wasn't sure if that mattered.

*Damn. I can't think of anything legitimate.*

*It's all right. Maybe something will come up.*

"All right. Enough." Wunik let the window of light fade. "Who's helping Aven back to his room? Looks like he needs it."

"I will!" she and Derk said simultaneously. Then they looked at each other in surprise, Derk's eyebrow raised, Miara frowning. What was he up to? She couldn't let him go off with Aven alone, that was for sure.

"Hey, wait. I have some questions for my brother before he sleeps," Dom called out. Siliana had been in mid-sentence, and he whispered an apology. Miara had to remind herself not to stare at Siliana's mooning eyes. They exchanged a few more words, and Dom joined them. "Tired, Aven?"

Aven started to lean forward and did indeed lurch to the side—unfortunately into Derk, who caught him.

"C'mon, let's help him back," Derk said pointedly to Dom, giving Miara a suspicious glance. Oh, as if *she* was the suspicious one. She couldn't completely trust either of them.

"I can help too," she managed weakly, knowing she had already lost.

Derk didn't even acknowledge her statement, just kept on pulling Aven to his feet.

*Damn it, I wanted to come with you at least.*

*It's okay.* Dom joined Derk in lifting one arm of Aven's over his shoulder, and Aven finally stood.

*Try to keep a little bit more energy next time. Just a little, if you can.*

*I'll try—it's like a whirlpool. Hard to resist.*

*Can you trust Dom? Are you sure?* The three men eased past her and toward the door.

*Oh—yes. Don't worry.*

*And Derk?*

*It's fine. Sorry we couldn't, I don't know...* His thoughts trailed off into images and swirls of thought, but she didn't pull back right away. For once, she let their minds mingle. Sorry we couldn't think of an excuse, he'd been intending to say. She let her borders drop further. He also felt sorry they couldn't sleep side by side. Sorry we haven't told everyone. Sorry I listened to my father instead of telling him to go to hell. Sorry we can't... And if she'd held doubts about his attraction to her versus his new suitor, those concerns evaporated as she watched the images circle and flash by—memories of his lips brushing her neck, his hands stroking her palm, her shoulders, her... The images shifted to moments that were not memories but sounded even more delicious. Sorry we have to wait. Sorry we aren't already married.

*Oh, that's all right, there's time, just rest,* she thought as she pulled away. Besides, if that were true, she would be close to being queen. And she was not sure she was ready to be. Or would ever be. Maybe she wasn't cut out for all this. Would she even be happy as a queen, with so many eyes on her all the time? And yet, she couldn't imagine being anywhere but by his side for the rest of her days.

As the men neared the door, Aven's head lifted with a strange, abrupt jerk. He glanced over his shoulder at her, frowning in puzzlement. A thrill of fear ran through her. He'd heard that, hadn't he. She'd let the veil drop farther than normal, and it had taken longer to pull away than she'd thought. He frowned as if unsure he'd truly heard her thoughts, but she knew he had. He just didn't want to believe them.

What kind of fool was she? A kind, intelligent man wants to give me more power than nearly anyone in the land, and I'm not sure I want it.

They lurched awkwardly through the door and around the bend, Aven's eyes trailing her till the last.

Of course, she was thinking about what he would have wanted her to think about, she reminded herself. The good of his kingdom—was she really the type of queen they'd need in the future? Would they ever accept her? Would she be able to do the job? If she believed she was entirely unfit, Aven would want to know that. Wouldn't he?

It was too late to ask him now. Miara rose to help Wunik put away his tools. Then, with a pat on the old elder's shoulder and an assurance that he needed no more help, she headed back to her rooms.

Alone.

Yet another laborious dinner. Daes yawned widely, not caring which courtier or hanger-on might notice. He'd maneuvered for years to be outside their reach, and he would enjoy the benefits of that effort now. No matter how many of the king's feasts he attended, he had yet to find a way to entertain himself. His presence was of course required periodically to maintain his powerful station and the king's favor. Too many absences would draw unneeded and useless attention.

As a younger man, before he'd been a Master, these events had been far more useful. But now they were more maintenance than anything else.

He surveyed the court. No one was worth talking to. What a tedious waste of time.

He rose and headed toward the promenade. A wide balcony stretched beyond the hall, built of cream and pink marble. He strolled along, gazing up at the setting sun, thoughts clear. The stars were just coming out. They brought to mind the prince and his growing ability to bring everything Daes had worked so hard for crashing down.

He had better hear back from his mages soon, or he was sending a dozen more.

Elegant staircases zigzagged down two stories to the manicured gardens, where hedges were sculpted into fanciful creations, real and imagined. The sound of water burbling graced the air as fountains stretched out into the gardens. He headed down the stairs. On this promenade so close to the hall, someone annoying was liable to see him and corner him with some inane conversation—or worse, a ridiculous request. He shouldn't be away too long, but enjoying the gardens was a perfectly acceptable feast activity. He must remember to compliment the king on them later, in case the fool noticed his absence.

Daes forgot about this plan, however, when he turned a corner of the hedgerow and saw the queen. She sat on a marble bench, face turned into the corner of the surrounding hedges and hidden by her hands. Her shoulders shook, and although she was silent, it was obvious to him that she wept.

Queen Marielle. He remembered her first days at court, around the same time he had begun his upward climb. Unlike Seulka, she was a clever and pragmatic type. Daes had to confess he'd felt a touch of jealousy at the old king at finding someone so... reasonable. Most women of her type were beyond annoying, whether because they had never really had a problem in their lives, or because of how insanely driven they were by their machinations. She was not typical, and he'd had more than one rewarding conversation in those early days. Of late, she often sat sullenly at the king's side or didn't attend the feasts at all. How many years ago had she come from Reilin, on the southwestern continent, to marry the king? He had no idea. She had borne no heir, and it had been long enough. It should have happened. Was this why she wept? Or perhaps something else was afoot.

He came closer, his boots crunching on the gravel. Her head hung low for a moment, indicating she heard his approach, but she did not turn or straighten. That bad, was it? He stopped just before her, now close enough to hear the faint sound of her weeping.

He took a calculated risk. He reached out and gently placed his hand on her shoulder, his thumb resting ever so softly on the back of her neck. He patted gently, then moved his thumb so softly, it only grazed the soft delicate hairs at her nape. Treason, perhaps. Or a way to win a powerful ally.

She turned, shocked, but did not jerk fully away from his touch.

"Daes—"

"Your Majesty, are you all right?" he said, filling his voice with as much concern as he could muster. He withdrew his touch, bent down to one knee, and drew a handkerchief from an inner pocket of his red dress gambeson. While some wore finer clothing to affairs like these, he would have preferred full armor, as much as he trusted any of them. But the thick cloth protection of the gambeson was the closest he could get away with.

She received the handkerchief gratefully, straightening. "Forgive me, Lord Daes—"

"I see not what you have to forgive."

She gave him a small smile for his chivalry. "A queen must always be poised," she said. She quoted someone who'd often chastised her thusly, he suspected.

"No one is always poised," he replied.

"Says the man who is always the picture of composure."
Huh. Interesting that she had such thoughts about him,
or any thoughts at all.

"We are not always what we seem on the surface," he
said. "Are we?" Her smile faded into a relaxed nod. If she
ever saw him wake up from his dreams in a rage, she might
think differently. She seemed to remember her troubles
but resist bursting into tears. Good. If he'd only calmed
her, certainly she would still remember his kindness. It
could come in handy later. But his gut told him there
was more potential gratitude to be created here. "Who
has wronged you?" he said softly. "Are you all right?"

"I am much better now, thanks to you," she said, dab-
bing an eye and looking at him with sincere gratitude,
but dodging his question. He let the silence linger for a
moment, giving her space to fill it. She fidgeted.

"Is there some way I can help you, my lady?" he
nudged again.

"Oh, you needn't worry about my foolish woes." She
waved him off. "You have a war to plan, don't you? I have
heard of your many great plans for this kingdom." She had?

The gravel was beginning to dig into his knee. "May
I join you on this seat, my lady?"

"Oh, of course," she said quickly, scooting over a few
inches as if to make room for him, although this put her
nearly in the hedgerow. Indeed, a queen should not be
so willing to give up her space and power so easily. But
many a queen was more battered than powerful. If such
had been Marielle's fate, it was no surprise she would

readily make room for a friendly face. He sat much farther over, leaving her ample room, and then took her hand and pulled her toward him.

"No need for hedges in your back, there's quite enough room."

She smiled, looking down at her lap and not meeting his eyes.

He should let go of her hand. He didn't. She didn't either.

"My mage armies are preparing for war, indeed. But I am taken away from such measures by this... delightful feast." She snorted a bit of laughter at his clear lack of enthusiasm. "But may I remind you, my queen, that my mages are forever at your disposal."

She looked up and met his eyes in earnest surprise. Was she shocked that he offered his power to her, or that he recognized her power as queen? Or was it something else? His hand clasping hers should have been much more surprising than a reminder of power she did in fact wield, should she choose to use it.

"Have your mages ever... No. Forget I said anything."

"What is it?" He squeezed her hand. "I am happy to educate you on my forces' capabilities. In a general manner, of course."

She straightened again, regaining her power by the moment, as if his hand's touch strengthened her. "Of course, of course. Are your mages equipped for smaller activities than wars? Such as... perhaps... assassination?"

Oh, ho ho. What have we here? Calculated risk, indeed! What gold mine had he just discovered?

"As a matter of fact, yes. They are not very common, but I have several…" He refused to think about the escaped mage, or the creature mage, or that the Tall Master had misplaced the brand, of all things. He'd focus on none of that nonsense at this prime moment. "Several mages who are skilled spies, capable of various forms of information gathering and intelligence activities." He smiled warmly. "Assassination among them, of course."

She stared hard at him now as if weighing his whole worth. It was not wise to trust him. He was clearly manipulating her in a weak moment to gain her trust, and he'd made no effort to hide his fairly transparent ploy. Many would not notice, but just as many would be fully aware of his potentially self-serving motivations. She did not know his loyalties or really anything about him. Or so he suspected from her reactions. If she had made any effort to keep tabs on him, to learn of his past or his present, it had been behind closed doors. But why should she? He tried to keep as low a profile as possible in terms of gossip, and aside from the war, there should not have been much worth knowing about him.

And yet, he was not being insincere. He did hope to comfort her. She was a beautiful, well-liked, and reasonable woman, thoroughly wasted on the king. Her ties to her homeland of Asraet—and their powerful navy—across the sea remained strong. Daes had kept his own tabs on her, and he'd heard reports of her addressing grievances of a minor noble here, a frustrated landholder there at least a dozen separate times. All were grievances the king had ignored. It was possible their agendas aligned.

"What about kidnapping… or perhaps, escape?"

"It might be best if you simply told me of your troubles, my lady."

"The king's mistress," she blurted, shoulders slumping as a few more tears seeped out.

His eyes fell to his lap as he shook his head. Fool. The king was a fool, but dallying with a mistress while he had no heir? But perhaps he called Marielle barren, and it was not just a foolish dalliance. "I am sorry to hear that the king does not properly honor you, my lady."

She straightened again and shook her head. "I no longer desire his affections," she said, although the words came out stilted. So she had hoped to love him once? Idealistic for a royal. Or perhaps it was simply innuendo for his heir-producing activities. "And it is all well and good, as *she* has produced no heir either." Her voice grew bitter as her hand clenched his tighter. "But she is insufferable. Constantly flouting her place in his bed in the court, with the servants. She thinks it's a matter of time before she conceives."

"You disagree," he offered.

"I have done my duties as queen. And she has done hers for nigh on two years. It has been long enough. If only he would find another mistress, it would at least buy me some peace. But I fear he loves her." She stared off into the distance as if hoping to see the answers to her problems.

She needn't look. He had a diverse array of options.

Time to seal the deal, he thought.

"My lady, dry those tears. This beautiful garden you maintain is so large and open." Her eyes widened as she caught the meaning in his words. "But were you able to visit me at Mage Hall, I would be able to better acquaint you with the capabilities of my estate and forces."

"I don't know if the king would approve of my interest in… your martial affairs," she said, fidgeting.

"Perhaps a visit to his cousin, our lady Seulka then. She has not attended tonight, *claiming* ill health. It has been too long since you visited; perhaps you should check up on her." He smiled, letting a little of his natural deviousness through.

Her eyes lit up. "Indeed. I am quite concerned about her health," she said. She was a good actress, sounding sincerely worried. Good, one less liability.

He stood, still clasping her hand in his. "I fear I have been gone too long from the feast. I must let the king know how much I appreciate the fine treasures I've discovered in his gardens. Will you give me my leave, Your Majesty?"

"Of course," she said, although she looked disappointed he was leaving so soon. But this was a promising start. He could not afford to raise suspicions of any connection between them before their plots were even begun. He could see so much potential here. Respected by the king or not, the queen held real power. While Demikin dallied, she had sown gratitude among many of those lesser nobles, and many would feel indebted, even if she hadn't yet realized it. Those seeds of appreciation could be reaped later. Although he had the impression she'd acted more out of boredom and duty than determined maneuvering, Daes could help her take advantage of these bonds she'd naturally made. The king was a fool to make an enemy of her. Another way the king and Daes were quite different.

He bowed deeply and brought her hand up, carefully pressing his lips to her fingers with a slow, soft kiss, leaving a trace of cold wetness behind. All the while, he watched her eyes flick from his gaze to his hand and back again, her mouth dropping open slightly. Then, before he could ruin it, he took his leave.

He heard no footsteps behind him, so fortunately she'd taken his lead not to return together. He found himself striding back to the feast with a spring in his step. This was good. Very good. And he was not the only one who'd struck gold tonight. Queen Marielle had received a valuable reminder of her actual power and comfort besides.

This could only get better.

# 7  INSTRUCTION

Jaena awoke to a knock at the door. Tharomar had been asleep beside her, apparently, because he roused with a snort and a start and stumbled to the door. Good thing he'd slept with his clothes on. A part of her had expected some sort of betrayal in the night, and she couldn't believe in the bleary morning light that he could possibly be just what he said he was. But it seemed so. He had treated her ankle and given her a place to sleep and nothing more. And he hadn't asked for anything in return.

He squinted and ran a hand over his face as he stumbled to the door and opened it. Jaena's heart leapt as reality rushed back into her groggy mind. It could be Devoted or others from Mage Hall looking for her. Should she hide, pull the cover over her head? She lay facing away from the door. She decided not to move. Motion might just draw more attention.

"Mornin', Ro. You wanted me to stop before I headed into the city?" said a gravelly man's voice. Apparently her host had a nickname.

"Morning, Nemin. Yes—one moment." Tharomar strode across the room, opened his cupboards, and rummaged around.

"Another share for the womenfolk?"

Jaena felt another leap and sputter in her chest. Perhaps he was not so unattached after all. Curse her, why did she *care*? She did not have time to moon after this man. Or any man. It did not matter if he had ten wives in ten different cities and a dozen children by each of them. It should make *no* difference to her.

"Aye," he said, striding back with a burlap pouch in both hands. Coins clinked against each other. "It's not much, but tell them…" He stopped, looking thoughtful.

Nemin laughed. "You're not trying to think up a reason why you aren't sending more, are you?"

Tharomar looked surprised. "I was, why?"

"They haven't even let me finish telling them your tales *the last three times*."

Tharomar grimaced but still seemed intent on thinking of something.

"No, no. Don't misunderstand me, Ro. They *don't care*. You could send them nothing. They're just happy you've made this life here at all. Better than many of their kids end up. They don't care about a single coin."

"They need it." His voice had an edge.

"They raised you without it somehow. I'll have to ask them if they know any way to get you to relax."

"Tell them I should be able to take an apprentice by

the spring." Apparently Ro was determined not to relax.

"Aye, well, that they'll listen to. But don't be so hard on yourself, all right, my boy?"

"I'm hardly a boy, Nemin." He finally handed the visitor the pouch of coins.

"I'll see this there safely, Ro. Don't worry."

"Blessed be, as the spring blooms, Nemin. Safe travels."

"May her sun watch over you, my friend."

And then the visitor was gone. Tharomar flopped back down on the cot, stretched, and seemed to consider sleeping more. But after a moment, he said quietly, "You're awake?"

She turned on her back to face him and was rewarded with a reminder of the horrible pain in her ankle. She stifled a groan. What a mess she'd gotten herself into. "How did you know?"

He sat up and rubbed the sleep from his face again, then shrugged. "I've spent more of my time sleeping near others than alone. You learn to tell."

She snorted. "I could interpret *that* more than a few ways, you know. Soldier? Patron of brothels, perhaps?"

He turned and gave her a grin that was entirely too charming. She should get out of here as soon as she could. "I was raised in a temple of Nefrana. Well, mostly."

Oh. That explained… a lot. The necklace, the pious fear of mages, the womenfolk Nemin mentioned. His generosity. His determination to help her, without seeming to seek a reward. She had never encountered much kindness from someone who was devout—except perhaps him—but the sermons *did* speak of caring for one's neighbor. Perhaps he was the one fool who had actually listened? He hadn't exactly denied or even flinched at her brothel accusation, though, she noted. "You were raised in a temple? To be a priest?"

"Yes, it was inside a temple, although it was more like an orphanage. They just didn't call it that. No, not to be a priest. They have enough priests, charity isn't a great way to feed a temple full of parentless children, and they were all women anyway. I'm happy to contribute in other ways."

She nodded and eased herself to sitting as he spoke. She winced but tried to hide it. "Like coin?" Or were there *other* ways?

"Like coin. They set me up with this smithy. I can never repay them for everything they've done for me. But—well, at least I can try. So when Nemin takes his goods to the city, I send help along. It should really be more, but it's hard to charge more for a horseshoe when you know a farmer needs it to survive and can't pay any more. But the temple has been struggling too. Some merchants have no trouble charging more, no matter who you are."

"You said 'mostly' raised there."

His smile turned sheepish. "Well—let's just say I know my way around alleys more than anyone really needs to."

She nodded. Alleys and maybe brothels too, she suspected. A gasp escaped as she tried to put weight on her ankle, and instead he helped her to the edge of the bed.

She swung her feet to the floor. Her head didn't pound, which seemed remarkable. What *was* in that mead?

"Did those priestesses give you those salves too?" she asked, putting the facts together.

"Exactly. Nothing gets by you, I see." He grinned. "And it looks—and sounds—like time for another application, eh?"

She nodded, scowling at her ankle in disgust as he squatted down to inspect it. She wanted to hide back under the covers so he couldn't see. It'd swollen up and turned black and blue and purple. Like a beaten hog's leg. Damn it to all seven hells.

After a thoughtful inspection, he grinned up at her, straightened, and headed back to his cabinet for the salve. He's a smith, she reminded herself. He's probably turned his thumb or his knee that color more than once. Nothing he cares about. Why are you being such a fool around this man? The sooner she could heal and get away, the better.

He handed her the salve this time. "If you can put this on, I can get us some breakfast."

She opened her mouth, thinking she should deny needing any breakfast, since she certainly had no coin. But that hadn't mattered before, had it, nor had he accepted any of her objections. And she wasn't healing and getting away any faster on an empty stomach.

Instead, she took the jar. "Got it."

Aven had woken with a headache after they'd freed the first warrior mage, but this morning was worse. He'd gone back to sleep for a while, his head pounding. Perhaps even with help, there was some cost to these spells that he wasn't quite compensating for.

He should probably just stick to one a night. If he got Wunik and the others doing it, maybe he wouldn't end up feeling like a mace was crushing his head from both sides. In between dreams and pained bits of sleep, he worried.

The thoughts he'd felt from Miara last night had scared him deeply. So much... doubt. So much concern. Her feelings for him were as strong as ever, if not stronger. But then in that one unguarded moment, he'd seen deeper. He'd felt her fears, her inadequacies.

Everyone had such feelings, of course. What worried him was... what was she going to do about it? Her affection was so constant, he had never questioned if she'd want to marry him. That was a bit foolish in hindsight. And of course, she *did* want him. But unfortunately he, like most men, came with a job description attached. One she seemed to think she was ill-suited and unprepared for.

She was wrong. So wrong. And yet, he knew enough about insecurity to know he couldn't just argue the point. He couldn't simply insist to her she would be an excellent queen, a strong leader, a steady and careful hand at his side. She would dismiss anything he said as biased, as said only out of love and not out of logic. But of course the things he logically thought would be good he also found terribly attractive. Was that so hard to believe?

No. He'd have to get others to convince her. Or help her find that in herself. Or put her in situations where she could see that she was more than the slave she'd thought of herself as for so long.

When the pounding had finally subsided—which might have been partially due to inhaling the dumplings, sausages, and tea that had appeared next to his bed while he was sleeping—he sat on his bed, scratching his jaw.

He'd hoped to show her his room last night, but again, that hadn't worked out. And he'd intended to head there to check in with her this morning, but… he found himself hesitating. He wasn't ready to talk about whether or not she wanted to be queen, and he didn't think she was ready to talk about it either. But the idea fogged his mind—and he didn't feel much like talking about some other topic.

He dressed and, with some mixed feelings, went looking for Wunik instead. There was time to figure things out with Miara, time to show her his room, time to talk about their whole situation when he wouldn't be so tempted to go to insane lengths to convince her of her worth. In a few hours, he had a feeling he'd be much more rational about it, and he'd have something else to talk about—namely, spells.

Wunik was delighted to see him so early, and they spent the morning practicing setting things on fire and then putting them out. Wunik also showed him the strange pastime of building up a static charge in one iron orb and then jumping the charge to another—exercises in tiny, well-controlled lightning bolts. The practical use of this, he wasn't certain, but it sure looked impressive.

By lunchtime, though, Aven was wondering where Miara was. And regretting he hadn't gone to see her. Would she be wondering what had happened to him? If he'd been okay? She hadn't been completely comfortable with his departure with Dom and Derk at his side. Damn, that was thoughtless. He should have already gone to see her.

Her rooms, however, were empty when he strolled by. Fayton had said she'd been at the Proving Grounds one morning. He'd never found out why. Perhaps she was there again, so he headed that way.

He stood at the top of the high stairs and surveyed the Grounds and the many seats that surrounded them. Off to the left, Thel sat with Renala, watching a group of young prospective wardens practice. Well, that was an interesting match—was Thel interested in her, perhaps? That would take the pressure off Aven, at least. At the bottom of the steps, Derk was chatting with Siliana and Dom. No Miara, no red hair anywhere.

Hmm. Where could she be?

"I heard you've been practicing spells with Wunik." Aven roused to realize Derk was talking to him.

"Uh, yes. All morning. Yesterday too."

"Well, come on then. Let's see. There's room down there, right?"

"What?" Aven blinked.

"Let's spar. Show those soldiers over there another

kind of battle, eh? What do you think?" Derk grinned and held up a hand like it cradled a ball. A flicker of flame burst to life in his palm, mildly threatening.

"When I spar with swords, I know how not to go killing my opponent. I've learned. I don't know how to do that with magic, yet. Just as importantly, do you?"

Derk shrugged. "We've got some healers. We'll be fine."

Well, that was encouraging. But Derk brought out a competitive streak in him, and he found himself nodding and following the blond mage back down toward the main ring. There was room for three times as many soldiers on the field as they had, so they shouldn't have to worry too much about hitting anyone. He hoped.

This was also a good excuse to live out the violent fantasies he got every time Derk looked at Miara. Or talked to her. Or was in the same room as her.

He sighed. Was this jealousy? He had nothing to be jealous of, did he? Miara had no interest in the fellow. Did she? He knew better than to let jealousy eat at him.

This is new to you, Aven, he reminded himself. You're no veteran. He would be more likely to get trounced by the more experienced mage than to live out any fantasies of jealousy or dominance or socking him in the jaw.

But then again, if he surprised the bastard, that would be delicious. Worth the risk of getting knocked on his ass.

Aven stepped out onto the field. "What did you have in mind? Obviously my sparring experience is strictly limited to blunted and slicing implements."

"Well, what has the old man been teaching you?"

"Farsight—"

"Not much combat use, I'm afraid."

"Fire—"

"Now we're talking."

"—and small charges, lightning sorts of things."

"Oh, balls of iron are my *favorite*." Aven had no idea if that was sarcasm, innuendo, or something else altogether. "Well, take your pick. Oh, and I also heard you know how to cast a breeze or two. You should definitely conjure us some pleasant weather, maybe a tropical breeze for our affair." He laughed now.

Aven gathered the energy inside him like a fist clenching and sent a rush of air at Derk's left.

Not expecting it, the mage stumbled and nearly fell. He recovered just in time, blinking and laughing. "All right, you proved your point," he said. "My turn."

A crackle in the air was all the warning Aven had. Lightning arced out of the air as if originating from the ether and stabbed into his left thigh.

He swore and stumbled backward, but thankfully he didn't lose his footing. Damn, how was he supposed to *defend* against that?

Another crackle. This time, Aven held up the palm of his left hand, which dutifully caught the brunt of the crack of lightning but failed to defend him in any meaningful way. Getting shot with an arrow in the hand was not really an improvement on getting shot in the thigh. His palm was black, like he'd been handling burned logs. Well, that was just great.

How could he defend against—

Another crackle. This time, Aven jumped to one side, but it was no help. An arc of light connected with his shoulder and sent the muscles of his arm spasming.

Well, this was far too lopsided to be called sparring at this point. Aven concentrated for a moment, ignoring the spasms as best he could, and lit the soles of Derk's shoes on fire.

The stream of curses was all that told Aven he'd succeeded, for he was busy trying to calm his arm down with his singed palm.

How did they defend themselves? Certainly there had to be a way, especially if you could see the spell coming. He wanted to bounce the lightning back to him, or catch it and—

That must be it. Something like that had to be possible.

Another crackle broke through the musty air. No, two this time.

Aven tried not to look for them. He didn't need sight or sound. He needed that extra sense, to feel the energy in the air as it moved toward him. He could sense an arc of mental energy mirroring the light that shot through the air.

He reached out and—

He missed the first. It slammed into his ear, of all places, and sent him spinning. But the second, he caught. It soaked into him like water into a sponge.

He felt hot, euphoric. Too much. He hadn't expended the energy, and it bounced around inside him now, jockeying for release.

He sent his own arc of lightning back, but it shot wide, connecting with the practice rack behind Derk with a small shake. A few of the warden students stopped and stared for a moment, then diligently pretended to return to their own activities. He could feel at least a few of them watching. Derk raised one cocky eyebrow at him, and Aven felt him readying something.

The air filled with more of a roar than a crackle, and Aven knew before he could see it that this meant fire. He was not afraid; he could do the same thing and catch it.

He snatched the fireball and sent it back like on a sling.

And Derk returned the favor.

They exchanged volleys like this three or four times before Derk gave him a grin.

"What?" Aven grunted.

"You got it. Now you know how to spar."

"You knew I didn't know, and you still wanted to?"

"You've got to learn somehow. Wunik waits forever. You don't have forever."

"You could have just told me."

"Nah, this was much more fun. Besides, you'll remember this better. It's how Wunik taught me."

Probably because he was a snide little bastard and Wunik longed to pummel him with a shovel. But perhaps he was right. No practice was as effective as when you truly believed your life was at stake.

"He's so damn delighted to be here, I don't think he's been of much mind to go shocking anyone or knocking them on their asses, least of all princely members of his ruling family. But like I said, you don't have time. Aren't you going to thank me?"

"No," Aven said. His pounding headache had returned, which made it hard to be terribly grateful. Plus, Aven was fairly sure Derk was more interested in having fun at Aven's expense than actually helping.

Derk rolled his eyes and sent a flame that spiraled unpredictably toward Aven's torso. Aven managed to catch and absorb it, but just barely. He glared at the other mage. "I have other duties to attend to."

"But we've only just gotten started!" Derk shot out two spiraling bolts, and one almost slipped by Aven's notice, but he caught it at the last moment.

Aven's glare deepened to a scowl. "We're done here."

He sensed Derk readying a shot anyway. Aven caught the arc of lightning and made his first attempt at multiple shots, three bolts at once directed at Derk's knees.

One made it through, and Derk cackled and swore in surprise.

Derk gave him an annoyed look. "Fine. You're no fun. You win." He straightened and brushed himself off, striding toward Aven and holding out his hand to shake.

Aven felt like this was some kind of trick, but he wouldn't be seen snubbing a handshake, especially not with impressionable wardens practicing nearby. They shook hands.

Derk wiped his brow, smirking. "My knees are burnt thanks to you. I guess I better go spend some time with our healer friend. Do you think she'll mind if I take off my shirt?"

Aven knew he shouldn't, but he scowled and stepped closer. "Find your own damn healer."

Derk sidled forward too, inches from Aven's face. "Why should I?"

"Stay away from her," Aven said.

"She isn't yours."

Aven opened his mouth but stopped himself barely in time.

"*Is* she." Derk stated it like a fact, but his eyes pierced Aven in question. He suspected something.

"I don't see how that's any of your business."

"You really going to make a mage your queen? A commoner?" Derk hissed, his voice hushed.

Aven almost said, "That's the plan," but he held back. He glared harder at Derk, willing him to back down.

"Are you going after her or not?" Derk pressed.

"What does it matter?" said Aven.

"If you aren't, I am."

Aven lowered his voice and said, deathly quiet, "I said, stay away from her."

Aven turned and started to stalk away, but Derk's hand thudded on his shoulder, stopping him.

Aven slowly turned back, barely concealed rage smoldering beneath the surface. Derk's eyes were hard as glass. "She deserves better than to be kept a secret on the side while you swive some noble wife." Derk jutted at Renala with his chin.

Hmm. Looked like this sparring hadn't decreased Aven's desire to punch Derk in the jaw. Or maybe the gut would be better. Not many had the gall to take that tone of voice with him, let alone a newcomer he didn't trust, let alone tell him how to live his life, and on top of it all insult his integrity. The only thing that stopped him from launching into an outright brawl was that, well, Derk was right. The man's intentions seemed almost noble, clad in the sarcasm of a cad. Was he a decent man disguising himself behind the veneer of a scoundrel, or the other way around? Derk, of course, had no way of knowing if Aven was an honorable man. And the mage must have been picking up on something between Aven and Miara, and yet he'd also noticed they were hiding something. And what possible reason could they have for hiding it?

"You forget yourself," Aven said, glaring down at Derk's hand. The mage withdrew it from Aven's shoulder, backing down slightly, but his frame was still tensed and ready for a fight. "And I assure you, that's not what's happening."

Aven stalked away, hoping Derk would finally drop it. He heard no steps following him, so he immediately headed straight for Miara's room.

This was stupid. Keeping it all secret was impossible and probably just looked worse in the end. He'd had enough.

"Oh, Aven—there you are." Miara sat on the bench by the fire, a book in hand, but she rose to greet him. A long, crimson tunic fell to her knees, belted with black leather. "I was worried when you didn't come by this morning. I talked to Dom about—"

He pulled her into his arms and kissed her fiercely. Her lips wasted no time in returning his affections, her intensity quickly surpassing his. Camil, not three feet from them, dropped her laundry basket.

"Please keep this to yourself, Camil," he muttered, and then returned his lips to Miara, pulling her closer as he ran a free hand over those soft, red locks. Camil recovered her basket and bustled into the next room. Well, there went the rumors. He couldn't bring himself to care anymore.

Finally he let their lips part, for just a moment, maybe two. He should probably explain this outburst, shouldn't he? "I'm sorry I didn't come by this morning. I should have."

"Oh, no—it's fine." She frowned, mystified, cheeks flushed.

"And I'm sorry about—this whole—everything." Her eyes darkened, knowing what he referred to. "I heard a few thoughts more than I think you intended."

"I'm the one who should be sorry."

"No. You didn't ask for this."

"Neither did you."

"I wish I could throw it off so you didn't have to even ask that question—"

"No, you can't. I wouldn't want you to either. Don't think that way. This is just… it's not what I'm good at. I'm good at sneaking in the shadows and not being seen and coming up with good excuses for being places I shouldn't be, like you said. And also curing horse stomachaches. Civil war? Fancy banquets? I am out of my element."

"That doesn't mean— Ah, damn. I promised myself I wouldn't try to push you on it. I know! Maybe I'll lose the vote and we won't have to worry about any of it."

"By the gods, Aven, have you gone insane? Don't think like that."

"I want us both to be happy." And he had felt her fear so clearly, her gut instinct that she would not be happy. Even if she denied it, he knew what he had felt.

"I can't be happy without you either, though."

He pulled her into a hug and breathed her in, catching different scents of violet, rose, mint on top of the lavender. He didn't know what to say, so he didn't say anything.

"This is a big adjustment," she said softly into his ear. "I've gone from having nothing to potentially having what feels like the whole world. I can't even take a bath without feeling guilty for those back home."

She was right. Maybe all she needed was time.

"Except that's *not* home. I have no home. I want this to be my home. But I'm still very much an outsider here."

He pulled away, frowning.

"No, no, don't argue that I'm not. Just give it time, Aven."

He sighed. "Patience is not one of my strengths."

"You were doing so well up until a few minutes ago, though." She grinned. He studied her face and decided she did not mean it critically.

"Well, at least it wasn't those banquet tables we talked about."

She chuckled. "That sounds uncomfortable anyway. But what brought this on? Last night?"

"Last night combined with my guilt over avoiding you this morning. Colliding with a nice chat I had with Derk."

She raised an amused eyebrow. "A nice chat, huh?"

"It could have gone worse. I didn't beat him to a pulp."

"Wait—is that a victory or a defeat?"

"A victory of my patience, but apparently I had none left after that. No, but more seriously. He must have picked up on something between us. He talks like an ass, but his intentions seemed good."

"Hmm. Sure they were."

"Well, he did want to find you and take off his shirt. But he seemed to be just goading me. He may think I've taken you for a mistress or am planning to. And he was rightfully offended by the idea."

She smirked. "Well, that is sweet in a way. But I'm sure he'd be a lot less offended if he found me more hideous."

Aven laughed. "Maybe so. Either way, at least I didn't eviscerate him."

"What happened to your hand?"

"Oh. That. Well, we did exchange a few magic-related blows." He gasped as he felt the skin itch, heat, pucker— and then his hand was back to normal again. "Warning next time, maybe?"

"We'll see. We should go find Camil. She may have a few… questions."

"Wunik, can you get closer to the tower? Look at that. Are they—" Miara pointed into the window of light. She, Aven, Wunik, and Derk had gathered on the starlit balcony to make another attempt at freeing a mage slave.

"Shackled? The mages are shackled to the towers? By the gods," Aven breathed.

A rush of excitement ran through Miara's veins. Perhaps, just perhaps, the Masters were afraid of something. And that something was her and Aven.

"The Masters must know Jaena got free somehow," Miara said, "although that doesn't prove she actually made it out. Or if any of those we freed did. The Masters could have discovered Menaha and Kae too, I guess."

Derk nodded. "The Masters need mages to guard them against external attacks—air and earth attacks, in particular. But those would be the easiest positions for a freed mage to escape from. They cracked down."

Again, the night was eerily still and silent. No one was about. "Gods," Aven grumbled. "We are never going to free *anyone* this way, let alone even a few."

Miara sighed, although she wanted to groan outright. She didn't want to let her discouragement with the situation show, though. "Over there, Wunik. Can you get closer to the temple? Maybe someone is near there. The columns are high and there are no shutters on some of those windows."

Wunik moved the window of light slowly toward the building Miara indicated. The high, pale columns of the temple came into view. "Try that garden over there," she said. Could Menaha have reached Sefim with her message? Was this simply wishful thinking? She was dreaming, wasn't she? The guards had ensured that no one was outside. "Argh, try the next one."

"I think no one's out. Their curfew is still in place," said Wunik.

"Gods, I hope they let them eat," she said. "Menaha said they hadn't let them out for dinner yesterday, even."

Aven folded his arms across his chest. "By Anara, I hope they're not suffering more without any of them even escaping. Damn it. Where else do you want to try—"

"Wait—there!" Miara pointed.

Three statues sat on a bench with wall fountains burbling behind them. The stone had been carved in the forms of monks, legs crossed in meditation.

"What about it?" said Wunik.

"There are usually *two* statues. Can you go closer?"

They drifted closer, and indeed, the middle statue was a bit stouter than expected.

*Sefim?*

The statue's eyes snapped open, startling Derk, who took a step back. Wunik let out a soft chuckle.

*Miara?*

*Thank the gods. I'm glad you… figured out a way. There's still a curfew?*

"Working on it," came Aven's voice. Sefim's eyes

closed again.

*Yes. But apparently the guards are rather inattentive to religious statues. Now I just have to sit here the rest of the night.*

*Well, at least you'll be free while you do it.*

*Truly?*

*We're working on it. What news?*

*Over a dozen new mages arrived today, but none have been branded yet. They're being kept in the dungeons, which are now full to the brim. Maybe they haven't branded them because there are so many. There have been more than usual each day, but this was high by even normal standards. They are actively trying to increase our numbers, I think. Also rumor has it at least one mage has escaped. Some rumors say two. I think those count your escape.*

*Jaena, Menaha, Kae?*

*Kae—no. Menaha told me to tell you he was summoned by the Dark Master this morning for some kind of mission.*

Miara caught her breath. What terrible luck. The knots would not work on him with the bond broken. Would he have to act the part? Would it even be possible to fool them? Kae hadn't seemed like he had much ability at deception. *Do you know any more about the mission?*

*No. But I think it must have been Jaena who escaped. Menaha was unable to find her anywhere, although she didn't dare ask specifically in case that aroused any suspicion by association.*

*Good thinking.*

"It's done," Aven said, voice gentle, almost forlorn.

"Is there any chance we'll find anyone else?"

"One more moment, and we'll look around. But I doubt it."

*There. You're free, Sefim.*

He took a deep breath, taking in the moment, an even more perfect picture of meditation than the statues at each side. Then she heard softly, *Thank you, Miara.*

*It's not me. It's my… friend.*

Sefim's eyebrow twitched, made all the more subtly humorous looking by his statue imitation. *Your… friend, eh? Should I be telling your father you have a 'friend'?*

He did not seem at all mystified by what she meant. Which figured. He had always seen right past her barriers and into her soul, and speaking this way doubtlessly did not help. *If you see him, certainly. Have you any news of his whereabouts?*

*None new. Menaha told me what she told you, and neither of us have seen any change in the situation. But wait—who is this friend?*

*The prince I kidnapped.*

Now a smile spread across his otherwise still face. *Didn't I tell you not to worry about your soul?* He sobered, probably remembering his disguise. *The Masters perpetrate this evil, and the Balance will bring justice back to them.*

*I hope you're right. But this whole bringing justice business personally is new to me.*

*You're going to be a natural. I can tell.*

Sunlight filtered through the dust motes that came through the library windows. Daes had hoped never to open this library. This wasn't somewhere he had ever wanted to be. It was a place of forbidden magic, the kind of magic that he wanted to destroy.

But when all your power rests on one thing, it makes a certain sense to have a backup plan.

Three air mages trailed him, ready for his orders.

"I suppose you'll need to clean this place up first. I don't know how long it's been since someone's been in here." Daes certainly had no desire to touch anything. The dust was a fingernail thick on some of these tomes. "If you think it will slow you too much, I can arrange for more mages to help you, although access to this room will be strictly controlled."

"What are we doing here?" the young blond one said.

The comment seemed a little out of turn, but Daes chose to ignore it. "I have a special mission for you," he said. "Something a little different."

He turned left when they reached the far side of the library and headed down to the stacks that were the farthest from the door. An alcove separated a handful of tomes from the rest of the collection. A shaft of wheat hung over the top of the alcove. Whether it was meant to protect or signify something, Daes wasn't sure, but it seemed a little decorative for his tastes.

The three mages followed obediently and stopped as he did upon reaching the alcove.

"What I have to tell you I command you not to repeat. I seek the creation of a second brand to further our mage control efforts."

"A second one?" said the mage that had spoken up at first. Again, the comment struck Daes as a little odd. But he couldn't put his finger on why. This boy had been a talkative one the few other times Daes had had the misfortune to run into him. Perhaps he just didn't like the boy or that peasant accent he had.

"Yes, a second one. For traveling." The Masters had enough rumors flying around; they didn't need these mages to know that the real brand was missing. No one needed to know that. He would find it. It wouldn't be long now.

But just in case he didn't.

"As you know, the Devoted Knights are working hard to bring more mages to Mage Hall, and we almost can't keep up with them. In addition, some mages have to be transported long distances from other kingdoms. It would behoove us to have more options, perhaps to enslave them first or to create a second major control site. And that's where you come in."

Daes spread his hands wide at the shelves of tomes behind him. "I am told that these books contain the knowledge that was originally used to create the brand. As you can imagine, these texts are quite old and fragile. You will use the utmost care and secrecy in dealing with them."

He pinned them under his gaze, studying their posture, their faces for some hint of what they thought of this assignment. If he had learned anything from dealing with the rebellious creature mage, it was that perhaps the mages' temperaments should figure into his plans. At least a little. He could have taken the hint, noticed her temperament as an indicator to watch her more carefully. Seulka had been right about that much, and that much only. Exactly why he'd sent her off on a fool's errand to keep her out of his hair. But if he'd listened to her and paid the mage's temperament more mind, been less arrogant, he could have sent other mages on that journey with the creature mage, and that might have prevented all that had transpired. He could have—

No, it didn't matter. He was second-guessing himself again. He had been trying to study the mages, but he wasn't even paying attention. He redoubled his focus.

None of the three mages looked particularly comfortable about the assignment, but none of them had that rebellious streak in their eyes either. The young blond one looked determined not to meet Daes's gaze. The oldest one stared off into space, shoulders stooped, long ago defeated. The tall, dark-haired one studied the room with curiosity. None of them gave him any explicit reason for concern.

Perhaps he should give them a reason for concern.

"You have seven days."

Now the oldest one looked up, slight alarm in his eyes. "Seven days?" He glanced at his colleagues nervously.

Neither of the younger men reacted.

"What, too long?" Daes said with a wicked smile. The fool blanched. "Seven days." Daes kept his voice hard as iron. The older man hung his head as if he'd accepted a death sentence. Daes wanted to give him a good shove. He barely held the urge in check. If one thought the battle was lost before it had even begun, one was sure to lose. Should he get a replacement for this one already? But this oldest mage was also the most experienced, so he decided to let it slide. If the spineless husk was still looking like he would have a heart attack at the end of the second day, perhaps then Daes might take some action.

Daes's smile grew to a grin. "You had better get to work."

# 8  DEMONSTRATION

Miara sliced another section of apple and held it out. The white mare chomped happily away. Her mane was striking, her demeanor calm. All these things steadied Miara's nerves. The demonstration was to start any moment now, but she'd stolen away for a few moments to herself.

She wasn't hiding. She was just... gathering her strength. Searching for a way to convince herself that she was not in far over her head and about to do something entirely stupid and dangerous. Of course, she'd been quite talented at doing some stupid and dangerous things and getting away with them.

But none of those had required an audience.

She forced a deep breath. Gods, what was she thinking? She was just a horse healer, and that glorified how she'd spent most of her life. It didn't take a mage to muck a stall. Right now, she would have preferred that chore to what she needed to do.

Someone's eyes were on her now, she realized. Warden

Asten had appeared at the back of the stall and was eying her.

Oh. "This your horse?" Miara said.

Asten nodded, approaching with more caution than Miara would have expected.

"She's beautiful. I gave her some apple, I hope you don't mind." Gods, she should have asked first. She hadn't thought she'd get caught, but she should have either way. And she should have realized they'd all be gathering down here anyway. Great, she was already estranging the very people she needed to win over.

"Thank you," Asten said, holding out a hand. Miara sliced another section of apple and gave it to her. Well, perhaps no harm done after all. The mare chomped loudly. "She's a fine steed, from the Delagosan line out of Dramsren." Did Asten expect her to know this, or was she simply making conversation? She could only hope it was just small talk.

"I never saw anything so fine in Kavanar," Miara replied. "Mostly Southern Beylans and Hepani Creams out that way."

Asten nodded again, smiling. "Makes sense, if you don't need a warhorse."

"No wonder she's so calm with a stranger feeding her an apple."

"She hasn't seen much battle. But we're ready, when the day comes. Which may be sooner than later, I fear."

Miara frowned. She hadn't been paying the horse's health much mind. Some horse healer she was. She needed her strength for what they'd planned, but...

Perhaps she could stave off an ailment that might critically weaken the mare in the battles to come. "Well, let me give her a look, eh?" Miara skimmed her mind over the mare, first her skin, then shoulders, stomach and all those inner workings, down to her legs and hooves. A fine steed, indeed, and in very good health. Oh, but the back hoof— "She having any problems with this leg?" Miara pointed at the back left one.

Asten frowned. "I noted a bit of a change to her gait on the last stretch of the way here, but nothing specific to one leg yet."

Miara nodded and handed the apple to Asten. "Takes time for the signs to show in the hooves, all too often."

"Indeed, it's a shame how many a horse is brought low by injuries so suddenly." Asten cut off her own slice of the apple to give to the mare.

Miara stepped around the warden and caressed the mare's side as she stepped back a few feet. There, she could grasp it now—tiny bits of life squirmed on the hoof's left side that didn't belong there. To her mind, the hoof felt fiery, oozing.

She beckoned the mare to lift the hoof and winced at the sight. "Ah, beginning of an abscess here. Well, lucky we caught this, or it might have slowed you down." The wounds were hard to catch until the horse was damn near lame and unwilling to walk, and could take weeks to resolve without magical assistance.

Should she wait till after the demonstration? No. The gods didn't give her these abilities only to raise eyebrows and drop jaws. She poured a small amount of energy into the natural resistance of the hoof and guided the tiny squirming bits out and away. Probing further, she'd probably stepped on something, maybe a nail. With a touch more magic carefully placed, the slice in the heel began to close. Even that small effort was more than was needed, as the mare attested by stamping the now hot foot.

Aven's voice caught her ears. Not calling for her yet, but talking to someone in the courtyard. Enough hiding—er, gathering her strength. Searching for calm. Right.

"It should be healed now, but keep a watch on it," she said, patting the mare. "If you notice something more, I can look at it again in a few days. I think they are getting ready for us."

"Uh, thank you, Miara. And I believe they're getting ready for you, in particular," Asten said.

Thanks for the reminder, she thought. She stalked toward the center of the stable ground, where the horses were turned out for exercise. Asten followed, half an apple in hand.

Aven caught her eyes from the back of the crowd. He was standing with that damn dvora, clad in a pristine sky blue. Miara had cast aside thoughts of queenly politics for her clothing today, not that she'd embraced them very well in the first place. She wore the leathers of a royal guardsman she'd convinced Camil to track down. She was not demonstrating magic in a courtly affair. This was war. Aven's gaze flicked to her hand—oh, she'd forgotten to sheathe the knife. Did that look odd without the apple as explanation? Oh well, too late now.

She stopped in the center of the ring before them. The king, Assembly members, advisers, arms masters, and a bevy of stewards and servants had gathered. Wonderful. Many were still chatting, although a few stopped and waited at the sight of her.

Siliana and Derk joined her, one on each side. Miara took a deep breath and squinted at the crowd, lifting her jaw, straightening her shoulders, and readying herself.

To her surprise, the rest of the crowd quickly quieted at this gesture.

"King Samul and Prince Aven have requested that the three of us give you some education in magic," she said. She chose her words carefully, wanting them to feel drawn in, that they would now have the knowledge all mages did. "We've prepared a few training tasks for you with relevance to war. As such, they may seem dangerous, and they are, but we assure you, you will be in no mortal danger at any time."

"Only we will be," Derk muttered.

Miara silenced him with a glance. She was the one with the riskiest task, why was he complaining? "Ready?" she said, glancing at Siliana now. Both mages nodded.

Time to light the firewood and see what happened.

"Siliana, something to burn, please?" Miara asked.

The other mage responded, raising a dozen patches of tall, dryish grass from the dull earth. It waved in the mountain wind. Or was it Aven's? She hoped it was.

"Derk," she barked. He stepped forward, thankfully

cooperative. "Light them."

A crisp nod, and the grass burst into flames. Forms in the crowd shifted, growing uncomfortable. Good. They should be.

"Care to put it out?" she asked.

The smile of a child invited to play with a flint striker took over Derk's face as the first peal of thunder rumbled above them.

"Siliana. Something more to burn. I don't think Derk's been adequately challenged."

"On it." Saplings of three young oak trees curled from the ground to the far left, startling the crowd. Even as they grew, flames appeared and licked the branches.

Drops of rain fell. He *was* an apprentice, and the storm wasn't so neat that it didn't hit the crowd. Sorin could have done better, but she was annoyed for even thinking of that fool. She'd much prefer Derk's company to Sorin's at this point, and that said a lot.

The rain fell on the flaming plants, gradually extinguishing them.

"And now the lightning, if you please, Derk," she ordered. And again, thankfully, he complied. A crack and flash of light split the air, and suddenly the sapling—which had grown into a small tree nearly as thick as her thigh—exploded, shards flying.

Miara opened her mouth but stopped an oath in time. Too hot. Figured that a mage like Derk would have little control. Thankfully, she had enough control not to curse him in front of all these people.

He surprised her by being competent enough to send a gust of air toward the lords. The gust sent some off-balance but also flung the wood away, keeping it from impaling anyone.

Dom stalked into the ring, bow in hand. She was worried the Assembly members wouldn't spot him as they watched the rain or stared at the shards of tree that could have killed them, but Beneral pointed out the new arrival.

Dom drew the bow back and fired three arrows at Derk in rapid succession. The air mage held up a palm as if it would shield him, and in seconds, two arrows met an early end in the dirt, and the third turned to cinder midair.

Miara's turn. She stepped forward and waited as the chaos calmed. Eventually, all eyes were on her. The rain had calmed, the flames were out. Only the wind clanging the stable doors met her ears. She'd never sheathed her dagger, she realized. Well, all the better to prepare them for what they were about to see.

Without hesitation, she plunged the dagger into her left side and dragged it to the right, slicing a gash the length of two hands across her torso. She staggered back as a wave of pain hit her, then dropped to her knees. Horrified gasps and murmurs flitted through the crowd.

Miara struggled to focus above the cries of warning from her body for a moment, but her eyes locked on the nearest dubious noble—Lady Toyl. The merchant wore a fine cloak of pale blue and a dress the shade of the sky before a storm, and her brown hair swayed in the mountain wind.

"Is this a real wound, my lady?" Miara called. "Would you care to come inspect it?"

"Real enough to get blood on my cloak," she grunted. Her gruff attempt at indifference seemed a cover for the shock and touch of unsettled panic lurking behind her eyes. Even Alikar's hardened visage had melted into horror. The king's gaze remained stoic. "I'll observe from here, thank you," Toyl said.

Miara withdrew the dagger from her gut and tossed it at the feet of the crowd. The blood came quickly now, and other things too, and she would have to heal herself soon. "Would anyone else care to examine it?"

Asten strode forth and fell to her own knees before Miara, her face creased with concern. Asten's gaze flicked from the wound to Miara's face and back, but the warden did not recoil from the blood. How often would lightning strikes come in handy in war, Miara wondered as she stared into the warden's icy blue eyes. Hopefully, the universal usefulness of healing should be inarguable.

"I don't doubt you," Asten said quietly. "But I must perform my due diligence." She crouched and rose, returning to the crowd.

Miara waited one moment longer. She caught Aven's eye, his expression one of near terror as he squinted in the harsh overcast light. The air around her twitched, jolted. Was this his energy, or the earth's? He gave her a nod of support.

Enough time. Enough pain. She shut her eyes and began closing the wound. Healing it seared almost more than the initial injury, although at least she had no bones to pop back into place. Organs globbed back together, skin pulling tight across it all, leaving no trace. She growled through the pain as she felt Siliana approach and rest her hand on Miara's shoulder, feeding her a slight stream of supportive energy. The growl grew to a roar before she finally fell forward on her hands and knees, panting, exhausted.

It was done.

Siliana continued to push energy, pillaging the mountain trees and flora to feed her. Miara accepted it gratefully. They'd made sure energy would be adequate here, plentiful even. If the plants did not fill the need, they could also tap the horses, the crowd, passing birds. They were as far as possible from the Great Stone.

But it was still a massive wound she'd inflicted on herself.

The pain eased, and she regained her composure. Still kneeling, she wiped away some of the blood with a red cloth Camil had dug up, particularly so the lords could see clearly her regrown skin. She was a bloody mess, and her insides were still sorting themselves out, but that skin was clear and smooth as the snow on the mountain.

"And now, my lady?" she asked Toyl.

Lord Alikar stood just behind the assemblywoman, glaring at Miara, as if he were still determined to believe this was a trick. Figured. Or perhaps he just thought he was in the presence of utter evil. She wasn't sure which she thought more moronic.

One of Toyl's eyebrows arched. "I see no wound. Impressive."

"Thank you." She bit the words out as if to say, you're right, you sure as hell don't. She glanced at the king. His expression was stern, unreadable.

Miara hoped this risk, this effort would be worth it. Energy continued to drain from her as her body reeled with the effort. If she lost consciousness, Siliana should be able to finish the job, and Elise could too, in a dire emergency. It should be safe enough, but the flow of energy could be hard to judge between two people, as she and Aven had seen so well. He had been inexperienced, and the wound they healed far more fatal and damaging than these. But still.

Miara felt herself lose her balance a bit and fall to one side. She had lost track of her body in the vicious transfer of energy. No. She did not want help from the real queen for this. It would do little to convince others of either the power of her magic or of her leadership potential if she collapsed unconscious, a husk bereft of energy, cast aside on the pale dirt of the stable.

And then—suddenly, to her relief—it was enough. Her stores were replenished, her mind clearing as she felt hands steadying her, lifting her up. Gods, let it not be Derk.

She blinked open bleary eyes—when had they closed?—to see Aven's face. She smiled, although she could feel eyes watching him touching her. Would the king disapprove?

*How did we do?* she whispered to him. *Should we keep going?*

*You are an extraordinary woman, Miara Floren. How many of* them *do you think could do what you just did? You scared the piss out of them. Gods and ancestors, you're bloody. I think that's very much enough for now.*

*No vines?*

*Oh, yes, let's forget those vines forever, unless you have other goals in mind for them.*

His eyes twinkled as she straightened herself. Thankfully, Derk had quieted the storm without needing to be told to and had helped Siliana to her feet as well. Miara felt too exhausted to stride over to the crowd. Hopefully the lords and ladies could see well enough from where they were. She leaned on Aven and closed her eyes.

"I hope this has been informative for all of you," Aven called over the whispers as they stared. "I believe our mages are quite exhausted now and will need to rest."

"Can you do all that, Aven?" Asten asked, an edge to her voice. Miara couldn't read if it was hope or fear, and the warden's deadly serious expression revealed little. Funny, she hadn't seemed so serious by her mare. A soft spot for her?

"Not all of that, not yet," he replied.

Oh, who cared if the man could call lightning if he could free an entire people? Miara wanted to snap. But it was a good question. And who knew which answer they had wanted to hear? They might fear a king who could start spontaneous fires, and she couldn't blame them. But

Aven would learn, and they didn't know him half as well as she did if they thought he would abuse such powers.

"My lord?" Toyl called now, her voice loud enough to be heard over the wind that was picking up.

"Yes, Lady Toyl?" Aven answered, a sharpness to his voice.

"May I speak with you privately after this?" she called. "With our attendants, of course."

Aven nodded. "I will find you shortly." On the surface, Aven remained composed, but she could see the smallest twitch in his eyebrow and the corner of his mouth. She could feel the hope he kept bridled under the surface.

"Thank you all for coming," Aven said. "Let us retire. Looks like our fine apprentice has stirred up more than just a baby storm for show."

"A baby storm!" Derk grumbled. He held Siliana's arm as they headed toward the main gate. She had given nearly as much as Miara in the end, although with less bloodletting. She leaned heavily on Derk as the thrill of the moment wore off. "That was a work of artistry! It takes *control* to keep it small and contained. I had nothing to do with this nonsense sweeping in. Don't you blame that on me; I wanted to go for another ride away from this stinking place after this!"

"Oh, shut it, Derk," Siliana grunted. Of course, he didn't listen. But the two mages had gotten far enough ahead of Miara and Aven that she couldn't hear them anymore. She leaned heavily on Aven too. This once she had an excuse, although she glanced nervously around, wary of disapproving glares from the king. But Aven's father appeared to be gone, headed inside more quickly than the rest.

Together she and Aven walked inside. Worrying about what her audience might think must have taken more out of Miara than she'd thought. She wanted to sleep for days. Shouldn't she have more energy back by now?

Something niggled at her about this new storm. It felt off. Too sudden. She stopped in the entryway and peered back at the sky.

"What is it?" Aven said.

"Something's not right with this storm," she whispered back to him. "Can you feel anything?" She tried to reach out, into the clouds, down the hills. Was someone building this storm? She couldn't feel it as directly as an air mage would, and Aven likely hadn't learned how yet.

"There is—something," Aven said slowly. "Someone?"

Who could be doing this? And for what purpose? She glanced around. Wunik had watched them like a doting tutor, and he had followed Siliana inside. Her eyes caught on Elise, who saw them stopped and came over. "Something's not right with this storm," Miara repeated to her. "Do you feel it?"

Elise frowned. "Derk—"

Miara shook her head. "He claimed it was not his doing just a moment ago. Besides, he's hardly even winded. He wanted to make sure he had every chance to show off. He wouldn't risk screwing up and getting shot by an arrow to brew this up after everyone had gone inside."

"But… who? Or why?"

Miara shook her head. "I don't know, but let's get inside."

Tharomar stoked the coals of the hearth and carefully placed the single shaft of wheat into the embers. A flicker of light and smoke went up, and he dropped to his knees in the smithy, offering up the morning's devotions to Nefrana.

He felt the holy connection open, divine joy and encouragement bathing him from within. He sighed with relief. Some days he needed to feel the gods more than others.

The mage had not asked about any altar, and he did not expect she would. She showed no signs of being the pious type, even when the subject of the temple came up. He couldn't blame her. If *his* only experience of Nefrana's favor had been the Devoted burning a hole in his shoulder and making him a slave, he would probably be pretty unenthusiastic too.

But if she would not pray for herself, he could pray on her behalf.

Only luck had helped him find her. He had had no idea where or how she'd been hiding under that bridge, but he'd nearly given up and turned back toward town. When those Devoted had come knocking on doors, he'd gone hunting to see if he could find whoever they were looking for first.

The priestesses would appreciate this news, even if the mage had fled by the time he returned. He'd been on assignment for his order here for nigh on three years now, and he had not yet encountered a mage he could actually help. They were all already enslaved, this close to Mage Hall. The Order of the Silver Grove was not a particularly patient group of women, and he wasn't sure how long they would let him hold this location. They'd argued it was too risky in the first place. But Tharomar was the most battle hardened of any of their order—well, street hardened, anyway—and when a smith had died and bequeathed his smithy to the order, Tharomar had argued it was not an opportunity they could pass up. Plus, it had made them more money than most locations, since he was in fact a half-decent blacksmith.

So much time had passed, though, that some days he forgot his mission altogether. Some days he forgot that he was anything more than a small-town blacksmith for these farms.

The sight of Devoted banging on his door had been enough of a reminder, though. Those hoods had called up memories he had spent a long time pushing away. He'd known many in the streets that had fallen to their brutality, as well as others who had fallen to those who ruled Evrical with more force than persuasion.

Sasha's face sprang to mind, eyes wide with surprise, blood on the cobblestones. He pushed the memory back down again. Not now. Well, maybe just a prayer in her memory.

He had to get more of the mage's story out of her before he explained this to her. She hadn't even told him her own *name*. If she proved worthy, he might be able to help her completely evade them. Were she a criminal, well, he would never turn her in to the likes of them, but he couldn't be so sure it was Nefrana's will to help her either. Still, she had seemed like a sweet person, quiet but confident in her way. Appropriately wary of him, but also… He had long ago set his course on a mission to help people like her, but he was starting to wonder if that was his *only* reason for charming her into his home. And his bed, for that matter.

The hot energy of the hearth surrounded him as it began heating up for the day's work. They'd take a quick meal, and then he had work to do. But before then he always let the hearth burn in honor of the great holy three for a few minutes, a few prayers.

He tossed in a rose petal for Anara now, and spoke her prayers, plus a few invocations of healing for the girl and protection for Nemin. They'd probably need it.

Would she even be in the house when he returned? She would have bolted away at first sight of him, if it weren't for that ankle. He found himself feeling a little glad that the injury had waylaid her, and then he realized that was a horrible thought. She'd probably be off and out of the Devoted's clutches by now, if it weren't for that.

Was that really true? On the road, they'd probably have found her. Did she have the skill to get to the forest, to leave no trails even in a wheat field? To outrun both men and the dogs he'd seen? She didn't seem the type. Her athletic frame seemed more strong than nimble.

Was she an innocent? A charlatan? A thief? A murderer?

You need to know more about her before you go thinking about her athletic frame, he told himself. He couldn't help criminals. The order only had so many resources and kept themselves secret, staying small to keep themselves that way. Being enemies of the Devoted was a dangerous thing to be. Temple priestesses hid mages from those bastards when they could. Of course, they encouraged them not to use their magic or risk corrupting their souls. But it was a free choice, something only the mages could decide for themselves. He sighed, watching the coals burn. One day, his brothers and sisters would stop the Devoted forever. Someday soon, the priestesses would find a way.

Perhaps he could even help his mage if she had done something. Escaping them this close to Mage Hall would be extraordinarily difficult. No one deserved to be enslaved. Or any of the other things the Devoted meted out to mages they captured.

As the last part of his ritual, he tossed in a nail for the god Mastikos. Mastikos received little worship in these regions compared to the two goddesses, but their only god of the trio was important nonetheless. The priestesses taught the value of all aspects of divinity, not just Nefrana's golden light, as well as all the holy languages, the ancient alphabets. He would make a fine priest, if he chose.

He was something like a priest, in his own way, although he had no intention of taking any vows of celibacy anytime soon. His dreams the night before had been proof enough of that.

He shook his head at himself. He *also* had far more important work to do in Nefrana's name than coordinate worship in the temple. The idea felt more like fact than conviction, like something he could sense. Even now, bathed in the holy connection, something somewhere urged him on.

Important work waited. Here. Now. The mage.

Why did his thoughts stray so easily to her? Were they really pushing him toward helping her, or was it just his own mind wandering back, as mischievous as his dreams? Was she a merchant, as she claimed? Perhaps she had been in the past. Had she come from Mage Hall itself and escaped, or was it merely a terrible coincidence that they hunted her so close to this evil place?

Had she gotten away, or had she not yet been captured? *That* was the real question, the real answer he needed to wheedle out of her. If she had been branded, there was less that he could do, if he could help her at all. But was it even possible for them to escape while branded? He thought not.

The nail was red-hot. He had been lost in his thoughts. Standing, he murmured the final holy words. With tongs, he lifted out the nail and placed it aside.

He said the last remaining prayer sadly, the holy connection reluctantly closing. He set off with a spring in his step for the cold cellar behind the house, gathering cheese and a slab of smoked meat. What did he have to be springing about? He shook his head at himself.

When he opened the door, she whirled, expression sheepish. She stood by his cupboard, leaning on her good foot. "I—uh—put back the salve."

He said nothing but smiled, wordlessly putting the cheese and meat on the table. Silence was often the best way to get more information. Did she think he might worry she'd stolen something? *Had* she been stealing something? He didn't think of any of these things as his. They were all given to him, mostly unearned, by the order. They were all simply in service of the mission and therefore ultimately free to her to take. But of course, she didn't know that yet.

"Are these… your books?"

Ah, was that what the fuss was about? "Yes."

She eagerly examined their spines. "You are a strange fellow."

He snorted. "You're not the first to tell me that."

"How many other blacksmiths do you know who've read *The Book of the Vigilant*?"

He laughed outright. A clue for her. What would she make of it? The books were one of the few things he kept that hinted there might be more to this story than that of a simple blacksmith. Mostly, he couldn't manage to part with either the beautifully crafted leather or the precious knowledge. "You told me I was different, I didn't deny it."

She smiled and returned to looking at the books.

"Have you read it?" he asked.

"What?"

"The *Book*."

"Oh. No." Of course not, her tone said. Who read obscure philosophical texts for fun? Crazy blacksmiths? And she was right. Why the hell did he feel disappointed by the knowledge? He already knew she wasn't the religious type, and he could thank the Devoted for that. Of course, the volume spoke mostly on the value of integrity, the nature of suffering. It was an important work in ethical and spiritual understanding, not just another tome of predictable parables. Although he liked those too.

And he was staring at her back like an idiot. He strode to her side and reached to the top of the cupboard, where his remaining stash of bread lay wrapped in linen. Two loaves still—plenty left until next market day. Then, bread in hand, he offered her his arm. She hobbled with surprising speed with his assistance, and they sat and began to eat.

He'd waited long enough. Time to get the truth out of her. "You know, you haven't told me your name," he began. That seemed like a fair start.

Was that a blush? She hesitated. "Jaena." It had the ring of truth to it.

"Well, you know all about my childhood—"

"Hardly."

"—what about yours?" How deep did her cover story go? How good of a liar was she going to be? She didn't seem like much of one, compared to the many thieves and charlatans he'd known in the past. But sometimes that, too, was an act.

Her brown skin faded a little, lost some of its rosy, blushing hue. He smiled to soften the question. He was just making conversation, after all, right? But he *would* get his answers out of her today. Too much time had already passed. "My father—is a diplomat in Hepan. But I always hoped to be a merchant. No endless parades of silly affairs, fancy festivals, and interminable banquets if I can avoid it, thank you very much." She sounded like she'd sat through more than a few of those. If this was a lie, she was very convincing. "I am starting my own shop with the help of my brother. Starting off on this journey, looking for items to trade back in Hepan."

He raised his eyebrows. Not even a native to Kavanar? How strange. And even as a foreigner, many would guess she'd be from Farsa from the darkness of her skin. She probably got that a lot, but she had no touch of the relaxed, jovial culture of the gulf about her either. "Hepan? You're a long way from there, indeed."

Her face fell. "Is it so far?"

"Well, we are much closer to Akaria. But if you've come on foot from Hepan, you must know how long it's taken you better than I."

She tore her gaze away and took a hasty bite of a hunk of bread. Yes, she had not come directly from Hepan on foot. He let none of his knowledge show. He knew he shouldn't even have called out the discrepancy, as it could put her on the defensive, but he'd been unable to resist. He would stop there, though. He'd been a street rat long enough to learn to hide a myriad of emotions on his face, and that calling people out on their lies was not always the fastest path to the truth.

"We're close to Akaria, though. With a horse, you can be in Anonil in a day's ride." Her face brightened at that. Anonil was certainly her real destination, if everything else in her story was falsified. He thought much of it was true, though. Maybe he was merely sensing an important omission?

"Do you have a horse?" she asked.

He nodded, pretending not to notice the edge of excitement in her voice. "Oh, yes. A good one, strong enough to pull a wagon."

"Where do you keep it? I've… always loved horses. I didn't see a stable about."

Nice try, but you're not getting away without me that easily, he thought. He stifled a laugh and realized even his smile was probably letting on too much. "Oh, nearby," he said as casually as he could. "Done eating? Good. Now—how about we look at that craft work I mentioned? I've got a few things worth selling, I'm sure."

She nodded reluctantly and took another too-long gulp of mead.

Thel ran up to them, Elise tagging alongside him. "Something's wrong," he said breathlessly.

Aven and Miara had hung back, trying to figure out the storm and failing. "Wrong with what?" Aven said.

"The mountain." Thel's eyes were trained on Miara.

This was very, very bad. She pushed away from Aven's embrace, grabbed Thel's hand, and pressed it against the wall. "Close your eyes," she ordered. He complied. "Feel for the mountain—the heartbeat, the breath of it." He nodded. His thin lips parted as she knew he was starting to sense it. "Now try to expand out, feel the rock in larger and larger areas. Which direction is the problem?"

"Like you're looking out over the horizon," Elise chimed in, "but one inside your head. Go out farther and farther, as far as you can."

"You feel it? Something off?" Miara wished at least *one* of them knew this art. Damn arrogant fools, living under here with no defense whatsoever.

He nodded. "Vibrations. Something is—shaking. It's unnatural. It's—angry. The rock is angry. It's been this way for ages. It doesn't want to be disturbed. It's… that way, I think?" He pointed back toward the storm—and the main entrance to Estun.

She looked sharply from Aven to Elise and back. "This is the area of the hold that's farthest from the Great Stone, correct?"

Aven nodded.

"And where are the most people gathered?"

"Well… What are you getting at?"

"If I wanted to do the most damage—kill the most people—and do it farthest from the Stone so I had the least resistance—"

Aven's gaze snapped to his mother. "The gate."

Elise nodded.

"Send word," Miara snapped. "Tell them to get out of there. Go out in the rain or wherever—but out of the mountain."

Aven didn't exactly listen. He turned and ran back toward the gate.

"Aven!" she shouted, reaching after him.

A hand on her shoulder stopped her. Thel's eyes had snapped open. "We need to get back. Come on." His voice was deadly serious, a tone she hadn't heard it take before.

"But Aven—" Elise started.

"Will kill me if I let you two get crushed along with him." He ushered them both back, eying the ceiling. Miara thought she could hear a distant rumbling. The thunder from the storm, or something else? A hundred paces back, they found an archway of keystone granite, more separate from the mountain. "Here," he said. "This rock is different from the others, and hopefully far enough away."

Miara looked back down the hallway, searching for Aven's running form. "Are there other exits out?"

Elise frowned. "Of course. Three. Not all convenient to travel, but they are there." She glanced around, but it appeared to be just the three of them. "There are also two others known only to the king." Her voice implied that perhaps others knew—her, Thel, Aven? Were there really even only two? The important part was that there *were* escape routes, and they were not all going to suffocate down here. She hoped.

Wunik trotted up beside them, spectacularly out of breath. "I heard shouting. What's wrong?"

"The mountain—" Thel started but was cut off by a sharp crack splitting the air.

"Aven!" Miara shouted into the dark, empty hallway in spite of herself and their stupid promises for secrecy. What would that matter if they were all dead?

Derk caught up to them. Others. She glanced at them in annoyance. Lady Toyl and one of her guards. Dvora Renala. What were *they* doing here? They were no help.

"They're attacking the mountain," she said as if only to Wunik.

"Who?" demanded Toyl.

"Who else?" she said through gritted teeth. "I'd wager Kavanarian mages. But it's not like they sent us a letter."

"This is because of that demonstration—the gods will punish you—" a voice started. Was that Alikar? Some other priest? She couldn't see who spoke in the throng, but the voice sounded familiar, almost like Sorin's. But that was insane; he was far away in Mage Hall.

"Derk, up here with me," Wunik ordered. "The rest of you get back. Get out of here."

The crowd didn't listen to him, but Derk did. The two mages braced themselves against each side of the tunnel. What were they planning? They seemed to know each other well enough to not need explanations.

Rumbling began again, then grew louder. Then another crack sounded, and another.

Where in all the gods and heavens *was* he?

She started forward. Elise caught her arm. She was probably right, but Miara was tempted to tear her arm free and run forward anyway.

Fortunately, before she had to, Aven's form sprinted around the corner. Another man, a woman, yet another followed. How many were there?

Another crack, lower in pitch this time and closer to them. The earth above the hallway shifted.

"Now," Wunik snapped.

The air vibrated bizarrely, strange and unnatural and moving away from them in a rapid wave toward Aven and the gate guards. Several of them started to cough—whether from the dust falling through the cracks in the hall or the strange spell, she wasn't sure. The air snapped back and forth in space, but not going anywhere; it vibrated in the tiniest bits, but all around them, pulsating toward the people running up the hallway. It tickled the hairs inside her ears, and she stifled a sneeze. It was like the air almost hardened, shifting back and forth every moment. Like the wind blew back and forth endlessly on the tips of her fingers.

The next crack, and the ceiling visibly began to sag. Wunik, too, sagged against the wall. Elise let go of Miara and ran to him.

He needed help. She had little energy left, so she reached for those around her, dug deep, and closed her eyes, demanding the strength of the oak to sprout before them, for its branches to grow low and wide and help hold up the mountain. There—she'd done what she could. That was all she could muster. She opened her eyes.

Aven was close now. Twenty paces.

A thick tree was pushing its boughs and tendrils up against the rock above, but she could also hear the wood snap. It was not enough. Most creature magic was not strong enough to withstand the weight of a mountain above it. Could she mend the tree? No, nothing left. And she couldn't pass out now. She had to know if Aven made it.

The loudest rumbling yet shook the earth beneath and the walls above them. She stumbled and, in her weakened state, fell to her knees. When she straightened and looked up, to her horror she saw that much of the hallway before them had collapsed.

Only a small tunnel at the bottom remained. She glanced at Derk, who was still bracing hard against the wall and sweating profusely. Wunik, too, had crumbled quite a bit, but they still strained.

They were holding up the tunnel with only the air.

It seemed like a lifetime passed before she saw that sandy hair crawl out of the tunnel, shaking dust off his head and reaching an arm back to help out the next person.

She wanted to shout at him to get the hell out of there, with her voice or her mind, but really she had hardly enough strength for either.

*You can't help anyone if you're dead, prince,* she finally managed.

He glanced at her with a twinkle in his eye. After a

few more were free, he got to his feet and staggered to them, collapsing into her arms.

Six more men came out, eight women. The last one looked back for a moment, but then said with a voice that suddenly knew death, "I am the last, I fear."

They held the tunnel for a minute longer, maybe two. But no one came.

"How many guards were there?" she whispered to Aven.

"Some may have gone out into the courtyard," he said, his voice hopeful. "But twenty."

Into the courtyard where an air mage waited, brewing a storm likely designed to keep them from running out into it. Those guards were likely no safer out there.

Miara had no doubt that slaves from Mage Hall must have caused this. Mages had finally been sent to attack. How many? And to what end? Had they hoped to trap the Akarians inside? Kill the guards? Perhaps they hoped to shake Akarian confidence, show them that even their strongest fortress was not impenetrable. Perhaps they were simply trying another tactic to provoke war. Or was there some other goal they had in mind?

Whatever they were seeking, it could not be good.

# 9     Disguises

Jaena hopped along irregularly beside Tharomar as he headed for the smithy. Could she really play the part of a merchant? It had been a long time. She'd have to bluff her way past having no coin, although in this bartering community, that didn't seem like it would be a huge obstacle.

"What is Hepan like?" he asked as they strolled. "I have never journeyed so far."

"Have you traveled much?"

"Not outside of Kavanar. And even inside, I've only lived here and Evrical. But I'd like to someday."

"Use those languages you know."

"Indeed."

"What languages were those, by the way?"

"Are you dodging my question?"

"No." She smirked.

"Takaran and Farsai."

"Were those your best guesses or just the only languages you knew?"

He narrowed his eyes at her, although he was smiling. "You ask a lot of questions to answer one simple one."

"My curiosity outweighs my loquaciousness, I guess."

"I speak about a dozen languages. Scraps of others. Can read a few more."

Her eyes widened. "That's—a lot for a blacksmith."

"And you?"

"Just this common tongue. I knew ancient Hepani once, but nobody uses it anymore."

"Finally something about Hepan."

She snorted as they arrived at the smithy, and he her found a stool. "Oh, it's not that different from here."

He took a key from his belt and made quick work of a lock on a cabinet on the far wall. "Not much pride for the motherland then?"

She shrugged. "We spent a lot of time traveling. To Detrat, Sverti, Farsa, here. My father spent some time delivering relatively unimportant diplomatic treaties."

"Which was your favorite?"

She raised an eyebrow. "My favorite of the treaties?"

"Of the kingdoms. Would you go back to one of them? Someday in your merchant travels?" Something about his voice made her think that he did not completely buy her merchant story. Or possibly any of it. If that was the case, then why was he playing along? He was drawing pieces out of the cabinet onto a long table perpendicular to it.

Hmm. She struggled to remember. It had been a long time since she'd thought about those days. About being able to travel if she liked. If she made it away from here—if she could destroy the damn brand—could she somehow make it to the other side of Kavanar?

Could she someday see her mother and father again?

She didn't like the news she would have to tell them. About Dekana. But they probably considered both their daughters lost. Perhaps getting one back, even if not their favorite, would be some consolation… But that was a long way off. Although—perhaps she could write them a letter.

She was still not answering his question, she realized. He seemed to be pretending not to notice.

"Farsa was very beautiful. If I could go back to one—perhaps there." The beaches had been Dekana's favorite. Jaena crushed back a wave of grief. No—no, she had never liked beaches herself. That wasn't her truth. Wasn't there anywhere else she remembered she might someday want to return to? "Wait, no. The great market in Leniya, western Sverti. How amazing would it be to trade there one day? But such a thing is a long way off, if it could ever happen."

"Oh, you never know," he said, with a twinkle in his eye. He strode back to her and held out his hand. She took it and made her way ungracefully over to the table, and she sucked in a breath.

The work was beautiful.

"So what I'm taking from this was that Hepan is very boring. Or you are mostly never there. Except right before you came here."

"These are stunning, Tharomar. What? Oh, well, it was very boring. The capital, Sicat, has a magnificent library, open for all to enjoy. You might like it, a lot of ancient tomes."

"That's what you think of me? That I like ancient tomes?"

"Well… don't you?"

He narrowed his eyes, but he was grinning.

She decided to carry on briskly, in case it had been a bit of an insult, stifling her own grin. "And it's well known for its public gardens, saltwater pools, and mineral baths. But outside that, it's mostly very crowded and dirty. And the rest of Hepan is much like Kavanar. Wheat fields, small villages. Nothing much to see otherwise until you get to the other side of the mountains and the rainforests, but we almost never traveled there. Did you make *all* of these?"

"Finally, I get it out of her, thank Nefrana. Now that you've actually answered my one casual question, yes. I did."

"How long have you been a smith?"

He shrugged. "I began learning in temple."

Door knockers, hooks, utensils, candleholders, pendants, hair sticks, knives, hammers, axes. Dozens of items littered the table, each with a similarly fine artistic touch. "I'd venture it must be a might boring here too," she breathed. "I see you've been keeping yourself busy."

He snorted. "Perhaps."

"You are very talented."

"You don't have to flatter me, I'll still give you a good deal."

She glared at him. "I would never say something if I didn't mean it. By Nefrana." There, perhaps that would assuage him more than her usual mutterings.

"Think you could make some sale of these?"

Gods. Here it came. She had no idea how to handle this. He would see right through her. "It... depends on how much you want for them," she bluffed. "But the quality is certainly high."

"How about this? These aren't doing me any good, sitting in my cupboard. Winter's on its way, and there will be fewer traders coming by until the snow and cold breaks. You take some of these with you to trade, and you can bring me back my share."

She raised her eyebrows, tearing her gaze away from the items. "I daresay you're far too trusting." Of course, his proposal was perfect. It would be a fine thing to have some items to start with, exactly what she needed to start off as a merchant. She thought she could get a good price in the White City or Takar, even. Perhaps he wasn't too trusting, because she would dearly love to make a profit for both of them. He just didn't know she had a brand to dispose of, the Devoted to escape, and revenge to wreak before she got around to that. "Do you always trust everyone to do the right thing?"

"No." He boldly met her gaze with a crooked smile and a twinkle in his eye. "But that ankle won't hold you here forever. Maybe the guilt will lure you back."

She let out a bark of laughter but then sobered a bit as the implications of his words dawned on her. He... cared that she should return someday? "What if I invest your fine profits a few times first? As you said, traders aren't fond of winter travel."

"All the more for the womenfolk."

She felt her smile fade a little but tried to hide it. Ah, yes. *The damn temple of Nefrana, the religion that would keep you from truly… caring for me. Oh, Tharomar, if you knew my whole story, what would you do? Would you still want to lure me back? Would you send me away or call the Devoted before I had the chance to run?*

Curse her stupid magic, yet again. Damn her for being born a mage. What had magic ever done to help her? It had only brought harm. She shouldn't be surprised. The only thing surprising was this new, subtle source of pain.

"Do you want to think of which to take while I work?" His voice was surprisingly soft, as though he'd read her change of mood. She liked him better when he seemed completely oblivious to what was going on in her head. This new perceptiveness was unsettling.

"Yes, yes. That'd be good." She had nothing else to do anyway. She almost offered to help him, but how could she explain, with her made-up story, knowing her way around a smithy? No part of a merchant or diplomat's life involved pumping the bellows, let alone trying to explain all the ways she was able to help with her magic.

But she glanced after him wistfully. The thought of working by his side was strangely appealing. And she'd been so excited to get away from those horseshoes. If only she could have told him the truth, and if he could have actually accepted it… what could things have been like?

She shook her head and tried to focus on the ironwork

before her. That was a dream, another life, an impossibility. And she was much more likely to simply get caught by the Devoted first.

Aven stared at the rock filling the graceful archways that had once been the grand entryway to Estun. To his home. Had the others gotten out of the guard towers and the tunnel in time? How long would it take to clear this out? To rebuild? Would it ever be quite the same? There were other ways out but none as large or direct as this.

Toyl and his mother approached where he and Miara stood, staring at the devastation.

"I really must speak with you, my lord," Toyl said. "Privately, please."

"It can't wait until after all this is… handled?" Aven gestured vaguely at the collapse.

"Unfortunately, no. If anything, this hastens my departure."

Aven nodded. He squeezed Miara's arm and let his mother lead her over to the group of other mages. They would all need to rest and recover. They'd meant the demonstration to be dramatic enough to use most of their energy—no one had thought an attack would happen at all, let alone that it might follow so soon after. With all that, he hoped they would get back to their rooms and rest. Who knew what else might happen? Aven was one of the few mages not utterly fatigued at this point. At least he was getting back into his training sprints.

Aven led Lady Toyl to the nearby military affairs office, waving for Fayton to join them. That should be plenty private, a place where visitors would expect to knock and request entry. The usual two guards, however, were not at their posts. They'd probably rushed to help in defense of the collapse, although he hadn't seen any helping the group outside the fallen rock. Could they have run into the tunnel too? Gods, he hoped not. He did not want to know how many were crushed under there.

Damn them and their foolish arrogance. They needed trained earth mages, and they needed them now.

"I must stop in Dramsren before heading on to the Assembly in Panar, so I had been planning to leave later today," Toyl said as they entered. The room was nearly pitch-black; this was not one the rooms in Estun with windows.

"Well, that may prove a bit difficult after that cave-in." Aven headed to the hearth and stoked the flames, throwing on a log, while Fayton lit several candles. While Lady Toyl examined the books above the record cabinets, he fed the flames a little extra, and soon the hearth was ablaze.

"I am still planning to take to the east gate on foot if need be. I will *not* be the one who doesn't make it to an Assembly."

"You may not be able to make it all the way to the horses, nor do we know what condition the stable itself or the storm is in. But at the very worst, you could trek down to the villages and get horses there." The two of them stood, one on each side of the hearth fire. Fayton busied himself straightening the shelves. The rest of the room seemed cold, as it was still dark. Aven could feel the oncoming winter in his bones.

"We will find some way," said Toyl briskly. "I've got a solid back to climb down from this mountain. I plan to beat that brat Alikar to Panar, or close to it."

"Wait, he hasn't left yet, has he?" Aven leaned against the hearth stone, letting the heat from the fire beat on him. The heat was barely enough, especially given the thin sheen of sweat cooling him from racing around under the falling rock.

"He's not left yet," she assured him. "Your father required us all to be here at least until this demonstration. But Beneral is preparing to ride as we speak. I plan to ride with him, if we can. Safety in numbers and all that."

"Understandable." Aven nodded, folding his arms.

"Watching all that rock crumble over your head hasn't left me terribly enthusiastic about staying here much longer either. Seems like that could happen again." She gestured at the ceiling warily.

"All the more reason we need mages to defend the hold from abuse like this."

"Hmm. Perhaps. At any rate, before I go, I wanted to speak with you about all this."

"Of course," he said.

"You must have wondered at my complaints." She clasped her hands in front of her, and he had the impression she was preparing herself to say something difficult.

Aven nodded, perhaps a little too quickly. "You've

never seemed a terribly religious woman. Although I suppose people change."

"Yes, they do. But I haven't."

"Then what is it?"

"I can read. You can read. I have read years of writings from the temples. Generations. The temples did not always condemn magic. Once, mages were some of the most pious followers, if you go back before the Dark Days. This condemnation is nothing but politics and manipulation. It's dishonest. And if there is *one* thing I don't like, my lord, it's dishonesty." At that, Toyl inclined her head slightly and paused to let the words sink in. "And so that leads me to ask, how can I possibly trust you, after all this?"

Aven let out a bit of a cough, not missing her point.

"I want to trust you. And your father. But I'm not sure that I can. And what are we voting for if not who we most trust?" Her hands were still calmly clasped, head tilted, demeanor placid. Funny how it made his heart race.

He swallowed. A fair criticism. It had never felt like much of a choice, though. The day when he'd realized he had magic—and that that was a bad thing—had been so long ago that he could hardly remember it, let alone choosing to try to stifle it. And he'd never denied he had magic either. But he'd known and had certainly never divulged it, although he knew people would have wanted to know.

Well, he was divulging it now.

He looked down for a moment, then back at Toyl's

dark gaze. What would she think if she knew about the *other* secret that he hadn't quite shared yet? Would it confirm her concerns about him? "I value honesty myself. I never set out to deceive anyone. I didn't want magic or seek to practice it; magic hoisted itself on me. I only sought to make it go away."

She took a deep breath. "It does help to hear you say that. But of course, anyone can say such things. I need to know, my lord, if I'm going to support you. Are there other secrets you're hiding from us? Any other snakes under rocks that will come back to bite me if I throw my lot in with you?" She arched an eyebrow.

No snakes under rocks. But there was Miara. But he couldn't just go against his father's wishes—or commands, really—and simply tell her. Could he? Damn it, this was exactly why hiding their relationship was a bad idea. People's trust had been broken, and he was not going to earn it back by failing to come completely clean.

"If? Is your support truly so tenuous?" Aven dodged her question with a smile, although his stomach knotted.

Lady Toyl smiled back, but mischief tinted the look as if to say, perhaps it is, perhaps it isn't. "I believe you are telling the truth about the nature of the Kavanarian threat. I believe you intended to tell us without any threat from Lord Alikar. I also believe that it's possible to learn things about men that make you realize you didn't *know* them after all."

Aven crossed his arms across his chest. "Rulers will always have secrets, Toyl. You should know that as well as I do." All governments held secrets, in different groups and from different parts, for better or for worse—but he hoped it was for the better. At the very minimum, to protect the realm, it did not make sense to tell anyone and everyone the location of every soldier, fortification, or armament. If the king's secret escape routes from Estun weren't secret, that could easily be used against him in an attack, like the one earlier that day. Keeping *some* secrets was simply required for being safe. More likely, it was not that Toyl did not want him to have secrets. She just wanted to be privy to more of them, as she was part of the government, after all.

Even if it didn't make sense for governments to control the flow of information, he would still never explain to Toyl that he'd found a map that would allow him—and *only* him right now—to enslave anyone and everyone in the land. Wasn't that a cheery thought? How quick would she be to trust Aven then? To support him? And who might he mention such a power to who might seek to abuse it? Such a "truth" could only come across as a threat, and Aven strove to avoid such intimidation tactics.

He sensed Toyl was only growing more suspicious in the growing silence. Aven needed some way to offer a token of trust, a symbol of his goodwill. "Listen. I understand your concerns, and I appreciate your honesty. But some amount of secrecy is part of keeping our kingdom safe. As a token of my trust, though, I can tell you something more, but only if you can keep it in confidence."

His father was going to kill him.

Lady Toyl narrowed her eyes at him. "I ask you not to keep secrets and tell lies, and in response, you ask me to do the very same thing?"

Aven glared right back. "If you think any kingdom operates without *some* secrets, you are a fool. Or, more likely, trying to manipulate me."

Toyl scowled, but muttered, "Fine. Your words will not leave this room, at least until you share them yourself." Well, perhaps his father wouldn't kill him if she kept her promise. But he knew he couldn't completely trust that. No matter, he would rather her know the truth anyway, and this was the only information he had to try to earn her trust.

"Good. I will take you at your word. Do you recall the mage I brought back with me?"

"The intense one who stabbed herself and nearly bled all over us this morning?"

Inwardly, he winced. Was that a good or a bad way for Toyl to remember Miara? "Yes, that one."

"What about her? That demonstration was informative, as promised. I am concerned the resulting cave-in was related, though."

"It was not. We don't even have any trained earth mages. She and the others you saw simply can't do that with their magic."

"Why do you mention her?"

Well after *those* comments, he no longer felt good about telling her this. But he was already too far down this path. "I intend to marry her," he said with as much blunt confidence as he could muster. As Toyl fit the pieces together, understanding spread across her face.

"I should have known, the way you two were clutching each other back there. I saw you watching her at the banquet, but I thought you were simply curious about the new mages. But why the secret? Why the lies?"

"I have *never* lied to you, Toyl."

Toyl pursed her lips, unconvinced. "You didn't send that lovely dvora away either."

"It's a *secret*, not a lie. I haven't promised to marry the dvora, *that* would be a lie," he said.

"A secret is a lie you haven't told yet, a lie by implication if you let it stand."

"Not true, at least not always. The king suggested that sharing the news at the same time as news of my magic might be a bit much for people to accept. Especially as she's a foreigner and a commoner."

"And a *spy*, don't forget," she said.

"Past experience that I believe is an excellent virtue in a future ruler. She's stealthy, can defend herself. Not exactly a warrior, but no stranger to fighting either."

"No stranger to fighting? She damn near disemboweled herself without even wincing." Toyl's eyes were wide.

He stifled a smile. What was that, pride? "A true warrior then. Just the sort who would do well at all levels of Akarian society."

"Maybe so. But I've heard rumors. Rumors that she didn't rescue you, but *kidnapped* you," she said.

"Both true, technically," he replied.

"How—"

"She was a slave. Kavanarians commanded her to kidnap me. She did—quite a feat, if you hadn't noticed. I freed her, and she freed me the very moment she was able to. The king has pardoned her from any wrongdoing for saving my life."

"How do you know this isn't some sort of enchantment?" Toyl said.

Because magic doesn't work like that, he wanted to say. But that wasn't entirely true, was it? There *was* dark magic that could enslave and enchant, but right now, only he knew it. If anyone were enchanting anybody, it would be *him*, not her. But he *really* didn't want to explain that to Lady Toyl just now. "She doesn't have the power to do that. And this kind of concern is exactly why the king and queen advised we wait to tell anyone, and I've gone along with it so far," he replied, running a hand over his face in frustration.

"So far?"

"Well, I just told you. Let's just say, your frustration with not knowing what's going on is not falling on deaf ears."

"Truly, though, my lord—can you be sure it's not a spell of some kind that binds you to her?" She sounded sincerely concerned.

"Yes, yes. I can be sure. As a creature mage, she cannot do it. But obviously I can't convince you of any such thing, because I suppose you can always wonder if I might have been enchanted to say so. Let me ask you this: am I acting any differently than I ever did in the past?"

Toyl frowned and straightened a little. "Well—yes and no."

"What do you mean?"

"In many ways, no. You are much the same as I remember you, not that we know each other well," she said.

Aven heaved a sigh of relief at that.

"But I can see you've grown," she continued. "I see darkness in your eyes, like those who have seen and felt real pain, deep suffering. Those who have begun to understand that things do not necessarily always turn out well. You seem different now. Older."

Aven straightened. Was that a compliment? He liked the words, in spite of himself.

"You have a mission now."

He nodded. "I do. A noble one, I'd like to think."

"Protecting and serving your land could be construed as simply self-preservation."

Aven smiled wryly. "Are you *always* so contrary?"

She relented with a small smile. "Yes, as a matter of fact. I didn't get where I am by being too agreeable." She cleared her throat before continuing. "Freeing slaves, though, I suppose could be considered universally noble."

"So, do I have your support?"

"We'll see."

"We'll see?"

"If I vote for you—"

"If? I've earned *none* of your support in the course of this conversation?"

"—I expect you and your future queen to keep the secrets to a minimum. At least from the Assembly. From me. Your Highness."

You and your future queen. He liked the sound of that. As much as she withheld the promise of an allegiance, she hinted at it in those words. "We will do our best, I'm sure, out of our eternal gratitude. *If* we have your vote."

Toyl's smile revealed nothing. "See you in Panar, my lord. May you have a safe and easy journey. You'll find out my stance when you get there."

"You have a safe journey as well, my lady." Whatever she meant by all that, Aven did not like the sound of it.

As Toyl left and Fayton with her, Aven sat down at the desk and surveyed the piles and piles of remaining work to be done. This morning had been one rush of fear after another, with close brushes with death sprinkled in for good measure. Not all had escaped either, he thought, wincing at the thought of the guards who might not have made it out. He shut his eyes and rubbed the bridge of his nose. He was exhausted.

He should probably head back out and help orchestrate—whatever needed to be orchestrated to reopen the main gate to the outside world. His delayed work, piled up here, would probably have to wait another day or more yet again.

And yet. He had a moment or two to rest. No one was rushing in, demanding his support. Many others were quite capable of figuring out what the hell to do next. To figure out who had survived and who had fallen.

But he didn't want to think of those losses now, that tragedy. He had to try to process what Toyl had said. Did he have Toyl's support? Hard to say. He'd certainly felt optimistic at first, but then why hadn't she just come out and given her opinion? If Aven *did* have Toyl's support, why hadn't she simply said so? If Toyl did not want to support him, what reason did she have to hide that? Why not tell him to his face? Did she fear Aven might try something while she was still inside Estun? Perhaps. Was that why she was so eager to leave?

Certainly Toyl knew Aven and his father better than that. Didn't she?

Some of those Assembly members tried to keep a semblance of neutrality, of separateness from the king and by extension Aven and his brothers. Especially those that were chosen through votes among the richest families, like Toyl. They seemed driven to demonstrate that they represented those who had put them in power.

The soft sound of a pebble tumbling off a ledge and hitting the stone floor to Aven's right cut through his thoughts. Quiet enough that he almost missed it, but loud enough that he realized something horrible.

There was someone else in the room. Hiding in the shadows.

Slowly, pretending he hadn't noticed but fearing he'd already betrayed himself with his tightened shoulders and tensed posture, Aven opened the drawer of the desk to his right on the pretense of putting a folded parchment inside.

The dagger that usually rested in that drawer was gone.

Who had been in here last? When he and Lord Dyon had been working, had the dagger been there? Was it long gone—or was its removal more recent?

He placed the folded sheet inside and slid it shut as casually as he could. Meanwhile, he tried to scan his peripheral vision, straining his ears for anything, any clue that would help him in whatever was about to happen.

The attack launched from behind with little warning. How had they gotten fully behind him? He'd only heard the final step as they jumped. He tilted his chair to one side and dove as the figure collided with the wood of the chair and the desk. He rolled and scrambled hastily to his feet, back to the wall, and saw—

"Miara?"

Crouched behind the desk, wielding a short sword and small hand ax, was a form whose face looked just like Miara's. Except, it wasn't. It held an expression altogether foreign to him—a curved snarl to her lips, a vicious anger in her eyes. She had all the expression of someone intent on his death.

Not Miara. It couldn't be. Could it?

Aven glanced at the wall over his head, then to his left and right. Usually, some old weapons hung here between candelabras on this wall, although they were more for honoring some distant past battle than any practical use. But the weapons were gone—and the candelabras too. They would have made a decent weapon, now that he thought about it. No matter now. Someone had cleaned it all out.

He thought of the missing guards in front of the room. That hadn't seemed so strange in light of the cave-in at the time. And it *had* been his plan to be in this room today with Lord Dyon, one of his most likely supporters.

Or was he? Could it have been Dyon who set this trap?

Miara—or whoever his attacker was—launched over the desk in three strides. The figure headed straight for him. He waited till the last second and spun out of the way and toward the hearth fire. He danced back a few steps, grabbing a fireplace poker mostly without removing his eyes from Not-Miara as she poised for another strike.

After his altercation with Daes, a fireplace poker was not a weapon he wanted to use against anyone, let alone *her*. He shivered at the thought.

No—bad idea. Don't think about that shit now. Focus.

"Miara, what's going on?" It couldn't be her. Unless—had some kind of spell been cast on her? Could she have been re-enslaved somehow?

Like a prowling animal, she'd sunk into a bent crouch and was stalking to his right, toward the desk again, as if planning something. Her form moved differently, crouched differently. His attacker's proportions did not quite match Miara's, at times too slight, too gaunt, too gangly.

"Miara, you don't have to do this. Is that even you?"

Suddenly, grumbling sounded from the other side of the door. Oh, gods, let that not be reinforcements for this assassin.

"Where the hell—should be three—"

The door opened, and Devol of all people puttered

in. Oh, the gods were indeed on his side today.

"Devol—" Aven started, but before he could issue any warning, a dagger hit the doorframe post behind the master at arms, narrowly missing the side of his head.

Devol swore and ducked, diving toward the desk. Aven took a risk and snatched the dagger from the doorframe, accidentally knocking into the door and causing it to slam shut again. But he'd found what he needed to know. It *was* the dagger from the desk drawer. Which meant it was unlikely the attacker had more of them.

He backed into his corner and looked to Devol, who was crouched on the closer side of the desk and eyeing a far dark corner. What was the attacker behind the desk waiting for? And what was Dev looking at? Dev glanced at him and then jutted his bearded chin at the darkened corner. He held up two fingers.

Two of them. Aven barely had time to catch sight of another impossibly familiar face before the first attacker launched herself again over the desk and at Aven.

Poker as sword in one hand, dagger in the other, he blocked her this time, parried, and engaged. Neither of them could be Miara. They were impersonating her to hide their identities. And fairly cleverly too, he had to say.

"Dev, it's creature magic," he said between breaths, dodging another blow. "They can disguise themselves. Very well, apparently."

Dev drew his long sword from his belt and charged at the one in the corner with a vicious shout. Damn, it had been ages since he'd seen Dev really fight. He hadn't risen through the ranks for nothing.

Aven put up a fairly good fight, but the ax as a second-ary weapon was a lot of trouble, and his weapons were not well suited to blocking anything, let alone axes, especially since fireplace pokers didn't come with handguards. Or at least, this one didn't.

I should really get back into the habit of actually wearing a weapon, he thought. He hadn't done it in ages, since he'd begun officer school. But perhaps he had been ignoring some practical realities. Estun had always seemed so safe.

The other mage did not appear to be fighting Devol, or at least not with weapons. No clangs came from that corner, and although he feared the worst, he could not tear his eyes away.

Finally, finally, he gained one slight opening and jammed the dagger toward the attacker's kidney.

It was stupid, but he flinched. He could not stand to see Miara's face twisted in pain he had caused. He did not need the memory of injuring or killing her. Certainly he wasn't killing this mage. If they were creature mages, they could heal themselves. But if they were creature mages, why wasn't this one using any creature magic at all? Was the disguise that demanding?

Or perhaps one was the mage, the other an assassin?

Before he could unpack this further, his attacker spun off the blade and toward the door. Devol swore as Aven realized his partner, too, had made for the door, now with a hood drawn. The hooded one flew out into the hallway, the injured one after her, clutching her side.

He and Devol raced to the door and out after them. Just as Aven came round the corner, he heard the *kathunk* of a crossbow firing and veered erratically to one side.

Not far enough to the side, apparently—a sharp pain sank into his left bicep. But his bicep was better than his chest.

He did not slow down. Lady Toyl was still in the hallway, speaking with Lord Alikar and Dvora Renala a few dozen feet from the door. Aven collided with Renala but spun her around, leaving her upright. Unfortunately, Devol was less lucky and sent Alikar reeling. The master of arms kept running and didn't look back, though. Probably glad to have an excuse to knock the bastard around a bit.

There were no longer two identical figures racing away down the hallway. Instead, two black birds flew faster than Aven's feet would take him.

He raced around the corner of the hall, heading away from the cave-in, the birds putting distance between them. What kind of birds *were* those?

They turned another corner. Several precious moments later, he turned after them.

Nothing. The hallway was completely empty.

Aven ran anyway, his eyes searching, desperate for some clue. Dev caught up with him.

"Gone? Really?" Devol panted. "I ran all that for nothing?"

"They *have* to be here. Maybe they've become something very small—like a spider or something."

They searched up and down that hallway and a piece of the next. Toyl, Alikar, and Renala strode up as they searched, looking at their frantic, panting forms with confusion.

Finally Dev said, "I don't see anything. There's nothing here."

"Was that—did they just try to kill you?" blurted Renala.

Aven nodded, too exhausted to form words for her.

"And you lost them?" Alikar said matter-of-factly.

"Was that—who I thought it was? I thought—" Renala started.

"Creature mages," Aven panted, cutting her off. "Both disguised. Probably hiding now. Tiny. Fly or something?" From the bewildered expression on their faces, Aven did not think they understood, nor did he care to explain it.

"Well, this is a hell of a day, isn't it?" Devol grumbled.

Yes, what a coincidence the cave-in happened so closely timed with this attack. Sure. Or—more likely—it was no coincidence. But he kept those thoughts to himself.

From behind Toyl, he heard footsteps. They all turned to see Miara and his mother approaching. "What's going on?" Elise started.

"Aven—what happened?" Miara lurched toward Aven, spotting his arm.

Lord Alikar stepped in front of her. "Wait just a minute. I know what I saw." Alikar leveled a dark glower at Miara.

"Guards," called Toyl.

"Take her into custody," Alikar ordered.

"Now, hold on there—" Aven started.

"What are you talking about, Vitig?" Elise glanced

around, deftly invoking Toyl's first name.

"My lords, there is more to this—" Devol started.

"I saw it with my own eyes. She tried to assassinate the prince," Alikar said, his words slow and measured.

Trap. This was a trap. Alikar hadn't been outside that door by coincidence, had he?

"It was not her, the mages were using her as a disguise," Devol said. "There were *two* of them that looked identical. At the very least, one of them was a fake."

"Release her now," Aven started, but he suddenly felt weak. He sagged against the wall, closing his eyes. An icy cold blossomed in his chest—was someone draining his energy even now?

"Let me heal him!" Miara's voice was savage. A scuffle sounded, and Aven tried to open his eyes, but they were too heavy.

"Stay away from him." Alikar's voice, by contrast, was calm, collected, a man full of hate.

"Come, now—two of them!" Dev pressed. "Looked just like her. And neither of them as bloody, by all the ancient ancestors. There's magic afoot, they're trying to impersonate her."

Aven reached out into the air around him, snatching a bit of energy to replenish whatever had been ripped away. He would really need to learn to not allow that to happen. Soon. He opened his eyes again, feeling a little stronger.

Lady Toyl had sobered and frowned, seeming to consider the situation. Aven took it as a good sign that she seemed to be defending him, or trying to. Why bother helping an heir if you didn't want him to sit on the throne? He supposed it could be just human decency or faith in the rule of law—no one deserved to be outright murdered, even if you didn't want them as your king. But then, Alikar's presence made him wonder. Could they both have somehow been involved? Was it all a ruse to distract from that fact, or to get a secondary outcome they wanted? Toyl angled to get him in the right place, and then they both waited to see the job had been finished? Toyl did not seem the type to work with Alikar, though, or take orders from anyone like him, but Aven did not dismiss the possibility. If Alikar could be bought, a merchant from Dramsren should have a price too, shouldn't she?

"It would still be prudent to arrest the mage until we sort this out," Lord Toyl said finally.

"Please—let me heal him first," Miara insisted.

Aven finally managed to speak up. "I'm getting better, Miara. It's all right, just a momentary weakness. Toyl, do you *really* think that's necessary?"

"My lord, it is up to you," she said, finally showing a bit of deference. "I won't go against your wishes, but for your safety, I think we must understand this situation more fully."

"We must detain her in the dungeon." The dark tone to Alikar's words twisted Aven's stomach. In the dungeon, others could gain access to her... in a variety of ways. They shouldn't, but guards could also be bought. Drugged. Hit over the head.

"Detain me all you like, but I'm a *creature* mage,"

Miara reminded him with disdain.

"I believe you've only just started my lessons on just exactly what that is, mage," Toyl replied sourly. Was there a hint of disgust in calling her a mage, or was it simply this situation?

"Creature mages can shift into any animal or plant. I didn't demonstrate it today because it's energy intensive and only really good for close-contact fighting. Not in a war. So for someone who can shape-shift into a mouse, bars are not a very reliable restraint."

Alikar scowled. "Doesn't sound like there *is* a reliable restraint for you." Aven couldn't shake the impression that he said the words with a bit too much relish, too much desire to restrain her. Was this just some barely hidden lust, or did he have more of a plan?

"You won't be able to trust or prove that I haven't escaped and returned, so that won't help you understand our situation any better. I *wouldn't* escape, mind you, but if you don't trust me not to have tried to kill *Aven*, then I don't expect you to trust me with that either." Her voice tensed over his name, crackling with an energy that those paying attention might understand. It gave away everything if one listened for such things, and indeed Toyl's eyes caught on his, holding nothing but concern. Miara's tone said, Aven of all people, Aven who I've risked my life for, you stupid fools. He didn't mind hearing it after seeing that twisted, snarling apparition of her face. This was the real Miara, here before him. He toyed with pointing out she could have also killed him a dozen different ways on the way here but hadn't. So that hardly made sense either. She was just a perfect disguise.

But… they had more pressing matters. He could demand Miara's freedom and dismiss their concerns completely, but at this point, that might be interpreted as irrational or irresponsible, especially by Toyl. Not the best way to win their good faith as their leader. And if Alikar had some scheme that involved getting Miara imprisoned somewhere and getting to her—Aven wanted to thwart that completely before he had the chance.

"Her rooms then, under constant guard," Aven ordered. "Devol will take up part of the watch and oversee. If we keep constant watch, we'll know for sure."

Miara's eyes widened, and he felt a pang in his chest. She didn't understand he knew she hadn't done this. The fear in her eyes spoke volumes, that even he might believe this was real. How could he give her some indication that this was all to spite any nefarious plan of Alikar's? If only he could dip into her thoughts the way she could dip into his.

"If she wanted to kill him, why would she come strolling up casually just after the attempt?" Devol grumbled.

"Perhaps she meant to throw us off by returning quickly," Toyl said.

"She's been with me the whole time," Elise snapped.

"Well, there *were* two of them." Alikar, damn him.

Aven sighed. "Enough. You heard my orders. Dev— choose the guards yourself, please. Don't worry, we'll get to the bottom of this, Miara. Toyl, will you escort Devol and these guards to her quarters so you can see that this is carried out?"

"Of course, my lord." Toyl gave a bowing nod.

"I'm not leaving until your arm is on the way to healed," Dev insisted. "Can one of these mages use that fancy magic on you now?" He was right. After that attempt, it probably wasn't the best idea to hobble around alone and injured.

"I'll stay with Aven too," Elise said, releasing Miara into the guard's grip. A knot in his stomach tightened at the sight.

"Fine," Aven grunted. The weakness returned, and he slumped against the wall again. Hell, who was doing it? Where were those damn mages? "Miara, will you…"

"I'll be fine." Miara nodded to the guards, perhaps realizing the queen needed Miara's captors to leave before Aven could be healed. "Will you come so we can talk about this later?"

"Of course." Aven sank to a seat and watched them guide her away as his stomach twisted into further knots. He had a sinking feeling that putting her under guard was exactly what someone wanted them to do. She was not in the dungeons, and Dev would handpick her guards, but… that was just a dungeon of a different kind. Whoever had attacked him could just as easily attack her. Especially if they were a fly on the wall nearby, listening to all their carefully made plans.

Who could be behind this attack? His legion of enemies grew every day. While Toyl could be either friend or foe,

Alikar simmered with hostility. And of course, the Dark Master would not be sitting idly by, accepting Aven's escape and moving on to a different plan. His shoulder throbbed in phantom pain at the thought of that bastard. The timing, so close to the cave-in, could not be a freak event. Mages had to be the cause. Who was more likely to employ mages, his Akarian enemies or his foreign ones? Certainly Daes had far more mages to wield than the others. If Aven were the Dark Master, what would he be trying to do?

But even as the idea formed, he knew. Daes would be trying to kill him. Aven wouldn't hire an assassin or force a mage slave to do such a thing on his behalf. But the Dark Master definitely would. And he would have more than one plan of attack in store so that if some of them failed, he would still have a chance at victory.

What would his other attacks be? How had they infiltrated Estun? Whose faces were behind those masks?

As he sat, pondering, his mother healed his arm without comment, only giving him a slight warning as she yanked the quarrel from his arm. For not being a warrior, she sure could handle blood. He put his hand over hers and squeezed it.

"We'll figure this out, Aven," Devol said, struggling to sound encouraging.

"Yes. We have to."

# 10  Truths & Accusations

Miara stripped off the bloody leathers and cast them aside, hoping they weren't totally ruined and Camil would know what to do with them. The blood rinsed away, and she found a fresh tunic that she happily put on alone for once. Its softness was welcoming, to her surprise.

She tried to wait patiently for Aven to join her, to offer some explanation of what the hell had happened that had led to them bringing her back here. She alternated between sitting and pacing. As the minutes ticked by, she gradually succumbed to exhaustion and the lure of the cushions and drifted off to sleep.

She awoke to a knock on the door being answered by one of her courteous new guards. *And if I hadn't wanted to get up just now?* She stifled a grumble to herself. It didn't matter. They were right—she would have answered to see if it was Aven, or someone similar. And really, who else could it be?

She sat up. The door-answering guard was none other

than Devol himself. And sure enough—her visitor was Aven, arm freshly healed, if still bloodied. He didn't look pale from the blood loss, though. Small wins.

"What by the gods happened, Aven?" she demanded, still rubbing sleep from her eyes.

"Some harpies disguised as you tried to kill him," Dev answered for him. "And I was lucky enough to walk in on the tussle. Good fun, if you ask me."

"Says the one who walked out without a scratch." Aven grinned.

"Oh, you liked it. You're probably out there waving that arm around at every captain and young recruit you can find. You look just fine if you ask me. Gotta say that healing magic is powerful stuff. We'd be fools to turn our eyes from that outta some foolish religious nonsense. Not sure how keeping people *alive* is so evil." Dev's eyes darted around to the guards as he spoke, as though he was keen to the fact that many might disagree with such words. Was he testing them? Perhaps looking for those who might not be such a good fit for this post? Clever.

"At least one of them was a creature mage." Aven came to sit beside her, and Dev joined them in a nearby chair. "Could have been both, but I don't think so."

"And you said they were disguised as me?"

Aven nodded. Damn. That was smart on their enemy's part and took planning, preparation. "Of course, the Dark Master would think of such things." Aven's pale eyes studied the fireplace as he rubbed his shoulder absently. She wondered if it was truly healed yet. He had not let her speed their healing or repair the scars, though she could understand why.

"The Dark Master?" Devol asked.

"He was one of four masters in control of the slaves in Mage Hall," Miara explained. "But the one most interested in Aven. The one who sent me on my mission—" She faltered, unsure of how much Aven and his family had really explained to anyone. "Also, he's far more cunning than the others. I think they'd be content to live out easy lives, ordering us around and abusing their power. But not the Dark Master. He seems intent on something—I'm not sure what. At the very least, Aven's death, although to what end?"

"Well, war with Akaria, for one thing," Aven muttered. "And my personal death as part of that plan, partly because I'm a prince of Akaria. And partly because… I know magic he doesn't want anyone to know."

"The magic to free the slaves?" Devol asked.

"Yes." Aven bowed his head. "So you think it had to be the Dark Master? What about one of these other lords, unhappy with recent revelations?"

"Why use me against you then? And how many of them have access to mages, let alone ones who could imitate my image well? You say it was convincing? Accurate?"

"Fairly. The face was, on both of them."

"Could have fooled me, if there weren't two of them," Devol grumbled.

"The bodies were off. I don't think it was a complete illusion," Aven said.

"They probably couldn't do that without having me in their custody to reference."

"Don't talk like that," Aven said, shifting uncomfortably.

"Why not? I'm just trying to teach you what's possible."

"I don't even want to think about it." He shook his head and ran a hand over his face.

She took a risk and laid a hand on his arm for a moment. Without the slightest hesitation, he laid his hand over hers and squeezed. She wanted to laugh but stifled it into the smallest smile she could. He was really not very good at keeping secrets.

"And they got away, it seems?"

He nodded, scowling. "Think they transformed somehow to hide. They can't just disappear, right?"

"No, they can't. There have been very rare stories of air mages figuring out how to disappear for very short periods of time, but they are probably just rumors. Who wouldn't want their enemies to think they could be nearby and invisible? But even if it is possible, it's not for creature mages."

"I think the one that attacked was not a mage. Unless they were also a *very* good fighter. They seemed dedicated to the study."

Miara shrugged. "It's possible there were some good fighters among the mage slaves. I just don't know."

Devol cut in. "The one I fought just tried to dodge me, make herself smaller, faster. She was definitely a mage, form shifting this way and that. Quite a strange sight to behold. Wouldn't fight me. But did you notice the choice of weapons on your opponent, Aven?"

"Yes, short sword and hand ax."

A chill ran through Miara. "The same weapons that I practiced with yesterday morning."

Aven frowned. "When?"

"In the Proving Grounds."

"You didn't mention it."

She gave him a half smile. "I was *hoping* to surprise you. Perhaps with a duel. Not at this point, apparently!"

"She was far better than you, though," Devol added. Miara glared at him in spite of herself. "No offense! You haven't had much practice!"

She sighed. "I only know the dagger."

"You'll get there—don't worry, my girl."

"Don't call me a girl."

"He calls me a boy too. And my father. But cut it out, Devol."

Dev wrinkled his mustache as though his nose were itchy and gave them a grin. "All right, all right. The point is, unless you're great at hiding your ability, which is damn hard, that attacker was far more skilled than you with those weapons. And a lot of other weapons, I'd wager. Seems like they picked them specifically to impersonate you more convincingly."

"Who else saw you two there?" Aven asked.

"Thel was there. Talking to Renala." Miara's gut twisted at the thought. Thel seemed like a good fellow, and rather innocent and naïve, as Aven had been—and in some ways still was. She'd hate to think he was behind this. And yet, he stood to benefit a lot from any downfall of Aven's. He could claim he didn't want the crown, but he could easily be lying. He had also sat talking with Renala—what if he had designs on the beautiful, graceful, noble dvora, and Aven was all that stood in his way? "How much do you trust your brother, Aven?"

"Completely," he replied quickly, without hesitation.

Dev was nodding in agreement. "Hmm. Renala and her lady in waiting were also there."

"The dvora?" Aven asked.

"Yes."

"But she arrived here before we did," Miara pointed out. "If the Dark Master sent her from Kavanar, she couldn't have gotten here more quickly than we did."

"Unless she was meant for my brothers?" He tapped his chin with his finger, thinking. "Or as a spy. What if Daes had already sent Renala before we'd even escaped?" Why did Aven call the Dark Master by his real name and not his title? What had he seen from the Dark Master? Had they spoken? There had been time to talk on the journey to Estun, and she'd seen the burn marks, many of which Aven had agreed to let her heal. But they hadn't talked in great detail. It wasn't exactly something she thought either of them wanted to revisit.

"One way to find out. Confront her about it!" Devol's eyes lit up with too much glee at the idea, and Aven snorted. But then he nodded. "I'll go and get her myself. *If* you two can stand to be alone without me while I'm gone." He jumped from his seat and was out the door with a snicker.

Miara raised her eyebrows. Then she glanced down. Aven's hand still covered hers.

"Is it that obvious, you think?" she said softly.

Aven smiled crookedly and gazed down into the fire, not meeting her eyes. "I'm not sure. Maybe. We'll tell my father, definitely not."

She snorted.

"I mentioned it to Toyl. She was not terribly surprised."

She shook her head. "You going to tell the king about that?"

He looked at her with twinkling eyes. "Hey, I'm keeping secrets as best I can."

"You're not so good at it."

"Never have been. Isn't that what got me into this mess?"

As if in mocking agreement, the air around them picked up, little currents of air swirling the room. The guards shifted uneasily. Miara grinned. And this time, it did not calm after a few moments but continued listlessly, stirring the air and teasing the flames and embers in the hearth.

*I thought the Dark Masters got us into this mess,* she whispered.

*But you got us out of it.*

*You give me too much credit.*

*No. I don't.*

"Did Toyl object?" she asked eventually as her mirth settled.

"She was noncommittal. Said I would find out her

vote at the Assembly. A lot of the Assembly members like to maintain an air of impartiality. Of distance. Probably good for them. She said nothing to make me think she didn't support us, though. Me, I mean."

Her smile broadened at that turn of phrase. How much were these guards picking up from the conversation? How much were they paying attention? At this point, he apparently didn't care.

The door creaked as it opened, revealing first Devol and then Renala. Aven took back his hand, and his face hardened. They rose in greeting.

"My lord, Prince Aven. Lady Miara. You wished to speak with me?" Her elegantly-painted eyes were wide, worried, far from cunning. No one had ever had kohl in Mage Hall. So many facets of the world open to Miara now, she didn't know what to make of them.

"I'm not a lady," Miara said quickly but returned the dvora's curtsy with a bow. Was she supposed to be curtsying? Had she offended everyone by bowing all this time? Certainly Aven would have told her. Wouldn't he have?

"Thank you for coming, Renala," Aven said. "We have some serious things to discuss. Would you sit down with us, please?" She nodded and sat in the seat as close as possible to Aven, and Miara tried not to clench her jaw at that fact.

"We know you were behind the assassination," Devol said abruptly.

*Gods, Aven. Can you accuse her so directly? Should we have talked to your parents about this?*

*It's a ploy. Wait and see. I do have authority, though, yes. We have to work fast, before word can spread.*

"What?" Renala blurted, horrified. "What assassination?"

"Don't pretend," Devol said calmly. "We know all about it. That's why you came here to Estun in the first place, isn't it?"

"What are you—no—" Miara had never seen the dvora's tan skin look so pale. She wore a low-cut violet silk gown that even Miara had to admit looked lovely and soft and maybe even comfortable, but it heaved dramatically as she started to take faster, panicked breaths. Was that the panic of being found out, or being wrongly accused? Or was it knowing how to heave your chest to distract men at appropriate times?

Renala stood, conscious of being about to lose her composure, and took a few steps away to face the fire. "Please, I had nothing to do with anything. I don't know what you're talking about, but I'm sure I can find some way to prove it. I was at the demonstration this morning—then I went back to my rooms—"

"It was shortly after the demonstration and the cave-in thereafter that the attack occurred."

She whirled. "I told you I don't know how to—"

"What were you doing at the Proving Grounds yesterday morning then?" Devol demanded.

"I—simply wanted to watch."

The master of arms glared fiercely at her.

"What? I'm sorry—what does that have to do with anything?"

"You were looking for clues to best impersonate someone, weren't you?"

Renala frowned in what seemed to be genuine confusion. "Impersonate someone? Who?"

"Then why?"

"I just… I wanted to ask for lessons as well." She scowled, casting a clearly jealous glare at Miara. "I was too afraid."

Oh. That made sense, with her behavior and her hesitation to ask if she could watch. By now, Miara was thoroughly convinced that she was uninvolved. But… then why the similar weapons? Could it have just been a coincidence?

The men did not seem similarly convinced. Devol leapt to his feet as well and strode toward the dvora. She turned as he approached, backing away with wide eyes. It was not the stance of a competent assassin, that much was for sure.

"You sought to take the prince's life," Dev thundered.

"No, I would never, you are mad—"

"I think you look like just the right type to offer a sizable reward," Devol said coldly, inches from her now. "A bounty on a prince's head would be enough to set you up anywhere comfortably."

"I would never—I thought I could make a place here away from—maybe not as a wife but as something. I would never have endangered that chance. I'm so stupid. I should have known this wouldn't work." She buried her face in her hands.

Renala's despair twisted knots in Miara's stomach. Perhaps there was more to this woman than her beauty. But then, of course there was. There always was. How foolish to have ever thought otherwise. How could she let her feelings blind her so thoroughly?

Devol scowled and strode away. "Well, either it wasn't her, or she's a better actress than I've ever seen."

Renala glanced up quickly, hope in her wet eyes.

Aven nodded. "Excuse our accusation, my lady, but we needed to be careful. Two attackers tried to kill me just a short while ago. They were both disguised as Miara, using magic."

"The attackers wielded the weapons Miara tried at the Proving Grounds the day you were there," Devol said. "So we believe they must have been there that day."

"But you were only learning." Renala spoke as if only to Miara.

Miara shrugged. "Indeed, I know how to use a dagger, but I'm not much with those weapons, certainly not good enough to defeat Aven."

"We're trying to figure out who's behind this," said Aven. "There weren't many other people there that day. I can't think that Thel would have anything to do with it—"

Renala's body went suddenly rigid.

"What is it?" Miara said. "Did Thel say something?"

"Oh, no. But my maid was with us—Pyandra."

"So?"

"She arrived yesterday. I thought it odd my brothers would send help after me, but her details seemed to fit.

They've never sent anyone to tend to me before, although I had servants at home. Perhaps—" She stopped and stared off into space for a moment, face pale.

"Perhaps they didn't send her?" Miara finished for her.

Renala's eyes came back into focus as she met her gaze. "Yes."

"But how would someone know our dvora was here, to pretend to be a servant for her?" Devol asked.

"Someone in disguise among one of the attendant noble parties would know. They could leave and return in a new disguise, knowing more than any arriving outsider should know." Aven scratched his jaw, thinking.

"We need to find this Pyandra. And fast. What if she's realized we're onto her because we're talking to Renala? Was she there when Devol came by?" Miara asked.

Renala nodded. Aven swore.

"Then we don't have another moment to lose," Aven said. "Let's go."

The three of them hurried off, leaving Miara alone yet again. She was just starting to feel bitter about it when they returned—entirely too quickly and alone.

"She's gone," Devol groaned as he came panting into view.

"Along with her things," added Renala, frowning. "My lord, I'm so sorry I let her inside. I must repay you somehow for this grave mistake."

Aven waved her off, then sat down on the bench beside Miara and scratched his jaw. "They were likely already inside, if our theory is correct. The more important matter is, what are we going to do now?"

Aven escorted Renala back to her rooms. The tension of unspoken questions was thick in the air.

Perhaps he should just be straight with her and let her go home. It was cruel to lead her on like this, although it might be equally cruel to reject her at this down moment. With the way the day had been going, and preparations to leave for Panar nearing completion, he might not have another good chance.

"I apologize again for accusing you, dvora," Aven said.

"It's all right. An attempt on your life is a serious matter."

"It's got me thinking…" How could he broach this subject? "I don't want to waste your time here. But I just… I don't think this is going to be a good match."

"Oh." She paused.

He studied her intently. Her face was placid, almost relaxed. If his words had hurt her, she showed no sign.

"You should just tell her, you know," she said.

"Tell her what? Who?"

"I think you know. Miara. The Kavanarian you brought back with you."

Aven blinked in surprise. Was it obvious to *everyone*?

"I had figured you would say this eventually. You clearly love her. You should just tell her. I would not want to stand in the way of that. And to think, a commoner as queen? I rather like that idea. I've known enough nobles to know the status is not synonymous with virtue or skill."

"I—ah—"

"You *do* love her, don't you? I see the way you look at her."

"Is it that obvious?"

"Perhaps I have had incentive to look harder than most."

"Or—"

"Or perhaps, yes, it is that obvious. Your face lights up at the sight of her."

He looked down, struggling to stifle a boyish grin and failing. "You are very perceptive, Renala of Esengard. It's supposed to be secret. For now."

"Oh, she knows? Returns your affections?"

"Yes and yes."

"Then why the secrecy? Because she's a commoner? Many great kings have had mistresses—"

"No," Aven said harshly. "No, not that. Miara will make a great queen."

"Not because of me, I hope?"

"No. She's just so new to this place, and of the enemy. We thought, well, the king suggested perhaps it'd be best if she earned more of a place first. Became more one of us."

She nodded. "I thought you were only just falling for her, so perhaps that plan is working." She paused. "Gods, I'm *so* relieved."

*"Relieved?"* He hadn't expected that, and he let out a laugh.

"Yes. I don't *want* to marry." There was more she wasn't telling him, something she left out. "My brothers sent me here. Busy with their new wives."

"New wives?"

"They want me out of the way. I've been running my father's household since my mother passed away. But now the eldest's wife will take over. And both my younger brothers have wives as well, fighting for lesser duties. I guess they didn't want me to add to the fray. All those years running things for them, and I'm left with nothing but my marriage prospects."

"Which you don't want."

"Precisely. I don't want to marry at all. But what can I do? I have no other skills. They wouldn't let me learn any. What am I to do, sell embroidery?"

He nodded solemnly. "That's not an impossible idea, honestly. I'm sure you have other skills you haven't realized. You're welcome to stay here while you figure it out. Just because I've said we're not a great match doesn't mean you have to leave."

"I'm sure they have a list of visits for me to make."

"Perhaps you can figure out something else here. We won't be sending any formal declarations of the failure of our union to your brothers. We have enough else going on. And hey, the Takarans are still here, you're not even coming close to the length of their stay, eh?"

She laughed. "I heard they were staying permanently."

"Perhaps. That might be the case." He was noncommittal, grinning.

They strolled in silence awhile.

"Thank you for being so understanding, Renala. I

hope you can find a man someday that is perfect for you."

"Indeed. I hope I can find… someone some day. Yes." There was meaning to the pause, but he was not sure what it was. Perhaps a man was not what she was looking for. Was that why she was so determined not to marry? With no independent money to rely on or skills, she had a hard path ahead. Perhaps Fayton could walk her through what skills she had. She might not realize some were actually marketable.

They reached her rooms. "Again—stay as long as you need. I won't even mention anything beyond us for now. But after all this, I wanted you to know."

"I should be the one thanking you, Aven Lanuken." She smiled and drifted into her rooms.

He bowed and fled before he revealed any more secrets to any foreign dignitaries.

The heavy pound of hooves outside. Jaena knew those sounds. Something about them told her this was no farmer and his wagon, no Nemin returning from the city.

The Devoted.

At least there seemed to be no dogs this time. Tharomar was sprawled on the fur at her feet, studying some leather-bound book she hadn't recognized. She sat as close as she'd dared to the fire—it was freezing when you couldn't get up and move around.

The horses stopped outside. Ro hadn't moved, but his

eyes had lifted, head tilted slightly. He, too, was listening carefully. The sound of men dismounting, footsteps approaching.

Gods.

Someone knocked on the door. Tharomar stood and strode toward it. She was out of his sight but not that of someone standing outside.

She threw herself out of the chair and onto the floor. She gritted her teeth to the pain and rolled into the only hiding place: under the bed.

Oblivious, Ro opened the door.

Seven hells. She could see their boots. This was it. They had found her. At least three Devoted waited outside in the rain.

"We're continuing our search for the renegade mage. Stand aside. How many here." The words were more demand than question.

"Be my guest," Ro said, turning away and making room for them. His feet moved as he turned toward her chair and seemed to freeze for just a split second as he saw it empty.

He would know what her disappearance meant. That *she* was the mage they were looking for. Without intending it, she'd just let her secret out. Not that she had much choice in the matter.

"How many," the knight demanded.

"I live alone," Tharomar said.

Her heart leapt in her chest. Not a lie. Also not the truth. But—he was covering for her.

"Hrm." One knight moved carefully around the room. He seemed to be carrying something magical, like the repression stones they wore—but different. She longed to move just a hair closer and sneak a peak at it. But—no, it wasn't worth the risk. Could it be what they had used to detect her presence near the bridge?

None of the other knights moved. They didn't turn over everything looking for her. But they were looking for a mage—*any* mage. Ro was standing *right* in front of them, although he didn't know it. He believed he had nothing to hide.

"It says all clear. No mages here."

How were they missing him? And her, for that matter?

"There's a slight vibration—you may have purchased a charmed salve or herb without realizing it. Might be wise to replace such things, if you value your soul."

Tharomar said nothing. He must had nodded or acknowledged them somehow because they seemed satisfied and turned to leave.

"Be on the lookout for this rogue mage. Here. She is dangerous and not to be trifled with. King's permission to kill on sight."

"You said as much before," Tharomar replied, his voice cold.

"We'll be back through tomorrow if you see anything."

"Nefrana bless your journey."

The door shut. At first, his boots just stayed near the door, unmoving. She heard a piece of paper unfold, and a chill shot through her.

I'm at his mercy, she thought. All he has to do is call them back in. But worse, what was he going to think? His half smile flashed through her mind, his implication that he cared for her to return here. That would likely be gone now. He apparently didn't want to give her up to the Devoted, at least not yet, but would he cast her out into the rain?

She was evil, Nefrana-cursed, an aberration, a danger to his soul. Not someone to be cared about. And he was a good man, a holy one—or as close to it as she had ever known.

Other knocks sounded. Other doors opened, closed. He remained by the door, unmoving. She remained under the bed.

Finally, the jangling of bridles and reins. Men's shouting voices. Then, hooves pounding.

The Devoted rode away. She was still here, albeit with her damn lame ankle. She could hardly believe it.

Silence for a moment. Then he strode straight to the bed and bent down. There certainly weren't many other places to hide.

His brown eyes were only concerned. He extended an arm, reaching a hand out to her. "Can I help you up?"

She stared at him for a moment, like a caged animal, unsure if she should bite or flee. Her eyes flitted around, then locked on his. He, who had shown her nothing but kindness. He, who had offered her shelter and food and medicine and warmth and asked for nothing in return. He, who possessed a pair of beautiful, shining, too-intelligent eyes that regarded her with only empathy at the moment. He, who had just lied on her behalf.

She reached out and took his hand. Scooting out and shimmying on her stomach hurt, but it could have been a lot worse. Once free of the bed, she pushed herself up to her knees, just as he was. Her face was barely inches from his, their bodies close, and his musky, earthy scent enchanted her.

Their eyes locked for a moment. He did not turn away.

She tore *her* eyes away, however, the intensity too much. It had almost seemed like— Was he thinking of— No, he couldn't be thinking of kissing her. Not now. Likely not ever, with what he had just learned. A ridiculous fantasy on her part.

She was smoothing her tunic with her sweaty palms, nervously straightening herself, when she glanced down and saw the paper unfolded in his hand. A rough parchment bore a drawing of her, painstakingly rendered and fairly accurate. A large bounty was scrawled below it.

"Oh, gods," she whispered. "Twenty thousand gold."

Miara read on her couch for several hours. Everyone was busy with the final preparations for the trip to Panar, even Camil. And who knew how they were handling the devastation of the cave-in. She would rather have been helping, but she didn't mind the time alone after all that mess. If only it had been by choice. It stung to lose that cherished freedom so quickly, but even this was a curious experiment. She had long been a slave but rarely if ever imprisoned. She'd hardly been free but never physically bound. Now she was technically still free—but her freedom had shrunk to three designated rooms.

Only the guards stood watch, watching her while she restlessly drifted about her rooms before returning to her book again. Camil finally delivered dinner to her room with an apologetic shrug.

After dinner, she took a bath, tossing rosemary and mint from her garden into the water. Camil had already scented it with lavender too, and the heat of the water did melt away some stress of the day. She stayed in much longer than she might have planned, with no reason to rush out. But finally she rose, dried herself, and found a warm, pale blue tunic and soft trousers that she didn't think were meant for sleeping, but she intended to use them that way. After everything that had happened today, she wasn't sleeping in the giant sack of a sleep shift, which was like wearing a sail from a boat so big it must be designed to catch the wind. The shifts also made it much more awkward to strap her dagger to her calf, but the trousers were better.

As she twisted her hair into a bun for the time being, her eyes spotted a scroll of parchment on the bed, and she froze.

What the hell… ?

Could it be from Aven? Some secret message? Any legitimate message would have been delivered by Camil or Fayton, and they would have announced its arrival. This had to be… something else.

She inspected the scroll carefully. Red wax sealed it shut, the symbol pressed into it reminding her of the twisting mage-knots. Gods. That could not be good. She investigated it for anything strange looking but found nothing, so she broke the seal and unrolled the strange scroll. It read:

*Miara Floren,*

*You know that I have your father and sister. I know that you have the location of the upcoming Assembly of Akaria.*

*Send me via bird the exact building, room, and time to ensure your family's continued safety. Tell no one.*

*If the information you provide turns out to be false, or you share this with anyone, consider your sister dead. Your father will watch.*

*Daes Cavalion*

She dropped the parchment on the bed, her heart pounding. She had to tell Aven. But how had this scroll gotten here? Could it have been Camil? Someone else?

Who would have access to this room and be willing to do this? What else might they be planning to do? Damn, she wasn't safe even here, by the gods. Not that she had entirely expected to be, she was no fool.

The Masters obviously had someone on the inside. She couldn't be certain, but the same person would likely know if she shared this information with Aven.

She had to find some way to tell him anyway, some way to figure out what to do together. Even as her heart ached in her chest, she knew she could not betray the true location. Her father and Luha would not want that, either. The blood of likely dozens of innocents hung in the balance, blood they would not want on their hands. The Assembly meeting would contain not only the members of the Assembly themselves, but their trusted advisors, family members, and lesser officials. An attack on the Assembly would cut off the head of Akaria in one blow.

Which was precisely the plan.

Those innocents were also the people in the world most likely to be convinced to fight for the freedom of mages everywhere, making such a betrayal all the more abhorrent. No, no, she couldn't do it. There was no way. Hands shaking, she picked up the parchment again. Perhaps there was some way out of this trap. Perhaps they could figure out a way to save Luha before the meeting. She needed to talk to Aven. He could think clearly. He could think of something.

She scrutinized the parchment for clues. Was it genuine? Could it somehow have been faked? That didn't help.

Even if it were, if she put the information onto a bird and sent it off to Mage Hall, the result would be the same. The Dark Master would be just as delighted. She was familiar enough with official missives of Kavanar, having stolen a few different letters and scrolls and replaced them with fakes during her years in his service. The seal wax was the appropriate scarlet color and consistency, the parchment a common thickness.

She rolled the scroll, folded it flat, and slipped it into her pocket.

Hurrying into the outer room, she approached one of her guards. She would give them nothing to be suspicious of.

"Can you possibly send for the prince for me? Or for Camil, so she can summon him? I grow bored."

One guard eyed her warily but did step out.

In the end, they did not produce Aven. A quarter of an hour later, Queen Elise arrived. Hmm, were they keeping him away from her, or was he simply busy with all the preparations and cleanup from the day? Again, a wave of frustration at being unable to help hit her.

"The guards said you had a question for Aven?" Elise asked. "I can take it to him."

Miara blinked. Did they sincerely think she was a danger to him, or was it a show? "Yes, I was wondering if he would like to play Rooks and Pawns or a dice game."

"Oh," said Elise, clearly having expected something else.

"But you'll do." Miara confidently strode to the small corner game table and sat down, not looking at Elise and wondering if she would take the bait or take offense.

*If you pretend to play,* she whispered to Elise, *I can give you my message. I can't let the guards hear.*

Elise joined her at the chess table, straightening her pale sky-blue dress as she sat. *What is it?* Elise was in some way even better than Aven, as she could send her thoughts back easily and with more control.

*Terrible news. I just found a scroll on my bed, signed by the Dark Master and sealed with Kavanarian red wax. Appears authentic. It demands the location details of the Assembly vote in exchange for my family's continued safety.*

Elise's eyes widened. *How... how do they know?*

*The assassins that attacked Aven are likely disguised as ordinary servants, allowing them to overhear much. There are certainly others listening and reporting back too, including our dear Lord Alikar.*

Elise picked up a piece. "Do you want to go first, or should I?"

"Feel free." She continued to speak as Elise considered a move. *The scroll says they will kill my sister if I don't tell them. Or if the information is false, or if I tell anyone I've received the scroll.*

Until that point, Elise had been managing it all with her typical composure. But at those words, she fumbled and looked up with wide eyes for a split second before continuing to make her first move. *Tell anyone, like you're doing right now?*

*Yes. Thus the secrecy. Can you tell Aven? I am not sure what they would prefer me to do. We cannot turn over the real location. Maybe there is a way around this, a way to save my sister. I thought Aven might be able to think of something.*

*And if he can't?*

*We cannot tell them. My sister would not want to live with the deaths of innocents on her hands—*

*It's the Masters who would have the deaths on their hands.*

*Either way there will be death, unless we figure a way around it. Two versus dozens? It's hardly a choice.*

*Even when those two people are all the family you have in the world?*

Miara picked up a piece. It was her turn, but she had trouble steadying her hand. A rising tide of anger came with those words. *Must you remind me?* Perhaps she was callous, secretly like her mother deep down. No. She was trying to do the right thing.

*I'm sorry. Putting the good of all ahead of your personal happiness… is admirable.*

She didn't know how to respond. *If anyone can find a way to appease both, it's Aven.*

*Too true. There are only so many buildings with big enough meeting halls. Even if we lie, they could simply try them all.* Elise was scowling at the board.

*They could do that right now anyway. Tell me a location and time to tell them. A false one. I'll send it back to them. Then, we can try to think of other options.*

Elise remained silent, thinking about more than the game as they went through several turns.

*I'll talk to Wunik and Aven and get their opinion.*

*As secretly as possible, please.*

*Of course.* A few minutes later, Elise rose, smoothing the dress's pale blue linen with her palms. "I should get back to my duties, I hadn't expected to stay long. Let's continue this later, or—oh. You've won."

Miara nodded and gave the queen a seated bow. "Thank you for taking a moment to entertain me, Your Majesty."

Elise gave her an uneasy smile. "My pleasure. I'll tell Aven he missed an excellent, although very quick, game."

*I will send word of what to reply before the end of the day.* And then, she was gone, leaving Miara frowning at the game pieces.

Later that night, the reply came. Elise knocked, and a guard opened the door before Miara could even stand up from her seat.

"Aven asked me to send this. Of course, he chose the contents, not me." Elise handed her a warm, red linen package. "He sends his regrets. He is busy with the trip's preparations."

"Of course," Miara said, her voice faltering only a little. Elise took her leave.

Was he truly busy? Were they keeping him away?

She took the red linen package into the bedroom and unwrapped it on the bed, where fewer guards could see her. Steam wafted up from a warm, fresh apple dumpling. A small scroll, unmarked with any seal or signature, rested quietly underneath the next fold of the linen, likely holding whatever location and time Aven and Elise had chosen to tell the Dark Master. She slipped it to into her pocket with the other.

Taking a large bite of the dumpling, she strode to the desk and penned the details in her own hand. She folded the piece and sealed it with stormy Akarian blue-gray. She even found an ursine stamp to press into the hot wax.

Now it was just a matter of finding some poor bird and sending it into danger. War was not an easy thing. If only these people would wake up and realize they were in one. Luckily, she had a room with windows—and guards who frowned on watching her while she took a bath.

And opening the window.

In the end, her large bathroom window held only a smaller window that could be levered open, possibly for ventilation but more likely to aim an arrow through. It wasn't much, but the scroll would fit.

She closed her eyes and spread her mind out across the mountainside, feeling a little guilty about asking any creature to fulfill this task.

A few sparrows flitted overhead. An eagle. A white hare jumped and rolled in the snow. A young falcon.

The falcon's attention turned toward her even as she noticed it. More curious than usual, she could imagine it tilting its head, considering this foreign presence.

*Can you help me?*

She let the quiet desperation, the sadness, the regret seep into her words. She wasn't entirely sure all creatures understood or even experienced such emotions, but she felt much better disclosing her regret and her dire need along with her request.

It—he—swooped down a ledge. He paused, listening

for danger, then swooped closer. He landed in a small, steep snowbank and hopped a few inches up the slope.

For a moment, Miara saw the window from the outside. A dark eye peered out the leaded blue, green, and white glass window. Wisps of red hair teased by the wind swished in and out of view. The bird hopped closer.

She saw him now—small, powerful, elegant. The falcon inclined his head, as though waiting.

Miara held out the scroll, then thought of the location of Mage Hall and pushed it to the falcon's mind. She thought of the Dark Master too, picturing his cursed face.

*I need to get this scroll to this man, or he will harm my family.* There, that should make sense to any creature. *I can't go myself. Can you take it for me? How can I reward your efforts? Although—I am concerned it could be danger-ous to you.*

The falcon hopped a few more steps forward and inclined his head the other way. Her mind and his mingled again, and she caught another glimpse of herself through the window. Strange, creatures usually kept more of a barrier between them.

The falcon found her… intriguing.

The thought of a reward flashed through her mind—food. Meat, in particular. Perhaps a nice tasty duck. Doves were nice.

Miara raised her eyebrows and tried to appear calm as she strode back into the bedroom. Good, her dinner remained, along with an untouched chicken leg. She snatched it, and brought it back to the falcon.

Ripping the flesh from bone with surprising agility, the bird made short work of the chicken as Miara stared with round eyes. Then he hopped closer and extended his talons.

Miara reached out, and the bird took the missive.

*I will return to you. More birds to eat would be good. I do things then. If you wish.* The bird did not exactly speak in words, but his intentions were clear.

*I may be in Panar. The city with the white towers in the south?*

Recognition in the falcon's mind. He'd already soared over the mountaintops. *Your mind is bright. It can be found.*

Huh. What a strange creature. She did hope she would see him again.

# 11    Drawing the Line

Tharomar said nothing as Jaena stared at the parchment, only turned his gaze from her face to the drawing with a scowling brow. She could not read his expression. What did he disapprove of? What was he thinking? Did he regret offering her sanctuary in his home?

"Twenty—I—" She stumbled over the words, struggled to rise, but found herself only grabbing onto him and stumbling awkwardly instead. Panic pumped through her veins. Should she run? Were the Devoted still close by? Could she even get away from the likes of Tharomar?

Did she even want to? Destroying the brand was a noble goal, and she'd made a valiant attempt at revenge, but dying to feed orphaned children wasn't the worst way to go. He could use the money for the temple. The damn womenfolk. Dekana might have even preferred that to revenge. Her sister would hardly have been disappointed by that end, right? If the Devoted were going to catch Jaena anyway, it'd be nice for *someone* worthwhile to benefit from it.

She had been so close to freedom, though. She couldn't give up yet. She couldn't let them have the brand back either. That would hurt more than her own death. She lurched to her feet and took a limping step forward.

"What are you doing?" He stepped right on after her and caught her elbow as she wobbled, supporting her weight. "They can't be far. We need to be quiet."

She met his gaze and tried to keep the fear from her eyes.

"They could come back. Someone will likely mention that you're here. The others won't think to—"

"To what?" she whispered.

"To *omit* that fact."

"And why did you?"

His chin lifted slightly, but he didn't immediately answer.

"Twenty thousand gold is a *lot* of coin for the women-folk," she whispered, daring him to sacrifice her to them.

"Do I really seem like someone who would do that? To you?" he whispered back harshly, finally showing a touch of anger.

"We've only just met. How do I know if I can trust what you say?"

"And yet, I'm already lying for you."

"Have regrets? Call them back."

Now he scowled even harder at her. Her eyes caught on the pendant around his neck and widened: the gold of the wheat had turned to silver. What strangeness was this?

"Why are they hunting you? What did you do?" His face was dark, as if he didn't want to know but needed to.

"I escaped. And I stole something… valuable to them."

"Why were you imprisoned?"

"Imprisoned? I wasn't imprisoned. I'm a slave. Er—*was* a slave, I guess." Well, if nothing else came of this, it felt good to say *that*.

"How did you become a slave?" he followed up quickly. Did the idea of slavery truly not disturb him at all? Or… did he already know? If he knew, why was he asking if she was imprisoned? "Were you a criminal?"

"No!" she snapped. "I was simply born a mage. They have an enchanted rod—a slave brand. Like they use for cattle. When they put it in the fire and brand us, we must do whatever they ask. And they *never* ask for anything good." She pulled free just far enough to pull down the collar of her shirt and reveal her scar, wincing inwardly at the thought of him seeing its ugliness just as much as she wanted to throw its existence in his face. Although still there and plenty ugly, she realized Menaha had been right. It was actually starting to heal.

"If you were branded, then how did you escape?" He peered critically at it as if evaluating it. As if this were no surprise. His demands came quickly, although he kept his voice quiet. Wait—if he knew about the brand already, what was going on?

"Someone figured out how to break the spell and freed me."

"What did you steal?"

"It doesn't matter."

"Tell me—what did you steal?"

"I'm not telling you. I don't trust you. And why do you even want to know, anyway?"

He looked taken aback, almost... hurt. "Because I'm not allowed to help you if you're a criminal, and if you stole something, it sounds like you're a criminal."

A pause. "Help me?" She frowned at him. "By the gods, I'm not a criminal."

"Then it shouldn't be a problem to tell me what you stole. Coin? Jewels? What?"

She scowled at him. Was there a way out of this? His determined expression said likely there wasn't.

"Wouldn't I have turned you in already if I wanted to?"

"Well, you hadn't seen that poster before."

"Damn it, Jaena, I'm trying to help you," he hissed, anger straining his voice as he struggled to keep quiet.

"What if I don't need your help?"

He held up the poster, then gestured at the door, then her ankle. Gods, she hated being injured. She kept on frowning at him stubbornly. He sighed at her. "Fine, don't tell me. You're free to go. Stay. Whatever you wish. I was trying to help you."

He turned to stalk away from her, toward the cabinet, and the floor seemed to shift out from under her at the sudden loss of his support.

"Wait," she said.

He stilled, but did not turn.

"Fine. I stole the brand the Masters use to make slaves. I want to stop them."

"You—" He turned wildly, his eyes flicking to her

knapsack, then back to her face. She nodded. "You broke the spell—and stole… You *stole* it? That's very brave."

"And don't forget stupid. And I didn't get very far, as you can see." She sighed, glaring down at her ankle.

He stopped for a moment, seeming to take it all in. "We have to get you—and *it*—out of here." He immediately grabbed a leather saddlebag from a hook on the wall.

"What, no—"

"What are the chances none of the others mention you?" As he spoke, he began moving around the room and adding things. The salve. The bread. *The Book of the Vigilant*, another of the smallest tomes. Was he packing?

"Wait, go? How? You've seen I can't walk."

"The horse. We'll take it and ride for Anonil—"

"Wait—we?"

He stopped and met her gaze.

"You want to come with me?"

He frowned again but a different one this time. He searched her face, but she had no idea what he was looking for or if he found it. "Yes. I'm coming with you." He resumed packing, not looking at her as he went.

He seemed sincere. How could he be sincere? "But why? You can't leave your smithy."

"It will wait here for me until I get you to safety."

She swallowed.

"Or another from the temple can inherit it. I'm sure. We're going. Now."

"Why are you willing to help me?"

"There's no time to explain."

"They could have ridden east. We could just be drawing attention to ourselves. Who in their right mind would be riding in this rain, in the middle of the night?"

"*We* will be. They won't be looking for people because it's a stupid time to ride."

"There won't be enough light to ride. We could wait till morning. They'll have tired and returned home. More people will be on the roads to blend in with."

"Or they'll come back and search harder because a neighbor mentioned two people were here."

"But they left. Surely no one must have mentioned—"

"There were three scrawny little men with that damn lantern. They could have just as easily gone for reinforcements."

"A lantern? What was it? And why didn't they find me?" She had heard that strange clanking, and the Devoted had taken almost no time to look around. Why?

"They had a metal cage like a lantern, but instead of a candle or oil, it held a purple rock. Similar to those they wear around their necks, but orange in the center, like a burning ember. They only looked at it. Seemed like they were waiting for it to do something. I assume it detects magic."

"Why didn't it work?"

He shrugged, and his eyes darted away from her gaze. Something he almost never did. He was hiding something. But what?

"Where did you get that pendant?"

"Why?"

"Was it from your parents?"

"I never knew my parents. I grew up on the streets. The temple gave it to me."

"So the priestesses gave it to you then?" Hmm. Interesting. Could they have known he was a mage somehow, found a way to protect him? Something similar to the magic-repression stones, but different in that they hid magic from detection instead of repressing it? Or perhaps it repressed the repressing stones, an idea so odd she'd laugh if she weren't in this situation. Whatever it was, the pendant didn't seem to be repressing *him*, with all the spellwork that swirled around them.

"We don't have time for this. I don't see why it matters."

How could she tell him? How could she explain that he was a mage too if he didn't already know? Should she, even? What if he didn't want to know? But wouldn't it be safer for him? If that pendant was all that protected him, and he lost it, he could end up in Mage Hall himself, especially living barely a day's walk from it. And yet—he had a whole bowl of them. Why? He wasn't telling her something.

"Look—we need to go," he said cutting into her thoughts. *"Now."*

She hesitated for a moment longer. She could not imagine what he could be hiding, but he had had every opportunity to turn her over to the Devoted. If he'd planned to, he could have done it already, more than once.

If they fled, at least it would mean an end to all the waiting. On horseback, it wouldn't be long before they

made it to Akaria—or not. It would end this just waiting
around for the Devoted to figure out she was here. There
had to be fewer of the bastards farther away from Mage
Hall, right? And if Tharomar was with her, she could
decide later whether to tell him he was a mage or not.
"All right, fine. Let's go."

Tharomar stalked out into the rain. He'd gotten some
fairly thick cloaks for them both, and they were lucky
it wasn't slightly colder, or this late fall rain would be a
heavy snow. But the rain was heavy enough that it splashed
everywhere and managed to get into places it normally
wouldn't otherwise. The deluge had opened up out of
nowhere, and if it kept up like this, they wouldn't get far.
The road would be black as pitch. But it was likely just a
short downpour. They could pack and prepare, and then
at least they would be ready to leave as soon as the rain
let up. Or they could hide out in the barn, which would
give them some warning if the Devoted did come back.

He'd packed one saddlebag with perishables and a
few of the precious books. He kept another ready with
the saddle, packed with the necessities that lasted—flint,
blankets, hunting knives. It wasn't a long ride to Akaria
and the next city anyway, where hopefully they could
hide. If they couldn't make it in one night, perhaps by
nightfall tomorrow…

He stopped and listened. Were those hoofbeats in the

distance? Or was it his imagination? Hard to tell with the heavy rush of the rain.

The last items he needed were in the smithy, so they made their way there as quickly as she was able.

By the gods, she had stolen the damn brand. The thing they used to *make* the mages slaves in the first place. It had been there, just sitting on his floor by the fire all this time. It had been nearby as those Devoted searched his home. He should have pressed her for her story sooner, he should have looked in her bag when she'd fallen asleep. They could have been long gone. The order would be furious with him if he lost either her or the artifact now. But not half as furious as he'd be with himself.

"Stay here just a second," he said as they stopped by the entry to the smithy, its wide-open mouth facing the farms. He hoped the farmers would find a way to manage without him.

"Do you have a staff or something?" she asked. He searched among some shovels propped by the entry. "We can't go far in this deluge."

He nodded as he handed her a rather large tree branch he'd used as a walking stick on a hike into town that summer. "I know. Hoping the rain will let up. Here—not a staff, but close as I've got. Should help steady you on your feet. Good idea. It will just be a moment."

He strode to the heavy trunk beside his hearth and took a knee next to it. He unlocked the padlock and heaved open the hefty lid. The hearth's embers cast a dim, warm light over the contents. The night itself was dark and empty, moonless.

Perhaps he had one thing he did consider his own—his weapons. First, he drew out the mace, dark and elegant with holy symbols inlaid in gold on the handle—grain, rose, and nail always underneath his hands. Then, he pushed more lambskins out of the way and found the sword and scabbard. Just as he lifted the carrying strap over his shoulder, a voice broke through the calm rushing of the rain.

"Stop, in the name of Nefrana."

Tharomar sucked in a harsh breath. He struggled to squash a wave of anger at the words; it would not help him fight.

And fight he would.

The voice belonged to the same Devoted that had been here before. Were these knights or lesser soldiers? They had not identified themselves. Had one of the others mentioned her—or had they returned of their own accord? Could they have been watching him and Jaena? Perhaps he should have listened to her—

"Put the sword down."

Ro slowly lowered the sword back into the trunk and began to straighten as slowly as humanly possible.

"This mage the one?" said another.

"Stay away from me," Jaena snapped. Had they tried to grab her? He hadn't yet dared to turn. He wanted them to come closer. Just a little closer.

"Aye, this is her. What'll we do with this smith then? Lied to us, I think. He's sheltering her." Two of them approached, he judged by their footsteps. How many were there? He had only heard two voices.

"We should take him back. The Masters can—"

He didn't let them finish. He snatched the mace from the hearth beside him and spun. He hadn't even laid eyes on the Devoted yet, but he made a blind swing, not daring to waste a moment of his surprise sizing up the situation.

He got lucky. The mace collided with the right side of the head of the first with a sickening thud. He felt a pang of nausea. By Nefrana, why had they chosen to return? He didn't want to kill them.

But he was going to. He would likely have to kill them, to get her and the brand away. He hadn't sworn that oath because this would be easy.

The second Devoted staggered back in shock as the first fell in a splatter of blood.

Ro circled the mace back up over his head with both arms, gathering momentum as he stepped forward once and swung. The weapon crushed into the second Devoted's left arm and ribs, sending him flying.

Hoping that was enough to incapacitate him but perhaps let him survive, Tharomar lurched toward Jaena only to find another Devoted lunging at him instead. He caught a glimpse of her swinging the branch, deftly knocking another Devoted to the ground with a blow to the side of the head. Ah, so the staff *hadn't* been just to steady her on her feet.

Tharomar ducked quickly and dodged as best he could. The knight missed him with whatever weapon had gone by in a blur in the darkness.

Ro returned the Devoted's attack with his own, crushing a femur and collapsing the man in the process.

His luck ran out when a blow pounded his right shoulder, sending him reeling forward and knocking the air out of him. Face in the dirt, he scrambled forward.

Boots he knew all too well blocked his path as another Devoted behind him fell to the ground with a thud. Feminine boots, one ankle tied poorly because it was swollen to twice the size it should be.

Whatever she'd done, she'd taken out the Devoted behind him. She stamped the staff on the ground beside the two of them, stirring up a slight dust cloud. Silence fell around them, no noise but the pattering of the rain.

More slowly now, he rose and straightened. He rubbed his shoulder and scanned the smithy and the night beyond.

"Do you think that was all of them?" she whispered.

"Four seems like an odd number. Why return with just one more?"

"There were six."

"Six? You took out three?"

"Yes." She nodded as he surveyed the fallen men.

"Just a traveling merchant, eh?" His eyes had finally adjusted and his head sufficiently cleared to see the competent way she held the branch.

"Oh, and you're just a blacksmith?" She narrowed her eyes at him, leaning on the branch with both hands. She was a beautiful sight in the dim ember light, powerful and lithe like a forest spirit, eyes keen and sparkling in their darkness.

And he was staring. He shook it off and glanced around. The second one he'd hit lay not far away, hands on his thigh, twitching every now and then. That one was only pretending to be out cold. He wanted to get away.

Or to listen and learn something.

He held a finger to his lips but couldn't be sure she saw him in the dim hearth light. He pointed at the suspected Devoted, and then after a moment's hesitation, he pressed a finger gently to her lips as well. They were warm, soft to the touch.

And he was a damn idiot, thinking about that at a time like this.

"Let's go," he said quickly. Thankfully, she didn't demand to know why he stepped over the bodies to grab the sword and mace he had just felled three men with. He didn't know how many were truly unconscious and how many were pretending, but he did feel confident none of them would be able to follow them right away. He did hope some would survive. He also hoped it would be very, very hard for them to call for help.

Tharomar muttered a quick blessing, both for their foolish sins and for forgiveness for himself if he'd ended any of them.

He took her arm over his shoulder and again steered her toward the barn, where his horse Yada lived with several of the other townsfolk's horses. They made even faster progress with the staff by his side.

"When are you going to tell me what is really going

on?" she whispered. "Where did you get those? What are those symbols?" They reached the barn door, which was closed but not bolted. He heaved the door open. The downpour had relented a bit but not completely.

"Holy weapons, blessed of the gods," he replied as they stumbled inside and he pushed the door shut. One dim lantern had been left burning, luckily. "They were a gift to me from my order when I swore my allegiance and joined them."

"Your *order*?"

"I actually never claimed to be *only* a blacksmith, unlike some people," he said, smiling. He strode to Yada and greeted her gently. "But you can interrogate me endlessly once we're on the road."

"I will be sure to do that."

He made short work of loading up the saddle, bags, and weapons as she did her best to gather a few horse provisions and tools.

He helped her mount first. A footstool was some help, but her ankle still made her too unsteady, so he found his hands on either side of her hips, lifting her onto the patient mare. Her body felt good underneath his hands, reassuring, strong.

Gods be damned, this was *not* the time. Get your head on straight, Tharomar Revendel, he chided himself. This woman is on the run with a very heavy burden. She has a lot more important things to worry about, and he would just be another one. Also, thinking about her hips and his hands instead of focusing on getting away from these damned Devoted would just make him sloppy. They did not have room for mistakes.

Still, clarifying his mind only got harder as he got into the saddle behind her. If only they had two horses, but he drew the line at stealing from the townsfolk. Her body pressed against his, fully of wiry muscle and tense for any new danger.

He led the horse out into the last of the drizzling rain at a slow walk, jumping down once to shutter up the barn and bar the door. They pulled up their hoods as he eased them down the road toward Anonil and hoped the Devoted who were left conscious would not figure out the direction they were heading.

"Can we go faster?" she whispered.

"It will only make it easier for them to hear us. Plus it's still quite dark." The mare knew the way well enough in spite of the lack of moonlight, at least. In the night's darkness, he could see the many intricate braids of her hair, Yada's mane, and a few feet around them to either side but not much else. He had to rely on hearing for now and hope the clouds would clear. He whispered a prayer and was not sure whether Jaena heard it or if he wanted her to. Nothing about his faith had elicited anything but fear from her. Understandable, but also saddening.

They pulled down their hoods to hear more as the rain stopped. She listened keenly as they rode, quick to turn toward any sound from the fields. He thought he heard shouts in the distance but didn't hear anyone following them.

Eventually the clouds *did* part just a little, letting a slight bit of moonlight past. Enough to see their way. Not enough to make traveling at night the best idea, which was just as well. Nefrana's hand, he thought, guiding us away from this evil place.

The swaying of the horse lulled them, and despite her claims, she did not resume questioning him. The night felt too silent. Could she tell if they were heading in the right direction?

"You're still certain we should head to Anonil?" he whispered, his lips accidentally brushing her ear.

"Yes. We should be able to find help there." He wanted to press her to explain more. But perhaps it was better not to give away their destination with idle chatter anyway.

She was nodding off a bit. Good. At least one of them should rest. Her head finally came to settle on his shoulder, her forehead pressed to his neck and puffs of breath warming his chest, a sense of relief washing through him.

Rest, my unfortunate one. We are on our way out of here.

The sun had set as Miara stared out her window at the snowy peaks. A knock sounded at the door. Again, the damn guard opened it without acknowledgment—or even a nominal amount of caution. Certainly *some* caution was warranted at this point. Although her heart leapt that it might be Aven, she had a feeling that it wouldn't be.

And it wasn't. Instead, King Samul stood before her, waiting as she pulled on a night robe against the serious cold of Estun at night and marched into the sitting room.

"My lord," she said, bowing. He gave her a curt nod. His temples and jaw seemed tense under his dark beard.

"Good evening, Miara. I came to speak to you about the attack."

"Of course, my lord. Would you like to sit down?"

He remained standing. "Where were you when the attack took place?"

"What? I was with the queen, exhausted from the demonstration before the attack."

"She says she briefly left you with the group of mages to tend to one of the injured gate guards."

"Briefly, yes. I waited there. I was with them. Why don't you ask them?"

"Unfortunately, their memories are a bit foggy in light of the chaos from the cave-in and being overexerted themselves."

She frowned. "You can't be serious."

"I am deadly serious."

"I would never hurt Aven. I—" She glanced around uncomfortably at the guards. She couldn't say more while they listened without disobeying him at the same time. "You *know* why I wouldn't."

"Do I?" The king inclined his head, his fingers stroking his beard thoughtfully. What an odd response. And come to think of it, why was the king here himself, with no one else even accompanying him? Where was Aven?

Could this be another trick, maybe even one of the assassins in disguise?

Audacious as it seemed at the moment, she dipped into his thoughts. She went as quickly, as briefly as she could and hoped he wouldn't notice. Untrained, he shouldn't, but he did have a creature mage for a wife. Certainly that could have come in handy in their years as rulers. Whether he could tell or not, she had to ensure he was indeed King Samul before she said another word.

An image of Aven approaching in a room she didn't recognize flashed through her mind, his arm soaked with blood. A memory of pain and fear shot through her veins, then filled her with anger, then rage. No. Not her veins, not her rage—Samul's, and the pain that of a parent seeing a child injured, nearly killed.

She reeled back as quickly as she could. It was... definitely him. His brow slowly furrowed deeper, the touch of suspicion growing in his eyes. She had a feeling she had not been as stealthy as she might have hoped.

"I don't know what to say. I was with the queen for all but a moment. Aven trusts me. Doesn't that mean anything to you?"

"Aven has many great qualities, and finding the good in people is one of them. But every strength has its opposite, its weakness."

"And what is that?" she demanded.

"Not seeing the bad in people," he replied.

"And what bad do you see in me?"

He frowned. "I don't see much of anything past that

wall you put up. You are hard to read. As a spy should be."

"I'm a spy no longer."

"But you've been one your whole life."

"I stole things. I eavesdropped. Against my will, mind you. Do you really think I attacked him?"

"I don't know what to think."

"If I wanted to kill him, I've had ample opportunity. I wouldn't have come back here. I could have killed him on the road. Or left him in Kavanar, for that matter."

"Aven believes he freed you from your enchantment. But I just wonder, what if your orders have only changed?"

She recoiled, her jaw dropping. Was he saying what she thought he was saying? Gods. She couldn't blame him, such a thing could certainly have been possible. Thank the gods the Masters hadn't thought of it and that she'd been free by the time they returned.

"I swear to you they haven't. But there's no way I can convince you of that."

"You're right, there isn't."

She waited, unsure of how to proceed.

"I won't bring this up with Aven until the dust settles on the rest of this. If the Assembly won't accept his magic, then we'll have a whole host of other problems, but you and he might not be one of them, unless of course your enchantment is truly unbroken. But I don't want that—or you—distracting him right now."

"They will support him, won't they? Do you truly think they won't accept him?"

"I think that he has a much better chance with you

out of the situation."

She flinched. She had once sneered at Aven's comment that his magic was inconvenient. While he'd never been enslaved for it, he also hadn't had it as easy as she'd thought. "What do you mean… out of the situation?"

"We walk a blade's edge. The stability of the nation rides on this vote. You do understand that, don't you?"

She nodded, a little bitter that he might think she wouldn't.

"You complicate the process. It's hard enough to get them to accept a mage as it is; we risk civil war if you—an enemy spy *and* a mage—are at his side." A jolt of fear shot through her. "You will remain in your quarters, and he will not visit, until we leave for Panar."

Miara balked. "But—no—my lord—"

"We leave tomorrow. After that, you are free to roam Estun as you wish until we return."

"You mean—I'm not coming with you?"

He blinked, probably at the panic in her voice, but his face hardened further.

"Please, you've got to take me." She fumbled for a reason. Because she'd been wrongly accused? Because she could help keep him safe? Because she dreaded being away from Aven for that long, not knowing if he was safe or what had happened? Those weren't real reasons to give a king. "I can—"

"No. Aven has spent his whole life preparing to be king. I will *not* have it stolen away by a woman he's known for barely a fortnight."

She flinched again at those words. "It's been almost a month," she muttered.

He turned to leave.

"I thought this was a kingdom of laws," she said to his back, some strength returning. Or perhaps that feeling was despair. "I haven't *done* anything."

"You—or a woman who looked *exactly* like you—attempted to murder the heir to the throne of this realm, in multiple ways, in front of multiple witnesses. We *do* have a law against murder, I'm afraid, and assassination in particular."

"Wait—I can't even say goodbye?"

"No. This has gone on long enough. This is where I draw the line." Then he stalked away, and the door shut behind him.

She stared at the polished oak of the door. She could not let Aven go to Panar alone. Hard to believe that the king and his lords did not see through this ruse, that they might actually believe it had been her, in spite of what the queen or any of the others might say. Being fooled by this trick showed how unprepared they were to deal with the threat of magic of any kind, let alone a mage army.

If the Akarians went to Panar without her, what mages would they bring? Just Queen Elise? Would they take Wunik? Even two or three of them could not be everywhere at every time, not to mention that neither of them was familiar with using magic for war.

She gritted her teeth. She should be at Aven's side. Now her moments of self-doubt about being a queen seemed foolish, juvenile. She had the skills, the knowledge, the temperament to help him better than anyone they knew. She was better suited to help him through all of this than most, and her loyalty to him was unmatched. He'd known that all along, but she hadn't known herself as clearly.

She sighed. Of course, when she thought becoming queen was a certainty to be feared, she'd questioned if she were up to it, if she would be happy. Now that the crown seemed more distant than ever, a fierce need rose in her. She might not be a charmer or an elegant diplomat, but she could stand by Aven's side and glower while he took care of those things.

But if Samul didn't let her be in the same *city* as his son, that was not going to happen.

No matter. Samul had told her when they would leave. She would just have to escape and go after them anyway.

If she could get out of Mage Hall, *this* should be nothing.

Aven was tempted to throw open the door to his father's meeting chambers. After the insane events of the day, who cared who the king was talking to? But Aven knew it would not help him convince the king how utterly wrong he was, so he settled for pounding on the door with his fist instead.

His father called him from inside, and Aven stepped in.

Fayton and two apprentice stewards stood by the king's desk, going down lists of parchment.

"What is it, Aven?"

"I think you know. We need to talk," he replied through gritted teeth.

Samul raised an eyebrow and took his pipe from his mouth for a moment. "I presume this is about Miara." His father beckoned for him to enter. "Do you have what you need to finish the preparations without me, Fayton?"

The steward nodded. "Things should be complete by morning, my lord." The stewards left and shut the door, leaving them alone.

"What the hell is this about?" Aven said coldly, surprising himself at the harshness of his voice.

Samul tilted his head forward, biting down on his pipe. "I believe you know exactly what it's about. Come, sit by the fire with me."

Aven didn't want to sit, or meekly obey commands. He wanted to pace. Maybe slam things. But he sat anyway. Expressions of rage did not help convince anyone of anything, least of all his father. He settled for the small rebellion of plopping violently into a chair.

"I see you're wearing your sword again," Samul began.

Aven nodded curtly. "It seemed prudent."

"I understand you're angry," his father said. "But I have good reasons for this."

Aven glared at him. Here came the patronizing parental voice, the "I understand you want a horse of your very own, to go to war with the men, to eat all thirty-five cakes, but you can't because you're only six" voice. He recalled it thoroughly from when Dom was young, if not from his own childhood.

But he was not a child anymore.

"She is not guilty of the crime you hold her on," Aven said, trying logic first. "If you can't trust the word of Devol and Mother, who can you trust?"

"She has not been proven innocent either." Samul narrowed his eyes at Aven.

"Are you saying you don't trust them?"

"I frankly don't care if it was her or not, we aren't going to sort it out before sunrise. There's not enough evidence to prove anything either way. But if it *was* her, she can't attack you again if she's here."

"You can't seriously think that likely."

"It doesn't matter if it's likely. If I make it impossible, we won't have to consider it. I'm taking that chance off the table."

"Miara has the most knowledge of Kavanar's magic and war plans. What if they attack while we're in Panar and she's here? We'll have hamstrung ourselves unnecessarily."

"We can't trust her knowledge, much as you might be wont to."

"Why the hell not?"

"You've barely known her for a month, how do you know she doesn't still have some other enchantment on her? Or bribe? You *know* they hold her family now. She has that motive alone or many others we don't know about, and she's the perfect person at this point to sabotage us from the inside."

Should Aven mention the scroll Daes had sent? Would

that help or hurt his case? "I've been through hell and back with her. She's had every opportunity to betray me and not taken it. She would never—"

"You can't prove that."

"Neither can you! With that logic, we can't know for sure Mother couldn't be bribed." The hell with sitting. He got up and started pacing.

"I am a year older than my father was when he died, you know."

Aven stopped and rounded on him, scowling. "And you're bringing that up now because… ?"

"It is very real to me that you could become king. *Will* become king. More real than it is to you because it's happened to me already."

"You think I don't take this seriously? That I don't understand what's on the line?"

"I didn't say that."

"Then what's your point? I don't see what this has to do with Miara."

"I want them to vote on you. And you alone."

Ah, so that was it. Aven gritted his teeth as he resumed his pacing. "But it's *not* me and me alone. If they get me, they get her too. They should know the truth." Hmm, perhaps Lady Toyl was not entirely wrong when she called a secret a lie by implication. For some secrets, anyway. If you let them stand.

"The Assembly members have had no time to get to know her as you have. *You* they have known their whole lives. Most of them, anyway. Which judgment do you think will be more fair, more well informed?"

Aven wanted to groan. Of course, his father was right in the sense that he was correct. Aven alone would be judged more fairly. But he wasn't right in the moral sense. They deserved to know, as Lady Toyl had so eloquently pointed out. Aven said nothing, pacing, thinking, searching for a way to throw why he was so wrong in his father's face.

"They do not understand her yet," his father continued. "They do not trust her. Hell, I don't trust her yet."

"Why the hell not?"

"She's a hard one to read, Aven. I trust your impression of people, but it's hard to see it myself. She's closed off. As someone with her skills and expertise probably should be."

"She hasn't had much incentive to develop an open and inviting personality," Aven grumbled. "Slavery doesn't exactly engender that in people, you know. And now we've locked her up, even though she was with Mother the entire time the attack was taking place."

Samul rose to his feet and stepped in front of Aven, blocking his pacing. "We cannot afford for the complexity of her situation to muddle a vote that could change your life and the lives of your brothers, and potentially start a civil war while we're at it. If they vote against you, neither Thel nor Dom will have a chance. Peaceful jockeying for a new heir would be *lucky*. More likely, the whole kingdom would fall back to warring cities and tribes. Our line would be destroyed. Hundreds if not thousands of lives could be lost. Do you hear me? If you're willing to risk all that over whether or not your *woman* is in the same city with you, you're not half as ready to be king as I thought you were."

Aven shook with barely restrained rage. "That *woman* has considerably more training in using magic for combat than anyone else we have. Not to mention she's the source of nearly all the intelligence we've been able to acquire, save my own. As to her loyalty, I don't see any of us stabbing ourselves in the gut just to get it through our thick heads that magic is seriously dangerous. This is war, and we're throwing our most powerful weapon aside. If you think this attack and this cave-in are the last things the Kavanarians will attempt, then *you're* not the king *I* thought you were."

From the look in Samul's eyes, Aven thought his father might beat him senseless. He braced himself, but it didn't come. He should back down now. He was way over the line, and this was a line he never toed.

But he didn't back down. He couldn't. Too much was on the line. Aven continued, "If we're to present a strong and unified front against Kavanar, we can't win the Assembly's support with lies and altercations. I *am* going to marry Miara, you're not going to stop me, and they should know the truth about it when they make their decision. If not, they'll feel betrayed again when they find out the truth."

"Not if you manage it right—"

"Please. And if we *fail* to 'manage' it right? What then?"

"Your idealism will be the death of us."

"You were the one who taught me the Code. You were the one who told me that principles matter. You were the one who explained that we must follow our principles, especially when they are inconvenient. And yet, you're going to stand here and tell me to throw it all out when the swords are drawn?"

His father said nothing. His body shook underneath his scowl, fists clenched at his sides, just as Aven's were.

"I *thought* that's when our principles were needed most," Aven said coldly.

Samul was silent, their hostile gazes locked with each other.

"This is not about idealism anyway," Aven said, more softly now. "War is coming. Whether we like it or not. Shutting Miara out weakens us. It's a poor choice, tactically, morally, and politically. It's your decision, but—"

"It *is* my decision. And I've made it. We're not going to resolve this now."

"I'm going to ask you one last time—"

"The answer is no. I forbid you to see her until after the vote has taken place."

Aven's scowl deepened. "You're wrong about this. You'll see."

He stormed out of the king's meeting chambers, then down the hallway, a spiraling staircase, and another bleak hall. Nearly everyone was already asleep in their quarters, everyone who was leaving for Panar anyway, which was most of them. He tried to collect himself as he stalked back to his rooms. Years had passed since he'd fought with his father like that, and it'd never been over something so deeply important. How had he missed the depth of his father's mistrust, his misgivings? Could he have done anything about it, if he'd noticed? A fresh wave of anger swept through him over the decision, the somewhat irrational feeling of betrayal. He'd been so focused on convincing others of his own worth, he hadn't thought he needed to tell his father what he thought was obvious. Could the Akarians succeed against Kavanar without her help and the help she'd already given them? Aven honestly wasn't sure.

When he got to the next corridor, he stopped. His rooms were to the left, back in the direction of the king's but a few floors down. The hall to the guest quarters waited to his right.

The king's words echoed in his head. Tomorrow, Aven and half the household would leave for Panar, and Miara would stay here in Estun with at least two assassins. Unless, of course, they tagged along with Aven. One or both of them would be left to face that threat alone, and probably others.

He regretted nothing he had said to his father. But Aven was tired of going against his own intuition. Of doing what he was told, every single time.

He knew what he needed to do.

Aven turned down the hallway to the right. He would see her whether his father liked it or not.

Reaching her rooms, he knocked. The guard opened the door without even asking who it was. "Shouldn't you ask your charge if she wants to see the visitor, not just let everyone in?" Aven's scowl hadn't left him, so he turned it on this guard.

"Prisoners are usually required to see members of the royal family, my lord. But I apologize." The guard glared back, his words insincere. "She's asleep."

"And you still let me in?" Aven didn't care. He stormed past the fool and made straight for the bedroom.

He slammed the door behind him, shutting out the guards and the rest of the whole damn world.

Miara looked up in surprise from where she sat at the writing desk, clearly not asleep. A pale blue tunic hugged her curves, a robe thrown over that and her wild hair hanging free and mingling with thin braids.

They were alone. Completely, actually alone.

He froze in the doorway for a moment, remembering a time not so long ago when they'd regarded each other this way. The music of flute and drum floated through his memory.

"You once told me to get as far away from you as I could," he said, his voice rough with emotion. "Do you remember?"

She nodded, her eyes wide, lips parted.

"I'm apparently very bad at following orders."

"Aven—" she started, standing as he rushed toward her. He took her face in his hands, kissing her hungrily, like there might not be another chance. The entire world be damned. He would have this moment, at the very least, with her. Her lips parted, opening beneath him and kissing him ardently in return. The taste of her was familiar, and yet not familiar enough.

*I thought—your father said you were forbidden to—* she started.

*I am. He did say that. I'm here anyway.*

*Oh. I see. Following orders. It's good to see you too.* She broke away for a moment, stealing a breath with a small smile.

"Do you have something to write on?" he asked.

Frowning and smiling at the same time, she reached for a sheet of parchment and placed it before him on the desk. He started drawing, her arm still wrapped around the small of his back.

"What is this?"

He tapped his temple to make sure she was listening. *It's a secret emergency path out of Estun. It goes past the cellars, where there are supplies.*

*Am I going somewhere?* Her mind's voice shook with laughter.

*I want you to come. To follow us. Something.*

*I was already planning on it.*

Of course she was. *That's why I love you.* He roped her in for another long kiss before he continued his map creation.

*Because I disobey my king? Because I'm good at escaping from places?*

*Because you do the right thing, even when it's difficult.*

*You give me too much credit. It would be harder to stay away from you. I have to follow. I have to know you're all safe.*

*Got one more sheet?*

She handed him another. *What will your father say*

*when he finds out you came here?*

*I don't know. Or care.* He paused for a moment, remembering the fight, wondering if recalling those moments would be enough to explain to her generally what had transpired.

*Oh. I'm so sorry I—*

*Don't be sorry. I'm not.*

"What are you drawing now?" she whispered.

*The roads to Panar. Do you think you can follow this?*

*Yes. But what is that?*

*This is Lake Senokin. If for some reason we can't meet in Panar, I want you to come here. What do you think?*

*A secondary meeting place is smart.*

He pulled her close and kissed her again now, turning over the idea that had taken root in his mind. Was this the right time? The right way?

What if they never got another?

*It's also one of the sacred lakes where by tradition Akarian kings and queens have married. The ritual requires two lovers, alone at night under the silent moon, and only a priestess in attendance. No grand state affairs, at least not till later.*

She broke away from his kiss, eyes wide.

*When this is all over, will you meet me there? Marry me, Miara. Not someday, not maybe—as soon as humanly possible. As soon as the vote is finished, we'll go straight there.*

Her eyes widened further for a split second, and he felt none of that connection that had scared him so, that fear of being queen. Perhaps he asked too much, perhaps he and his father had ruined her trust in Akaria already.

His heart jumped to double, then triple time.

*If you'll still have me,* he added, not even sure if she was listening. *If you think you can stand to be queen.*

"Oh, of course," she whispered, snapping out of her daze. Ah, she was only surprised, not trying to figure out how to throw him out of the room. Thank goodness. She dove into his kiss again. *Yes. Yes, of course. I'm sorry you thought I doubted you.*

He guided her away from the desk and toward the wall, pressing her against the climbing vines, roses blooming around them as their lips met again, feverish. He had held this back for so long… and soon enough he'd be leaving again. *Tell me what you're planning. We don't have much time.*

*I'd almost think you find plotting insubordination alluring.*

*When you do it, I do.*

She let out a musical laugh. *I'll wait until you should be on the morning road, then I will get out of Estun with the help of your map. If that doesn't work, I can always try my window, then try to acquire some supplies on the way. Of course, I'll have to borrow a horse, but that shouldn't be a problem.*

*We won't be going terribly fast. That may give you a few hours' head start. You might be able to catch us.*

*Maybe, but I'd rather reach you closer to Panar,* she said. *Too late to send me back, you know? And I'll head to the palace you marked—isn't that the address you told Daes on the scroll?*

*Yes. Let him go ahead and try. Most heavily fortified*

*building in the city. We'll think of a way to get to your sister, to stop Daes somehow. I promise you.*

*Don't promise the impossible.* He felt her ache like it was his own.

*You're right. But I'll do my best to think of something.*

*And I'll do my best to get to that address. If I can't make it there, or you aren't there, I'll leave and head to the lake and wait there.*

"Good plan," he whispered in her ear.

"Be careful, Aven. The mages who caused that cave-in, those assassins, they'll likely follow you."

"I know. Try not to worry."

"I don't worry about such things. I prepare for them."

"Of course." He gave her another small kiss and nestled into her neck. Lavender, cinnamon, and rosemary.

*You can't stay, can you?* she said softly.

*I shouldn't. We ride in a few hours. But I'll spend those hours here with you if you wish.*

She clung harder to him for a moment before saying, *No, no, you should go. We needn't try so hard to point out this visit to your father. And… I can't imagine your stay here would be very restful.*

*No pillow is as restful as your arms.*

*Ah, but my arms do not have restful activities in mind.*

He let out a muted rumble of a laugh, still conscious of the guards outside and potential eavesdroppers.

*I… did not entirely mean to share this line of thinking.*

*Let me in again, like you did the last time. One more moment, and I will go.*

The walls of their minds fall away, thoughts mingling together in curious harmony, a sea of flashing images, most of them plans for future minglings that would be slightly more physical and slightly less abstract.

*I need to never let you go,* he told her. *Ever.*

*But you must.*

*I know.*

Finally, he stepped back from her, reluctant but exhausted, afraid and yet also relieved.

"See you in Panar," she whispered, taking the maps from the desk and folding them. Her sleepy eyes twinkled, a smile gracing her lips.

"I'm counting on it."

The sound of the door creaking open woke Miara. Aven was gone, of course, and the fire had burned low. She didn't open her eyes as the door creaked shut again. She lay on her back, left arm over her head, the other straight by her side. The handle of the dagger under her pillow was unfortunately readied for her right hand, but her left was the one close to it.

It could be just a servant.

But she had a feeling it wasn't. She reached out gently to check.

A mage. Someone who seemed—familiar. She mustn't let them realize she'd awoken. She eased her left hand over the top of the pillow and closer to the blade, all in the guise of sleep.

The edge of the bed dipped. Whoever it was had climbed onto the bed.

*Could* it be Aven? He'd have to be crazy to come back at this early hour, before the long trip. It wasn't unthinkable, but he could also have just stayed and never left. She was tempted to reach out further, but that would alert them to her wakefulness.

Her instincts blared danger, and she eased her hand further under the pillow. That said, she did need to figure out how to be sure it *wasn't* him, but that would cost her precious moments.

The form eased closer. They made their way up the bed, coming toward her. Over her.

Good. Fine. Better to get them in range. Her first strike would be the easiest, as they wouldn't expect it.

Except—gruff hands suddenly seized her forearms, yanking her right hand up over her head. She ignored that and pushed her left hand further under the pillow, getting her fingers at least partially around the handle of the blade. It was an awkward angle, and she had to reach farther, but she almost had it—

She bridged, lifting her hips into the air, sending her attacker flying over her head and colliding into the bed frame. While their balance was off, she twisted beneath, scrambling to land a blow or slide away. A lucky kick made contact, sending them rolling, and she scrambled to the other side of the bed, dagger in hand.

Hearth light fell across a familiar face.

"Sorin! By the gods, what are you doing here?" That son of a bitch.

"Just my duty. Tell me how you got free, and I'll make this easy on you."

"Make *what* easy on me? You getting a beating?

"You're dangerous. You need to be stopped."

"What? Why would *I* need to be stopped?"

"Nefrana teaches we are evil. Without their chains on you, who knows what you will do? You must be stopped, for all our sakes, or there are even greater dark days to come."

"Did the Dark Master send you here for this?" No, he was not her master anymore. "Did *Daes* send you?"

"The Masters sent us for the prince. Coming for you was my personal choice."

He leapt over the bed and lunged at her again. She was faster, though, easily dodging and scampering across the room, taking cover behind the desk.

"How did you get free?" he demanded.

"What does it matter? Do you want to be free?"

"Was it that damn prince—the one just in here plowing you—"

"He was not—" she started. Wait. "How did you know he was just here? He was *not* plowing me."

"Sure, he wasn't."

"How did you know?"

"I was right outside, dutifully guarding you," he said, his voice sickly sweet.

He sauntered slowly across the room toward her,

trying to intimidate, perhaps. She readied herself to dodge in the direction of the main door. Didn't need to be cornered. Where were the guards? "How can you not want to be free?"

He had reached the other side of the desk and stopped. His voice was breathy, just above a whisper. "I don't need freedom if I have Nefrana's eternal favor."

"You really believe all that?"

Suddenly, the desk lurched before her. He heaved it, sending it toppling over and to the side and leaving no barrier between them. She recoiled another step. "How can you deny it, Miara? Who are you to question the gods?"

"Who are *you* to know their will perfectly?"

"See, I told you, denial. You must accept—"

He lunged, mid sentence, seeking to catch her off guard. It worked, partially. He captured her wrist and swung her with her own momentum. She flew into the nearby wall, and he rushed to pin her.

She rode the momentum of the spin and stabbed. The dagger gored into his neck.

The spurt of blood covered everything, it seemed. That sickly, hot wetness was answer enough that she'd made contact in the darkness. Still, she thrust him away from her. He collapsed to the floor. One gurgling breath, then another. Then nothing.

"Let me know what they say," she whispered into the silence.

She stared at his still form for a long time, feeling hollow. The Akarians were leaving her, her family had drawn the Dark Master's ire. Now this. Was Sorin truly dead?

After a while, she blinked, trying to snap herself out of the shock. It was over. She was safe for now. She'd had to defend herself in a way she'd never wanted. But for now, it was done.

Miara made her way to the bath, which felt like an entirely too cold and unfeeling thing to do right after you'd murdered someone. But she wasn't touching his body again if she could avoid it. She was unsafe here, and she would be even more so once Aven and the others left in a few hours for Panar.

Looked like the time for escape had come. An hour or two earlier than she'd planned. But there was no way she was staying here now.

Water remained in the pool from earlier, and although it was as cold as the rock it sat in, it would wash off the blood. It would have been more frigid without the slumbering coals that still heated it a little from beneath. She scrubbed with the rosemary and lavender, again and again, and yet again, even after the blood was mostly gone.

She didn't call for help. Part of her feared that she'd discover more bodies in the outer room if Sorin had dispatched them. She doubted he could have bested them, though. At least not alone. But he must have gotten through somehow. Had he truly been hiding as one of the guards all along? Could the assassins have been helping him? Perhaps the creature mage assassin had transformed him or created a distraction. Either way—she would enter the outer room with caution and see what awaited her.

Something about seeing Sorin brought the seriousness of everything back. This was not a game played for votes. If Sorin could get to her, past all those guards, what would stop the assassins from getting to Aven?

It was time to go.

Shaking now, she climbed from the water and dried herself as best she could. Were her old leathers here? Yes. Not the cleanest, but she knew them best for traveling, knew they wouldn't vex her, knew the pockets without a thought. She pulled them on quickly and twisted her hair back into a bun. Camil wasn't there to use Miara's hair as her canvas for creative expression, nor would that be ideal at the moment, but she felt a pang of sadness. Would she see Camil again? Would King Samul be furious when he found out she'd left? If the king discovered how Aven had disobeyed him and helped her? Some might try to twist her escape as a sign that she *had* been the assassin all along, and if they hadn't believed her about the assassination attempt, how would they believe her about this? But it was a risk she had to take. Hopefully Sorin's body would be a clue that foul play was afoot.

At least, she hoped so.

Lastly, the dagger. She yanked it from Sorin's neck as best she could and returned to the bath to clean it. Gods, how could he do this? She had once counted him a friend. Someone she had come to believe was a bit of a fool, but she'd had no idea this hatred simmered beneath the surface. She had never realized he'd been indoctrinated into the Masters' ideology so completely. That he'd truly believed that mages *deserved* to be slaves.

She swallowed as she wiped the blood away. Anara forgive me. You steadied my blade against him. I will not waste this opportunity to fight for the other mages who are enslaved. Even the indoctrinated and foolish ones.

Once clean, she tucked the dagger into its sheath on her calf, hidden by her boot. Then she strode as silently as she could to the door, took a deep breath, and twisted her body into the shape of a small black spider.

Creeping under the bottom of the doorframe, she peered out as best she could with her strange arachnid eyes. There—one guard lay on the ground just ahead of her. She pushed the rising dread aside and stalked slowly forward, trying to survey the room as best she could, first with her eyes, then her mind.

No, it was not the guard, it was only the guard's clothing. Nine points of energy remained in the room. Eight were clustered near the door, entirely too close together.

One was sitting near the hearth. And now her odd eyes could see the ninth—a woman. A creature mage *had* been helping Sorin.

She stopped. Where were the guards? She spotted a wooden box by the door. Tiny squeaks issued from it. Mice. The creature mage had changed them all into mice and deliberately neglected to transform their clothes with the spell. That was one way to get a person naked.

Miara turned her focus toward the mage. Should she confront the intruder? Continue forward and sneak away? If this mage was here, then it was unlikely more were attacking Aven. If she could capture them, she could prove her innocence. Or could she? If assassins had disguised themselves as Miara, she had no way to prove it had been *this* mage specifically that had impersonated her and not someone else. Indeed, it was technically possible this was an entirely different mage. In fact, Sorin could have lied to this mage, and they might not even know his nefarious purpose. That meant Miara didn't feel justified in killing this mage too, if she could even accomplish such a thing.

The idea hit her all at once. The soul chain, that spell she'd bound Aven with not so long ago. She could trap this mage here and let the guards and whoever found Sorin's body in the morning sort it out.

First, Miara crept as close as she could to the door. Then, she plucked a bit of energy and twisted. Done. She'd spun a chain around the mage's wrists and then looped it through the workings of a heavy, ornate iron candelabra. That should take her a while to figure out.

The mage did not seem to sense the spell or react. Good. Sorin hadn't noticed it the first time she'd tested it on him either. Until it held its captive in place, it was a quiet little invocation. Preparations for her mission to kidnap Aven just kept paying off. She had never learned such a spell in any class; indeed, it probably ought to be on the questionable list, if not outright forbidden. But it had been there in the tomes, if you knew where to look and looked hard enough. She would have to remember to tell Wunik about it. Assuming she ever saw him again.

She inched her way out the door and toward the main entrance. Time to put her plan and Aven's maps into action.

# 12 THE ROAD

Jaena awoke to a glorious sunrise. Bands of purple and pink hues danced across the horizon before them. So they were indeed heading east. Toward Akaria. Toward freedom.

"Are we close yet?" she croaked, voice groggy with sleep.

"No. Unfortunately, it's probably a half day's ride away," he said. "We're not the fastest, two to a horse like this."

She nodded and realized suddenly she was nuzzled against his neck. How long had she spent like this? How uninvited, and she'd dozed off and left him to do all the work of getting them there. That said, he was enough larger than her that it was unlikely he could sleep resting on *her* shoulder.

"We need to stop and rest," he said. "Let's camp out in these woods for a few hours and then get back on the road when there are more people on it."

She only nodded.

"You can sleep some more or watch for trouble. Or

a bit of both."

He led them off the edge of the road and dismounted, leading Yada by the reins into a forest of tall oaks and ash and low ferns and other leafy things. The forest was thinner here but grew denser up ahead. But if they could get through it, it would also help to hide them from the road.

He found his way around it easily. Though he'd grown up on the streets, he seemed to know the forest well enough too. He helped her down, watered the horse, set down two bedrolls, and promptly went to sleep.

Why had he insisted on coming with her? She had a lot of questions for him when they were back on the road.

She lay beside him and considered trying to rest or listening for trouble. They were fairly concealed from the road, and the Devoted would have little reason to look for anyone at *this* particular spot. She and Tharomar had tried to leave no trail, but even if they had, any two lovers could have made a path back behind these brambles, not just a renegade mage and her—what was he, even? She had no idea.

She found herself blushing at the thought of two lovers hiding back behind these trees. Her imagination flirted with the idea for a moment before she brushed the heated thoughts aside. As if he could ever love a mage, with all he believed. Even if he *was* one, she seriously doubted he would ever consider someone like her. He was probably betrothed to some temple priestess anyway.

Besides, she could never love someone who could be convinced that something as beautiful and natural as magic was evil. Never, ever, ever.

Could she?

It was probably best if she didn't tell him of his powers. He didn't need to know, did he? It'd be best if he remained ignorant. She had seen self-hate do terrible things to mages in Mage Hall, her sister included, although for different reasons. She didn't wish such a fate on someone as good and kind as him.

Her sister had been good and kind once too. Gentle, until the Masters had gotten their hooks in her. She had still been a gentle person, but not when doing their bidding. For a while, Dekana had told her sister of her missions. They'd started as petty theft or eavesdropping, then slowly built up to more. One day, she'd come home and refused to tell Jaena where she'd been. What she'd done. No news reliably reached Mage Hall, so Jaena had never been sure what had been the deed that broke her, but her sister had never been the same after that.

Three months later, she'd been dead. They all said committing suicide was impossible, that someone must have killed her. Many eyed the Dark Master with suspicion when his back was turned, and he certainly deserved that. Jaena did not know which story she preferred to believe.

She hated her sister sometimes, for leaving her. For caring more about death than about surviving this hell with her little sister. For wanting to get out more than she loved Jaena.

She hated Dekana a little because deep down, Jaena knew. She knew that no one had killed Dekana. They'd had no incentive to; she'd been a valuable tool. She was of no use to them dead. She had just been strong and beautiful and fragile in her own way, and the Masters had pushed her beyond what she could take. And in many ways, Jaena liked to think that her sister had beaten them. Found a way out. That when it had seemed impossible to escape their torture, Dekana had figured out her own way.

Of course, if only she had held on. Just a little longer. Perhaps she, too, would be free. Jaena tried to blink hot tears out of her eyes and thanked the gods Tharomar seemed to be quite sound asleep. Why was she letting herself think about this now, as the morning light played cheerily through the trees? It must be the exhaustion.

None of it mattered. Nothing could be done now. She had to focus on what she could control. She couldn't save Dekana or stop the Masters from what they did.

But she could get revenge. And if the gods were willing, she would.

Without really intending to, exhausted mentally, physically, and emotionally, she drifted off to sleep.

Aven eyed the circling crows as he rode with the procession toward Panar. A month ago, he might not have thought anything of them. Knowing what he'd learned in the last few weeks, he couldn't help but wonder if they'd been sent by mages to watch him. Or perhaps were mages themselves.

Miara could have sent them. Wunik, his mother, or Siliana could be keeping watch via these friends from within the carriage.

Or they could not be friends, but enemies.

He sidled his way forward and to the center of the group, where the carriage bounced along, to ask if they had noticed the crows too. An annoying, icy rain fell over the group as they made their way. Too bad that it was against the Balance to twist the weather for his own convenience. It was one thing to tolerate an icy mist flying into your face with each gust of wind; it was another to know you *could* do something about it but probably shouldn't.

Aven had been riding toward the back of the procession, and his father toward the front. Thel swayed on his mount toward the middle of the pack, trying to read a small book even in the rain. Dom had stayed behind, as it was pure folly to have all three heirs on the road together at the same time. He would join them in a week or so, when the cave-in repairs were complete. Their mother rode with Siliana and Wunik in a carriage, but what kind of leaders would he and his father be if they relaxed in relative comfort while their men slogged along in this shit?

That said, he was regretting his "leadership" at this point. This far into the fall—almost winter—the cold of the wind and the rain combined could seep into your bones. He'd slept barely three hours, and most of that had been filled with feverish dreams, stoked to greater intensity by recently holding Miara in his arms. On top of it all, his boot would not stop rubbing his calf raw.

If Miara had been with them, she'd have figured out what the damn crows were about five minutes ago. He'd better get on that.

He finally reached the side of the carriage. "Any of you notice those... overhead visitors?" he called.

His mother leaned toward the window, peered up, and frowned.

"I'll take that as a no," Aven muttered.

She didn't reply to him but turned toward the other mages, though he couldn't make out what they were saying.

He ran his eyes along the mountaintops on either side of them. Three roads led out of Estun, and all of them took rather risky paths through the valleys and passes, curving their way down into the somewhat flatter forests. Following the riverbeds down the valleys was often easier riding, and it was also easier to keep the roads travel worthy, even this late into the year, when the rain turned them muddy but they hadn't yet frozen.

But what Estun gained in security in its mountain home, the roads gave up in exchange. They were not the safest way to travel. This was not a position any of them would have picked for a battle.

Since his mother hadn't yet replied, he extended his senses outward, as Miara and Wunik had begun to show him, to sense for mages. Not toward the crows, as his carriage-bound companions were already concerned with them, but rather toward the ridges above and down the hills on the other side.

His father had sent scouts ahead, of course. But they were ordinary soldiers. All their scouts needed to be mages from now on, Aven realized, or there could be forces in hiding that an average soldier was simply unable to sense. Unless they could find some kind of stone like those Devoted used to repress magic, but one that would detect it instead... He pushed the idea aside for now. He needed to deal with the task at hand.

On the range to his right, he felt nothing but the usual wind sweeping over the crags. But on the left one... What was it? Was something there? He couldn't specifically identify what he felt, but he caught a whiff of something... wormy, maggot-like, squirming. Could it be that peculiar yet familiar taint?

Slaves.

He couldn't feel them for certain, but he didn't need to to know they were there.

"Those crows are mages, aren't they." Gods, he hoped they were coming up with something.

His mother reappeared, face white. "At least three creature mages overhead—not animals under their control, mages shifted into crows. We think there are more—"

"Over that ridge?" he pointed.

She frowned. "We're not sure—there's something odd about their location. There are definitely more not far away."

As much as he wanted to press her for details—how many more, what type?—he urged his horse forward instead, weaving through the procession till he reached his father.

"We may have a problem," he told the king.

Samul raised an eyebrow.

Aven glanced pointedly up at the crows overhead, then bent to adjust where his boot rubbed his calf. Damn thing. "Mages. At least three overhead, more maybe beyond the next range. They haven't been able to—"

He never finished his words. A sudden bolt of lightning cracked somewhere close by. Aven's horse flung his head back, slamming her neck into Aven's forehead, knocking him backward off the saddle. Another loud crack sounded behind him.

Aven hit the ground with a thud, left shoulder first, his breath flying out of him.

Bloody hell. What was that?

He blinked, but all he could see was white. Another blink, then another, and the world came back into view, although the world seemed muffled and dimmed. The deafening sound left his thoughts and hearing cloudy.

He struggled to sit up. Another sharp crack, then another accompanied by a roll of thunder. Aven cursed, a sharp pain diving into his left side as he tried to right himself. Broken rib? Broken shoulder? Damn it, this was *not* the time for an injury to slow him down.

His mind raced as his pulse quickened. Lightning. Way too late in the year for storms with lightning. The storm—it must be unnatural. Damn it, he should have tried to sense for such a thing.

He may have only been trying to use his magic for

a few days, but he needed to get better at this, and in a damn hurry.

He finally made it to sitting. His horse lay on the ground before him, convulsing. To his right, his father readied his weapon. Thel and three more soldiers to his left drew their swords and readied their shields, swinging their mounts outward to face the ridges surrounding them.

What good was *that* going to do?

The thunk of an arrow bouncing off a shield made him eat his words. He should get to his horse—get his shield, or at least roll behind it for some shelter. He twisted onto his hands and knees with a groan as pain shot through him, and he had to stop for a moment and catch his breath.

"My lord—take my shield!"

Words finally cut through to his mind, and he looked up in time to catch the shield tossed by a lieutenant, who dismounted and came toward him.

"You're hurt?"

"Rib, maybe. Hell."

The soldier heaved him to his feet as Aven let out something between a growl and a cry. He gritted his teeth, but glancing at the horse, he knew it could have been worse.

That lightning had probably been meant for him but had struck the horse instead.

"You six, Asten—with me, up that range," Samul shouted. "Dyon—with Aven, Thel, and the rear platoon, secure the carriage and the far side. Go!"

Dyon trotted up on his horse, ushering them back. Aven let the stream of curses come, if it helped him get there faster.

"At least a dozen mages," his mother was calling as they ambled up. "We just found them. Mostly creature and earth. Just one air."

"One was enough, apparently," Aven grunted. "Can Wunik—"

"He's out cold, Aven. Derk too. The other bolt hit them both."

Aven winced. Those targets were not accidental. Someone had sought to take out all the air mages before the battle had even begun. "Can you save my horse?"

"I'm sorry, Aven. Wunik may be all right, Derk is breathing, but I don't think I can help—"

*May* be all right? Gods damn those mages, they would pay for this. "Get me inside the carriage," he barked.

He would be no good for fighting now. But he had a better idea.

Another stream of cursing later, and he was collapsed inside. Siliana leapt toward him. "Don't heal me," he said. "Keep it for the fight. It's just a broken rib."

She froze for a moment as if checking if his claims were true. Which, come to think of it, was probably a good idea. Every breath ached, so perhaps the rib was too close to a lung. But if the earth mages that had filled Estun with rock could also fill this canyon, Aven would much prefer Siliana and the rest save their energies for battling their enemies. If they even could.

Aven had something else to do.

Siliana turned back to the carriage window. Outside, vines thick as his torso shot from the ground and clenched around the carriage, then suddenly froze. Did his mother and Siliana have a way to stop their attackers? He had to trust that they did.

He slumped against the back carriage wall and closed his eyes. He had no idea if this would work, but there was no time like the present to find out. He drew himself out and up, toward the sky and the storm that the air mage had probably wrought. Even if the mage hadn't, it didn't matter.

He reached the rumbling energy of the clouds and the pattering energy of the rain, nearly turning to ice at this temperature. Outward, upward, a little farther and…

It was his.

He pushed the storm back, away from the carriage and his warriors and toward the mages. He poured energy into the cloud, stealing it as quickly as he could from what wind and sun he could find, rolling and tumbling the storm larger, the rain heavier, into a downpour.

The mountain floated by underneath him. A handful of archers were perched at the top, but he ignored them. He drifted along as the land fell away. There, at the edge of the forest—a dozen people hunkered down behind boulders and fallen trees.

Could he find the air mage?

A collision with the carriage snapped him back into his body. He was flung to the side—his left, of course—and groaned at the fresh agony. The carriage seemed to have slid several feet, and light peeked in from the corner up and behind his right side.

"Damn it," his mother snapped. "We've got to stop that, or we've got to get out."

"Weave a protective barrier. They're not the only ones with vines."

"No—trees."

Aven closed his eyes and seized control of the storm again. He had to trust them to try to protect him—and if they couldn't, to rouse him with the vicious pain of dragging him out of the carriage.

There—he found the mage force again. As quickly as he could, he ignited the fallen trees.

They burst into flames. Mages scattered, running. He threw flame after them without aiming or seeing if he made contact. He had to keep his mind on something else.

One mage remained still.

Then, for the first time, he felt something like what he'd felt battling Derk, but inside the storm. The other mage reached for control of the storm and nearly took it.

He shoved them back. They thrust forward again.

Aven ignited the ground beneath the mage, the tree behind him, but the mage snuffed out the flames. Damn. Aven had a lot less practice at this. What could he do to stop this mage once and for all?

The image of his horse convulsing on the ground flashed through his mind.

No—the thought turned his stomach. To kill with

his magic? How could he claim magic was not evil if he took a life with it? How could he—

Another loud crack snapped his concentration like a twig, whirling his mind back into the carriage. Did he smell... smoke?

*No.* He couldn't let go yet. He hurled himself back into the storm and again found the mage, who had by now seized much of the storm for himself.

He had to stop hesitating. He had to act. He knew the Code. This mage had nearly killed him, and this mage's companions were fighting to kill the rest of his family and all of their forces. If he'd had a sword in his hand, he would not have hesitated. To kill in self-defense was not evil. Indeed, he could not help anyone if he was dead, struck by this mage's lightning.

Still, he hesitated.

"Samul, no!" his mother screamed, breaking his concentration again.

Aven's eyes snapped open. His father rode toward them. Abruptly, the earth cracked apart, yawned like a gaping mouth before him.

The king and his mount almost made the jump. Almost.

Instead, they tumbled down into the earth.

Aven closed his eyes. There, the mage. Aven gathered all the energy he could muster and struck. Lightning sizzled through the air, once, twice, three times. Flames danced up from the earth.

The world whirled and went black.

Tharomar awoke to sunlight blinding him from a fresh new angle. The sun had been rising higher as the day wore on. Still, he lay unmoving with his eyes shut, hoping to sleep just a little longer if he could.

Next he became aware of the warm body curled next to him. Jaena. Her slow breaths meant she was asleep. A cold wind blew across them, and he was glad for her warmth. He opened his eyes for just a peek and discovered her arm stretching over his chest, wrapped around him. Her dark, elegant fingers rested against his ribs, an unfamiliar but beautiful sight.

Well. It was too cold for sleeping outside comfortably. He, of course, would never take advantage of such a situation. But he allowed himself a moment's flight of fancy, imagining sweeping her into his arms, pulling her close, burying his face in her neck and her braids, feeling her body against his. He noticed now, suddenly, details he had somehow missed before—a small scar above her left eyebrow, a tiny silver earring in her ear, the way one side of her mouth curved just slightly higher than the other.

Nefrana's blooms. He forced himself to sit up abruptly. Enough, Tharomar, enough. Not now.

He stalked away to relieve himself behind a tree.

When he returned, she was rubbing her eyes and showed no sign of remembering she'd slept with her arm around him. Good. They didn't need that awkwardness on top of everything else.

Or was it already too late?

No, damn it, he told himself. Get the brand out of Kavanar, get this woman to safety, and then you can find a dozen girls to sleep with. But not *this* one. Not that finding someone else sounded at all appealing at the moment.

Unless… unless it was her idea. He hadn't been the one putting his arms around her, after all. With that ankle, she was depending on him to get out of here, and he refused to put her in any kind of tough situation.

But if she put her arm around him again, he wasn't going to push her away either.

"Ro? Everything all right?"

Gods, he was just standing there, staring. "Uh, yes, just listening for the road. Ready to get going again?"

She stood, although it required a bit of lurching. "Listen, before we go *one* step farther, you are going to tell me what in all the gods' dreams is going on. Why are you helping me?"

He scowled. "Can't it wait until we're away from them? On the road?"

"No." Her voice was suddenly cold. No, she most definitely didn't remember throwing her arm around him last night.

Damn Devoted. "Well, can we talk while I roll up these bedrolls?"

"Yes."

He nodded and set to work. "Look, I apologize for not

explaining myself sooner. But I didn't want to press you so hard that you ran away, and I needed to understand who I was dealing with. I serve the Order of the Silver Grove, a sect of Nefrana's worshipers whose mission is to find and protect mages and to end the Devoted blight."

She blinked, incredulous. It was probably a big jump to make, he couldn't blame her.

"The Devoted... blight?"

"These 'Devoted' corrupt Nefrana's good name. They preach evil. They commit heinous acts in the goddess's name. They will be punished in their day."

"*The Book of the Vigilant.* The pendant."

He nodded. "The pendant is a symbol of my order. We keep ourselves secret until we are poised to take on the Devoted menace more fully. But in the meantime, we help folks like you. I was stationed at Mage Hall four years ago, waiting for my chance. But there's been nothing in all that time. That is, until now."

She blinked again, clearly struggling to sort through his words for truth, for any incentive to lie. He hoped she would believe him.

"Now can we get on the horse?"

"So you're telling me you're a priest of Nefrana who doesn't hate mages. And in fact, you hate the Devoted instead."

"'Hate' is a strong word. But yes." He shrugged.

She rubbed a hand over her face and looked as if she wanted to say something more but then stopped and shook her head.

He pointed at the horse, and she finally nodded.

Once they were on the horse and on the road, all packed again to go, he remembered one more thing. "Oh, and well, I'm not a priest." Definitely needed to be clear on that. There were no vows of celibacy for *him*.

"What *are* you then, exactly?"

"Oh, I'm just a blacksmith." He grinned.

"With a really dangerous hobby?"

"You might say that. But it led me to you."

"As I said, dangerous."

He smiled. "Danger has been a bit… lacking in my life as of late."

"Well, I happen to have an overabundance. I'm happy to share."

"Nefrana blesses you, my good woman, for your generosity."

She winced. Hmm, her definition of Nefrana did not include a benevolent, loving deity. He would have to work on that. Another example of the Devoted blight, driving a wedge between mages and the gods. "I don't think she'll bless me if I get you killed or captured by these Devoted."

"You're not responsible for the evil acts that they commit."

She pressed her lips together, as if she weren't so sure. "I still brought them on your trail."

"How did you become a slave?" He kept his voice soft.

She glanced down at the horse. "Knights attacked my family on one of those treaty voyages. Kidnapped my sister and I. She's—she's dead." Her voice broke on the words. The passing must have been recent.

"I'm sorry to hear that. But then it is *those* knights who put themselves on my trail. Not you. You were on a diplomatic voyage with your parents."

She blinked rapidly again, then rubbed her eyes. Were those… tears?

"And it's my mission to stop them, remember?" he said gently. "I chose this path."

"Why? Why did you choose it?" Yes, definitely tears, from the roughness of her voice.

He hesitated. He didn't like *thinking* about Sasha, let alone talking about her. But… "An old friend, from when I lived on the streets. She wouldn't come to the orphanage with me."

"Not the religious type?"

"No. And she had a boy. An older one, one she loved, who said he would protect her."

"Gods, let me guess. He didn't?"

"Turned her in for a bounty. I don't know how he figured out she was a mage. They slit her throat and left her body in the streets of Evrical."

Jaena sucked in a sharp breath. "Not… they didn't enslave her?"

He gritted his teeth. "Some Devoted only kill the mages they capture. Not all of them work with Mage Hall, especially those not in Kavanar. I guess no one in Evrical cared enough about an alley rat to capture her. She wasn't the only friend I saw killed, mage or no, just the one I cared for the most. Kavanar's colors must come from the blood that runs so red and thick in Evrical's streets."

"Oh, Tharomar." She twisted and met his eyes, concerned. He blinked. How often had she said his name? It sent a thrill through him. How often had he found himself, his lips just inches from hers, and resisted the temptation to kiss her? More than he would have expected in their short acquaintance. His eyes flicked to her mouth—no, damn it. Did he have no self-control left?

She seemed to notice something in his gaze, but he had no idea what. She leaned her head against him and nestled it into his shoulder again, this time not to rest, but as a sort of hug, since she couldn't turn as they rode the horse.

He took one hand from the reins and risked one soft caress of her back, the cloak rough beneath his fingers. Nothing more than a kind gesture of comfort, he told himself. Nothing more.

She straightened, and they rode farther toward Anonil in silence, his neck cold.

# 13     INTO THE DEEP

"Aven! Aven!"

His mother's voice. Still, he felt tired. So tired. He needed to sleep.

"Aven, damn it, wake up!"

A rush of energy flooded into him, and he snapped his eyes open. He sucked in a painful breath, as if it had been a long time coming. She was crouched over him, cheeks wet as she cradled his head in his hands.

"Don't you ever do that to me again!" she shouted. "You're going to kill yourself. You *stopped breathing*. You're going too far, damn it."

He sat up—or tried to. She'd infused him with energy but hadn't healed anything yet. The agony of his left side was plenty strong. He let himself fall back to the wet, muddy earth with a squish.

"What happened?" he coughed. Even wheezing that out felt like hell. What was that in his mouth? Blood?

"We fought them off. Dyon and several other warriors

took out the archers. Siliana and I kept them away from the carriage, just barely, until they lit it on fire. Then we had to drag you out—"

"Father?"

She looked away, up at the ridgetop, wouldn't meet his eyes. "Did you—did you take the storm?"

He nodded.

"Damn, Aven. You left a *crater*," Dyon said. "Those mages are either dead or thoroughly run off by now."

"Father—I saw him—" Aven insisted.

His mother's face twisted. Did he really need her to answer? He knew as well as she did. Something had happened. The question was what, and how serious.

"Is he dead?" Aven said quickly. Gods, let him not be. The heated words of the evening before flashed through his mind. This attack only proved his point, but would he have said the same things if he knew they were the last words he'd ever say to his father? His voice sounded strange, hoarse. He tried not to groan, but the ache grew. Yep, that was definitely blood in his mouth.

"Is that—I need to heal you, damn it." She ignored him, shutting her eyes and placing her hands on his chest. Siliana rushed to her side. Behind her, a fir tree abruptly faded from green to brown to black and crumpled into dust on the forest floor.

Gods. She was taking the tree's energy, for him.

So much death.

"Is he dead?" he shouted now.

"We don't know," Dyon finally said. "Thel and the

others are looking for him. The king fell into a ravine they opened up. When we went to try to find him, the horse was there, legs broken. But Samul wasn't. The canyon those mages opened stretched all the way to the river, and water had just reached us, so we couldn't quite tell."

"If he's dead in the bottom of that thing—" He cut himself off. He didn't want to finish. Heat built in his side, in his neck, at the base of his skull.

"I don't think he died," said Siliana. "I didn't feel his light go out, I tried to watch. I helped the horse let go cleanly, it didn't deserve to drown. I think the king was swept out into the river. Of course, that doesn't mean he's alive *now*."

"Now," his mother barked. Siliana bowed her head, and Aven discovered quickly why.

If he'd thought breaking the rib was painful, or falling from the horse, this was a dozen times more so. He could not contain the scream of agony as muscle, bone, and nerve rearranged themselves.

He must have passed out again because again someone was rousing him. Gentle slaps to his face and a muffled, "Aven, Aven, wake up."

He forced his eyes open a second time. Probably shock, not any kind of magical expenditure. The mind could only take so much pain before it shut off.

So this is what that boy had gone through. It was good to be alive, but... what a cost. Beyond worth it, but "agony" did not seem like a strong enough term.

He tried to sit up now, and succeeded, although his

head spun. He looked around for his mother but didn't see her.

"Where is she?"

"Siliana is feeding her some energy down by the forest's edge. They're okay. There are others to heal, so—"

He swore. "She should have healed them first."

"Beg your pardon, my king, but I believe she did the right thing. She knew exactly what she was doing."

He snapped his gaze to Dyon. Had he heard right, or was he just that dizzy?

Dyon lowered his head, acknowledging Aven's questioning gaze without words.

"He could still be alive," Aven said quickly.

"He could also be dead."

Aven swallowed.

"Until we know for certain, you are our king," Dyon said. As his mother was not Lanuken blood, the power to rule passed directly from father to son.

Aven sucked in a breath, mind racing. "What does this mean for the Assembly vote?"

Dyon shrugged. "Did that damn vote ever mean anything? Even if we vote against you, Samul always had the right to ignore the Assembly."

"He wouldn't have. Doing so could destroy everything."

"I'm not so sure. So could putting the wrong son on the throne, no offense to your brothers. But either way—it is up to you now. You could let us vote, perhaps abdicate if you feel you do not have our support. You could tell us our Assembly gathering is no longer valid, as you are no longer the heir, but the king. Which is probably what I would do."

Aven stared at his boots. When had they gotten so muddy? His whole body was nearly covered in mud.

"You could go in and slaughter us all, even."

Aven looked to Dyon with wide eyes.

"What?" Dyon shrugged. "I prefer to live, but lesser kings have done such things. And for good reason. If you let us vote, and more than half the Assembly votes against you, we could be looking at civil war. The death of a few nobles might be a lot more merciful than letting them pressure the poor into throwing their lives away for those nobles' own power. Think of the fighting that would ensue."

He did *not* want to think about it. He would make sure it didn't happen. Although Dyon did have a point. From the perspective of protecting his people, perhaps it was an option he should consider. He had no intention of seriously doing anything about it, though.

At the very least, he would wait to see how they voted. What was the sense in killing them all if some of them willingly gave him their support?

Gods be damned, what was wrong with him? He hadn't even been wearing the crown for a full minute before plotting the deaths of his enemies. These were *people*, damn it. People he'd grown up with, like Asten and Dyon. Even damn Alikar had a family to return to. Which reminded him.

"Where's Alikar?"

Dyon gave him a look that said he'd followed Aven's line of thinking. Damn, he hadn't meant to be so transparent. He'd gone straight from Dyon talking about murdering a bunch of nobles to asking for the location of his primary dissident. Smooth, Aven, very smooth. Fortunately, Dyon seemed to have no problem with this line of questioning. His nod said, *that's exactly what I was wondering too. That's what you should be worried about.*

"I'm not sure, sire. Let me look. Can I help you to your feet first?"

With Dyon's help, Aven straightened and brushed himself off. Then the lord circled the edges of the group, asking for Alikar's whereabouts. His mother and Siliana strode back from the forest's edge, looking full of life and ready.

Aven staggered to the gash in the earth left by their enemies. He stared down at the water lapping over the poor horse's dead form.

*Rest in a better place, in Mustaik's fields, my brother.* At least he'd fallen in battle. But the noble horse deserved a better end than this—long years in a green pasture, not a tragic, sudden death in this place.

And so did his father.

*Gods, let him be alive.*

Aven sat, head propped in his hands, under the temporary pavilion they'd erected against the rain while they searched. Footsteps approached, and he raised his head. Thel stopped just outside the canvas enclosure. His brother's blond hair, which usually hung to his chin, was tousled in all directions, and his normally pale blue eyes were dark, heavy. Thel shook his head, grim as the overcast sky.

No sign of their father. Aven sunk his head back into his hands as Thel strode away.

Moments later, Dyon strode up with Alikar at his side. Was he pulling the younger man by the fur on his cloak?

"You wanted to see me, my lord?" Alikar said, voice dripping with disdain.

"You've been helping our enemies. Tell me what you've told them."

"I have no idea what you're talking about."

"All right, if you won't simply tell the truth, we'll go bit by bit. How did they know when we'd be on the road and exactly which road we'd take?"

"They could have watched all the roads."

"Please. All of them?" That was possible with the crows overhead, but Aven wouldn't admit that just now. He wanted information, not to educate his enemy on the finer points of magic.

"They'd already attacked Estun. Clearly they were in the area," Alikar said.

"They knew when we left. You're a traitor."

"That's certainly one way to deal with your opposition, but you won't shut me up that way."

"The letters you've been receiving from Kavanar. Just

*who* are those letters from, might I ask?"

"It's none of your business—"

"Yes, it is, as a matter of fact. If you're feeding Kavanar's lies to our Assembly, I have every damn right to know whom you're getting your information from. And possibly whom you might be sending information to. Sounds like treason to me."

Alikar sniffed. "I won't tell you. Nefrana protects me and guides my hand." His words were sarcastic, proudly flaunting how little he meant them.

Aven would have liked to run the man through with his sword just then. Aven wouldn't, but he wanted to. "You can pray to Nefrana all you want, but Daes can't protect you here." Aven's bet paid off as Alikar's eyebrow twitched with recognition and surprise that Aven knew the Dark Master's name. The lord strove to hide it and keep his face blank, but Aven had seen enough. "I know you're working with Mage Hall. I think *you* delivered his scroll to Miara. I think *you* brought those assassins with you, at Daes's request." At that, Alikar paled, although his expression did not change. He hadn't known they were assassins, had he? He could have thought they were only spies. "I think you told them about the demonstration so they knew where and when to attack. *And* I think you told them when we left and which road we took."

"Those are tall accusations for a *mage* to make."

For a moment, Aven saw himself punching the bastard in the jaw. But he kept it together. "You're playing a dangerous game, Alikar, and I don't think you know what you've gotten yourself into."

"Neither do you."

"I am not the one whose choices led to the possible death of the king."

"Aren't you, though? We wouldn't be on the road if you'd simply abdicated your position."

"You forget your place," Aven thundered at him. The whole clearing fell silent. "If you're lucky, we'll find my father. But until then, I am king. You'd do well to remember that."

Alikar opened his mouth, but Aven cut him off.

"And if we *don't* find my father, I will hold you personally accountable."

"For what? You can't—"

Alikar was right. He had no proof. But that didn't mean he couldn't find some. Alikar would slip up eventually.

"I'm watching you, you bastard. Make no mistake."

Jaena didn't recall dozing off, but Ro's voice in her ear roused her. "Knights—up ahead," he whispered.

She blinked, trying to clear her eyes, and she could see them. Lucky that this section of road was fairly straight, but trees had begun to appear. The mountains that waited inside the Akarian border neared; they must be close. "Are we nearly to the border? Are they watching for us?"

He nodded. "And anyone else your friends might have freed."

He turned the horse off the road casually, as if they were stopping to rest it.

"If we can see them…" she said softly.

He gave another crisp nod. "They can see us."

She took a deep breath, steeling herself for battle. "What do we do? I wish I had my staff."

"Well, we could probably go through them." He squinted over Yada's back as she happily began searching for something edible in the late fall foliage. "We've taken six before. Know how to use a sword or mace?"

"I hadn't gotten to sword yet, but I'm probably less likely to injure myself with that than the mace."

"Here—put it on just in case." He handed her the weapon with the strap bunched up in one hand. She pulled it over her head and one shoulder and hoped she wouldn't need to use it. She was used to the longer range of the staff and hadn't gotten comfortable with opponents in close quarters. It would come with time, she was sure, but it was not something she'd mastered yet. "Alternatively," he continued, "we could try to go around."

He glanced to the north, and she followed his gaze. Her stomach sank with dread as she saw how the trees thickened. The density would help hide them, but none of the typical oaks or firs of Hepan's forests grew there. Strange, broad-rooted trees rose out of murky earth below them, roots poking out like fingers into the muddy water.

"Is that… a puddle?"

"Yes. Well, more accurately, I think it's a swamp."

"Seven hells," she swore.

"What?"

She waved him off. "Hepani have a different concept of hell than Kavanarians, I believe. Now is not exactly the time."

"Just when I thought I'd get something interesting about Hepan out of you." He grinned. "I'm joking. What do you think we should do?"

She kept her glance over her shoulder at the Devoted as veiled as she could. Even if there were only six of them, she would rather not risk it. It was not hard to get injured, or worse, as her ankle so delightfully illustrated. Maybe if they had a healer with them, or knew one would be waiting in Anonil. But they really had no idea what awaited them there.

Funny how easily she'd gone from worrying for herself to worrying about both of them.

"We might be able to handle them, but we could still be injured in the process. Possibly gravely."

"I'd prefer not to kill them either, but we may not have much choice if it comes to that."

He was a better man than she, clearly. Not that she longed for such a thing, but they wouldn't have blinked an eye at killing *her*. Self-defense was a completely different matter. "That swamp does not look promising, though. Any other ideas?"

"We could delay and see if they stay all night? Perhaps we could sneak by them in the darkness."

"Where's a creature mage when you need one," she muttered.

"What?"

"Nothing, it doesn't matter. Just trying to think if there's a way to involve magic somehow. Let's sit down like we're having lunch, and I'll think about it. Out of sight, if we can."

He searched a little farther into the woods while she monitored the Devoted. He checked out a few locations before beckoning her forward. "A lot of wet ground, but I think this will be not too terrible with a bedroll down."

She nodded, but her mind was working. What could she do that would not hurt the knights, but that would somehow allow her and Ro to pass? She'd survived her first altercation with Devoted by tunneling away—could she bury them in a cave of her own making? Something they could dig out of, but that would delay them long enough? Of course, that would also be a rather terrifying experience.

Breaking open the earth beneath them would likely kill them. But maybe she didn't need to actually trap them. Could she just… scare them a little? Or a lot? Enough to make them run away?

"Maybe I can frighten them away," she said.

He cocked his head, eyes twinkling. "I assure you, neither of us is that mud covered or rain drenched that we will frighten anyone." He sat cross-legged on one end of the bedroll and appeared to be waiting for her to join him on it.

"No, I meant with magic."

His brow furrowed, and he opened his mouth as though he might object. But then he glanced at the swamp and shut it again.

"If we go into the swamp, I might be able to bring earth up so that we don't have to trudge through the water, or at least less of it. But it's not easy, and the swamp is not a great place for a horse. And I'm also not keen on disturbing the swamp. That's against the Balance in its own way. I could try to return it to its natural state as we go, but it would be exhausting and imperfect."

He shook his head. "I know. I—I can't condone using magic, but if it avoids us having to kill them, or risk Yada... that seems worth trying."

At least he was practical. She wanted to point out that killing them would definitely be more evil than scaring them away with a few earthquakes, but she held back. It'd be better to make such a point when she was sure her plan had actually worked. For all she knew, they could end up in an altercation anyway. She lay down on half of the bedroll beside him, knees bent and feet flat to the earth.

A good position to connect to the soil.

"You watch, I'll work."

She had no interest in arguing the point further, since they had few alternatives, so she closed her eyes before he could respond. She sank her mind deeper into the soil, feeling the immensity of the water in the swamp that lay beside them, the way the roots of the trees curled down into the earth, the burrowing of the creatures clawing through it.

She couldn't quite feel the mountains, and she had no landmarks beyond the swamp's water to work with to know exactly where the knights were while she was this deep down. A creature mage would have been able to feel them, but not her, not at this distance. Not unless they started digging a hole or something. She would just have to guess.

She took in a slow breath, steadying herself. And then, as she breathed out, she pressed more energy into the earth, into the soil, activating it with her power. Letting it get... excited. Angry. Tense. She found the deepest plates, where the earth turned to rivers of heat that no one quite understood. Some thought this might be the first hell, but she doubted it. It felt like earth and only earth; there were no people there, at least not to her.

She searched for a seam, a rock, an edge, a boulder in the rivers of heat and earth. There—a fragile crevice. Anara forgive me for meddling in these things, she thought. And then, with a slight inward wince, she twisted, pushed. Rock slid over rock, shuddering and skidding, breaking.

Back in her body, she felt the ground shake. Ro grabbed her shoulder, probably out of instinct, and Yada whuffed. Horse hooves shifted uncomfortably.

She relaxed for a minute, two, maybe longer, simply allowing her mind to ride the flows of the deep earth.

Then again, she set one bit of the world against another, and the collision shook the ground beneath them again.

Now she let go fully and opened her eyes. He was staring straight at her, gaping a little. When he realized it, though, he looked away quickly.

"That was—you did that?"

She nodded. You could do it too, she thought. But she said nothing. She sat up. "Do we have any food? Let's eat, and I'll do it again. Maybe it can frighten them off the path. If not—I have a second idea. But it's best to leave it for nightfall."

He opened a saddlebag, withdrew something folded in waxed paper, and handed it to her. "For nightfall? Why?"

"You'll see," she said and took a bite of sausage. "Don't you want to be surprised?"

"By something you intend to frighten them away with? I'm not so sure about that."

Miara urged Lukor into a gallop in the direction of the storm forming in the distance. The tightly clustered, swirling clouds were too small to be natural, hanging low and close to the ground, nearly covering the valley ahead.

Aven's quickly sketched map had worked perfectly, and she'd managed to filch a few supplies before heading out the long, narrow tunnel. Flying till she found the stables, she'd discovered only a few horses were not already being prepared for the journey to Panar, and so she'd hidden in the stable's eaves as the horses and single carriage had been loaded and then led away. More than once she'd been tempted to see if she could spot Aven, but she'd been too wary of being noticed and imprisoned again in her rooms. She'd finally spotted him as the procession departed, riding down the long stone bridge into the early morning sunlight. Two hours or so later, she'd saddled up her gelding, the amiable and sweet Lukor, and taken off after them. The stable hands had all retired by then, as they'd been up all night preparing for the departure.

She hadn't yet made it all the way through the valley when the churning, bleak clouds had drifted behind a peak and faded from her sight. A column of thick smoke, dark as pitch, rose in its place, then another farther in the distance.

Damn.

Lukor pounded down the mountain road, fast as she dared to urge him. At the ridge just before the smoking valley, she slowed. If she simply rode straight out, she would reveal herself to gods only knew whom. What was over there? Or more importantly, who? And how could she figure it out without alerting them to her presence? She could dismount and check the place out, perhaps by creeping from the crest of the ridge to her left, but that might lose her precious time. She could transform them both, but she had a feeling Lukor was not quite ready for that yet.

She eased her mind out into the surrounding trees until she found a nearby robin. She tried to calm herself as she whispered a soft, musical greeting, warming it to her presence. It focused on her immediately, always keen on new creatures in its territory. It huddled with a group of other robins against the icy rain that had just passed.

*It's all right,* she whispered. *I just want to see over the ridge. Can you help me see what's there?*

In answer, the little bird jumped into flight. It—no, he—was happy to help, especially if it meant keeping an eye on his woods and rocks and worms and things. They were his, of course, and he needed to watch out for other robins anyway. She hoped he couldn't sense her amusement. The individual concerns and motivations of different animals were so interesting and unexpected to her, while at the same time universal—safety, security, companionship, curiosity. Common needs and motivations for people too.

She followed through its gaze. Her stomach twisted a little at the movement, but she forgot the sensation when she saw the wreckage.

A carriage lay broken and smoldering off the side of the road. One side had been smashed by a boulder that rested a few feet away. The first column of smoke came from it, twisting lazily into the sky.

A mound of fir branches lay over a large heap to the side of the road, the typical harried treatment of a fallen comrade during a rushed battle. Or perhaps the battle continued somewhere else?

The heap looked large enough to contain three or four bodies, maybe more.

Stranger still, a ravine ripped through the earth and split the road down the center. No such gash had existed during her and Aven's journey *to* Estun.

What the hell had happened here? And by the gods, where was Aven? And all the others?

The depth of her concern for Elise, Samul, Siliana,

Wunik, Thel, Dyon, all of them, even Derk, surprised her
a little. She hadn't known them long enough to realize
she might care so much what happened to them.

The robin hopped forward a few times, jogging Miara's
mind from her reflection and dizzying her a little.

*Let's look over the next ridge too,* she whispered. *There's
another column of smoke. Don't you want to see what
that's about?*

Indeed, he did, but not before he snatched a nearby
juniper berry and gobbled it down.

Over the next ridge lay an even more mysterious
scene. A fire had indeed scorched the earth here. Fallen
trees crackled as the hollowed shell of one collapsed into
mere embers. Flame must have spread to the surrounding
brush too, as much of it was blackened. The cold and rain
must have eventually put out much of the blaze. Strangest
of all, though, were three great black spots on the earth,
each about a horse length's width. They were all within
a few feet of each other, but not touching, randomly
dotting the earth among the charred trees and branches.

Lightning had struck here. Three times.

Or more precisely, a mage had caused lightning to
strike here. The real question was: to what end, and had
they achieved their purpose?

She had rarely seen lightning spells cast, at least not
of this magnitude. What occasion did anyone at Mage
Hall have to practice magic on that scale? The lightning
must have been brought down from the storm, which had
now dissipated, leaving weak, late-day sunlight shining

down on this desolation.

What the hell had happened here?

Whatever had happened, no one was left. She reached out more broadly across the valleys, sensing the usual mix of mountainous forest life, but no humans. She could ride on safely and investigate.

*Thank you,* she whispered to the robin, and he burbled a bit of song as he flew back to join his flock. As concerned as he was about his territory, it *was* cold, after all.

Now she urged Lukor around the bend of the road. Tackle the toughest thing first. She headed to the fir branches, her mind probing for life. Nothing, save a few flies. Death was the last thing she wanted to see. But hesitating would not bring whoever was under there back to life. Get it over with, see what worlds had been destroyed this day.

Who had fallen?

Could one of them have been Aven?

If the crown prince had died, the Akarians would have spared more time for a true burial, wouldn't they have? Or taken him with them? He could *not* be dead and just lying by the side of the road here for her to find.

Could he?

What if he had been betrayed? What if *all* of them had been betrayed? What if Alikar had taken control of the procession somehow, and she found the whole royal family cast aside here in a hasty coup?

By the gods, she hoped not.

She dismounted and strode to the heap, flinging back

a branch and refusing to let herself slow or hesitate. If he was here, she needed to know. Whoever might have fallen, she needed to know. Hesitation would not make it easier.

A horse. Chestnut colored and finely bridled, much like the mare she'd seen Aven riding into the distance.

They hadn't even taken the bridle.

Gold inlaid into the supple leather shone in the weak sunlight. Not a piece readily abandoned. Had they been in such a hurry? Or was this a matter of burial rites, of leaving some fallen warrior's weapon behind? Clearly they could have left the horse where it fell, but it looked like it had been dragged here. There were many footprints leading from the road and a wide trail of mud she hadn't noticed initially.

So the Akarians must have been attacked. The gash in the earth, the lightning strike marks, the strange vanishing storm—all these indicated magic at work.

Perhaps the mages that had caused the cave-in had followed the procession once it left Estun. Was it possible someone on the inside had told them when they were leaving and which road they were taking? And—then what? How could she divine what had happened from what she could see?

The Akarians must not have fallen, or their bodies would be strewn around the road, right? Instead, they'd had time to drag this horse aside and give it *some* burial and honor. But not a complete burial. And she was only a few hours behind them, so they could not have dallied long. But they had paused. Why? Had it been only for the horse?

She left Lukor looking for nibbles of grass while she strode to the rift that gashed across the road. Nothing about it was natural. If the same mages who attacked Estun were involved, likely many of them were earth mages capable of this sort of thing.

Water from a nearby river flowed into the bottom of the ravine. At the bottom was the murky outline of another fallen horse. Or was that her imagination? The weak sunlight did not adequately reach the bottom of the newborn canyon.

She traced the edge of the ravine down toward the river, whispering to Lukor to follow. Footprints covered the banks of the small river, perhaps the length of four horses across. People had searched here for something. Something had been lost in the battle.

Or someone.

She looked down the river, where willows dipped and hung lazily over the flowing, now unusually shallow water. What troubles would be wrecked on the animals living in the river by this sudden offshoot? Those mages should be ashamed. The gray willows swayed, peaceful and relaxing in a lulling scene of tranquility, the former chaos of battle indicated only by the altered water level.

Upriver, the water ran more normally, spilling down violently around a few boulders when it hit the detour of the ravine. The forest grew denser uphill. The river flowed out of the next valley to the west. Two smaller streams combined in a marshy area a bit up the hill.

She almost missed it, but then—up along the mountain, a weak column of smoke.

A campfire. Could surviving Akarians have retreated there?

Or their assailants?

*Stay here,* she whispered to Lukor. *Going to check this out, I'll be back.* She had to go as quietly as she could, and no horse would be anything close to quiet in the forest underbrush. If he could even fit under all that. He huffed a quiet acknowledgment. For a moment, she missed Kres and wondered where he was and who was taking care of him. Damn, now was not the time to get emotional. Focus.

She muffled her footsteps to some degree and began picking out a path toward the smoke. After a dozen steps, she caught the presence of a fox nearby and slipped into a similar form, careful to get it right and hold onto her clothes and equipment. Being smaller and lighter would make her both quieter and faster—and if she were spotted, not such a concerning sight. Just a fox, really. A wandering forest creature, nothing more. With the dried leaves crunching underfoot in spite of her best efforts, she was going to need all the help she could get. The mages—if they were who awaited her up the mountain—would have to be paying close attention to notice anything more than an ordinary forest denizen.

As she got closer, three voices caught her ears and were making no effort to keep quiet.

"We should head back now. We've lost too many."

A man.

"But what about him?" A woman with an unfamiliar accent. "We can't just let him go. We got lucky."

"Not lucky. Nefrana blesses us." A different man now, older and with more gravel in his throat.

"Oh, shut it. *Lucky*, with six of us dead? That's not what I call it."

Miara reached the edge of their gathering. Three figures sat around a campfire, while one stood pacing back and forth. She inched closer, squinting at those seated. Hmm, this fox's eyesight was blurrier than expected.

The woman shook her head, running a frustrated hand over fair skin and blond hair. The gravel-voiced man stroked a braided, straw-colored beard. The pacing one was jittery and nervous and pacing so fast she couldn't get a good eye on him, nor the fourth figure farthest away. This fox's eyesight was *not* its best quality. Perhaps she should have found a model creature that had sharper eyes, or simply improvised. Her vision could likely be tweaked and fixed, but there were also other things to spend energy on.

"Let's take him with us," the woman suggested. Miara struggled to place her accent but came up with nothing.

"On foot? With no horses? We wouldn't make it far."

"With so few of us, we should just head back. We've more than completed our mission. We've got no supplies for transporting a prisoner."

Prisoner? So the fourth one she couldn't make out was an Akarian? Miara wanted to snort to herself, but she kept quiet. The cowards were whining away about how hard it would be to keep the prisoner, and there were *three* of them. Alone, she had kidnapped Aven just fine. Although she hadn't had to do it on the spur of the moment.

She was a little too familiar with the task they were considering. Time to get more rescues than kidnappings under her belt.

"Plus those Akarians are still out there," the cautious, pacing one continued. "You want to run into them again and get toasted too? I'm not even sure how far inside Akaria we are, but we still have to get out."

Miara skirted the clearing as silently as she could. The mages did indeed seem familiar, probably warriors she'd passed within Mage Hall. The Masters would be proud; this nervous one was certainly a fine example of what they looked for in warriors—someone with absolutely no taste for battle at all. Hopefully that would come back to hurt them.

None of the mages turned out to be as familiar as the fourth figure. Getting closer, she finally made out who it was. Sitting silently beside them was Samul. His hands were bound with the heavy vine of a creature mage's making, no doubt. His majestic armor was smeared with smoke and soot and blood, and his hair and beard were slicked flat to his head. His helm was gone, and blood soaked the left side of his face and into his beard. He looked a decade older, and his eyes stared into the distance as if ignoring these mages. She could not tell visually if they had healed him and just not cleaned him up or if he was still injured. One of his legs jutted out at an odd angle, semi-straight, and she had a bad feeling it, too, was injured.

"I can change *you* into a horse. Perhaps that would help, or at least shut you up," growled the gravelly voiced one.

"Let's let him go," said the pacing man.

"The Masters would want him," said the foreign one. "Obviously."

"They didn't order us to take him. We don't have to do it. It's our *choice*."

Foreign Woman rolled her eyes. "They'll *kill* us if they find out we had him and just let him go. Don't be a fool."

"Let's kill him then. Don't have to take him back, don't have to tell them we let him *go*, of all things." Gravel Voice brushed his hands off each other as if washing his hands of the matter.

"Oh, like that's easy," sputtered Nerves, scowling.

"We can transform him into something else, make it easier to transport him," Foreign Woman said. "We don't need to have that debt on our hands. I thought you were concerned with the Balance."

"Of course I am," said Gravel Voice.

"You think Nefrana doesn't frown on killing people, but she's *definitely* against all things magic?"

"Don't oversimplify. You're just being emotional, after all the losses we've experienced."

"Eat shit, Harum. How's that for emotional?" She scowled at him.

"He's an enemy of Nefrana, of course. That makes

it allowable."

Why was Samul not reacting, trying to convince them of anything? She probed cautiously toward his mind, carefully avoiding the others. He seemed alert. His head did not seem injured anymore, but his leg was. Not broken, but something was wrong inside the knee. There, she found it—a spell binding his throat. They'd taken his voice so he couldn't call for help. Or argue. They had *that* taken care of.

*Samul. It's me, Miara.*

To his credit, his face barely reacted. A slight awareness flickered in his eyes, nothing more. He had been ignoring them all, lost in his thoughts, and she had awoken his attention. His thoughts whirled, and she backed away quickly.

*You can't speak to me. But I can speak to you. Focus on a thought, and I can see it in your head.*

*Elise has… a few times. Not a stranger to this.* Still, he wasn't entirely comfortable with the idea that mages could simply peek into a king's thoughts whenever they pleased. The one time Miara had done it had already been too many.

*I know. You're not the only who's felt that way. It doesn't help people get comfortable with us. But it's not without cost—*

*What are you doing here?*

*Rescuing you, apparently. What the hell happened?*

*I could ask the same of you. I thought I left you under guard in Estun.*

*Can we deal with the immediate threat first?*

*Fine. Mages attacked. Six or eight of them were killed, these three are not sure. I fell into a ravine trying to save Aven.*

Her heart jumped into her throat. If something had happened to him because she hadn't reached them in time, she would never forgive herself. Or Samul, for ordering her to stay behind. *What do you mean, save Aven?*

*Lightning struck his horse, threw him off.*

Mage lightning? *They were probably aiming for him and missed.* The exact arc of the lightning could be difficult to control at a large scale, and there was no reasonable way to practice.

*Oh. I didn't realize. That makes sense. Well, I don't think it hit him. The horse knocked him off, went into convulsions.*

*I saw the horse. It was dead. But there was no one else there. No human bodies.*

*Good. Good. That is good to hear. They all must have lived then.*

*They searched for you, I think. What happened after that?*

*Dyon dragged Aven back to the carriage. He seemed alive, although in serious pain. They were targeting the car-riage—both with fire and rock. I went forward to—I don't know. I don't know what I expected to do. To try to help? I had no way to help. But he's my son. I had to stop them get through to them end them somehow…* His thoughts started to unravel for a moment, and she pulled back, both for her sanity and his privacy. The tumult calmed a little. *The earth opened beneath me. I fell. Washed down the river. I think I lost consciousness at some point, maybe when I fell. I'm not sure, it's foggy. Then these bastards found me.*

*Are they the remaining mages from the ambush?*

*I think so.*

*What happened to the others?*

*They seem to think Aven killed them.*

*Aven?*

*I think so. Lightning struck and killed them. Six, eight? Seven? They're not sure. They didn't look to find the bodies, just ran.*

Gods. She reeled her mind away from Samul's for a moment, not sure he needed to feel what she felt at that revelation. *Aven* had been the one to leave those char marks on the earth.

She wasn't sure if it was awe or horror that filled her most. To kill with magic was what all the priests insinuated mages would do, if they could. They'd been accused of much, in the Dark Days. They'd all heard enough stories to fear there might be some truth to them—a vicious killer secretly lurking inside, ready at the first whiff of insanity to fly into a rage and level a city.

Brother Sefim's words sprang back to her again. Magic was a tool like anything else. Nobody was outlawing spears or swords or arrows or catapults any time soon. What was the difference between killing with magic and killing with a sword? She would not have been appalled if Aven had run these mages through with a claymore in self-defense. Such deaths were sad, regrettable, but not avoidable. If an equally—or better—equipped opponent was trying to kill you, you could die or fight back, but there wasn't much room for middle ground.

Self-defense is different, she forced herself to remember. Just like with Sorin.

Not that she didn't feel horror for killing him and splattering blood across Estun's pristine floors. Aven had been protecting himself, and so had she.

Back to the matter at hand. The Akarians had lost their king in this horrid attack. Fortunately, that loss was only temporary, although Aven and Elise would not know that yet. They had to be distraught. Sitting around feeling guilty about her and Aven defending themselves from people who were trying to kill them was really helping no one at this point.

She *ought* to be able to rescue Samul from here—somehow. These mages didn't seem like much opposition. If she could escape Estun, kidnap Aven, and then rescue him from said kidnapping—she should be able to make this work.

Just a little clever thinking and creativity…

She waited, but no ideas showed up.

Abruptly she realized that Samul could be trying to talk to her, but she was no longer listening. She dragged her mind back to him.

*They dragged me up here and healed the gash on my head. But… your arrival is well timed. Which reminds me, are my guards dead?*

*What?*

*Did you kill Devol and my guards to escape?*

*Are you serious?*

*Am I laughing?*

434 › R. K. THORNE

She struggled for a moment to formulate a response that wasn't dripping with vitriol. That he thought she would casually kill innocent guards and the honorable and sweet master of arms simply to gain her freedom infuriated her. How could even think such a thing? *Devol and the guards are fine. Devol is my friend and has been far kinder to me than* you *have been. To think that I would hurt him is pure absurdity.*

*I have not been unkind to you.*

*I guess that's a matter of opinion. This is not the time to discuss that anyway. I have work to do.*

*Are you going to kill* them?

She was so annoyed at this new accusation that she couldn't even bring herself to answer. Instead, she turned her attention to the mages. She picked at that bit of their souls she could reach with her magic and began to spin her chains around each of their wrists, one by one. When she had enough chain to work with, she hooked it around a nearby tree and bound it back on itself, once, then again. None of them were going anywhere, although they didn't know it yet.

Now what?

She *could* simply step out of the forest, help Samul to his feet, and stroll away. But they did all still have command of their magic. The woman seemed to be a creature mage, so it was possible she might find some transformation that could twist her out of the chain or even figure her way out of it with a bit of time. One of them was likely an earth mage—she was betting on

Gravel Voice—and if he could open one ravine, he could likely open another.

It would still be best if she and Samul could sneak away. But what could they do? Should she distract the enemy somehow? Could she transform Samul to somehow get away?

They continued to argue Samul's fate, although she'd lost track of their conversation during the king's recounting of events.

She glanced back down at the river. It wasn't far away. It could be an excellent and unexpected place to hide, if they could make it that far.

She felt around until she found Lukor, still patiently waiting and munching on a willow leaf, a selection he regretted. *Downstream,* she told him. *I'll meet you down there.*

Another mental chuff of acknowledgment, and he trotted off.

As she drifted back to her fox body, she groped around in the surrounding woods, looking for something to work with. Rabbits, owls, foxes, ants, snails, potato bugs, butterflies—no, no, no.

And then she found him. A stag.

No time for musical overtones and gentle greetings, she spoke quickly and prayed she wouldn't spook him. *I need your help. Some humans nearby have kidnapped a man and mean to kill him. Can you help me free him?*

*How do I know they won't kill me? Or you won't?*

*I swear by—by—* What deity did a stag pray to? *I*

*swear by the Balance I will not. I will do my best to protect you and heal you if injured.*

The stag chuffed for a moment, considering. And then, he said, *Fine.*

*I simply want you to cause a distraction. Show up in the clearing over here for a few moments, then flee. I'm going to make you—much larger. Then I'll shrink you back down.*

The buck liked the sound of that, at least the first part.

She pulled energy from the lively forest around them, a little here, a little there, and poured it back into the stag, his antlers broad enough already to interfere with the tree branches. He grew, ducking his head and dodging the entangling limbs. His hooves stomped in their direction, close enough for her to hear already.

And now for her part. Just behind Samul, she concentrated carefully. A fox would have to do for him too. Would the armor be too much burden? Would it matter in the transformation or act simply like clothes, which would come along for the ride if she worked carefully enough?

She was going to find out, apparently.

*I'm going to transform you. I'm disguised as a fox behind you. When I transform you, turn around, leave the circle, and follow me.*

*Got it.*

She waited for a moment, then another, only the sounds of their arguing over the late fall forest sounds—a few birds singing, winds shaking the last brown leaves from the trees. The stag's approach grew louder, hooves rustling the fallen leaves and thudding against the ground.

The mages finally heard it a few moments later. First Nerves heard it and tried to stagger back, but the chain caught him after only a step. He squinted at his wrists, confused. Then the blond turned toward its approach. Her hands caught on the taught chain now too, and she frowned down slightly at them, not yet understanding.

This was the time if ever there was one.

She spun the transformation quickly, and perhaps a little more carelessly than she would have liked. Some of the armor came along, but the breastplate clanked loudly to the ground. Nerves stared down in stunned, frozen shock, but not for long.

The stag had grown so tall his antlers spread as wide as two horses; he was larger than an elk now. Any larger, and he might have had points reaching beyond the tops of the closest trees.

He stomped viciously at the earth, huffing and snorting at them in genuine irritation. Then he slowly turned, as best he could through the trees at his enormous size, and leapt gracefully away.

Thank the gods, it was just enough time. Samul had raced past her, an orange-brown streak flitting down the mountain and through the brush and leaves. She raced after him, catching up quickly, their scampering somewhat hidden by the noise of the great stag striding away in the other direction.

Cries came quickly, though.

*To the water. Ever fancy finding out what it's like to*

*be a fish?*

*No. I haven't.*

*Today is your lucky day, my lord.*

Perhaps they didn't need to. It was an extreme measure, a stressful experience to breathe water for a time, even if it came mostly naturally while you were at it. As they reached the shallows of the water, she padded in, and the king followed her. They trotted downstream. Shouts sounded, but from how far away?

*Ker-thunk.* An arrow splashed into the water at her side. Oh—damn it. She hadn't seen any weapons among them, certainly not a bow, but her vision had hardly been good.

*Shunk.* Another arrow flew, scraping past her hindquarters and shaving off a chunk of skin.

Guess there was no avoiding it. She dove further into the water, water that as a fox, she could not swim in. But transforming while on the bank would not end well.

*Come on. This will feel a little weird.*

*As if this doesn't already.* To his credit, though, he followed her without question.

Just a little farther, and she began the twisting transformation, her furry body whirling away to be replaced with slick scales, flapping fins.

Gills. She forced herself to breathe the water anyway. The instinct that she would drown this way soared, but there was no way around the water rushing in. The river was dark and murky, and the current spun her this way and that, tumbling her downstream and bouncing her off rock and pebble.

After what seemed like an eternity, she calmed. There were her fins. And the water's surface. Where was the king? And the stag? If she'd known they had a bow and arrow, she wouldn't have involved him.

She groped around in the wet darkness. A few crayfish lurked, insects, frogs. No predators that she could see, thankfully, nor many fish. This would only be a brief swim, to hide them way and get a little farther downstream. But where was Samul?

He was not upstream. Perhaps he'd been swished farther on, or hadn't righted himself yet. She moved her mind ahead of her as she began to swim downstream, hopefully toward her waiting steed.

There—she caught his presence.

*Are you all right?*

*This is insane. And yes.*

She caught up with him and saw why he was farther downstream than she. Not only had he righted himself, but he was swimming energetically away from those bastards.

*You make a fine fish, my lord.*

*Thank you, my lady.*

*I'm no lady.*

*You seem to be making this rescue thing a habit. I believe rescuing kings and princes is a good way to earn yourself a title. We should have thought of that sooner.*

She blinked, although with her fishy, translucent eyelid, she wasn't sure what the heck that was supposed to accomplish. Well, maybe if he hadn't been so busy distrusting her, he might have thought of it. Would he say the same thing when he was no longer a fish? *If we're making a tally of valiant deeds, your knee should be healed too when we transform out of this mess of a creature.*

She left Samul's mind and groped back behind them, looking for the stag. He had escaped them but had finally succumbed to a tangle with a great blue conifer and a pine.

*Ah, it's you. Good. Turns out this great size is not as useful as I thought.*

She stifled a laugh and brought him back to his original size slowly, swiping energy from the algae and plants growing beside them as they swam. *As long as you're safe. Thank you for your help. May the gods smile on you.*

The stag chuffed and sprang away, newly thankful for his more agile, original size.

As fish, they swam downstream for what felt like an eternity. She groped for Lukor periodically, torn between hoping to get out of this form as soon as possible and hoping to hide from them indefinitely.

*I have a horse,* she told him as they swam. *He was trotting downstream. As soon as we reach him, we'll get out of the water.*

*You said there was more to explain about your escape. Care to explain why you defied your king's direct order?*

*My king? I'd begun to suspect I would never be more than just some spy from Kavanar to all of you.* Except Aven, of course.

*Answer the question.*

*A mage tried to murder me.*

*What? What about the guards?*

*They had been transformed into mice and trapped. Alive, though, thankfully.*

*What happened?*

*I killed the mage, bound the creature mage who'd transformed the guards, and escaped.*

*I understand why you'd kill a mage who attacked you. But why follow us?*

*Because I knew Aven would need me. Appears I was right.*

*Point... taken.*

*I'm not willing to lose him over politics. Or anything else, really. No offense.*

Samul didn't respond with words, but she saw his thoughts, likely ones he was not intending to share. A realization was spreading through him that she did truly love Aven. Probably not because of her words, but because he could feel, mind to mind, the emotion behind them.

She should pretend she didn't notice what he was thinking. She should brush it off, hide it away. What business of his was the depth of her feelings? That was between her and Aven. Although... if the king didn't trust her enough to allow her to protect Aven when she needed to and vice versa... then it did matter.

*He is the noblest person I have ever known. If it were the right thing to do, he would face down any foe for his people. And for you. And for me. And for that, I would do pretty much anything for him. Fortunately or unfortunately, it turns out that the greatest monstrosity at the moment is not that far from home.*

*Are you referring to me? To the Assembly? To Alikar?*

I'm referring to the Masters.

I see.

All right. I feel the horse. Let's get out of here and back into ourselves.

Indeed.

Well, this calculated risk had gotten a lot more risky than he'd originally calculated.

He sat down at his desk and began looking for his quill. The curve of Marielle's hip caught his eye, sensuous underneath the red linen of the bed. They *had* discussed their options for dealing with the king's mistress at length.

But it seemed the queen's problem was less about seeking the king's affections and more about seeking any affections at all.

Well, he shouldn't paint Marielle as indiscriminate. Impossible to say if he in particular was attractive to her or if he'd simply presented her with the opportunity. He hadn't even intended to plant the idea in her head. Such a thing was a little more risky than his usual style. But... she had large, endearing eyes and a reserved laugh that lit her face pink when she was pleased. She was a beautiful woman. It *was* possible he wasn't the only man to have taken advantage of the situation. He would have to question her on the matter. If this was a hobby of hers, everything became more dangerous indeed.

If, perhaps, she were actually taken with him... that

would be much safer. And much more preferable.

Gods, was he growing soft? Was that the slightest hope kindling that this *was* personal, that she fancied him and not just revenge on that retch of a king? He was a right idiot, letting himself think like that. Such attachments were a sure road to disaster.

Another possibility was that he was one of the few men in a strong enough situation to be worth this risk. A man with some forces to his name that would definitely obey him and not necessarily the king. If King Demikin found out about this dalliance, he could certainly try to have Daes hanged, or some other, more colorful end. But Daes also had a few ways to prevent that from happening.

And now it was time to ensure he had a few more. He finally located his quill and began to write.

There were alliances to be made. A plot was coalescing in his mind, and if he could reach Evana, she would play a part in it. With those mages working on a brand, he would have a replacement soon. Or he'd slit their throats and try three more. It would work out. His forces in Akaria had to be making an impact by now, and more would be headed there soon. Even the creature mage had delivered the address he'd requested of her, although it had come attached to a falcon that had dived at him and nearly torn off part of a forearm. He didn't expect that the address was the truth, although the building *was* the primary Akarian palace in Panar and a logical choice for such a meeting. More likely, it gave him one place *not* to look. But he had been more interested in whether she'd respond to threats, and it seemed she might be persuaded to, with the right ax hanging over the right person's head.

In general, things were good.

He glanced back at Marielle's softly sleeping form. Hmm, companionship of this type did have a way of making people feel more optimistic than usual. But he was certainly being objective. This was merely turning out better than the pessimist in him could have hoped.

He tore his eyes away from the luscious curves of her body. If he could finish these letters, he could return and join her.

This was treason, of course, but he had no regrets. Why was it perfectly acceptable for the king to cheat with a mistress, but he'd try to have them both hanged for doing the same exact thing? Well. No way Daes was letting that happen.

He hadn't intended to take on King Demikin directly—Daes's activities against his lord had stuck more to verbal criticism than anything that would actually undermine the king's sovereign power and authority. But Daes was probably being unrealistic. Conflict with Demikin had likely been inevitable. Destabilizing the kingdom through a war the king was ill-equipped to lead would make it all that much easier and play right into Daes's hands.

Was it possible to topple King Demikin? Or at least, set him off-balance? That could certainly only be good for Kavanar in general—and Daes and Marielle in particular.

Damn. He was a damned idiot.

He continued to write.

# 14 DREAMS & NIGHTMARES

Aven took a sip of ale in his room and studied his notes. No news of any mages reaching Anonil had been waiting, so he could do nothing on that front. Instead, he'd made a careful list of the Assembly members and was trying to think through what their reactions might be to the news.

His father wasn't dead. He hoped. But… what if he was? What were they going to say when Aven told them?

Their chance to demand that Samul change his heir had been stolen. Aven was now the de facto king. Scary as that was to think.

He had never been frightened of *being* king. But he hated to think that they would feel their voices were being ignored, that their chance to *choose* him as their king had been brushed aside. He had always hoped and planned to win their support. Realistically, he still needed to, but this wouldn't help clarify anything.

At the same time, it really didn't matter. Aven was not going to abdicate. Both of his brothers were mages anyway, no one else made any sense, and being a mage was not a good reason to give up the throne in a time like this, if at all.

But. He had hoped to let them have their say and *convince* them.

Dyon wouldn't regret the meaninglessness of the vote. He'd probably never wanted it to happen anyway, and this was all a giant inconvenience. Asten might feel the same way. She'd never been a rebellious one; she valued the chain of command, and the throne was part of that. But he still felt unsure of her vote; Shansaren's loyalty rested above all that. Generals could be bribed or hate mages just as easily as anyone, and she represented them quite faithfully. He hoped he had Beneral's support as a fellow mage, but he hadn't had time to broach the subject with him. There could be obstacles Beneral hadn't mentioned—or wouldn't. Just as Toyl had refused to give her final say on the matter. Aven had no idea how the two of them would react to losing their chance to deny him rule of the kingdom. They might not care. Or they might care a lot.

Alikar and Sven were likely past winning over anyway. But what exactly did that mean? Would it come to war exactly, and if so, when? Would Alikar try to withdraw his territory from the kingdom? Aven had thought that if the men had voted and voiced their objections, Samul would then have likely ignored them or chastised them, and eventually they would have either gotten used to the situation or the increasing conflict with Kavanar would have changed their minds. Well, maybe Alikar's mind. Sven was a depraved fool, but he was busy with his wine and women and therefore rather harmless. He was also the farthest from Kavanar with the smallest territory. He could easily spend all day with his head in the sand—er, more likely the wine barrel.

But Alikar would be on the frontlines of any battle with Kavanar. Unless he had already chosen a side—the other one. Unless he already planned to fight against Aven and the others. Then Toyl and Dramsren would be at the brink of the conflict.

Unease shifted through him at the thought, but he wasn't sure exactly why.

How could Alikar be taking this position? Did he *really* hope to gain power from it? Could he perhaps have more mundane motivations than power or religion? Could he simply have been bought, the way he had bought his seat? And if he had—what did that mean? Would he aid Kavanar in a war, as Samul had suspected? If he'd been paid, Aven hoped he'd been paid well for that kind of treachery.

He sat within Alikar's territory even now. He glanced at the door, listened, but heard nothing. Thankfully, there were plenty of forces with them from Estun, and he didn't need to rely on any kind of local protections. Aven would breathe easier when they reached the White City, though.

If Alikar had been bought, then he could turn his own men inward. He could promptly attack Toyl in Dramsren.

Unless… Toyl had been bought off too.

*Now* Aven knew where that uneasy feeling came from. He stared at his map, although he didn't need it to understand the implications. If both were bought, the treachery would slice deep into the heart of Akaria. Nearly every territory shared a border with Dramsren. Northern and southern forces would be fairly divided, except for a stretch of extremely rugged forest terrain in Shansaren in the far east.

Gods, let it not be so. Aven wished Toyl hadn't gone on ahead of them, that he could go and talk to her now and convince himself he had nothing to worry about.

But, of course, he was a king now. He would always have things to worry about.

Like the fact that Alikar already knew Samul could be dead. If he truly was a traitor, could he have sent the word into Kavanar already? Maybe even now Daes was lifting a goblet of wine to celebrate the news. Maybe even now they moved to act again.

Yes. He had no proof, but he knew it must be true. Even if it wasn't Alikar, there had to be some spies, especially in Anonil. If any of the mage slaves forced into the attack had survived, they would likely report back the results of their attack. He winced. He hoped some of them had survived, as none of them had chosen that path, just like Miara. He shouldn't even have killed the one that he had, although it had hardly felt like he'd had a choice.

He refocused his thoughts on Kavanar. On Daes, the Dark Master. If he were Daes, what would he do?

If a more serious attack were an option, if he had control over the forces or could convince the king, this would be a good time. They wanted to draw Akaria into Kavanar, but as yet, Akaria hadn't taken the bait. Perhaps he was eager to get things started. Things wouldn't get any more unstable than this.

Instability that one could easily argue had all been caused by Kavanar, exactly according to Daes's plan.

He turned his gaze to the map of Akaria. Where? Where did it make sense to come into Akaria?

Anonil, this very city, made the most sense to Aven. If Alikar had been bought, he was probably offering little resistance. Kavanar could likely wipe out the Assembly and Aven with the right attack while they traveled. Luckily, they hadn't been traveling that long, and Kavanar didn't have the most mobile military.

Then he thought of the scroll Miara had received, requesting the details of the meeting place for the vote. If Kavanar knew the meeting was happening, they would attempt to target the event somehow. The White City was not as small as Anonil and was better defended, but it was no fortress. The seaside merchant city had walls and gates and guards, but it was a hub of commerce. Many came and went everyday as a matter of routine.

If he were Daes…

So far, Daes had favored the clandestine route and the use of mage slaves in all of his attempts. He'd expressed disdain for such tactics, but perhaps King Demikin still stayed his hand. Or perhaps he acknowledged it was the smart way to fight the early battles in a war with a superior force. Either way, Kavanar's traditional army remained at rest. The cave-in, the assassination attempts, the ambush—although it'd been the most straightforward, even the scroll left in Miara's room. He felt uneasy at the thought of that yet again but pushed it away. If Daes remained consistent, he would send some kind of ambush or assassin to the meeting place. If he could figure out where exactly the meeting took place. He still needed to think of a way to save Miara's family, but he grudgingly set the thought aside for now. One problem at a time.

And even with the false information Aven and Miara had sent, Alikar could be—and probably was—still in Daes's pocket. Any number of people could betray the meeting point, although of course Dyon hadn't chosen it yet.

Aven sighed. Getting them all together was inherently risky. This was partly why his father had ordered Dom to remain in Estun. Someone had to, Miara not included, in case of extreme disaster. Perhaps Aven should have more seriously considered using magic to be present, as his mother had with the light images Beneral had helped her create in order to visit him during their journey. Apparently he had done it from a great distance, while traveling to Estun at her request. He, Miara, and Beneral may have even passed each other on the road. How the spell worked, though, Aven did not yet understand.

But not showing up in person and only in the form of eerie blue light did not exactly emphasize that he was the same warrior they'd known for his entire life. And it did emphasize his newfound, questionable abilities.

No, they had to get together in person, and it would be risky no matter what. Aven would do his best to secure the location with their forces, but there was no way around the danger of everyone gathering in one place.

A knock shook the door. "It's me." His mother's voice sounded ragged.

He hung his head for a second. He didn't want to answer. He had to make sure he had figured this all out. He had to make sure he knew what he was doing on all these different fronts. He had to stay one step ahead of these people.

He could not stop and think—or feel—about what it might mean for his *father* to be dead, especially with how they'd last left things. But he had a feeling that would be a lot harder staring his mother in the eyes.

"I have news," she said, as if she understood his hesitation.

"Come on in."

She opened the door. Another haggard-looking woman accompanied her, hair hanging limply and riding leathers drenched from either sweat or rain or both. Two soldiers escorted her and waited outside the door while the two women came in.

"The riders you requested will be leaving within the hour to return and search for Samul," his mother said. "Also, we've received news from Kavanar."

The wet woman bowed. "I've seen troops mobilizing,

sire. From the central fort. Soldiers, cavalry, and siege troops, headed south."

"Not this way?"

She shook her head. "No, my lord. Of course, they could have changed direction. But they didn't take the East-West Road that leads here. They started out on the Tryalt Road toward Evrical, but I do not think that's where they are going."

"Anything else?"

She shook her head, then hesitated. "Well… some soldiers speculated they were headed toward Evrical, my lord. Others speculated the White City. But they did not seem to really know. They only had orders to start to move south, from the queen."

"The queen?" his mother started.

The spy nodded again. "I thought that odd as well, my lady."

"Thank you—what is your name?" Aven asked.

"Shanse Rego, my lord."

"Thank you, Shanse. See to it that you get a hot bath and meal and whatever you need before you head back."

"Thank you, my king." She bowed and left them, but not without the words shaking Aven a bit. He had hoped to hear those words eventually… but not like this.

His mother shut the door after Shanse. "My bird returned from Estun after relaying the news," she said. Dark circles hung under her eyes, their color dark like the ocean, without any of their usual sparkle.

"Did she bring back news as well?"

Elise nodded and sank into a nearby chair, as if she needed the support but hadn't quite even made the decision to do so. "I don't... I have some bad news."

His heart thudded against his ribcage.

"Miara?" he whispered.

His mother closed her eyes, pain creasing her face. "A dead man was found in her room, stabbed in the side of his neck. Another, a woman, was found dead in the sitting room. At some point, the guards had all been transformed into rats. Someone transformed them back, but it's unclear who." She opened her eyes.

"Did they— What about—"

"There's no sign of her specifically. One horse in the stable went missing the afternoon after we left. No one is quite sure what happened."

Aven cursed. He should have stayed. He'd been there only hours before that. He pushed his chair away from the table and propped his head in his hands and his elbows on his knees. Was she okay? Had Daes figured out they had no intention of hosting the meeting at the location Miara had provided? How could he, if they weren't even set on a location yet? Was this simply revenge for her escape from him in the first place?

By the gods. Not his father *and* Miara. Not—

Before panic and despair could overwhelm his thoughts, he forced them still. He didn't know anything for sure. She'd been planning to escape and had his maps, and one horse *had* disappeared. She might be fine. And right now, people needed him. A damned war was still about to start, and traitors lurked in their midst.

And he would have to face it without Miara *or* his father.

No. He forced his mind back to the practical matters at hand. He couldn't process that now. Wouldn't. Didn't need to. Didn't matter.

"So she could be…" He couldn't bring himself to say it. "She could have escaped from them?"

His mother nodded. "Yes. Or she could have been captured or killed, and we just haven't found evidence yet. Dom is organizing a search. But either way, we don't know where she is at the moment. I thought you would want to know."

He nodded. He appreciated her choice of the word "is" there. Of course, she probably knew exactly how he was feeling but on a magnitude he didn't yet understand. His mother came closer, patted his shoulder for a moment, and then gave him an awkward hug. He leaned into it but couldn't bring himself out of his slump.

"Also, one of the riders seeking our elder mages returned. Elder Staven was dead, seemingly of natural causes. The other rider is still out and long overdue to return." She squeezed his shoulder. "I'm sorry, Aven. I'll be next door if you want to talk." And with that she left him. He breathed a sigh of relief. It really was easier to pretend his father was nearby when she wasn't in the room.

Damn it all to hell. Where could Miara be? And if they'd taken her, where could they have taken her to?

He knew the answer to that immediately. Mage Hall, of course. They'd enslave her again.

Wunik was long asleep by now. Would it be worth it to wake him so they could look for Miara in the pool of light? Aven hadn't yet tried the spell alone, although he'd heard more than a few explanations of how it worked. No way was he asking Derk for help, even if the lout was mostly recovered from the damage from the lightning strike.

He glanced at the water basin. The innkeeper had brought up steaming water, a bundle of lavender, and lush towels that Aven had as yet ignored. The lavender only made him ache for her. This inn was nicer than any he and Miara had stayed in on their journeys. Why hadn't they lucked by this one? Perhaps because of timing; the larger group traveled slower. Or perhaps the larger group needed a larger inn, but one off the fastest route. It didn't matter. How silly, though, that he wished he were back on that journey toward Mage Hall. At least then, he'd had Miara by his side.

And known she was alive.

He eyed the water again. Could he try the farsight spell? No harm in trying it, was there? Wunik hadn't mentioned any risks to avoid.

He stalked toward the water, then remembered Wunik's blessing. Optional, he'd said, but it couldn't hurt to have a bit more luck on his side at the moment.

A bunch of small mums were gathered on the desk in a small vase. Did the inn put flowers in all the rooms or just the king's room? No matter. He plucked a petal from one and tossed it into the water with a silent prayer, then shut his eyes.

Wunik had spoken of the task like opening a window into the air itself. He pictured opening a window in the middle of the sky outside the inn. If he could just get that working, it'd be a miracle. He struggled to imagine it, add detail to the picture. Nothing happened. He didn't even need to open his eyes, he could feel that no energy had been released.

Wunik had also described it as similar to opening your eyes. Or more accurately, another eye, a third one that you could move wherever the air reached.

Aven squeezed his eyes shut, picturing the sky above again.

And then, slowly, he opened them again.

He'd thought the bowl would fill with light, as Wunik's had. But instead, a darkness spilled across the bowl and opened outward, filling the formerly cream-colored water basin as though the water had turned to ink.

But there in the center, he could see it. The inn. It was working.

Did he remember the road, after the last few times going there? Could he slide his way all the way to Mage Hall? If he recalled, it was a fairly straight shot along this particular road…

Miles flew past. Although night, the occasional rider or wagon was still visible. Could any of them have been the mages he'd tried to free?

The road and night grew darker as he went and clouds covered the moon. He lost track of the road in the darkness. He had no idea what he was seeing, which way he was headed. He just had a feeling, a direction. He'd just have to listen to his gut.

And then a village floated by, then another, and then he could see it. Mage Hall and the sea of wheat waving in the wind around it.

Wait. Miara wouldn't be here yet. She and her captors would still be on the road, or they would have passed his party. Wouldn't they have? How long would it have taken if they'd flown the whole way? He had no idea.

But much as he was concerned for Miara, he had to admit he knew why he was here. It was not because he expected to actually spot her there.

Daes.

Could he catch a glimpse of what the man was up to?

Aven moved the eye toward the Master's Hall, the great hold where he'd spent such a lovely time. His shoulder panged, and the image wavered for a moment. He rubbed the spot with his hand and tried to brush it off. Oddly enough, it wasn't the brand that still gave him phantom pains, but the burns on his shoulders and chest, long since healed away with Miara's magic. No one would ever know from looking there had been a wound there. But apparently his body—or his mind—had not forgotten.

No activity in the grassy fields in the center. Pairs of guards patrolled—two, three, maybe more? Far more than when they'd started. If Aven couldn't spot Daes or Miara, he could at least try to see if Menaha, Kae, or Sefim had escaped.

He swung the eye around the other side of the building

just in time to see figures getting into a carriage. Odd. Why would they be leaving at this time of night? A secret departure? Who could it be? And where could they be headed?

Aven swooped closer as the carriage door shut and the horses started off. It took all his concentration to follow behind the carriage and move closer. Perhaps if he got alongside the door, he could see through the carriage window.

A bead of real-life sweat rolled down his forehead and into his eye, breaking his concentration. The image faltered as he fell behind the carriage.

Aven wiped his brow with the back of his hand and quickly grabbed hold of the basin, willing his mind to focus, to hurry up.

He caught up with the carriage again. The carriage windows were drawn shut with a curtain. Damn it.

He almost gave up and let the image dissolve. To stop chasing the carriage at that precise rate was very tempting, to say the least. But—air mage, right.

He directed an overzealous gust of wind toward the carriage's door, which banged against its fastening a bit. But his ploy worked. The curtain was blown aside, and he caught a glimpse of three people. An older man, a girl, and Daes.

Could it be…

Sure, the man and girl could be Daes's family, although he didn't seem like the type of man who had any family or who spent any time with them if he did. Or simply some other folks related to one of the Masters, or even Daes's servants.

Or... could they be Miara's father and sister?

Perhaps Daes *had* received word of the attack from his mages and the confusion over Samul. Perhaps they *were* moving to act. The spy's confirmation supported this theory as well. If Daes meant to strike while chaos swept Akaria, he could be headed south with the troops right this very instant.

If he'd had Miara killed... if he knew she were no longer a threat... he wouldn't bring her father and sister with him somewhere.

Of course, he had no real proof that these people were Miara's family. Aven pulled back and followed the carriage from an easier, less precise distance. They could simply be his servants. But a young girl? No, this must have to do with the scroll. What if Daes was keeping her family with him so he could make good on his threats?

Aven followed the carriage doggedly for some time. It rode straight south and did indeed pass a fort, where many additional soldiers were camped outside—not their permanent accommodations. Some of Kavanar's forces were indeed moving south. The carriage traveled even farther south, it seemed.

Just outside Evrical, in the swampy marshes that dominated the southern borders of Kavanar, the carriage finally reached its destination. Daes, the man, and the girl got out of the carriage and headed into one of the king of Kavanar's three residences—Trenedum Palace. As far from Estun as it could probably be, the white marble building lounged amid the marsh and swamp, mosses and ferns draped across it like scarves. Vines crawled up the sides, and many-paned stained glass windows alternated between majestic white columns.

What were they doing here?

A woman strode down the front steps to greet them. Aven peered closer. It was nearly pitch-black in the night, save a few guards and torches. The woman wore a green dress and her eyes were round with… excitement, joy? A gold crown, adorned with rubies and horn-like spikes, circled her brow.

The queen of Kavanar? Greeting them, alone at night?

Daes took both of her hands in his with a bow and a kiss. Not a wholly inappropriate greeting… but Aven's gut told him something more was at work here.

The four of them went up the stairs and into the mansion.

Exhausted anyway, Aven released the spell and collapsed back onto his bed, closing his eyes. What did any of *that* mean?

He had so many pieces. How was he supposed to put any of them together when—

No. He couldn't go there. He had to keep going, keep thinking straight. There would be time to process after they reached Panar, after the vote, after everything settled down again.

If it ever settled down again.

Miara might be there waiting for him. Everything might be fine. Perhaps she'd just encountered unexpected resistance in her escape. If she wasn't in Panar, he would have time to head to the lake and see if she waited there. And if she didn't… there would be time then to fall apart and try to figure out how to put the pieces of his life back together. He rolled onto his side, kicking off his boots, and willed himself to just collapse in the oblivion of sleep.

Not so long ago, he'd have been tied to this bed, he thought. And he'd have had Miara at his side. He opened his eyes and stared at the dull, silver-gray wool blankets that lay too undisturbed and neat beside him.

Gods, what he wouldn't give to have her by his side again. He should have never agreed to let her stay behind, despite his father's concerns.

What if something had happened? What if he never saw her again?

There were no answers to these questions. He struggled to tamp them down and urge himself into the oblivion of sleep. He tossed and turned for what seemed like an eternity, and when sleep did come, his dreams were flooded with the same dark, unanswerable questions.

Jaena's earthquakes had rattled the Devoted a little, but their dark hoods remained at their posts in the center of the road.

"What are they doing?" she asked Tharomar.

Darkness had fallen, so their locations were unclear. "I think they're still there, just sort of clumped together," he said.

"Damn."

"About time for that other idea of yours?" He raised an eyebrow.

She nodded. "Let's get our stuff together. We might have to follow them, or at least be ready to run."

"Run toward them or away from them?"

"Either."

"Seems like a very detailed plan. You give me such faith."

She shrugged. "You seem to have plenty of faith without me giving you any." She had no idea if this would work. Of course, venturing into the swamp now that darkness had fallen would be much harder, so she hoped she'd get lucky. She couldn't imagine her and Tharomar attacking the Devoted at the moment, not when heading into the swamp could avoid it. So if her ploy failed, the swamp was next.

As he gathered up the belongings that they'd scattered in the course of the afternoon and early evening, she gathered her thoughts and marshaled her energy. She didn't know what to expect or if this would work, but that dog that she had dredged up certainly seemed to have scared off the Devoted in their first encounter while she'd hidden in her man-made cave. Maybe she could do the same thing again.

But another dog? Would that do the trick? One lone dog approaching six men, and no other dogs to send after him? That didn't seem like enough. What about...

maybe a form more like a man.

But bigger.

Yes, that would be it. A lot bigger. And the swamp was full of plenty of muck to meet her needs. She closed her eyes, bunching the mud together, visualizing a giant. Much taller than her, taller than Ro, although they were both tall. This creature would be taller than three men high, maybe a little more.

Although she couldn't yet see it, she could feel the muddy form rise from the swamp. Globs of dirt dripped from it, splashing back into the water as it rose. It took a step forward, the earth trembling beneath her.

She beckoned it forward another step, then another. The thuds grew louder as it neared them and staggered toward the road.

"Is that... Are you doing that?" Ro had sunk into a tense crouch; he must be hearing it, maybe seeing it too.

"Yes," she whispered. "Don't worry. It's just mud."

"Last I heard, mud doesn't exactly get up and walk on its own." He took a step back, then another. She wondered if he realized what he was doing. Yada shifted nervously nearby.

"All right, well, it's me and the mud. Unless you want to go clobber them with that mace?"

He winced. "Point taken."

"Can you comfort her? If the creature just scares the Devoted farther down the road, we may need to walk along behind it."

He nodded, remembering himself and creeping over

toward the horse.

All the while she brought the mud man forward, step by step. Maybe she should have started closer because now it seemed like an endless hike to get those damn Devoted. But it was too late for that now.

She ducked low and crept closer to the edge of the road to see better.

The Devoted all turned to face her abruptly. She stifled the urge to hide. They couldn't see her hidden in the dark. They could, however, see the outline of a monstrous black form against the early night sky. She could see it too, for that matter.

She picked up the pace, but the concentration required was grueling. One step, then another, then another. All of her mind strained to bind the creature together, to grip each piece as it moved forward, to make it as intimidating and menacing as possible.

Gods, let this work. After this effort, she would be drained. She and Ro might end up sleeping by the side of the road for the night anyway, having made no progress. It was much too cold for that, unless they huddled together for warmth. That didn't sound so bad…

Focus, girl, focus. But what the seven hells would this group of Devoted do if the creature actually reached them?

That might be a weakness in her plan. She'd counted on frightening them away first. If she—the creature—reached them, she had no idea what to do. Well, she'd cross that bridge when she came to it. Maybe she wouldn't need to.

*Thud. Thud.* The creature thundered forward. The

Devoted Knights clustered together. Did they have weapons raised? She squinted into the night. Crossbows? It was too far to know for sure.

Not that crossbows could hurt mud.

However, it would be good to know if they had ranged weapons. If she and Ro were thinking about making a run at them. Much as they both wanted to avoid that.

The creature was about fifty yards away now. One of them stepped forward, shouted something she couldn't quite make out in the night. He raised something in both hands.

A crossbow bolt struck the mud. The creature felt no pain, just one more bit of debris sloshing around inside its glopping body of wet clay, sand, and stone. She made certain not to react and simply took another step forward. Then another.

She was getting closer now. More bolts fired. Another step. Another.

Her mud monster was only about ten paces from them now. They staggered back a few paces, reeling, but intent on holding their ground. Two weighty logs blocked the road, a barricade to slow down any who approached. Maybe she could use those logs for something.

She focused on the creature's arms, the hands that until now had been unformed. Via the creature, she crossed the last two steps before their barricade and seized one of the logs. The men scampered back, out of reach. Just as well, since she didn't want to hit them. Well, maybe only a little.

She heaved the log into the air and then hurled it off into the forest, as though it weighed nothing, as though it were no strain at all.

The second former tree she seized and lifted up over the creature's head. She held it for a moment, wondering if they would perceive the threat or if the intentions of a monster made of mud were too hard to read.

Apparently they could figure it out. Four Devoted scampered back, twisting and breaking into a run. Someone swore.

Two still remained. She thundered another step forward. They responded with more bolts fired.

Hmm. They seem determined to stand their ground.

She could hurl the log at them. That didn't exactly accomplish the goal of not hurting them, but it probably wouldn't kill them. Probably. Hard to judge weight or the creature's strength via the mud. Was there something else she could do? Why wouldn't these damn men get out of her way? What had she ever done to deserve any of this? What could possibly motivate people to devote their whole lives to simply hunting down other people for their magic? Were they jealous? Bored? Had they been personally wronged? She doubted it.

Any personal wrongs were unlikely to measure up to *her* personal wrongs. Had *they* been torn from their families? Had *they* lost a sister to this mess? She wanted to scream at them, roar out her frustration—

To her surprise, a horrifying sound erupted from the creature. Neither scream nor roar, exactly. Which made sense, considering the creature didn't have vocal cords. In fact, she wasn't sure exactly how it created the sound. Rocks tumbled around amid the mud, and they shook and collided as the creature shouted its rage at them.

She slammed the log to the ground just before their feet. It collided with the earth, dust rising and shaking everything around them. The two men finally stumbled back, arms askew, struggling to keep their balance.

She lifted the log again. Another bellow erupted from the creature made of mud.

Finally, finally, they turned and ran, racing toward horses that yanked and pulled at their tied-off reins.

Back in her body, she breathed a sigh of relief. Her mud man thundered after them a good hundred human paces, but they didn't stop. Some freed their horses and took off at a gallop farther down the road, and others lost control of their mounts and fled on foot.

Where would they head? To Anonil? Probably. She doubted she'd seen the last of them.

But at least she and Ro could make their way farther now, without killing anyone and without trudging through the swamp. She waited just a moment longer to be sure the Devoted meant to put some distance between them and the creature. They never slowed.

She coaxed her creature back to its swampy home and gradually released the spell, letting the mud slide apart, finally laying its hefty mass back to rest in the mire of the swamp.

Odd how it had felt almost alive, like a real

flesh-and-blood creature, enough so that she ached to let it slide back into oblivion. But it was not the Way; the creature was not a natural thing by any stretch. About that much, Ro was right. She'd disturbed the Balance by creating it, but hopefully she'd only offset the imbalance those vile Devoted had created in the first place. After everything that her gifts had cost her, couldn't some good come from them?

Other mages grew flowers and cleared thunderstorms. She made mud monsters. Not exactly what she'd hoped to excel at, studying to be a warrior mage, but she wasn't complaining.

Miara found a fruit bat hanging high in the tree. Good. One more, and that should be enough. *Hello, there,* she cooed. *Might you be able to stand watch for a friend and I while you hunt? Just keep your eyes open and tell me if there are dangers in the area. New humans, wolves, the like. I have some dried berries you can have in exchange.*

It made an audible squeak of delight. It was happy to alert her—and also to scoop up her berries.

Miara heaved a sigh of relief. She had begged the help of six separate animals now, and this fruit bat should be enough. She and Samul could have veered into town a few hours ago and looked for an inn, but she hadn't wanted to risk it. Too predictable. If those mages searched for them, the nearest inn would be the most obvious destination and therefore the first place to look.

So instead they would camp in the woods, where the trees stretched for miles and offered a million hiding places, so many that it would be impossible to search them all. She hoped the pursuing mages were either smart enough to realize they couldn't search every corner and nook of this dismal forest, or stupid enough to try looking, because it would take them *forever*.

"It's set. I have a fox, a deer, an owl, a bat, a mole, and a cougar, all on the look out to alert us for danger." She spread out nuts and berries she'd foraged from the destroyed carriage and from her pack as her offering for those that helped. The cougar, luckily, had eaten not long ago.

"A mole?" Something about his tone made her think he might doubt whether she actually had any animal on alert. She almost shook her head. His suspicion knew no bounds.

"All of that, and *that's* the one you pick on?"

He shrugged but said nothing. Yes, very unlike his son. Not that Samul was stoic or wordless, but Aven never missed an opportunity to talk.

"I will stand guard as well. But you should rest and heal."

"I'm fine." Samul waved her off. "I can watch part of the night too."

Miara had no idea if this was some kind of test or how to pass it and was too tired to care. "What part of the night do you want? First or second or… ?" Perhaps offering him the choice would allay his mistrust.

"I can watch first. You were the one working magic all day."

Her turn to shrug. "There's plenty of life around here to replenish energy." But in truth, she was tired. No, after so much time with them both as fish, she was utterly exhausted. She'd spent as long as they dared, long enough that part of her had been afraid the king had forgotten he was not a fish nor had ever been one. They'd also traveled as humans, a pair of foxes, and as blue jays—sometimes perched on Lukor's back, although that hadn't been as restful as she'd hoped.

Samul had been fashioning a fire pit, which looked a lot easier now that his leg was healed, but she didn't remind him of that fact. "You don't have a flint, do you?"

"Of course I do." She withdrew the flint and dagger from her belt. Samul's eyebrows rose a bit, but she had no idea how to interpret the expression.

Samul was a much quieter companion than Aven had been. He lit the fire without much commentary and settled back into his seat. Perhaps he was just lost in thought. Or perhaps this was not his usual self, but a different him spawned by his near death. Maybe he was contemplating the irony that her disobedience of his orders had saved his life. She hoped he was.

Mostly, though, he watched her every move, seeming to judge each choice.

It didn't change anything. Judge all you want, old man. She had things to do to make sure they didn't die out here.

"Fine, I'll sleep first. Wake me when the moon has moved a few fingers, and I'll watch."

"That's hardly the midpoint of the night."

"I know."

He met her gaze for a few seconds, then shrugged again. Whatever was he thinking about? It was almost tempting to dip into his thoughts again to find out.

She lay down on the makeshift bed, contrived from a saddle blanket and the one fur that had remained in the stable from her earlier pack. Why had she even unpacked the old one? She should have kept it ready for an emergency, by the door. Then she remembered—Fayton. He was the charitable soul who'd helped her so... unhelpfully unpack everything so that now she didn't have most of it. She smiled a little to herself anyway. He'd meant well, and with Aven's map, she'd come out of there with *some* supplies, at least.

Had Samul and Elise ever camped like this together? Had they ever traveled across the realm, alone with just each other and the wilderness? She couldn't much imagine it, but that didn't mean it hadn't happened.

She missed Aven, with a sudden, heavy weight. If only she had been with them during the attack. But then again, by following behind later, she'd been able to find Samul when the other Akarians had failed.

Her separate journey would be a boon *if* she and Samul survived. If they got mauled by a bear, well... And while she hadn't found one in the area—a fact that certainly helped encourage her sleep—they were still close enough to the mountains for an ursine visitor.

She tried to close her eyes and sleep, but the image of Sorin creeping up over top of her on the bed flashed before her. Her eyes snapped open. Perhaps sleep would be harder to come by than she'd thought.

When she finally drifted off, Miara's light slumber was not restful. She tossed and turned and kept waking, thinking she'd heard something—a stick breaking, a door creaking open, soft footsteps on a stone floor? Other times, she dreamed.

She was back in Mage Hall again, standing before the Masters, awaiting orders. Sometimes she just stood and stood, the hours passing, interminable waiting for something that she just knew wouldn't be good. Sometimes they'd order her to kidnap Aven, and she'd march off dutifully. Her legs moved against her will, and she couldn't even feel them.

Sometimes, worst of all, her father and Luha stood with her. Daes would slowly approach each of them. He'd scowl into her eyes, then into her father's, then lean down to scowl into Luha's, then side-eye Miara. He'd step back like he was preparing something, but what, she wasn't sure. She'd be overcome with the need to rush forward. To stop him from whatever he planned to do to her family. To knock him out of the way and *run.*

Each time, she never achieved it. Her body was always still, frozen, stuck—still enslaved, nothing more than a prison that held her mind.

After yet another of these dreams, she sat up, panting with the effort to resist the irresistible orders of the brand.

It's all right. It's not real. You're free. She repeated it over and over in her mind.

"You all right?" Samul asked.

She shook her head, then propped her elbows on her knees and hung her head in her hands. She pressed her palms to her eyes. Why, why, why would her mind not rest? It's all right, it's not real, you're free now, it's all a dream. Why must it torture her so?

"Are you going back to sleep, or can I make you some tea?"

Miara peered over her shoulder at the king. "You... make tea for people?"

He smirked. "Like Aven, I wasn't always a king."

"Well, okay. Tea would be nice. Then you can rest some before we take to the road."

She sat silently, staring with round eyes into the surrounding woods but not seeing them, while he made use of the pot and tea and water she'd stolen against his orders before leaving Estun. She was free, and the Masters were far, far away. They couldn't hurt her—at least not right now. She was sitting with the damn king of Akaria, of all people. Not something she could have foreseen even a few months ago.

"Here you go," Samul said, handing her the tea. "I believe I owe you an apology. Perhaps tea will make it go down easier."

She accepted it awkwardly, bracing herself for what

was to come. True, he did owe her an apology, but she was a bit shaken at the moment to receive it.

"I was wrong to forbid you to come with us," he said slowly.

Part of the tension in her eased. While that didn't exactly change things, many people simply could not admit they were wrong, even when it was obvious. "Your mistake seems to have worked out in your favor."

He winced a little. Her words might have sounded harsher than she'd meant them. "That's not lost on me. The Balance has a way of occasionally throwing such things in our faces, I guess. But I hope you can accept my apology."

"I do," she said, nearly sure her words were true.

"You have clearly proven my suspicions unfounded. As Aven reminded me, you'd proven that to him repeatedly, but apparently, I had to see it for myself to understand."

"Much as I might have tried to convince you, I can't blame you for being cautious."

"Well, perhaps you can blame me for not wanting you present at the vote?"

She pursed her lips. "Hmm. Perhaps."

"I can't say I regret that choice. I still believe you could destabilize the situation. But Aven made a long list of good reasons why you were worth having there anyway. Even if I wasn't ready to accept them at the time." His voice was tinged with regret. She took a sip of the tea, having somewhat forgotten it. "But I should have explained better. If you set my ultimately false suspicions aside, I was not really concerned about you in particular. I was only trying to look out for Aven, in my way."

She gazed at the tea, not meeting his eyes.

"He has worked hard for the throne his whole life. I don't know what he would do if it slipped from his grasp."

She swallowed another sip of tea. A sudden determination to make sure that didn't happen filled her. "He will be a great king," she said solemnly.

"He's a natural." Samul sighed, a smile cracking his lips for the first time. "He takes to the crown readily. Not everyone is so... graceful about it. I've never gotten used to the throne, personally."

She raised an eyebrow, catching his eye. "What?"

"I always feel like I'm making a mistake. And frequently do, as you've seen."

"I've never heard anyone consider you anything but a great king. Trust me, I've seen King Demikin. I don't think you need to worry."

"Coming from you, the subject of my latest mistake, that does ease my heart."

"I had many missions eavesdropping on those royal halls for—" No, she would not call them the Masters any longer. They were not her Masters anymore. "For Daes and the others. Demikin is a worthless monarch, deaf to the cries of his people. Everyone acknowledges this. Not that it's much of a comparison. I haven't watched you order Aven's death, so he'll always be quite worse in my book."

The way Samul's expression darkened and his fists

clenched chilled her.

"I'm gathering Aven didn't mention that part of our journey."

"No. Apparently, he skipped over that little detail. I suppose it was implied."

"It's Daes, the Dark Master, in control of everything anyway. He plays like he is listening to the king, but he seems to be holding all the puppet strings. He uses the mages as valuable capital for trade."

"You honor Aven more and more, my dear."

She blinked. "I don't follow, my lord."

"He argued quite fiercely on your behalf, the value of your knowledge about Kavanar. I didn't give him enough credit. Rather... harsh words were said."

"I gathered that," she said before she froze, realizing what she gave away. Her stomach dropped.

But Samul smiled, an eyebrow raised. "He came to see you, didn't he."

She looked down into the fire, then back up, her eyes revealing everything.

Samul snorted. "Boy is as rash as he is noble."

"He's no boy," she said quietly.

He stilled, looking at her more deeply, it seemed.

"I know you love him, I see that now," Samul said slowly. "But I also see your hesitation. You're a hard one to read, and so the fact that I can see some fear in you is telling. It certainly didn't ease my suspicions. I didn't expect either of you to so forcefully object, honestly. I thought the time apart might help your mind... settle some things."

"Like what?" she said coldly, more exposed than she'd like at the moment. A fierce desire to stay by Aven's side, to rule with him, had kindled within her. She didn't like to focus on the fear and doubt that lingered, not after she'd promised him she was certain, that of course she wanted to always be by his side.

"You want the man, but you're not sure about the throne that comes with him."

She gaped at him. Hmm. Apparently Samul could be almost painfully frank too. It must run in the family. Her turn. "I don't *not* want it. I just… don't want to disappoint him in it. And I'm not sure I'm cut out for the role. Look at Renala. One glance at her shouts her nobility. No one would be surprised to find out she was a queen. Me they'd probably mistake for a royal guard. If I'm lucky. A stable hand, more likely. And Elise. They are all so amiable and elegant and diplomatic and…"

"And what?"

"And I am not."

Samul shrugged. "Aven has more skill at diplomacy than ten men need. He doesn't need any of that."

She leaned forward, setting down the empty cup. "I've spent my life doing three things, my lord. Healing horses, learning magic, and not being seen. I don't think any of those have given me any helpful qualities for the role of queen."

"Aven seems to disagree. You know, many who have held the throne have thought themselves unsuitable for it at times. I know I have."

She frowned. "Why?"

"Sometimes it's easier to see our flaws than our strengths. You worry if you are suitable. If you are good enough. Well, so do I. Since it hasn't gone away with age, I have decided that it's a desirable attribute in a ruler. It keeps me trying to be better. I keep wondering when they will realize that I'm just another man, just like any of them, and that there's nothing special or 'kingly' about me. I have wondered for years when they will realize it's only luck and chance that made me a king and not a shepherd."

She blinked. The fire cracked as a log popped and embers flitted into the early morning sky. If he didn't rest soon, they would talk all their time away. Perhaps he was concerned what dreams awaited him as well.

"I keep wondering when they will throw me out for someone who won't make so many mistakes," he said.

She ducked her head, not wanting him to see the emotion on her face.

"You may never feel you are good enough. I certainly don't feel like I am much of the time. That does *not*, however, mean that the idea is true."

She searched his face for judgment, some hint of his own estimation of her for the role, but found nothing. "You should rest," she said softly. "Before morning comes."

"You're right. Let's see what can be done."

They switched places, and she quietly made herself another cup of the tea, hoping it would give her the energy that sleep hadn't. She rubbed a palm over her face as he settled in. That man. You wouldn't really know he was a king, if not for the weight of the world creasing his brow. She struggled to digest what he'd said.

She had never felt good enough when the Masters gave her missions. Yet she'd always found a way. Daes had always been gleefully, defiantly confident in her abilities. And he'd been right, she grudgingly admitted. She'd *always* achieved her goals, some of them more easily than she could have ever expected. To this day, most of the tasks she'd already completed still sounded daunting, if not impossible. The only thing that had ever come naturally to her had been tending horses, and how much of that was she doing these days?

Speaking of which, she wandered over to Lukor to check on him. He had roused and was happily chomping on some nearby foliage. She ran her fingers over his pale mane and thought of her father, of Luha, of Kres. She'd probably never see Kres again, never get him out of that awful place. She sighed. She doubted she'd even free her family at this rate, unless they split Mage Hall clean open with a full-frontal assault and leveled the place.

Such an attack sounded like an idea almost as crazy and impossible as kidnapping an Akarian prince or stealing from King Demikin. Both things she had done if not with ease, then nearly so. Perhaps things were not so impossible as they seemed. Or impossible things could sometimes surprise you. Maybe Samul was right. Was it her fear speaking, rather than logic or knowledge?

Did she *know* she'd make a bad queen, or did she simply fear she might? But even as she asked the question, she knew—it was impossible to be certain until it happened. Samul was right. But... there was one more thing.

"My lord, are you awake?"

"Yes. What is it?" He didn't turn, simply speaking into the darkness, his back to her and the firelight.

"Do you really think they would accept me? A foreigner, a commoner, a... woman not very skilled in the courtly arts of dresses and meals and subtle turns of phrase? Tending horses and concealing myself from enemies did not require these sorts of skills."

He twisted to his back to study her face now. "My concerns have rested primarily with your magic and your loyalty. The former remains, but how the Assembly votes on Aven should illuminate that point. But otherwise, skills can be learned."

Miara hesitated, wondering if he really understood.

"Also, expert advisors can be sought. Or did you think I handle every decision of the realm all alone? Ha, far from it." He grinned.

"Queens get attention," she said softly. "I am very skilled at *evading* people's attention."

"You did just fine with that demonstration of magic."

"I had a willing attention magnet in Derk."

Samul laughed. "And you think Aven is *less* of one?"

She snorted. "I hadn't thought of that."

"I think you'll be fine." He turned his back to the fire again.

Miara tapped her chin. Interesting. Very interesting. Some part of her heart had relaxed, quieted at those words. "I'm sorry. Get some rest. I'll wake you in a few hours."

"Any sign of it?" Jaena and Ro had been searching for the inn for about an hour. Anonil's narrow streets wound in twisted, odd patterns, doubling back on each other. Was the city that large, or were they just getting repeatedly lost?

Ro shook his head. "Not down there. Have we been here before?"

"I thought the same thing." She scanned again to make sure she hadn't missed a sign bearing an apple and arrow. They huddled in a side street, and not for the first time, she felt a little like someone was watching her, someone who had noticed that they were looking for something or were having trouble finding their destination. Or at the very least, noticing that they were from out of town. She had traveled enough to know that made them a target, but so did asking for the location from random passersby. They'd tried to play the part of natives as well as they could, but if they had truly doubled back, they might need to break down and just ask someone soon.

"Let's try to go to the town's farthest edge and work back from there. Maybe it will help us figure out if we're going in circles."

He nodded crisply. He strode on one side of Yada,

leading her by the reins, while Jaena strode on the other. Each watched the side streets for signs of the inn Miara had mentioned.

As they reached the far town wall, they finally found the inn. Practically leaning into the wall itself, the white-washed exterior had cheery weavings of colorful fall leaves in the window boxes and hung on the front door.

"I'll look inside for a contact and get us a room if I can. You look for a stable," she said.

"No, I'm staying with you." He looped Yada's reins around a nearby post. She shrugged and let him follow. He was probably right.

They stepped inside, and the pleasant heat of the tavern hit her. She searched the room, wondering—what was she even looking for? How was she going to find it? She took a deep breath.

To her left, an innkeeper yelled out something in a language she didn't understand, looking hopeful. Jaena stepped away to her right, pretending not to notice him.

Ro squeezed her shoulder, then stalked toward the man, tossing words back in the same language. Good. If he could get them a room, she could focus on finding their contact. Perhaps he'd even get them a better price, chattering away as they were. She leaned against the wall and studied the patrons of the tavern that took up the lower floor of the inn.

As she watched, several of them met her eye warily. Too warily. It made her uneasy. A man in a gray vest, a woman in brown robes. A red-haired, bearded man sat by the fire. All seemed to be watching around them rather too intently.

A man wearing a midnight-blue tabard got up and approached. "Are you looking for someone, my lady?"

"Perhaps." She folded her arms across her chest. "Why do you want to know?"

Words from Ro's argument with the innkeeper drifted toward her, *Farsai* being among them. Oh, by the seven hells, she was *not* from Farsa.

"Come from Kavanar, perhaps?" The man in the midnight tabard caught her attention once again. Now that he was closer, she could see the faint embroidery of a bear, sword, and shield in the same dark navy color—the royal Akarian symbols. "My lord and his... friend, a Lady Miara, sent me to be on the lookout for friends arriving."

His lord? Was Miara with an Akarian noble? How had she ended up there? Still, a wave of relief washed over her. "Indeed, that is who I seek." She hated to admit it so blatantly without thinking over ten different ways this could be a trap, but she had no other way. Miara had given her no secret sign or symbol.

He nodded. "You just missed them; my lord left here but an hour ago."

She cocked her head. Were they talking about the same thing? Now she felt less sure.

"My orders are to send word. Your room at the inn is covered. Refresh yourself while I catch up with them and request further orders. Our original orders were to leave for Estun immediately, but they have left Estun and apparently had some… troubles along the way. We may wish to ride south." The way the man's face darkened twisted the knots in her stomach. What could he mean by all that? But it seemed a fair enough plan.

"My companion can join me, I assume?" She waved with a relieved smile at where Ro was still chatting with the innkeeper. Both looked almost nostalgic, as if their minds had drifted elsewhere.

"Of course. Shev, show them to a room, on my coin, please."

Tharomar blinked, eyebrows raised in surprise, and the innkeeper—Shev—froze a moment before he processed the response. Then he nodded and hurried to snap up a set of keys. The blacksmith followed the innkeeper toward the stairs, Shev continuing to enthuse over something as they climbed.

The man showed them to a room, all smiles and bows, and then handed them their own key. Must be a fine inn to have locks and keys. She had come to expect them in her travels with her father, but most inns did not have any way to secure their rooms. Her father had traveled with several armed soldiers, although obviously not enough. They hadn't been able to withstand the Devoted when they had come. As the innkeeper sauntered away humming, Ro shook his head, smiling.

"What was that all about?" Jaena asked.

"Our dear innkeeper is missing the warmer winters of Farsa just about now. Heard we were foreign 'merchants' and hoped we'd come from there with some sugared violets or vanilla from the southern kingdoms."

She snorted. They were all foreigners here, weren't they? Because they weren't in Hepan or Kavanar or even Farsa anymore. Her heart gave a little jump. They *had* made it to Akaria. One small victory. They had made it this far. "He probably couldn't afford such things even if we had them."

"A man can dream."

"Think he'd be interested in any Kavanarian iron?" Six of his smaller pieces had fit into her knapsack along with the brand.

"You're the merchant. I warmed him up for you."

At that, she couldn't suppress a smile. "Guess we should stable the horse before we settle in here?"

He nodded. "Did you find the right person?"

"I didn't have any sign or symbol to go on. I guess knowing this inn was where I should go should have been enough of a sign. He approached me. I hope he really is who he says he is. He said that my... friends were just here an hour ago. He left to pass word to them."

He frowned, thoughtful. "Well, not much other option. Keep your guard up."

"As always."

They headed downstairs. She glanced at the room. The red-bearded man by the fire was gone. But then again, he could simply have been finished with his meal or ale or whatever he'd been doing there. It *was* a tavern, after all.

And yet...

"What is it?" he said as he unhooked Yada's reins.

"One man from the tavern is gone now. It might be nothing, but…"

"But our 'friends' from last evening headed this direction when last we saw them."

She nodded, scanning the area around them again. "Exactly."

"Let's go." She didn't know when he had ascertained the location of the stable, or if he even had. They looped back and to the left, around the outside town wall that was also the back wall of the inn. A massive stable waited. They led Yada inside, ears perked, watching.

Once inside, Ro moved more quickly, guiding Yada into the stable swiftly as he pointed at a nearby ladder. She headed for it, going up into a loft where bales of hay waited to be eaten by equine guests.

A window let in light off to her right and looked out over the inn's roof, down a long street that cut nearly straight through Anonil. She could see all the way to the far wall and the southern gate. Damn, if only they'd tried *this* road or the southern gate first, she thought numbly. There was no time for that, though, because something much worse approached.

Six Devoted, marching neatly in three rows of two men, crossbows on their backs and headed their way.

As she just stared, trying to think of what to do, Ro joined her. She pointed, and he swore.

"Gods… They're coming—you have to go."

"What are you talking about?

"Follow that man. I'll stay here to delay them."

"Not a chance." But even as she watched, more Devoted poured from the building these ones had left. Four black hoods. No, six. Now ten. Gods. She and Ro had a few moments to debate, as the Devoted were still several streets away, but it wouldn't be long before the knights were upon them.

He swore again. "I bet that damn innkeeper ran and got them as soon as he left us. You have to get the brand out of here."

"No—I can't leave you to them."

"Yes, you can. They're not looking for me, remember? The most important thing is that they don't retake the brand. Clearly someone told them we're here. You've got to get *it* out of here. And they might know your face, with that drawing going around, but mine is less likely."

"But—"

"You also know the ones who freed you. I don't. I'll fight them. Get it to your friends. You've *got* to do this, Jaena."

"I can't leave you—"

"Come on, let's go." He put a hand on her arm, gentle but firm, urging her toward the ladder with him. She relented and followed him down the ladder. "You've got to get the brand to someone powerful enough to stand up to them, and that's not me. Besides, I'm more equipped to fight them. And I'm uninjured."

"That— No. That doesn't mean you should take on a suicide mission, we could both run—" Gods, not again. The intensity of the panic and emotion that swept through her shocked her.

"Yada can't do two of us again, not after all this, not with any speed. She might be able to manage you." He was getting Yada back out of the stable, the streak of white in his hair picking up more than its share of the dim stable's light. Calm, gentle, hardworking hands patted Yada's neck, comforting the mare even as the horse sensed their unease.

Gods, if she never saw him again… She thought of the moments close to him when he'd discovered she was a mage, the way he had looked longingly at her lips in the morning light, the way his fingers had lingered for just a moment when he'd helped her onto the horse.

"Come on, you need to go." He held out his hands to help her into the saddle.

Instead, she grabbed onto him, pulling him closer to her.

"I'll follow," he whispered, his lips inches from hers. His eyes said he knew he couldn't, but she didn't blame him for saying so. Perhaps he *could* outsmart them, though, or hide. Whatever he did, it would delay them and buy her time.

"They are too many. We could fight them together—"

"I'll find you, all right? I'll find you. This is not goodbye. Don't even say it. Just go. Now. They've got to be almost here."

She didn't listen and instead leaned closer. He stiffened, but she pressed her lips to his, soft, but insistent. There was no time, and this was foolish… but what other chance would they have? She threw her arms over his shoulders, the brand in its knapsack probably jutting into his back.

His lips parted, and she nearly dropped her burden as he returned her kiss with a surprising hunger. His arms wrapped around her, pulling her hard against him. A flood of heat shot through her.

Just a moment longer. She needed to remember this moment, and his mouth, for all of her days.

She broke away first and hesitated only a split second before she hobbled straight for the horse. He helped her up, and now more than ever his hands lingered on her fingers, her hip, her thigh. She squeezed his hand one more time. "In case guilt doesn't lure you back to me, maybe *that* will."

He snorted.

"Promise me you'll follow." Damn, she'd hoped to hide the note of desperation in her voice. "Don't let them catch you, Tharomar. There's no telling what they'll do."

He nodded, squeezed back, and stepped away. "I'll do everything I can to delay them. And I'll do my best to follow. Now, Jaena—please. Go."

She dug in her heels, ankle aching, and the horse surged forward. She bent close to the horse's back, clinging to the mane to avoid prying eyes.

South. She could only hope the man in the midnight tabard had been telling the truth.

Chapter 15   The White City

Tharomar spared himself a single moment to stare

after her, struggling to process what had just happened. All this time, she had longed for him as well? Or had that kiss just been some kind of good-bye born of passion and fear that would fade in the light of day? He had met her advances, hungry for her, eager to admit that he'd felt the same way. Regretting he hadn't done so sooner.

South. Hopefully she was headed that direction for a reason. And… hopefully he could follow.

Tharomar climbed back up the ladder into the stable's loft. He would need every advantage he could muster if they figured out he was here. He ducked behind stacks of hay bales, quieted himself, and waited.

If they heard Jaena racing away, there were no shouts after her, no horse hooves. Likely, they were still searching the inn and their room. But now, a woman's voice called out from the front of the inn.

"Search the area. Find them."

How many Devoted would check the stables, all of them or just part of the group? Would they be thorough? Would they use their lanterns, or actually check? Had they realized their lanterns had failed them before?

Unfortunately for him, it looked like his luck had finally run out. They, very logically, headed straight for the stables, and while he couldn't see all of them enter between the slats in the loft floor, at least eight drifted in, scanning for him. A lot for any warrior to handle. A chestnut-haired woman followed them with a severe expression, murder on her mind. He had a feeling she looked that way often.

As two of them started up the ladder, he made his move. He launched his two throwing knives and took one knight down but missed the other—knives were hardly his forte. With a swift kick, he sent hay bales toppling onto the other knights below.

Ro charged the one remaining knight in the loft head-on, taking a wild slash at the Devoted's neck and chest before diving into a roll toward the stable wall. Hopefully that would put him out of projectile range from those down below. Perhaps if he could slowly lure the Devoted one at a time up the ladder, maybe he could pick them off one by one.

Three more flooded the loft. Damn, they'd found a second ladder. He glanced around, frantic. How could he use this loft to his best advantage? A crossbow quarrel thunked into the wood just above his head, interrupting his thoughts. The three had narrowed in on him and just about had him cornered.

He kicked at the closest one's stomach and got lucky, sending him toppling. The next lunged at him, then the third, though, sending him down hard. He thrashed, but two against one, they easily managed to wrest his sword from his grip. Now the blows came, and he braced himself, twisted, kicked. These Devoted seemed more interested in pummeling him into submission than actually killing him, but he would give them no such quarter.

He managed to get to his knees. The bigger one was a bit overconfident, and on his next swing, Tharomar caught the fist and pulled, sending his attacker reeling off-balance. In nearly the same motion, Tharomar darted forward, over the Devoted's body, lurching for the nearby window. Maybe if he could just get out of it, he could get away from them or delay them just a little longer with a wilder chase.

Without entirely thinking it through, he thrust himself at the window, the wooden shutter swinging wildly and clanging, and he fell.

He hit the ground hard on his back, the air flying out of him. He needed to get up, but for a moment he was barely able to focus on breathing. He gasped for one breath, then another, then heaved himself up. He staggered three steps forward and around the corner of the barn, darting into the darkness between the buildings.

If he could make it to the end, then turn left, he could just maybe—

The tip of a blade met him, its point hovering in the air somewhere between his neck and his nose. The woman who so longed for death. He raised his gaze to meet hers.

She had eyes of beautiful crystalline blue beneath that murderous glare. Someone so dark didn't deserve such eyes. "Where is she, and where is the brand?" she demanded.

"I don't know what you're talking about," he said.

"Throw him back inside and torch the place," she ordered.

He gaped, in spite of himself. "But the horses—"

She gave him a withering look as another Devoted grabbed him, dragging him back toward the stables. Tharomar wasn't above an underhanded attack and sent a fist deep into the man's gut, but five more swarmed him, pulling him toward the stables.

They threw him to his knees amid the tumbled hay. One leveled a cruel kick at his temple, sending him reeling and into the dust and chaff, black splotches flashing before his eyes.

"I'll give you one more chance. That renegade mage you were helping. Where is she? Tell me, and perhaps you will go free." The woman and her sword had returned, leveled at his neck. She must be the knight, he thought. Were these others even knights, or simply her squires? "I said, tell me if you want your freedom," she pressed.

Freedom? No chance of that now. He highly doubted he would even survive. Fine with him. He'd gone down in the battle he'd chosen to fight, and not without causing them trouble along the way. He would die in service of his mission.

It would have been nice to find out if anything waited on the other side of that kiss, or if they would regret it after the danger had passed. But it was too late. For him, the danger was not going to pass.

He shook his head. "I told you I don't know what you're talking about."

She lifted the blade point and sent a swift kick to his shoulder, rolling him from his side to his back with the force of it. Then she put one booted foot to his neck and pressed ever so slightly. "You'd forfeit your life for this mage? This seed of corruption? Tell me where she is."

"I don't know now," he whispered. That much was indeed true. "And even if I did, I wouldn't tell you."

"Get those torches ready." She leaned forward, pressing her foot down and slowly closing the airway. This was it, he thought. He gasped for a breath to buy him time, but he had no hope. She was going to crush his windpipe and leave him here to die.

It was worth it if the Akarians could destroy the brand. It was worth it if Jaena got free. He'd done what he could. More than he could have hoped or imagined on that day he'd first sworn allegiance to his order.

He'd never expected to live forever.

Her eyes caught on something, and she stopped. Then she removed her foot entirely. He gasped for breath, more desperate for it than he would have liked to admit. She squinted at his neck and squatted down beside him.

"This necklace—I've seen it before. What does it mean?" she demanded.

He blinked at her, then shut his gasping mouth. He likely couldn't even speak. If he could, he certainly would not tell her anything about it.

She grasped it and yanked it from his neck, dangling it in front of her eyes. She scowled at the pendant, then at him, then handed it to one of the other Devoted. "Hold. No flames today. Put that in my bags for later. We'll have to torture this out of him, I suppose."

Torture what out of him?

Did that mean he was going to live, for the moment?

Another cluster of Devoted arrived, most carrying flaming branches and torches, but one carried one of their strange lanterns holding a purple-orange stone. As the squire strode away with his pendant, the rock suddenly flared to life, shining brightly enough to fill the whole of the stable as though it were the midday sun.

What the…

A dark smile curled across the woman's mouth. "Well, well. Is *that* what that's for?"

Tharomar frowned as he struggled to right himself and back away from her. What was going on? There was no one here but these Devoted and the horses.

And him.

"Looks like we won't have to torture him after all. Don't look so disappointed. Shackle him. We'll take him back to Kavanar. Once we capture that renegade and the brand, we'll get what we need out of this mage easily. Take him."

His mouth fell open for a moment, then he shut it again hastily. Revealing his surprise would not help him. But inside, his mind was reeling. Did they— Could they—

Nefrana's blooms, were they right? Could he be a mage, just like Jaena?

Before he could wonder, or think anything, really, the hilt of a sword collided again with his temple, and everything faded to black.

As Jaena raced south, she struggled not to look back behind her. He's not coming, girl. Not for a while, at the very least. But a part of her was afraid that deep down, she knew the truth. Those Devoted weren't going to let him follow if they found him. Although what exactly they *would* do, she didn't know. Slavery seemed like a terrible thing to hope for, but at least he'd still be alive.

And she still had the brand. It prodded her back and shoulders, a constant reminder of its presence. Damn, it'd feel good to get rid of that thing. Maybe she could even destroy it. If she could figure out how. If not, perhaps she could toss it into the deepest sea.

She wasn't entirely sure where she thought she was going. Her damn ankle ached with every hoofbeat. She'd tried riding with it out of the stirrup, but that wasn't much better. She had to hope the man's word that they'd left only an hour before was correct, because she wasn't entirely sure she could get on and off this horse alone. Maybe with the other foot, or with some serious pain. She'd figure it out. Or she'd ride the whole way to Panar, or as far as Yada was willing to go.

It wasn't like she had any money to pay for a room or food anyway.

More than an hour had passed, then two, but before the sun crossed the zenith in the sky, a large procession came into view on the road up ahead. She studied it at a distance. Three or four dozen horses carried men and women laden with armor, weapons, and supplies. One woman riding toward the front wore a dress of emerald green that made Jaena long for such things, irrational as that might be at the moment. There had been a day once…

Those days were over now, though.

Another woman was dressed in a tidy crimson shirt and breeches. Did that mean Kavanarians? Nearly everyone else in the group wore armor of some kind, and fine armor at that. She squinted, trying to make out the symbol on any shield or breastplate. A bear, roaring mightily into the night.

Ah, they *were* Akarians, at least. Thank the gods. Neither of these women had Miara's red hair, but perhaps someone among them knew her or could help Jaena find her.

She quickened her weary horse's pace, whispering, "Just a little farther, I swear."

As she neared them, the rear soldiers—for she realized now they must be soldiers—turned and faced her.

"Who goes there?" one voice called out, stopping. Several other horses turned and joined them.

Well, that seemed like a lot of soldiers to face one woman on a horse. She would not be cowed, though. She needed to find Miara and fast.

"Jaena Eliar, mage of Kavanar." She was pleased her voice carried with a strong echo, even after all the day's exertions.

At the mention of mage, however, the women and men shifted uneasily, horses stamping. Another horse carrying an armored man with shaggy, blond-brown hair rounded and trotted toward her. The rest of the procession had stopped.

"I have news and information. I was freed with the request to share it. I'm looking for another mage from

Kavanar—Miara Floren."

The riders exchanged glances. They knew Miara. They weren't sure how to react to Jaena's arrival, though. The grayish eyes of the blond-brown-haired man cut into her with a keen stare.

"Who did you say you were?" he said.

"Jaena, mage of Kavanar. Slave, until just recently. Miara told me to meet her in Anonil, but we were ambushed, and I had to flee."

"Ambushed, eh?" His voice was weary. "That seems to be happening a lot these days."

"I need to see Miara as soon as possible."

"Welcome, Jaena," he said with a slight nod. "I'm the mage who freed you." Her mouth dropped open as relief washed over her. Miara hadn't mentioned anything about her "friend's" identity, but at least she'd found someone she could—hopefully—trust. The armored mage looked to the other men. "Let's take a pause, rest the horses. I am sure Jaena has much to tell us and could use a rest herself."

The escaped mage slave—Jaena, was it?—followed Aven off the road with the others. Thank the gods they'd run into her. In all the tumult, he'd completely lost any thought or hope of connecting with her, at least not until much later.

Near a stand of trees, Aven dismounted and tied off his horse. Jaena hesitated for a moment, then dismounted herself. A hiss of pain reached his ears. She was wincing. Must be injured.

He caught his mother's eye. She'd heard it too, and she looked to Siliana, mumbling something Aven couldn't hear. The journeyman dismounted and stalked straight toward them.

Jaena turned, favoring one leg as she did. "Is there somewhere we could speak privately?"

Aven glanced around. "Not really."

The mage frowned, then her eyes caught on Siliana approaching her.

"Your ankle—may I?"

Jaena's eyes pierced the other woman with a tough stare. What was the escaped slave estimating? Then she heaved a sigh of relief and nodded, shutting her eyes. Siliana squatted down to look at the mage's leg. Gods, it was idiocy *not* to have mages on their side, if only for their healing abilities. Jaena's eyes opened, accompanied by a relieved sigh.

"Thank the gods for creature mages," she said, smiling.

Siliana straightened. "Siliana," she said with a bow.

Jaena bowed in return. "Well—you heard my name. Jaena."

"I believe Miara said you were an earth mage?" Aven said, joining them by Jaena's mount.

She nodded.

"We're in dire need of earth mages. We've got a number of them with no training. And yet, enemy earth mages are wreaking havoc left and right. I'm glad you're here."

Jaena looked a little stunned at that but smiled again. "I have something to show you... but I'd really rather not everyone see it at this point."

She had no idea who she could trust. And that was fair. He wasn't entirely sure who they could trust either, and Alikar still rode with them. Although... glancing around, he didn't see the bastard's horse anywhere. He scratched his chin. At the same time, how could he entirely trust *her*?

"We can go off a bit from the others. We don't have time to set up tents. Our plan was to reach the next inn before we stopped."

Jaena pressed her lips together, apprehensive, but then nodded. What other option did they have?

"May I join you?" Siliana asked. Aven looked to Jaena, who looked uncomfortable.

"Can you fetch my mother and then join us in a few minutes, please?" Aven said instead. That would give them at least a little time. "This way. Can you walk?"

"I can now." She beamed a warm smile at Siliana as the creature mage headed for the queen. "You said she's not here. Is Miara all right?"

Aven swallowed the lump in his throat, wishing he could smack the emotion down at the moment. "We... don't know." Damn it, his voice had faltered.

"I see," she said softly. "What is she to you? She said you were her... friend." The lilt to her voice said she understood more was at work.

He glanced at her, unsure how to deal with the direct

question. Was he still beholden to keep their secret? Should he keep it now more than ever? He stole a few moments to think, picking up several nearby fallen logs and twigs and arranging them for a fire. He closed his eyes for a brief moment, visualizing the heat. He opened them and smiled as the logs sputtered into flame. At least he could do that now, although it summoned up a memory of another time, another fire...

He settled on the ground by the fire and patted the earth for her to join him as he chose his answer. He couldn't continue along his father's path. He was king now, and he had to make decisions without looking over his shoulder. His father had taught him as much and would have wanted that. Er, would be glad Aven had done so when they found his father alive. That said, Aven hardly knew Jaena. He chose his words carefully. "She's one of the finest women I've ever known. She and I escaped from Mage Hall together, after I figured out how to break the spell."

Jaena's brow furrowed, as if she was putting the pieces together. "You were in Mage Hall?"

"Your former masters sent Miara to kidnap me. And she succeeded, I might add."

"Former. I like the sound of that."

"Definitely former. Hopefully no one's masters by the end of this."

"Menaha mentioned something seemed to have changed after her last mission. That she thought she saw Miara's scar healing."

"Yes. That would be me."

Jaena was still frowning. "Why you?"

He tilted his head, questioning.

"Why was she sent to kidnap you in particular?"

Oh. She didn't know anything about him, other than that he'd learned to break the spell. That was surprisingly pleasing. How interesting to have someone know him for an actual accomplishment as a mage and *not* know him as royalty. He rather hoped he could keep it that way a few moments longer. "I can fill you in on our journey till this point, but we may not have much time separate from the others. What did you want to tell me privately?" He glanced over his shoulder at the rest of the procession to emphasize his point.

She nodded brusquely, although the crease between her brows said she hadn't missed his dodge. She pulled the pack off her back. As she opened the strings at the top, his nose caught the scent of charred fabric, and in a moment, he understood why. She pulled out a long rod of iron with a simple handle, at the end of which squirmed another twisted circle of metal. No, the metal itself didn't move, but with his mind's eye, he could feel the enchantment. What looked like an ordinary piece of iron to his eyes was a disgusting, squirming mess to his mind, as if it craved new flesh to enslave.

The brand.

Reflexively he skittered back a few feet before he stopped himself. Her eyes flicked from it to him. "You know what this is. Don't you."

He slowly nodded. "How did you... Menaha said you disappeared a day early. And the place was locked down. Was this why?"

"I got lucky. After you freed me, I was determined to go about business as usual. Sometimes my business as usual includes assisting the mage smiths with their craft. They brought in a new mage to enslave, but he escaped. I was nearby and knocked down, and there it was on the floor beside me. I couldn't pass it up. Even if it meant no one else escaped, it seemed worth it."

"That was quite an opportunity. I'd have done the same myself." He was quick to reassure her. "This means they can't make any other slaves?"

"Well, they can still chain people up. But not as they have done with this. We must destroy it."

He stared at her. Gods, after everything that had happened, things had only gotten worse and worse. And now, a victory he could have never hoped for had fallen into his lap. "We'll need help from the others. Other Akarian mages, I mean. There's not many of us, and we're not as well trained as you."

She shrugged. "I was enslaved two years ago. Most mage slaves have years of training on me."

"And yet—you seem to be effective enough." He grinned. "Can we show the others? I can't destroy it by myself. Besides, we're already Kavanar's prime target. Having that brand won't make us any more so."

"I'd still prefer to make it as hard as possible for them to find it again."

Hmm, true. If mages assaulted them again, it would be ideal if their attackers were unaware of the brand's presence. If fewer Akarians knew about it, their enemies couldn't discover its location and go hunting for it so easily. Maybe it would be safer if she went on without them and met them in Panar, or if they broke the party in two so the brand traveled separately from him. But then if either group *was* attacked… The Masters may also have connected Jaena to the brand's disappearance, so they might be looking for her specifically. In that case, Aven should give it to anyone other than her, such as a non-mage that no one would expect to have such a thing. But he doubted he could convince her of that just now. He rubbed his chin, thinking.

"Wait—why are you already Kavanar's prime target anyway?"

Aven grinned at her. "Because, in addition to being able to free mages like you, I am also—for the time being—the king." He tried not to laugh at her wide eyes.

"For the time being?"

"I was the crown prince until we were ambushed by mages earlier in this trip. My father fell into a canyon roused by one of your fellow earth mages—"

"I'd rather not be associated with them."

"—and we lost him. I still hope he will be found."

"But he could be dead. Or you wouldn't be calling yourself king."

Aven winced. He couldn't manage an immediate reply.

"I'm sorry. Was Miara with you? Was she also lost in

the attack?"

"No," he said, shaking his head. "She stayed behind in Estun, for reasons too long to explain now. But she's disappeared from there. I hope she's snuck away unseen, but two were found dead in her room."

"Dead? By the gods."

"Yes, dead. As far as I can tell, she's nowhere near those mages who attacked us. And that's all the better."

After a short break, the procession rode on, Jaena joining them. They camped out along the side of the road in a meadow, too eager to reach Panar to take the time to find an inn large enough to hold them all. In the morning, they made it far enough to see the fair towers of the capital rising on the horizon.

The White City. Aven had visited it a few times, especially when he'd been very young, but each time he saw Panar from afar, he caught his breath as if it were the first time. Pale towers spiraled toward the horizon, all waving flags of pearl and the pale blue of the sea that lay beyond the city in the distance. The walls and ramparts, all the color of bone, rose the height of four or five men, and three gatehouses guarded impressive entrances on the north, east, and west sides of the city. Homes and small hovels crowded around the city as if for comfort or shelter, their dark thatched or tarred roofs peppering the grassy, flat landscape. Fields of crops and pastures of small herds dotted the countryside.

Thank the gods, they'd made it. He hated to arrive without his father, but arriving at all felt like an accomplishment after all they'd been through.

The king's Panaran stronghold had sprung to life as word had reached it of the Assembly meeting. For the first time, the head steward of Ranok took him not to the rooms he'd visited as a child and young man, but to the king's suite. The castle boasted a meeting room, an extensive collection of maps, a private library, and many other things useful at a moment like this. But Aven couldn't bring himself to take advantage of any of them. Everywhere he looked, when he tried to think of what they were going to do, of what awaited him in the Assembly's vote—all he saw was his father. And his absence.

So he was relieved when a knock on the door sounded to announce Jaena. Good. Someone who thought of him as a mage, valuable for things he'd actually done, like freeing her. The servants of Ranok treated him with a reverence beyond any in Estun would have, and it was driving him crazy.

"Your Majesty, I'm sorry to disturb you, but I was hoping I could ask for a small favor." Jaena poked her head in the king's door, her heart pounding. Gods, was it ridiculous to bother a king about this? But what other choice did she have? She knew no one else here to ask.

"Uh, you don't have to call me Your Majesty. Aven is fine. Or sire or what have you. But, of course, come in. What is it? Have a seat." King Aven sat at a large oak desk in the main room, one leg bent with his boot resting on the seat of the chair, an arm propped on his knee. He gestured to the seat across from him. She approached slowly, taking in the plush room around them. At least three servants were busy with unknown tasks in different parts of the room, maybe more she couldn't see. Dozens of beautifully bound books lined the walls behind the desk, golden inscriptions catching the midday sunlight. What would Tharomar have made of them? She swallowed the lump that rose in her throat.

"A man helped me in my escape," she said. "A local blacksmith. When the Devoted found us in Anonil, he stayed behind to slow them down. To fight and hopefully follow. I'm concerned he hasn't joined us. I was wondering if an air mage could help me find out what happened."

"Yes, of course. Wunik's rooms are just down the hall, and I believe he's mostly recovered by now. Sanai, can you—"

The door shut as a servant slipped out, already heading out to find this Wunik without waiting for the request. The king frowned at the closing door.

"Thank you, by the way," Jaena said as they waited in slightly awkward silence.

He glanced up in surprise, having been lost in his thoughts. "For what?"

"For freeing me. A mere thanks doesn't seem like enough. But it's a start."

He smiled wide. "No thanks are necessary. It's my privilege to right these wrongs. Just wait, we'll make the

Masters pay for this in the end."

Wunik mustn't have been doing anything terribly important because an older man in an exquisite dark blue robe rushed in before Sanai could properly finish announcing him.

"Anonil, you say?" Wunik said. "Do you know the name of the inn? I could help you find it."

King Aven bowed slightly with a grand flourish in Wunik's direction from his casual posture in his seat. "The elder air mage Wunik, my lady. You're welcome. Glad to see you're feeling better, Wunik."

The mage set himself up oddly with a bowl of water before him, but she certainly wasn't going to criticize. She leaned out of her chair and over the view of the countryside sliding away as he guided the view to the Apple and Arrow.

"He planned to hide in the stables," she said, "so look over there, around the—" She stopped short as a jolt of pain shot through her. Tharomar lay near a campfire, still, eyes closed, and wrists bound behind his back. A bloody gash marred his temple. "There. Gods, is he alive? Can you get closer?" The window floated toward him. The necklace was gone. Gods, in all the seven hells. They must have discovered he was a mage somehow. She hadn't told him; the Devoted had.

The sense that she'd failed him overwhelmed her.

Although… perhaps the fact that he was a mage had kept them from killing him. More than a dozen dark hoods patrolled the area. Others were loading up horses, pulling up tent poles.

"Is that him?" Aven asked.

She nodded, remembering suddenly that she wasn't alone.

"He's breathing," Wunik said.

She let herself start breathing again. "Damn. Are they leaving? Can we figure out where they are taking him?"

"We can stay on them and follow."

"Are you sure you have the time? I can feed you energy," Jaena said.

"I have nothing else I need to be doing," Wunik replied. "Sire?"

Aven frowned at him. Not yet used to his newly acquired title? The king pointed back at the glowing circle of light. "Look there." A tent had been pitched behind the inn.

"Odd, since they could simply stay in the inn," Jaena muttered.

"Perhaps it was full?" Aven said. "Can you get a look inside that tent flap? It looks familiar."

Peering at the tent flap closely wasn't necessary, though, because just as they inched closer, the flaps flew open and a black-cloaked woman wearing a beaded headband of sapphire and gold strode forward.

"Evana," King Aven growled.

"You said that man was a blacksmith?" Wunik asked.

"Yes, but he was also a mage," she said. "I never got to tell him. He didn't know yet. Do you recognize her?"

"We've had a few run-ins. She'd like my head on a platter, I think, and I nearly return the sentiment. She's a princess of Isolte but more importantly a knight."

"Do you think they're going to kill him?" Jaena said softly.

"I think if they were planning to, they would have done it already," Aven said, his expression grim. "Wunik, watch them as closely as you can. If she's working with the Masters, then they will head back to Mage Hall with him. But let's make sure. I want to know where she's going."

Wunik nodded.

Jaena watched as the Devoted camp unpacked and took to the road with Tharomar in tow. She leaned back in the chair. Exhaustion washed over her. Perhaps she would just close her eyes for a moment while Wunik rode…

"Ho, ho. What have we here?" Wunik's voice roused her from sleep. She sat up, shaking herself awake as King Aven strode in to join them.

"What is it?" she said.

"They aren't taking him to Mage Hall, my lord," said Wunik.

"Where did they take him?" the king replied.

"Trenedum Palace."

Aven frowned, looking shocked. "Truly? When we were stopped in Anonil, and you were still healing—I tried this myself, and—"

"You did! And it worked?" Wunik said.

"Yes, and—" Aven tried to start again.

"She's right, you are a fast learner."

"Who's right?"

"Miara. One of the first things she said to me."

The king's expression darkened with worry. "What I saw was Daes taking a man and a girl—possibly Miara's family—to Trenedum Palace. Why would they go there?"

"Perhaps the king requested an audience?"

"Daes might have an audience with King Demikin, but Evana? A random mage captive? Maybe Daes is there to see the king, and Evana is there to see Daes."

Jaena frowned. "Maybe the dungeons in Mage Hall are getting full?

"Hmm. Or could this have something to do with the troop movements?" Aven muttered.

"What troop movements?" said Jaena.

"We've had reports of Kavanarian troops mobilizing, heading south. We're not quite sure to what end."

"Coming after us, perhaps?" Wunik said.

Aven nodded. "So I assume."

"But wait—back to this palace," said Aven. "If the mages that attacked Estun captured Miara, might they have taken her there as well?" Wunik and Jaena both shrugged. The king leaned forward, peering more closely at Trenedum Palace.

Wunik eyed him. "What are you thinking, Aven?"

"I'm thinking... what if we paid this palace a visit?"

"And did what?" asked Jaena.

"And broke them all out of there."

"Them *all*?" Jaena said quickly, grinning, but Wunik looked stunned.

"I have a hunch Miara's family is there. Maybe Miara too. And we can save someone who helped saved Jaena.

The blacksmith, correct?"

"Well, actually he wasn't *just* a blacksmith. He belonged to an order of Nefrana, like a priest, but they sought to protect mages. I'd never heard of such a thing. But there must be others in his order. The temple is based in Evrical, I think."

"Hmm, Kavanar is full of surprises these days," Aven murmured. "A potential ally inside Kavanar would be valuable too. And look at this place. Highly unfortified. It's practically just a sculpture. An Akarian would never live in a such a pathetic excuse for a building." The king looked to Wunik.

Wunik hesitated, glancing from the window of light to Aven and back. Then he sighed. "Do you really think Miara is there too?"

"Sanai, can you fetch Siliana and Derk, please? And my brother Thel?" His attendant vanished without a word or acknowledgment. "I have no idea if Miara is there. It's a wild hunch. But Daes did make an attempt to blackmail her, saying he would kill her sister if she didn't provide the correct location for the Assembly meeting. Of course, we sent something back but not the correct location. We have until tomorrow before the girl is likely killed."

Wunik winced. Jaena sucked in a sharp breath.

"If we go and rescue them, we thwart Daes. We had planned to try to rescue them somehow, or at least to explore the option, before all the chaos set in."

Before Wunik could argue further, the woman in the tidy red shirt who had healed her foot arrived. Another mage followed, with a tall, blond, slightly awkward fellow only a minute or so later. Was everyone in this castle sitting around wishing for something better to do?

King Aven gathered them around Wunik's pool of farsight and explained his idea. "Siliana, do you think you could you fly us there?"

She nodded. "That looks maybe an hour or two in flight from here, by this map. Maybe a little more."

"That's fast—are you sure?"

"Do I need to be able to do anything once I get there?"

"Yes. At the very least, fly us back."

She shrugged. "Better consider it two hours then, but yes, I can do it."

"How will you get in?" Jaena said. "You'll need a distraction. I can create one." If she could create something like her dogs, or her mud monster... but bigger...

"A distraction?"

"Yes. Shake the ground a little, perhaps frighten them out of the building."

King Aven smiled ruefully. "That'd be a nice twist of revenge."

"What? Never mind, not now, you can explain later. I have an idea of what we can do." Her eyes had been scouring the palace as her brain raced while the king had explained his plan. She gestured at the palace while she spoke. "This here is likely their dungeon, correct? Where they are probably held? You will need to get through there. Well, what if I blow out the earth on the side instead? Then you can just walk in."

The king nodded. "That would be… excellent."

She hesitated, studying the building.

"I can tell you have more," King Aven said. "Go on."

"If I make a distraction on the other side, over here, it should draw people's attention. We can set down by this willow, and Siliana and I can hide under it. Do you think you could also defend me or at least stand guard while I work?"

Siliana nodded. "Of course. Lots of creature energy is in reserve here if we have an emergency—between the pond, the trees, the gardens. Should be easy to refill for the return flight too."

"I'll need someone to go in with me," King Aven said. "Not necessarily a mage, I guess."

Wunik cut in, "Sire, you are now the *king*. Even as the crown prince, this is not something you should attempt. What if you don't return?"

Aven gave him a firm look. "I have to know if Miara is there. If I don't return, I have two excellent brothers I've heard many would prefer to become king anyway." He smiled and gestured at Thel, the tall one.

Thel fidgeted under his gaze. "I don't know, Aven."

"I'm partly joking," the king said. "But I do think the risks outweigh the rewards here. Allies inside Kavanar would be immensely valuable. Jaena's smith may know much that could help us. Not to mention he played a critical role in… saving Jaena from the Devoted. And who knows, there may be a chance to throw off Daes, while we're at it."

"We can't use those allies or fight Kavanar if you're all dead," Wunik said.

"We won't be," Jaena said. If all they needed to do was get some people from a room on the outside of the building… that seemed relatively simple.

The king grinned at her ready support. Wunik frowned at him. "Your mother is not going to like this."

"And that's why we're not going to tell her. And why we're going to go right now."

"Right *now*?" Wunik was scowling now.

"Well, as soon as we feel we're ready. By tomorrow night, they may have left Trenedum Palace. Plus, we can't afford to keep watch via farsight on this building for an entire day. If we are able, we need to strike now."

Derk yawned loudly and stretched, clearly trying to get their attention. "Fine, well, I guess I could go and help save your asses."

Jaena raised her eyebrows, and King Aven glowered at him.

"Well, if *he's* going, I'm going," Thel said suddenly.

"Are you that just that determined not to be king that you'd rather risk your life instead?" Aven asked. Thel eyed the mage who'd volunteered with suspicion.

"If we all go and we all get killed, Mother will hunt us down in our graves," Thel muttered. "But I'm not going to be left back here like some horse put out to pasture."

"Well, we best not get killed then, so she doesn't have to kill us a second time."

"Also, she'd probably kill Wunik too, and that's not

fair," said Thel.

"Who says *I'm* not coming with you?" Wunik glared.

"Well—uh—" Thel stumbled.

"I'm just teasing you. Someone has to stay behind and tell your mother of this tomfoolery when it goes awry." The doubting nature of his tone was gone now, replaced by a more playful one. Perhaps their plan seemed plausible enough.

"All right then. It's decided," said the king.

Jaena pointed at the view of the palace. "Let's talk about what could go wrong in this plan of ours. We need backup plans."

"There could be a wall made of something you can't move," Wunik offered. "Wood or something. Under that rubble you plan to blow away."

Jaena nodded. "Okay, if there's another wall, we may be able to dig under the door."

"Or a wooden wall could be set on fire," Derk added.

"Good, although let's make sure noone's chained to any walls we destroy," she said. "Another potential problem. The distraction may not be enough, and someone could notice we're in the dungeon."

"And lock us in," Thel added.

"Your optimism is duly noted." King Aven laughed.

"Or people could flood toward the dungeon instead of paying attention to the distraction," offered Thel. Nervous, was he?

"I could create additional distractions if that happens," Siliana said. "Maybe bring some bees or wasps."

"Hornets," Derk offered. "Bet there are some sizable beetles around that pond to use too."

Siliana nodded encouragingly. "Lots of birds usually in this kind of environment as well. We'll be on the same side of the dungeon as you, so I should be able to watch for interlopers. And I can reach out and warn you."

"Another thought—what if Tharomar and the others aren't in the dungeon when we get there?" Jaena said.

Aven nodded gravely. "Then the choice is—do we search the palace, with the violence that comes with that? Or do we abort the mission and return?"

"If you have some reason to believe they've gone into the palace, that would be one thing," Jaena said. "I think my distraction should be enough to bring people out and cause serious disruption inside. But if there's no sign of them or where they went, it might be better to abort."

"We won't know for certain if they're even still in the palace. We can't watch while we fly," Siliana pointed out. "We will only know what was true just before we took flight. Wunik could watch, then Derk could farsee to him, and *then* I could ask him. But that sounds like an awful lot of energy, and we could get caught just sitting by the tree doing all that."

"Yeah, count me out for that. We might as well just blow the side of the building, whether we know they're in there or not." Derk jutted his chin at Jaena. "I like your style, by the way."

She gave him a sidelong glance. "We'll see if you like it after you see it in action."

Aven held up another hand. "We'll go in if we have some concrete clue that any of the four we're looking for are still there. But if we see no signs, we'll turn back. Understood?"

Nods all around.

"Good luck to all of you," Wunik said softly. "And I hope you don't really need it."

# 16 Distractions

The sound of Siliana's black wings flapping had been constant and regular for what had seemed an eternity. Aven knew it could only have been an hour or two, and it was not much different than when Miara had flown him out of Kavanar the day of their escape. The only difference was that this was at night, and being a tiny creature in a box with several other tiny creatures in complete darkness was both better and worse in some ways.

He could have opted to be a bird himself, but he preferred to save all his energy for what was to come. Aven wondered what Thel was making of all this.

Finally the wing beats changed, and he felt them landing. Moments later, Siliana drew his little form out of the box and shifted him back. Had he been a chipmunk again? Seemed so. Only slight nausea accompanied the transformation. Either she was taking more time than Miara did, or he was getting used to the feeling.

Human again, he surveyed the land around them. An

hour or two in the air had taken them across the border of Kavanar. Trenedum Palace glowed a ghostly white on the other side of a willow and a small, foggy pond. He squatted down with the others and looked them all over. They were prepared. They were as ready as they'd ever be.

"All right. Everyone ready?"

Nods all around. Jaena had sunk to the ground and crossed her legs to sit with her back against the tree trunk, preparing. Aven strode over and crouched in front of her, catching her eyes. "Will I know when this... distraction is happening?"

"Oh, you'll know." Was that excitement? A chance to torment her tormentors for once?

"Care to share what it's going to be?" Since she hadn't taken his hints, he might as well ask directly.

She smiled, her dark eyes glinting. "I'm going to... Hmm, no. You'll see. I'll give you a minute or two to get closer, then I'll move the dungeon wall, then it will come not long after. Wait for... the next loud noise after the earth stops moving." He nodded. She shut her eyes.

Aven straightened and strode to Derk and Thel. "Let's go."

The bright moon of the night might have made it easier to spot them, but none of them were particularly experienced at creeping silently through the underbrush in complete darkness, so it was probably for the best. They were relying on the distraction to hide them, not stealth.

Aven crept first, keeping low as he moved from cover to cover. Derk followed, then Thel. Aven might have rather had Dom at his back—they all knew which one of them was burly from wrestling dogs and which one of them had… extremely dexterous fingers from repeated page turns? Aven snorted to himself. Thel would be blessed when he found the lady who cherished these unique facets of his personality. Aven wasn't entirely sure how effectively his brother would be watching his back, but at least it gave them a chance of catching Derk if he tried to betray them.

Because how much could they really trust Derk? He had never given Aven a specific reason for worry, besides his attitude. And, well, his interest in Miara.

They reached the side of the white marble palace and ducked behind a hedgerow.

Aven listened. Nothing but the normal sounds of the night—the slapping of water against the bank, the wind rustling willow branches against each other, an animal lapping up water not so far away. Muffled voices emanated from inside, like a large, festive gathering. What in the hell was there to celebrate? But no loud cacophony met his ears.

Was something wrong? Was Jaena able to do what she'd planned?

He risked a peek around the corner of the building along the dungeon wall and—earth moved as if some giant mole beneath the ground was digging its way out.

Thel appeared beside him, peeking around as well. Aven almost elbowed him back for leaving their cover, but no one was in sight. Thel's blue eyes were wide as saucers.

"So... I could do *that*?" he whispered in Aven's ear.

Aven shrugged. "That's what they tell me. If Jaena survives this mission so we have someone to show you how."

Thel looked irritated at his practicality but gave him the slightest nod. He understood. "I forgot to tell you, we did find *one* book in the library on earth—"

"Not now, Thel."

The moving earth stopped, and Aven was glad for it. He had been completely unable to quell the notion that the earth would *never* move that way unless some giant creature was about to rise up upon them.

A slight thud, now. Then another, then a decisive crack.

Rock flew from the wall and splashed into the pond. Gods, he hoped *that* wasn't the distraction.

But he need not have feared. The sound of the cracking to follow was much, *much* louder and behind him. He didn't wait to see what she was doing exactly, but it sounded like the building itself was coming apart.

He rushed around the corner, the two other men in tow, and through the blown-out wall. Two men had stumbled out into the clearing but were too busy looking at the other side of the building to slip inside. Six men in shackles leaned at various points along the wall. The little girl was not there, and none of the men seemed to be the one that had accompanied her. The prisoners were apparently all in one cell, the door of which hung open. The guards must have entered the cell to see what the commotion was about.

"Any of you named Tharomar?" Aven raised his voice

as loudly as he dared.

Several eyebrows rose, but one man frowned. That had to be him. Aven rushed toward him.

"Who sent you?" the man demanded as Thel helped Aven get the man to his feet.

"Why does that matter if we're getting you out of here?" Derk said.

That only deepened the man's frown.

"A man and a young girl—have you seen them? Damn it, they're not here," Aven said instead.

"Was she youngish, maybe eleven?"

Aven nodded.

"He took them. The leader."

Aven swore. "Wearing all black?"

"Yes."

"Damn it. Do you know where they went?"

"No. Well—he said *he* was going up to the ball. Would he have taken them with him, or just moved them somewhere else? Who are they?"

Aven looked from Thel to Derk to the men outside. "Friends of friends. Thel—get Tharomar back to the others and see if you can get these shackles off. Derk, you and I will go in."

"In?" Tharomar started. "You're going up there? And I'm not going *anywhere* until you tell me who sent you."

"Jaena sent us. Come on, this way."

Tharomar's jaw dropped, but that didn't stop any of them from rushing back out. Aven had hoped to slip back along the side of the building, but one of the guards had unfortunately realized how thoroughly he'd abandoned his post. Spotting them, he cried a warning to the other guard, although Aven wasn't certain the man heard anything.

The soft rumble of voices from inside was gone, replaced with more frantic voices, cries, and a strange, deep, grinding noise. But Aven had no time to discover the origin of that sound. The one attentive guard rushed at him.

"Get him over there," Aven barked.

"Hurry up and get those shackles off. Shift just his hands," Derk added.

The guard appeared to be unarmed. As the guard reached him, Aven crouched slightly and dove for his attacker's midsection, using the momentum to hurl him up and over. The guard flew through the air and narrowly missed Derk, thanks to a small sidestep on the mage's part. The guard landed with a thud on his back.

Derk surprised Aven by being quick with a dagger. He had it at the man's throat before Aven had barely blinked.

"Don't do it. I'll cut you and roll your body into this pond, and no one will know the difference."

The guard froze. Aven felt himself freeze too, realizing he had no idea if Derk was perfectly rational or a completely cold-blooded killer. Aven forced himself to take a breath.

"You had a woman, a girl, and her father in your cell," Aven bluffed. "Where are they?"

The man's eyes strained to turn his face toward Aven

without pressing his neck against the knife's edge. "The mage slaves?"

Aven gritted his teeth. Not for long if he had anything to say about it. "Yes," he said instead.

"I saw no woman, but Daes Cavalion took the other two up to the main ballroom."

"Are you sure?" Aven glanced at Derk as if giving him permission to press harder.

"I escorted him up there, I swear it."

"How do we get up there?"

"Well, it looks like you can walk right in, with the front of the building torn off—"

Another large grinding screech finally drew Aven's eye. He took two steps to the side, and he could see... what by the gods *did* he see?

Columns and stones from the palace had torn themselves apart and reassembled into a huge stone creature. The palace was lush but low, perhaps three stories. The giant towered at least five stories above the earth. The elegance of the columns and the white marble was not entirely lost, and there was something strangely beautiful about the being. Where eyes should have been, no stones rested, only dark hollows that seemed to come alive and see straight through him.

So. Distraction. Yes. That *was* very distracting. Even to him.

The creature reached down with an arm-like appendage to grab something. Aven forced his attention back to the man.

"Go back in there, shut the cell door, pretend like nothing is going on, and we won't have to kill you."

Both Derk and the guard looked at him like he was crazy.

"Like nothing's going on?" the guard sputtered.

"Like he'll do that?" Derk said at the same time.

Aven wanted to pummel them both. He just wanted to get on with the mission and not have to deal with this bastard.

"Get up and *run*, or I'll make sure that you can't." Aven grabbed Derk's shirt and pushed him away from the guard before quickly hauling the guard to his feet and shoving him in the opposite direction.

The guard hesitated. Aven raised a fist over his shoulder and took a warning step forward. The man turned and ran.

Derk snickered. "Nice, I think he wet himself. Let's go."

Aven was relieved that Derk seemed perfectly fine with that solution. He didn't need a bloodthirsty bastard at a moment like this, as pleased as he was that Derk seemed capable with a dagger.

Aven drew his sword, and they ventured around the corner. Indeed, the front and side of the building were gone, as was most of the ceiling. The interior revealed a great dining hall where it seemed people had been eating. A multitude of pillows and cushions in the center of the palace suggested possibly more. Tiny shards of glass and beads of lead covered the ground around much of the outer edges. The windows must have shattered. Slabs of stone that made up the roof and ceiling edge looked unstable, and one teetered and crashed as Aven watched, smashing a table beneath it into splinters.

Seeing the interior and imagining King Demikin not so far away made his heart thud in his chest for a moment at the enormity of this act. They might not yet know Akarians were behind this, but Aven did. This was essentially an act of war, and *not* a subtle one. He hadn't exactly thought of it like that when they'd been conceiving their scrappy little rescue mission. Freeing mages had been Aven's goal, and this romp had just seemed like an extension of that.

It hadn't occurred to him that they were perpetrating the equivalent of a direct attack on the Kavanarian king, inside his territory. He hadn't known the magnitude of Jaena's distraction. No point in worrying now; they were already across the threshold.

Even with his sword drawn, Aven crept unnoticed around the corner, Derk behind him. Many had fled the outer room, but some were salvaging valuables, though the marble creature seemed bent on further destruction.

Where could they be?

Wait—he could feel them, through their brands. He could look for their squirming, tormented knots of energy. He spread his senses while trying to keep moving but found he had to stop to concentrate.

He felt dozens of slaves hiding in the rooms to his left, before him, and in the levels below. He felt each of the hearth fires in each of the rooms. How could he pick them out of these masses?

"Damn it."

"What is it?"

"Where do we start looking? I tried to feel for them, but there's dozens of mage slaves here."

"Maybe we should go back."

"We came this far… We have to…"

Aven groped around again, trying to think of something. Maybe… a small group of them felt separate from the others, smaller, off in front of him and up the stairs. If Miara's family was with Daes, then they could be alone or with only a few other servants. Might the larger groups be those in sleeping quarters or those hiding from the monster or ones who somehow worked in the castle?

He thought all mage slaves had been in Mage Hall. Why *were* there so many here now?

Because they're moving them, he realized. To hide them from *you*.

"Let's try this way." Aven started forward, and Derk offered no objection. They took a nearby staircase that looked at least somewhat stable, though a large chunk of it had been torn away by either falling roof rock or the creature's hands. The first door he opened led to a dark hallway with just one torch burning. Had others burned out? Strange.

They stalked carefully down it to the next door. Aven listened. Voices came from the other side, and footsteps—

Footsteps coming their way.

He spun away, just barely missing the door slamming into his face.

A man stalked past, leaving the door open. Voices

murmured inside, but he couldn't distinguish any of them.

Aven pivoted on one foot and spun round, entering the door with sword drawn.

Derk did not follow him.

He gritted his teeth. That smart-assed traitor. Had he come *all* this way just to screw Aven over when it counted? He shouldn't be surprised. Would Thel or Tharomar find the way to this spot and follow him? They might, but it could well be too late.

He was on his own.

"Well, well, we meet again, star mage."

Daes's voice threatened to make him shudder, but he steadied himself and leveled the point of his sword in the man's direction. Aven took in the room as quickly as he could.

It appeared to be an ordinary royal sitting room. A man and a girl stood to the far left, near Daes, who sat stiffly in a dark brown armchair.

"Brown, I see? Changing up the color palette a bit?"

A hint of a sardonic smile curled Daes's lips. "It was the closest to black they had."

In the far right corner of the room, King Demikin gaped out the window, a guard on one side and a woman in a red velvet gown on the other, her hand on his back. At Aven's voice he turned, his eyes wide.

"What are *you* doing here?" he demanded. "Are *you* responsible for this?"

Aven did his best to look incredulous. "Do I look like an earth mage? It seems you've mightily pissed one off, though, I must admit."

"What do you want?" Daes demanded.

"Miara's family," Aven shot back.

"Not going to happen."

A flicker of awareness caught in the eyes of the man and girl now. And was that hope? Or greater despair? They hadn't realized this mess was about them.

"Where is Miara?" Aven demanded.

Daes tilted his head and looked mightily amused. He didn't know. Wherever Miara was, Daes had heard nothing of it.

And maybe had had nothing to do with it.

Although those dead bodies hadn't just shown up in Miara's rooms on their own. At least… he didn't think so. Daes had probably had something to do with *that*.

"You don't know? That's… Why, how entertaining. Demikin, Marielle, we're getting quite the show with dinner thanks to these Akarians." He said the last word with notable disgust.

"Let them go, or I'll run you through," Aven demanded.

Daes's gaze flicked to Miara's family. "Defend me from this lout," Daes said to the man. Face twisting, Miara's father moved between Aven and Daes.

Damn. He hadn't counted on that. *Now* what was he going to do? He shifted his weight from foot to foot, trying to think. The older man didn't look like much of a fighter, and Aven could probably subdue him without any permanent injury, but that would be a chance for the others in the room to get the drop on him. He couldn't take them all at once, most likely. He had *thought* he'd have a companion. He pulled a dagger at his belt.

"The king. I'll kill the king if you don't let them go."

Leaning around Miara's father, Daes raised an amused eyebrow and smiled. "Oh, please do. Go ahead. That was my plan tonight anyway."

For the first time, Aven realized that the guard was not *protecting* the king, but *restraining* him. Oh, by the gods. What plan was afoot here?

"You're outmaneuvered, boy. Where is my brand?"

Now it was Aven's turn to smirk, although of course he wasn't going to tell Daes anything of the sort. Aven needed a plan. Perhaps if he could keep Daes talking, he'd have time to think of something. "What brand? You've lost something, I take it?"

"Oh, you know what brand. Come clean, and perhaps I'll only sear you to medium instead of well done this time. We will find it, you know."

Could Aven free them while they talked? That seemed highly unlikely, he doubted he could keep up a conversation at the same time, but what if he could? No, he'd pass out at the end by himself. It was just too much.

He wasn't even keeping up the conversation very well now as he struggled to think.

"You won't find it, because it's been destroyed." There. That should give him some heart palpitations.

And indeed, Daes's face turned an even paler shade of pallid. "You're bluffing. It can't be."

Was the girl commanded to defend Daes too? He

could probably club Miara's father over the head and get his forgiveness in the long run, but Aven wasn't sure he could render a young girl unconscious and forgive himself for it. But perhaps if he had no other choice.

Aven stepped to one side, closer to the king and skirting around Miara's father and Daes.

"It has already been destroyed," he said as coolly as he could muster. "You'll have to get your power from actually *leading* people instead of enslaving them."

That seemed to get under the bastard's skin, and Aven felt a bit smug. Not so fast with the back pats, though. He still had no idea how they were going to get out of this mess.

The grinding, rumbling sounds outside intensified.

"Well, your lies don't matter anyway," Daes scoffed. "We're making a new one."

No. No—they couldn't know how. Could they? Perhaps they had their own forbidden knowledge, tucked away for this very emergency. No. Damn it, he hoped it wasn't true.

"Now you're bluffing," Aven said, voice as flat as he could muster. "You don't know how."

"It's already in production." Daes waved him off like a gnat bothering his wine.

He *had* to be bluffing. But—

The grinding sound grew deafeningly loud, and Aven took a reflexive step back.

The outer wall of the room crumbled away, white granite fingers crushing the stone. The king, who had been leaning against the wall up until the last moment, tumbled out of sight with a surprised cry and fell. The red-dressed woman—the queen?—started to lose her balance, teetered on the edge, but then caught herself on the edge of a jagged granite slab.

Aven acted quickly, using the disruption to lunge at Miara's father and, with an inward wince, clubbed him in the head with the hilt of his sword. The girl rushed toward her father as he fell, and so did Aven.

Daes, interestingly, rushed to help the woman.

As Aven bent down, he heard a telltale swish over his head. A knife thrown.

Aven ducked but realized quickly the knife hadn't been for him. It'd been aimed at Daes, but the bastard had moved aside at the last moment to get a grip on the woman's arm. The weapon *did* find a home in the guard's chest, however, while he attempted to back away from the chasm. He, too, tumbled over the edge.

Derk swept into the room beside him, grabbed the girl's arm, and started dragging her from the room. She winced in pain, clutching her shoulder, compelled to try to stay, but fortunately, Derk ignored it.

His eyes caught with Aven's. "Are you coming?"

Hmm. Maybe not such a traitor after all. Still smart-assed, though. Aven bent quickly, not bothering to answer, and heaved Miara's father over his shoulder, racing back out the hallway, down the stairs, toward where the others waited.

"Where the hell were you?" Aven snapped as they ran.

"Covering your ass from the hallway. We both run

in there, and we've played all our cards. And how hard would it be for them to surround us and turn us both into rat meat? Not hard. No, thank you."

As Aven approached the willow, he was glad he'd sent Thel and Tharomar back. The two of them fought with four oncoming but fairly incompetent guards. Thel fought off two with his short sword and Tharomar the other two with a—was that a table leg?

Father would be pleased to see Thel's lessons actually being put to some use. Aven's gut twisted at the thought of his father, but he pushed himself faster. His father would also be damn proud if they got out alive.

They had to keep going. And finish this.

Derk handed the girl off to Siliana, who wrapped her arms around the child's struggling form. Would they need to free her before they left? Would it even be safe to fly with her being compelled to return like that?

Aven dumped Miara's father next to Siliana too, who looked at him with wide eyes. "He was compelled to defend them, had to do it. Can you fly with her like that?" He drew his sword and lunged to join Tharomar.

"I—I think so."

"Can you transform her now then?"

"Yes. I'll do it. Both of them."

Aven took a careful grip of his blade, twisted it, and half-sworded the man in the head, the hilt of the sword hitting the man's skull with far more force than he'd used on Miara's father. The guard fell, at the very least dizzy.

Tharomar sent his man reeling into the pond as Thel

and Derk dispatched their attackers as well.

"I've got them—let's go! Who's next?"

Jaena still sat, eyes closed in concentration, by the tree. Tharomar rushed to her now, falling to his knees and looking like he wanted to—what? Hug her? Kiss her? Shake her awake? He settled for just staring.

"Jaena last," Aven barked. "She's holding up our distraction. Thel, Derk, go."

But Derk had his eyes closed too. "I'm working up some cover. The smith, then me."

"Fine, just go, go, go."

The men all crowded around Siliana and Jaena. Aven searched the ruins of the palace. Where was Daes? The gash in the room they'd fled lay empty. Aven glanced down and saw Derk's distraction. Fog rose slowly up around them. Through the growing mist, the king's body was just visible. He had fallen two stories and lay crumpled, half across rubble, half submerged in a fountain.

By the gods. Demikin was dead.

It hadn't even been that far of a fall. Could Daes have had some other plan afoot? Could he have had him drugged? How could he have separated the king from his guards anyway? The woman. The queen. She must have been in on it too.

Would they blame Aven? Akaria? A giant marble creature that had risen out of the mist to wreak havoc on everyone?

Earth mages were supposed to be the *weaker* ones. By the gods.

Derk signaled he was ready, and his form twisted away beside Aven. The rising fog concealed them fairly well. Aven scanned the area, and his eyes caught on Daes.

The Dark Master and a dozen guards stood at the corner of the palace walls, searching around them for Aven and Derk's tracks. Aven crouched down, but it felt too late. He swore he could feel the Dark Master's eyes boring into him even then.

Siliana met his eyes.

"Guards," he whispered. "A dozen. Get Jaena first."

"My lord, you *have* to go. You cannot risk being left behind."

"There's time. Go—both of us."

Siliana lunged toward Jaena, shaking her arm. Her dark eyes snapped open in surprise.

The creature collapsed, thundering to the ground with an earth-shaking boom. They all winced, ducking their heads. Damn, they had known it was coming, why were they wasting time reacting?

"Go, damn it," he urged them.

How far away could the guards be? Siliana's face looked white, but Jaena twisted and joined the others in the box.

"Get more energy—go. You can't risk running out now."

She nodded, eyes looking a little frantic that she'd needed the reminder, but that was the last thing he saw. His body twisted again, and this time the nausea was intense. Well, that answered that question.

He looked down at tiny hands and soft brown fur as

she lifted him into the box.

Now he just had to pray their enemy had no arrows and that Siliana completed her own transformation before Daes arrived.

Or they'd all be served up to the Dark Master in a tidy little box, convenient for the squishing. At least Miara wasn't with them for the squishing ceremony.

But if the Masters hadn't recaptured her... where the hell was she?

The flight back to Panar seemed unending. The shift had nauseated Jaena, and her work had exhausted her, and the swaying of the tiny box in the darkness did *not* help any of that.

But they had freed Tharomar. Just that thought made relief and contentment swell in her small rodent chest. The discomfort of the ride was not important by comparison.

Siliana alighted on the balcony of the castle, gradually transforming them all back with greater control this time. Or perhaps she was going more slowly because she was afraid. Those had been great feats for one lone creature mage. If only Miara had been there to help.

Jaena didn't immediately find the energy to get up after the shift was complete. She sat and simply waited, watching them each reappear. She noticed one chipmunk had a stripe of white fur on its head and smiled.

Indeed, that creature transformed back into Tharomar,

and she beamed at him. She couldn't help herself.

"By the gods—Jaena!" He ran to her, then crouched and threw his arms around her. "Was this your idea?"

"Partly. Partly Aven's."

"Did you—what happened? I have so many questions." He stood, then held out a hand and helped her to her feet.

"I'm honestly exhausted, Tharomar—"

"That was *amazing*. It was like with the mud, but by the—"

She lurched to one side. "I think I need to lie down."

He jumped to her side and threw her arm over his shoulder. "Do you have a room here? Cause I sure don't. This time." He grinned.

"If it's all right with everyone, I think we'll take our leave to rest?" Jaena said.

Wunik was just rushing out onto the balcony. "Is this the smith, the priest?"

Tharomar winced. "Just a smith."

She snorted. "Hmm, is that so. We can talk in the morning, right, Wunik?"

"Oh, yes, of course."

"Go and rest," King Aven added. "The Assembly may vote first thing in the morning, so we may need to rise in only a few hours. Or the vote may be later. We'll see."

"That way," Jaena pointed with an elbow, as one hand was around Ro's waist and the other clasped his hand on her shoulder for support. And... maybe for more than support.

It felt funny not limping this time, although she did

indeed feel very weak. They left the king's chambers—she was still having a hard time processing that her mage savior was also their king—and headed down the hallway toward the room they'd given her.

"You knew, didn't you?" Tharomar said softly.

"Knew what?" she said.

"You know what." He narrowed his eyes at her, and she winced. "That I'm a mage," he said.

"Yes," she admitted.

"Why didn't you tell me?" he said.

"Why didn't your temple tell you?" she countered.

"A good question. My, you are good at dodging questions with questions."

"I was going to tell you. And I was going to answer you. I just don't always answer you promptly, that's all. I thought there would be time—and then we ran out of it. And I wasn't sure how you'd react."

"I'm not sure how I'm reacting either." He laughed.

"Oh?"

"A week ago the answer would have been simple. Even if I knew I was a mage, I would have thought the answer easy: abstain. Now..." He drifted off.

"Not so sure?" she said.

"Well, it's hard to recommend such an approach with the group of you saving my ass from slave labor, likely torture, and probably eventual death, using not much more than magic."

"Doesn't feel so evil *now*, does it?"

"Well, it doesn't feel against the Way. I mean, what

was the alternative? Kill them all?" He threw up his one free hand.

"Probably. Well, yes," she said.

"That would not have been better."

"I suppose we could have tried to capture and tie up everyone. But that sounds like a recipe for disaster. Well, there's time to think on it later."

"Yeah. I mean, I can't do any magic yet anyway," he said, sounding a little relieved at that idea.

"Oh, you were already doing it. That's how I knew," she said.

His eyebrows shot up.

"The smithy was full of it. You're lucky you had all those pendants. Where did it go, anyway? Is that how the Devoted figured you out?"

"Yes. Lost the pendant. Well, a knight ripped it off my neck."

"Gods. I worried something like that might happen."

"Well, now I know, and I got out. So that's a good first step. But I will need to reach out to my order in the morning, tell them the Devoted know of the necklaces."

"And why were they harboring you as a mage without telling you?" she asked. "Do you think they knew? Or maybe they didn't? But then why would they give you that type of necklace?"

He frowned. "Indeed. Why would they give *all* of us those necklaces?"

"Oh, here, this room," she directed. He opened the door, and they made their way inside. The small guest room contained little more than a bed, a small hearth, and one table. No chairs. "Perhaps it doesn't matter. But we're not out of here yet. We couldn't have gotten here without Aven's help. We have to help him get those he was looking for too."

"Indeed. Well, you have my arms if you have a sword I can borrow. Otherwise, I'm not bad with my hands."

Why was she blushing? Why were they still holding onto each other, as though she needed help to walk, even though they'd stopped? Even though she could sit down on the bed and… he could leave. But where would he go? The stewards would likely find somewhere for him, but…

"Who is this Aven, by the way?" he asked.

"The crown prince of Akaria. No, the king. I keep forgetting."

He stared at her. "You're joking."

"No."

"Well, even more then, I'm sure my sword or my hands can be at his service."

"I just want them to be at my service… and only mine. Is that too much to ask?"

Smiling, he turned and pulled her close, wrapping his arms around her. "I think that could be arranged." He bent to hug her and nuzzle his face against her neck.

Her breath a little ragged, she risked a kiss against the powerful muscles of his neck, then a nip on his earlobe. His arms tightened around her, molding them together as his lips brushed against her collarbone.

"Is that so?" she whispered. "Then… show me."

Miara and Samul had taken turns overnight, one walking, the other resting as Lukor carried them. She'd led them further into the forest, hoping to lose those damn mages by moving through the night so far afield. With morning came exhaustion, though, and as they neared the end of the forest and headed toward the more open grassy plain, Miara winced at the lack of cover. This was *not* going to help matters. She kept her senses outstretched, trying to pick up on their potential pursuers, but she felt nothing.

The last trees of the forest were falling away when the soft twang and the whistle of an arrow through the air caught her ear. Entirely too late, of course.

*Thunk, thunk-thunk.* An arrow stabbed into her left shoulder. Then the right torso and left thigh exploded in pain with simultaneous punctures of their own.

Pain threatened to overwhelm thought. Knowing she had to get to some kind of cover, scarce as it was, she staggered off the trail.

"Miara!"

Samul's footsteps followed, and then he was pulling her further into the few remaining trees. He must have knelt because he came into focus above her.

"I think they're trying to kill you." His face was grave.

"I think—you'd be right," she coughed. A warm liquid that wasn't saliva sputtered into her mouth. Great. This was not going to be easy. She struggled to assess the damage, figure out what they were going to do.

"If they kill you, you can't heal from *that*, can you?" Samul said, as if he had guessed the answer.

"I think that's the idea." She wanted to say more but couldn't. Those mages must know she could defend Samul fairly well and heal him when necessary. Clearly they weren't good enough shots to reliably kill from a distance. Thus they were seeking to eliminate her first so she couldn't save him. But she had no breath for all that. Instead, she said, "I can heal this, but it's going to give away our location. After I do it, you'll have to move me. Think you can?"

He nodded. "Go. You're losing blood."

"You'll have to yank out the arrows. Start with the top one, move down. Go."

She closed her eyes. The left shoulder wound was the worst, but the one in her right side wasn't much better. On top of impeding movement, it had hit something important. They had to be healed, and it was going to hurt like a thousand daggers raking her insides.

Anara help me, she thought. Nefrana even. All of you.

Samul yanked out the first arrow, and she gritted her teeth through a cry. She sucked in a breath and held it, and with it, she began the spell. Life drained from a nearby elm, a poplar, a juniper bush. Perhaps she could leave them a little alive to recover—she hoped—but even as it began she knew she lacked the conscious control to do so. The agony was too great.

She heard herself scream as though it were someone

else. For a moment, she could see her body cradled in Samul's arms. The greenery around them darkened into black as her mind stole the life of the creatures around them. Stole was a painfully accurate word, a heartbreaking, horrible word. But there was no time for regret yet, only pain, only survival. A pine tree dropped its needles, then shuddered into dust. She strained to avoid Samul himself, and a chipmunk scurried away, but beyond them, her magic had a mind of its own now. It knew she was determined to live. Her body was determined to heal. And it acted accordingly.

She opened her eyes as her body was jostled. Samul carried her in his arms like a child and was charging into what remained of the tree line. What other cover was there to be had? Lukor followed. They needed to mount up, get riding. If the mages were close enough for arrows, they would reach her and Samul soon. But—riding would put them out in the open too. They needed something else, something to buy them time.

And she was barely conscious, let alone able to think.

And yet she *was* thinking, wasn't she? Her mind was automatically assessing the situation, looking for ways out. The deep, determined part of her that had controlled her magic. The part of her that was determined to survive.

Samul set her down by another set of evergreen bushes. She squinted down at herself. The blood and holes remained, covering half of her at this point, and her thigh was only partially healed. But the wounds to her torso were repaired, and she had enough energy for more if needed. The trees weren't so lucky, of course. The thought made her heart ache, but it couldn't be avoided.

The Masters couldn't have given these mages orders to do this so quickly. They hunted her on their own initiative. Sorin was a painful reminder that not every mage might be looking for ways around their orders, as these arrows made all too clear.

Her eyes darted around. No cover anywhere. Maybe there was a way to slow or stall them that would help instead.

She reached her senses out, searching for the mages, and all too quickly caught one racing toward them along the road's path. Gravel Voice. She had to act while she could, he was not far.

Vines erupted from the earth, snagging at his bow, his arms, his ankles. They coiled about him and dragged him down face-first into the rough road.

The earth shook beneath them. Please, she thought. That earth mage simply had no idea where they were. What a sad attempt at a threat.

She groped around for the others. There. Following, but not so quickly. Not so ardently. The nervous one hung back a little. The creature mage was the problem. She could undo Miara's spells when the others couldn't. She must have succeeded with Miara's shackles, which meant she was thoughtful, creative, observant. Miara would not trick her with cleverness.

Well, perhaps where cleverness failed, brute force would have to do.

Her vines erupted again, but around the creature

546 ›          R. K. THORNE

mage, she raised a dozen-fold more than her usual effort and added thorns for good measure. Anything that might slow the enemy down a bit more. Again the vines caught the bow, then the mage, and tightened her into the earth. A faint cry caught on the wind. That was probably the thorns. But then another screech sounded, that of a falcon. By the gods, could it be? Had the same falcon returned?

Vines continued to coil around the creature mage, another layer and another, but another avian shriek rang out. Amazing. Her falcon had indeed come looking for her near Panar. She spared an expensive glance back at the fierce creature arrowing in a steep dive toward the road, likely at one of the two mages.

Probably hoping for a duck leg this time. Or maybe something bigger. He'd get it too, if she ever got the chance.

She found the nervous mage staggering back, uncertain. *Run,* she shouted at him. *Or I'll do the same to you.* If she could scare him off, that might leave them with only two pursuers. A vine snatched the bow from his hand, and she felt his energy bolt in the opposite direction, beyond where she could feel him.

"Let's go," Miara said quickly. "I've tried to slow them down, but it won't last. On the horse, both of us."

Samul swung himself up. "Get in front," he grunted. He relinquished the stirrup so she could mount.

"No, you're the king—"

"And you're the only one who can heal me."

"But—"

"You can't heal me if you're dead. Now get on." When

she hesitated, he added. "That's an order, mage."

She nodded briskly and hiked herself up. Riding in such close physical proximity to Aven's father was definitely something she'd hoped to avoid. But survival would be nice too.

She urged Lukor as fast as he could manage. *Not long now, friend.* They were almost to Panar. If they could just make it the last few miles... Miles of unfortunately open, grassy fields upon which they were easily visible and even more easily targeted.

# I7 IMPACT

All eyes rested on Aven, on the king of Akaria, and they waited for his last few words before their voting began.

Members of the Assembly circled the tan stone table, wide and pitted with age in the center of the tower room. Well, all the members except Lord Sven, who had still refused to appear and had sent his daughter, the priestess Niat, instead.

On all four sides, graceful arches framed dramatic views of the city, bitterly bright in the morning sun. Advisors, arms masters, and Alikar's precious archivists and chroniclers hovered near the walls; his mage friends Jaena, Tharomar, Wunik, and the others were among them. The mages didn't necessarily need to be here, but he preferred having them close by, particularly with Jaena carrying the brand. This situation had the potential to devolve into chaos, and if that happened, it would happen fast.

When Aven had first joined them, striding in from

the vicious brightness, he'd arrived without his father and wearing the simple crown of platinum and sapphire on his brow. The room had fallen silent, still. He'd hardly needed to explain. The faces of those who hadn't yet heard wore grim recognition, sorrow, a touch of fear.

Troops from Ranok had swarmed the place, searching for potential assassins and other betrayals. Aven didn't have much hope that they'd find anything, even if threats awaited them, but the soldiers that staffed Ranok were some of their best, specifically chosen from their own Elaren Territory for their loyalty to the king. With the king living in Estun, they'd so rarely seen combat on his behalf, but Aven was glad to have them with him. Daes likely now had his hands full with the aftermath of last night's chaos, but any attack he made on this meeting had likely begun days ago. It would shock Aven if Daes *didn't* try something.

The room secure, the Assembly of Akaria had been called to order.

They'd taken his news as well as he could have asked, listening tensely as he explained their journey, the king's disappearance. Dyon and Asten's eyes had locked as they discussed the news received from the watch towers—siege troops were approaching the city and would reach them soon. Surely Asten and Dyon wanted to be elsewhere, preparing for battle. So did Aven. But they had business to attend to first.

He'd hardly slept three hours, let alone had time to think about what he was going to say. And yet, he knew what he needed to say. He'd known from the day he'd stepped foot in Estun, and his only regret was that he hadn't been more determined to say it sooner.

He took a deep breath and began.

"Before you begin your vote, I have one more matter. Many of you know I returned from Kavanar with a companion, Miara. We've received word she has disappeared from Estun. We are not sure of her location or if she is even alive."

A quiet stillness settled further on the room.

"You've heard about her role in my rescue. She has provided valuable intelligence to us on Kavanar's mage troop preparations, as well as what we can expect from mages in the coming war. But there is more to our story. Miara is not only a talented mage, but she is also one of the strongest women I have ever known. In slavery, her moral fiber has been tested to a level most of us have never experienced, and I trust her as much as any member of my family. While on the course of our journey together, I fell in love with her, and I have asked her to marry me."

The room's silence exploded into a flurry of murmurs tinged with excitement, outrage, shock.

"I think her strength and experience will make her an excellent queen, should you all choose to support me." He stopped again to let it sink in. Beneral's and Asten's eyes were wide. Toyl smiled, looking pleased. And if he didn't know better, Aven would mistake that look on Dyon's face for pride. Directed at him?

"If I can find her," Aven added.

Alikar was smirking. "As if one mage wasn't enough, *now* we have two."

Aven ignored the comment. "Begin, and have your vote."

He hadn't intended to imbue his voice with any emotion, but the final words came out edged with disgust. That *was* how he felt, but he hadn't meant to share it. He took a step back, ceding the meeting to the Assembly with a nod to Dyon.

Dyon nodded in return. "All right then, Lord Alikar. You heard the king, the ballistae approach even now. Let us go with haste."

Alikar straightened. "You all know why I have called you here. Our finest religious leaders, our priests and priestesses, our clerics and scribes, all agree on this matter. Magic is a perversion of the world, an abomination, a twisted abuse deeply against the Way."

The first time sunlight had filled him with the power of magic flashed through Aven's mind. The joyous elation, the way his soul had soared, the way Miara had laughed at his exuberance. His gut twisted.

"Magic is a power humans are not meant to wield. As such, no man who chooses to wield this power should lead our kingdom. Nefrana condemns it, our priests condemn it, and you should condemn it as well. I call on *all* of you to make the difficult choice in this matter, the choice of light, the choice of heaven, lest we lose the favor of the gods. I called you here to vote on this man's fitness to be our crown prince, but the situation is now even more dire, as he already holds our throne as king.

I now request your vote. Do you find this mage fit to be our king, to support with gold from your treasuries and troops from your lands?"

Warden Asten glared at the last bit— by no means did she control her territory's treasuries or troops, exactly, although others like Dyon did. Of course, Beneral had glared through the whole thing. Perhaps having Alikar saunter into his own city and piss all over it with his foul words was making Beneral rethink his decision to keep his magic secret. Either that, or he didn't realize he was scowling.

"I'll start," Alikar said. The Gilaren lord almost glowed with even this slight bit of control. Did he really hope to gain any power from this spectacle? "I find any mage unfit to be king of Akaria. Gilaren withdraws financial and military support while Aven Lanuken sits on the throne."

Aven gritted his teeth. Of course, this was unsurprising, but his father's disappearance had escalated things. Aven hadn't expected him to formally withdraw support right away. It had seemed more likely that Alikar would have waited to see the result of the vote and his father's—now Aven's—reaction to it.

"Lord Dyon—your vote."

Dyon's slightly raised eyebrows indicated he was a little surprised by the severity of that statement too. "Liren supports the throne unequivocally, as we always have. Our king cares more about the Akarian people than all of you combined. That alone will make him an excellent ruler, even if he wasn't so well qualified militarily and diplomatically. Far more prepared than any of his brothers, cousins, or any of *us*, I might add. I find him very fit to rule. I would support no other, in fact." The threat in his words didn't seem to register with Alikar, but Aven did not miss it. Dyon beckoned civil war if the vote failed.

Alikar waved off Dyon's words as if he were a doddering old man. "Priestess Niat. Your vote."

She sat frozen, tense, eyes the size of saucers. Of course, Alikar presumed he knew her vote would be against Aven, and that was why he'd chosen her to go second, to weaken the impact of Dyon's words. Lord Sven's bigotry was also the only vote Aven was certain of beyond Alikar's as well. But the poor priestess did not understand any of that. She looked discomfited at having been given such a very prominent position in the order of votes.

She raised her chin and recovered her composure. "My father regrets he cannot be with you today," she said. Her voice rose in volume, as if she was picking up courage as she went. That did not at all sound like something Sven would say, so Aven guessed she was adding that bit on his behalf. "And he thanks you in your understanding for accepting me, his daughter, in his stead." She unrolled a small piece of parchment, as if that somehow made her word more valid or more directly from Sven. Had she embellished this too? The parchment was unsealed or unstamped in any way, as any kind of official document would be, especially coming from one as grandiose and pompous as Sven. "His vote is no, a mage is unfit to be Akaria's crown prince and heir."

Alikar gave her a withering look. "The vote has changed, as you well know. We're voting on our support for the *king*. Or haven't you been paying attention?"

Aven was rather sure that Alikar knew she *had* been paying attention, that he just wanted to see her squirm. Part of the power trip?

"I can't—"

"Amend the vote." Alikar's eyes hardened into black coals.

When she hesitated, Dyon lowered his chin and folded his arms across his chest. "He sent you in his stead. That's what he gets. You are his representative, *you* choose your vote."

She glared at him, then glanced with concern at Aven. Ah, that was exactly the problem wasn't it. She had counted on awkwardly relaying her father's vote. She was even less comfortable with insulting the king to his face, not when he had the power to have her hanged.

Alikar narrowed his eyes even further, as if he wanted to pin her to the wall and force her to vote. "Now, please, before we all get pummeled to smithereens by the approaching catapults."

Catapults. Aven had been very careful to say siege machines. Dyon had repeatedly said ballistae, for some reason, even though he'd *seen* the enemy's forces via farsight this morning too. None of the oncoming troops were in sight of the city yet, especially not from this room. And all of them were catapults.

Alikar already knew what type of troops approached the city. And how could he know that? Aven had never had such concrete proof the bastard was a traitor. Had Alikar given the Masters this location? Or did he hope to escape himself before some kind of attack? Damn it.

She lifted her chin even higher, defiantly glaring at Alikar. "My *father* votes no, he is not fit to be king."

Alikar nodded, looking round the table, as if he wanted to highlight Sven's agreement.

"Asten—your vote."

Did he choose her next because he knew her vote? Was he trying to alternate between positive and negative? How many of these votes did Alikar feel confident in? It doesn't matter. It doesn't matter. They can all vote no, and *technically* it doesn't change anything.

Except the armory budgets, or where troops are assigned, or…

Asten looked at each of them in turn, then at Aven for a long moment. The length of her stare rattled his nerves, and his stomach sank lower each moment she stared at him. Was that apology in her eyes? She looked back at Alikar.

"Aven is already our king, and I wouldn't have it any other way. Slag off, Alikar."

The rage that filled Alikar's face was even more intense than Aven had expected. "Shansaren will regret this. How—" Had he struck some kind of deal? He had expected her vote to go another way, hadn't he?

Asten dropped her chin, glaring at Alikar and leaning forward on the table. "The use of magic has already provided invaluable aid to us in this war so far, and yes, it *is* a war. From healing to attacks to intelligence to planning for the oncoming siege weapons." Was it Aven's imagination, or was there an emphasis on the final words? "We would be fools to turn away mages even just as weapons when such weapons are being turned against us. And they happen to be good and honorable people to boot."

Alikar pressed his lips together and acted as if she hadn't spoken. "Beneral."

"I believe a mage is especially qualified to be king in a time such as this. I find him a fit prince, king, and leader."

"Toyl."

Three in favor, two against. And Alikar had chosen her last. Why exactly had Toyl withheld her vote from Aven? The question haunted him. She had acted friendly, on Aven's side. Perhaps she was no enemy to Aven but a friend to money. Asten would be hard to buy, and yet it seemed that Alikar had tried. Toyl could be much easier, as trade agreements would benefit both her and her people far more than they would a warden.

Toyl glanced at Aven, her dark eyes glittering, then to the others.

"I have no particular love for mages. I have worshiped at Nefrana's feet, as she teaches us the error of those ways." A small smile grew on Alikar's face as Aven's stomach sank even further. But didn't that contradict what she'd said in private? And she'd admonished *him* for lies. "I do, however, have love for my coffers. And also for those who tell the truth. I would never deign to side with a man who could be *bought* by our enemies, even if I thought a mage would make a terrible king."

Alikar stilled, his expression frozen. "I fail to see what pertinence these preferences have to this vote—"

Calmly, Toyl turned and accepted a dark canvas sack and a scroll from an attendant. At the same time, Asten beckoned a soldier forward and did the same. Alikar's eyes grew wide with some recognition Aven didn't understand. Lady Toyl continued, "As a matter of fact, these preferences are highly relevant. How did you know that catapults were approaching the city?"

Hope flickered in Aven's chest.

Alikar scowled. "Aven said as much."

"The *king* said siege weapons approached," Asten said coldly.

"And I said ballistae. Not catapults." Dyon unfolded his arms and leaned forward over the table too, balancing on his knuckles.

"It does not matter, I just assumed one siege weapon over another. Your *vote*, my lady."

"You only had one way of knowing if they are ballistae, catapults, or bears riding horses," Toyl snapped, "and that's because you knew of them in advance. But you are right, that could be excused as an honest mistake. Perhaps that does not matter. This, however, does."

She dropped the sack to the table, the sound of coin clinking like a slap across the face. Asten followed suit, tossing the sack like a gauntlet thrown. Beside it, she placed a scroll with a broken seal of scarlet Kavanarian wax.

Alikar froze.

Toyl folded her arms across her chest. "Assembly members, I submit to you that last evening, Lord Alikar approached me with this bribe and message from King Demikin of Kavanar, attempting to purchase my vote."

"I received this offer as well, as Lady Toyl warned I would," said Asten. "She suggested we both accept so as to offer the Assembly this proof. Their offer stands in writing in these scrolls."

"Clever," said Beneral. "I rejected the fool. Never thought of accepting to acquire proof."

Dyon snorted. "Well, now I'm starting to feel left out."

"Oathbreakers," Alikar spat at Toyl and Asten in turn, ignoring the men. "Nefrana will not forget this. The gods will curse your souls."

Toyl laughed in his face. "You accuse me of breaking oaths? And yet you've betrayed us all and your sacred duty to the people of Gilaren. This morning, you also sent more than a dozen messages by servant in less than an hour once we'd learned the final location of this meeting. I charge you with treason, for your bribery and sharing the news of this meeting's location with those who would kill us all."

Well, by all the ancient ancestors. Aven's mouth fell open. The Assembly itself had beaten him to the punch. He'd thought to wait until after the vote. He'd had no real evidence, and he hadn't wanted to look like he was bullying them out of their say.

Aven stood. "I'll add to those charges of treason that I believe he shared the location of the king on the journey here with our enemies, quite possibly resulting in his death."

Alikar took a step back, then another, scowling like cornered prey. Thel and several nearby soldiers began to approach and circle him. Alikar's attendants tensed behind him, and hands reached for sword pommels.

"But if you insist on my vote, I find King Aven perfectly fit to rule," Toyl said, smirking.

"Seize him," Beneral ordered. "Take him to the—"

But the lord of the White City never finished that sentence. And in fact, the troops never quite reached Alikar.

A slight whistling sound was the only warning preceding the boulder. Rock smashed through the tower wall, glowing with heat. Rubble tumbled down around them.

Kae stared down at the worn parchment of the leather-bound book with wide eyes. By Nefrana's blooms. He'd found it.

Dozens and dozens of pages scrawled in an antique hand detailed in excruciating, mournful detail how the original brand had been created. A gathering of thirteen mages of specific types in a specific configuration, activating the right magic in the right order. Elaborately complex, technically beautiful, morally horrifying. He'd found it—the process the Dark Master was searching for.

And also the process that could make Kae a slave again.

He'd hidden his freedom so far. Turned out he knew

all too well how to act exactly like a slave, and he hadn't even caught a flicker of suspicion yet. He'd hoped to find this before the others and then… well, he wasn't sure what he should do next. He was still shocked that he'd actually succeeded.

Now what?

He glanced at the other two mages. Thank the gods he had been the one to find it first. The others searched hopelessly. He couldn't blame them. Idle conversation had revealed that his companions didn't think they could find what the Dark Master wanted, doubted it even existed. And Kae knew that in spite of their looming deadline, neither of the others wanted to be known as having created a copy of the brand if they did find it. They were doomed either way.

Of course, Kae had more incentive than they to stumble on the information. He'd tried to act as they did—calm, studious, rather bleak—but he knew that his best chance to keep his freedom rested in being *much* more efficient than these two.

And it had actually worked.

All right. What to do next? First, he needed them to leave. He'd have to stay until they both retired. Then maybe he could set this book aflame or otherwise destroy it without any guards noticing. He glanced at the hearth to the left. Could it be as simple as that? Toss it in, and keep watch until it'd gone to ashes? It was at least a good starting option.

He flipped back dozens of pages to where the section

on the brand started and pretended to study the knowledge. But as he read, he started to notice things that he couldn't help but be intrigued by, and he found himself at times actually studying it.

The brand used the magic of the stars. Of course, of course, that must be why all study of stars had been forbidden, but it was still unexpected. Was that why those Akarians could only free people at night? It must be.

He glanced around at the other two. The older man had fallen asleep, and the other stared out the window. Gods, would they ever leave?

Kae skipped to the end, looking for any indications as to how to break the bond. What if he could do it too? What if he could free these two men, and then the three of them could set this whole damn library on fire? Kae wouldn't mind going down with the building if it took the power away from these bastards and ended all this madness.

As he searched, the younger of the two men inadvertently woke the other as he rose and stretched. With a nod, the younger headed off to end the day with a meal. Kae hoped his remaining partner would take his lead and be gone soon. He wasn't looking forward to faking another prayer in front of this man. But he would do it if he had to.

He reached the last crinkling page. No mention of how to break the spell after it had been in place. Damn. That seemed another matter altogether, maybe contained in another volume. But what he did find, to his surprise, was some speculation as to how the brand could be *unmade*, just as it had been made.

Huh. Could this information be useful? Was there some way that Kae could get his hands on the brand on the way out as he made his escape?

Why did they *need* another brand anyway? Sure, Daes had given them a reason, a new mage site and bringing mages from other lands, but it felt off. The effort rushed. It didn't ring with the truth.

Could Jaena have stolen it? Those alarms had gone off the day that she had disappeared, the day after she'd been freed.

The day Kae had seen her in the smithy.

Which was the same place that they enslaved inno-cent mages.

It had to be true. Jaena must've stolen the brand. They needed a replacement, not a copy. They *had* been bringing in more and more mages, but they hadn't been enslaving any of them. They were all actually shackled or in the dungeons, which worked poorly, especially for the creature mages, who seemed to be giving them trouble left and right. It seemed so obvious, how could he have missed it?

If the brand was gone, and this book was gone, then he and Jaena had the potential to stop the Masters forever. Kae himself could stop them from replacing the brand forever. Sure, mages would still need to be freed. But if they couldn't make new slaves? What a victory that would be.

His other companion rose with a stretch. "Calling it a

night, Kae," he said. "See you on the morrow. Hopefully the Dark Master will see to ignore us once again, with our task unfinished."

"Indeed. Have a restful evening." Kae nodded and smiled, more out of relief that the man was finally leaving than anything else.

As soon as the door shut again, Kae dashed to the fireplace and tossed in the book.

The flames did not lick as quickly as he'd hoped. The leather binding apparently wasn't the most flammable thing in the world. He watched as the dark black leather curled and started to smoke.

As he stared off into space, waiting, a new idea popped into his head. If Jaena *did* have the brand, did she need to know how to destroy it?

He could destroy the book. Or he could try to escape *with* the book and find Jaena and then truly end all this. One option was significantly harder and riskier than the other.

He didn't care.

He sprinted to the fireplace and grabbed the book from the blaze, wincing as the flames nipped at his skin. He tossed the smoking book into the water pail that waited in case the fire got out of control.

"Damn the seven hells," he swore, fishing the book out of the water as quickly as he could. He'd probably destroyed it with that alone. He tried to open an early page. Some water smeared the ink, and some was intact, but opening the pages was smearing it all the more. He snapped the steaming, smoky pile of rubble of a book shut. By the gods. Well, it had already been done, he couldn't undo burning or submerging the book now. He'd just have to take his chances.

He didn't have time to hesitate. He spotted a scarf and cloak the younger air mage had forgotten on the bench nearby. He grabbed it and wrapped the book in the scarf, then tucked it into his jerkin. Then he pulled on the cloak. He would need to run soon, before the guards wanted to shut the library and go home. But he had a few moments to prepare. He searched around the table for anything that could help him. A bone folder, a small knife for fixing and adjusting the bookbindings, charcoal. Hmm.

Suddenly the peal of the prayer bells, high and musical, broke out across the growing night. The prayer was beginning.

By Nefrana. This was his chance. All would be knelt in prayer, and the mages of the guard towers would be compelled to submit to the goddess, rather than resist him.

Kae crept on tiptoe to the door of the library, waiting as the prayers progressed just a little further into meditation. And... yes, peeking around the corner revealed the guards were not looking at the door.

Hoping the smell of smoke that remained did not reach them, Kae slipped out into the hallway and the darkness on the other side. If the gods were with him, the evening's prayers might give him what he needed to slip by.

And if they weren't, he'd just have to fight.

Jaena, I hope you're out there, he thought. Have I got something to show you.

"Everybody out of the tower!"

"Down, down, down."

"To the cellar."

Jaena squinted up at the oncoming boulder, then looked around frantically. Someone—something—there had to be something they could do to stop it. The cocky blond mage passed in front of her on his way toward the stairs.

She grabbed his arm. "No. You're an air mage, right?"

He squinted at her for a moment, then nodded briskly.

"They're pushing the catapults with magic. Two can play at that game. Come help me."

His eyes narrowed further as he thought it through, then nodded. He followed her out onto the ramparts.

"Hey, now. You're not going anywhere without me." Tharomar charged after them, and she smothered a smile, hiding it with a turn of her head. She and the air mage would be busy with magic, too busy to notice any oncoming projectiles. Someone needed to stand watch over them. And she really had no intention of losing him again, especially not after last night.

"Wait—" Aven jogged up behind them. "What are you doing?"

"Get on down there," she said. "Figure out what to

do next. I think I know a way we can fight them off."

"She's got a mind to give them a taste of their own medicine, I think," Derk chimed in.

"I'll help—"

"No. We need *you* alive and well to free the rest of them." Jaena held up a flat hand, stopping him.

Aven hesitated.

"And also to lead this country against them, I might add," Lord Dyon said, jogging back to them. Had he overheard the conversation? "My lord, come."

Lord Beneral trotted up behind him. "You all need to get down from here. We're rolling out our siege, but it will take time. It's far from reaching them. Our riders will reach them first. The catapults are still several miles away."

"No. We have a plan." Jaena started backing away, wondering if they'd actually try to stop her. "Aven—go with them. Tell us how to join you down there. If it's not working, we'll follow."

"Fine. Take this." Beneral handed them a spyglass and gave them a few quick directions.

The three of them trotted along the ramparts and back up the stairs of the next tower. Where had the first few projectiles landed? Could they see the catapults at all from this distance?

She squinted, then took up the spyglass for a good look. "Let's try to fling it back at them. Ready?"

A massive boulder flew through the air. They readied themselves, and she caught its essence, trying to lighten the load as Derk sent a great gust of air behind the catapult. The stone flew, crossing the great distance. It cratered a few hundred yards short but continued to roll. Jaena winced as it leveled part of a farm. At least it was after harvest time.

She tried to shove it along, but she could not quite reach it. The roll slowed, and then slowed some more, and then stopped. It came to rest just short of the catapults without doing any damage.

"Oh, that's just great." Derk swore.

"We meant to use their weapon against them, and instead we politely returned their ammunition. *Damn* it," said Jaena.

"It was only your first shot." Ro put his hand on her shoulder. "Try again. They have the help of the catapults, and you don't."

Even now she could see them reloading the same boulder.

Derk grumbled as he seemed to ready himself for the next volley. "It's not fair. We're much better for getting it that far."

Should she give up their plan? They could try to meet up with Beneral's catapults, but they were sorely far behind them now. Much damage to the city would happen in that time. Should they just keep trying? She and Derk hadn't been that far off. The next time, they might get it. Or they might tire further and not make it even as far as the first.

"I have another idea. Can you make a wall of air?"

"Not one solid enough to stop a boulder like *that*."

"What if I smash it into tiny pebbles first? Can you

keep the debris from hitting us? Otherwise I think the roofs should be able to handle it much better than a boulder that size."

He pursed his lips. "That I can work with. I'd rather clobber them with their own boulder, but let's try it."

They'd decided in barely enough time. The whistle of the next projectile already approached.

She would have to be very precise. Too late and the effort would be for nothing. Too early, and she might miss the boulder and waste her energy.

She leaned back against Ro. His arms circled around her body as she closed her eyes, her mind reaching out to find the rock in the sky.

An arrow thunked into Samul's back. Miara wished it had come as a surprise, but the only surprising thing was the timing. She and the king had made it perhaps a half mile from where she'd trapped the mages in her vines, and clearly at least one of them had gotten free. She'd had no idea how much time her vines would bring them, but delaying them indefinitely would have been nice.

"Where are you hit?" she shouted over the wind. Lukor sensed her urgency and picked up his pace further into an all-out sprint.

The king didn't respond immediately, and she feared the worst. She could heal him if he was injured, but if they'd hit him in the neck or the heart—

"Should probably have tried to bring that breast plate with us, I guess," he grunted.

She swore, but at least he was still alive and joking. "I'm sorry my fins failed you, my king. I shall strive to do better next time."

"See that you do." Bleak laughter followed.

She needed to do something to stop them—something more. Vines weren't enough. She couldn't just heal him over and over again. If he passed out from blood loss or the healing or the pain of the arrows, she wasn't sure she could keep him in the saddle. She swept the grassy fields around them—squirrel, rabbit, chipmunk, sparrow. Gods, nothing that could help them unless she wanted to swarm them with small, adorable mammals. She heard the shriek of the falcon in the distance but couldn't feel him anywhere. Perhaps he was too high up?

The city was closer now, though.

"Should Aven be here by now?" she shouted.

"Yes."

Could she reach him? Find him amid the many denizens of the city? If she swept her mind far in that direction, she might just barely be able to reach. She'd be taken away from the battle mentally… but then she could call for help.

But many people lived in the White City, which did indeed live up to its reputation as a shining beauty on the horizon. Could she really find Aven amid the mess of a city?

Another arrow collided with Samul's thigh, and he

gave a muffled groan. At least there were no vital organs in the thigh. Except the arteries. And well, at least they hadn't hit Lukor, which could take them all down in one fell swoop.

Hmm. What if those mages figured that out?

*Hold on, Lukor. This is going to feel… weird.*

She recklessly went with the idea as it came into her mind. Lukor sensed the urgency, the danger, and braced himself. On his flanks and shoulders, she grew a strange armor, like a turtle's shell, then poured calm and trust back into him. *It will protect you from them.* He didn't much like that, but he didn't like getting shot either.

She swept her mind out forward, searching for any large predators. Or Aven.

The city was on fire with life, people teeming here and there. Panicked. They were panicking. Why were *they* panicking?

Inadvertently she brushed minds, seeing glimpses of sound and light. A boulder had hit the city. A large tower crumbling. Important people had been inside. Bad, that was bad. Fear quaked, whipping anxiety into panic.

Important people? The Assembly meeting. Had the Masters attacked it?

She could see the tower, but she groped further. People had fled down into root cellars and catacombs, wine cellars and sewers. They were in the ground, waiting to see if the buildings collapsed above them. Even having only seen the White City for a moment or two, she hated the thought of it coming to this. How were the Masters doing this? She hadn't seen any troops.

Could that have somehow been where the arrows had come from?

*Thunk.* A groan.

No time to think. Only time to search, maybe heal just a little.

Dozens of people flew past her, and then—

One underground area vibrated with magic. The other mages—Wunik, Siliana, Derk—they would be with Aven. That area could be *them.*

She narrowed in on it and—yes! His familiar smoke-sulfur twinge caught her senses, pulling her toward him.

*Aven!*

*Gods, Miara, you—*

*I have your father. We're on horseback en route to the city, but we're under attack. We need help.*

*My father! Where are you? Troops are headed toward the catapults, can you see them?*

*No.*

*You must be farther east then.*

*We had to go off the road to evade the mages pursuing us. I'm stable for the moment. But your father is badly hit. I can heal him, but he might fall off the horse from the pain, or—*

*I'm coming.*

*No–*

But he was gone; she had lost him again in the crowd of the city.

She reeled her mind back into her body. "I found Aven. He's going to send help."

"As long as he's not fool enough to come himself," Samul grumbled.

She winced.

"He's coming, isn't he."

"Yes."

"Well, let's just hope he doesn't come alone."

"Beneral—I need a horse. Now. Miara just contacted me. She's found my father."

The lord dropped the map he was holding to the table. *"What?"*

"Horse. Now. Asten, come with me. Get your bow. And one for me. Ben—two horses. Where's Thel?"

"He was on the other side of the tower with Alikar and Niat. They had to take a different way down."

"But where is he now?"

"He hasn't reached the bottom yet. We don't know."

Damn—was Thel missing? If he'd last been with Alikar, that would be a bad thing. "Find him," Aven ordered. "Send some men to look for him."

"Yes, sire."

Asten returned at a jog. "Where to?"

"Up these stairs," Beneral said quickly. "We've gotten two horses off a carriage. They're nervous, but it'll have to do."

"Oh, wonderful, no saddles." Aven took the stairs two at a time.

"Shouldn't be a long ride." Asten mounted up. "Let's go."

Aven urged the horse toward the east gate, only a few blocks away. Beneral hastily ordered several men to mount up and follow them. That was probably wise. Asten brought her mount even with his as they neared the gate and drew her bow.

There—Asten had already spotted them. Aven found her fiery red hair, tied neatly back, and the glint of his father's pauldrons. Something was… very strange about their horse.

The men that followed them surged forward too, probably on orders not to let Aven be the first one on the field of battle. If they could do it, fine, but he wasn't slowing down for them, not in the slightest.

Another mage on horseback followed behind them, arrow trained on his father. Aven slowed his horse, drawing his own bow now. The others would be closer, so he would be steadier. He nocked an arrow and carefully aimed, but waited a blink, another, to see if they would fire first and true.

Asten's arrow found its mark in the mage's neck, and strangely, he seemed surprised. He must have been so intent on Miara and the king that he hadn't noticed additional company. The man lost the saddle and tumbled to the earth, his own shot flying wide. Blood spurted as he went down, and Aven had the sick certainty that he would quickly be dead.

The others all turned their horses, narrowing in on Miara and the king. But to Aven's shock, he watched as the enemy mage's horse itself started to suddenly twist.

It was transforming. Gods, it wasn't a horse at all.

Even as the blond woman began to take shape, Aven fired. Asten's eyes caught on his shot, and she nocked a new arrow of her own, turning back to the mess.

The creature mage was only half human, half equine. She yanked Aven's arrow from where it hit her in the thigh, which seemed like a foolish move, although perhaps she planned to heal herself. First, though, her hands melted from hooves to fingers as she drew her own bow up and back and—

Asten's arrow flew, and the creature mage fell, a crumpled mess beside the first.

Miara's horse had nearly reached him. "Aven!" she shouted.

"Are they dead?" he called. Would she hate him for killing them? Perhaps he should have found some other way to stop them. As slaves, they likely had had no choice but to pursue. They hadn't chosen this fate.

She paused, checking. "Yes." Nothing in her voice held reproach or regret.

He steered his mount over to her and his father. The old man's face was white, and he leaned heavily on Miara. An arrow protruded from his thigh near Aven's face as well as his lower back. "Is he… ?"

"He's not dead yet, but I'm not sure how long we have. Is Siliana with you? I can't—"

"Of course. We'll lead you to her." He turned to their escort. "Surround them," he ordered. "No gaps."

The men needed no encouragement. The horses sidled as close as possible to the brave—and apparently armored like a turtle—steed that bore two of the most precious people in Aven's world.

When this all blew over, he'd have to get that horse a carrot. An apple, even.

He snorted at himself. What an inane thought to have at a moment like this.

As they entered the city's walls, the boom and whistle of another catapult launch echoed off the empty streets. The volleys were aimed at the west side of the city right now, but Aven urged them along faster anyway. Who knew when they might change direction?

"What was that?" Miara asked.

"Catapults," Asten replied.

"But—we didn't see any close enough—"

"They're using mages to extend the range," said Asten, voice hard.

Miara winced.

"Asten, can you ride ahead and warn Siliana? And the queen. Get a bed ready or—"

"Yes, my lord." Her horse galloped the last few blocks remaining ahead of them.

"Are you hurt?" Aven said.

"Nothing I can't handle." Miara managed a brief smile.

They reached the cellar just as Siliana and Elise charged back up the stairs. His mother's face paled. Aven jumped off his horse and helped Siliana get his father down, with more than a few groans. It took two more men to help him inside and down the stairs.

"Make way for the king!" Miara bellowed from behind them.

The corner of his mouth twisted into the slightest of smiles at that. He'd be glad to toss off the title if it meant the old bastard would live, especially hearing Miara say it. But *would* he live? He'd feel less anxious when the old fool wasn't bleeding, full of holes, and semi-conscious. They reached the table Asten had cleared to serve as a makeshift bed. The cellar wasn't meant for supporting troops in battle.

"Get the arrows out," Miara ordered, collapsing onto a bench against the wall. Elise joined Siliana at the other side of the table as they prepared to work. "Asten, you and Aven do it, let the healers save their energy. Count of three, ready?"

Miara counted, and they pulled, Aven gripping the arrow at the thigh and Asten at the back. Samul let out something between a groan and a howl. They lowered him to the table, and cloths from unseen hands were pressed into the wounds. Siliana and Elise leaned over him, eyes searching, intense, then closed.

He could feel them working now, though it was different than his own magic. He realized numbly he was getting more sensitive to it.

Samul let out a tortured wail, and Aven staggered back. They were working now. Good. Nothing else he could do.

He slumped down on the bench where Miara had been only to discover she was no longer there. Gods—where had she gone? He couldn't lose her again, not so quickly. Why was he always losing her—

As he lurched to his feet, searching for her, he caught sight of his hands. They were covered in blood.

His father's blood.

Everything around him froze for a moment. Somewhere, another boom shook the building. Somewhere, someone shouted, screamed. Somewhere, he needed to do something—help someone—stop all this. But for a moment—he just stared at his hands.

Hands joined his. Wet cloth slid over his palms, wiping them clean. He looked up.

It was her. Of course it was her. Of course she would make it to a moment like this, to a place like this with him. Of course she was steady. Of course she was calm.

"You made it," he whispered.

Her gaze fed him, fortified him, those brown eyes silently, patiently studying his own. Those eyes that said, I know. I did.

Samul cried out again, and Miara ordered someone to—he wasn't sure. He just focused on cleaning the blood off. He glanced up. She was sending for more water now, ordering them to shut the doors, board the cellar windows.

She returned to his side, again a pillar of calm, the shouting complete. She led him to the next room with her hand in his. A basin filled with icy water waited, and he washed off the rest of the blood. Asten's voice cut through the fog around him as she shouted directions to someone. She was glued to Wunik's side now, obsessed with the view of the catapults and troops attacking in the circle of light. What was she saying again?

"Our riders have almost reached the catapults. Half a mile more, maybe. Tell those mages upstairs to keep it up!"

His eyes caught on Miara now. Her usual leathers were also soaked with blood, torn in the shoulder and the thigh. The shoulder, she'd healed; smooth skin peaked through the torn leather. Her thigh was still wounded but didn't seem to be gushing blood.

He threw his arms around her and crushed her body and the soft leather against him, burying his face against her neck. Huh. Still lavender under all that blood, sweat, smoke. Her arms tightened around him.

Someone cleared a throat. Oh. They were standing a bit awkwardly close to the officers working… Asten was staring now, eyebrows raised, Wunik looking amused.

Aven withdrew, pulling them away from their audience as short a distance as he could manage before turning back.

Her lips covered his with a kiss. He pressed hungrily against her, and her mouth opened eagerly, their bodies molding together. For a long moment, he forgot everything around them, everything that was wrong, everything that he needed to do, every obstacle they faced. There was nothing but the two of them and that kiss.

How could he have come so close to losing her? He had to make sure such a thing never, ever happened again.

The thunder of another crash shook the building above them. Voices shouted outside.

"That one was close—"

"By the gods, are the riders nearly there?"

"A quarter left—"

Another boom thundered, but this one was followed by a strange sprinkling, almost like hail in a rainstorm.

He eyed the ceiling, then her again. He moved one hand to stroke her cheek, chasing the line of her jaw, the edge of her scar with his thumb. She mirrored the gesture, cradling his face in her hand. She leaned her forehead to touch his.

"I thought—"

"Shh."

"I thought you might be dead."

"I'm not." She pressed her lips together. "But I thought the same."

"That you'd be dead?"

"No. Well, yes, that too. But I saw the carriage, the lightning strikes."

"Oh." Had she figured out he'd killed a man with them then? Maybe more than one? Did she care? "Then you saw—"

"Let's just say if that damn demonstration happens again tomorrow, you are *not* getting out of it this time."

He let out the slightest snort of laughter but quickly sobered. "They said a… body was in your room? Two bodies?"

"Sorin," she whispered. His eyes widened, even as he felt a sudden rush of rage. "But I left the other one alive."

"Wait, did he… hurt you?"

"Nothing like I hurt *him*, that's for sure."

He drew her close to him again, burying his face in her neck and her scent for just one more moment. Another boom thundered. The strange hail followed.

"Is that... the catapults?"

He nodded, not releasing her. "Yes."

"We should try to stop them."

"Riders are on their way. Oh, and Jaena—"

"Jaena reached you?"

"Oh, yes. And she brought—"

Another thunderous boom and more hail cut him off for a moment. "Wait—what about her?"

"Her, Derk, and Tharomar are trying to do something to hold the catapults back—"

"Do what?"

"I don't know exactly. The king needs to be directing the action, not off in some tower—"

Her eyes widened as she processed the events in her mind. "Wait—the king?"

"Yes..." No, gods, no. The fear still lurked there in her eyes. "Having... uh, second thoughts?"

"If Samul lives, will you still be the king?"

"If I am, does it change anything?" He felt fear shoot through him now too. Any other woman would jump at this chance. How many suitors had been after him for this reason, for exactly this power he'd been born into? Not her.

She loved him. She'd said she wanted to marry him. Had the last few days convinced her she needed *not* to be queen more?

What could his father have said to her?

His heart skipped a beat as the moments passed, growing his fears.

Her mouth opened, then closed, and she pulled away slightly. She glanced around the room. He ignored it, only intent on her. His instinct said to pull her back against him, tighten his grip around her, but he fought it. He could never *make* her stay, even if he wanted to. If she walked away now, though, what would he do? King or no king, he might collapse just as soon as she was out that door.

Her eyes met his again, an unexpected hardness in them that he didn't know how to interpret. She's still here, he realized. She hasn't run off yet.

"If I am, does it change anything?" he said again, softer but more urgent this time.

Something shifted in her shoulders, and her chin lifted. Here comes the fatal blow, he thought.

"It might change a few things."

What for the love of Anara did that mean? "Like what?"

"Well, maybe we better get to our lake sooner, rather than later. Don't you think?" The corner of her mouth turned up in a half smile. We. Our.

Gods.

He kissed her again, softer this time, awash in relief and joy. After a moment, she pushed him away firmly. "Why are you so surprised? Did you really think I could walk away from you?"

"I just—I feared the worst."

"Don't." She kissed him again, gently this time.

"I'm a king, it's my job to worry." He tried a comic shrug and earned a slight laugh. Relief washed over him. If they could joke about it, it would probably be all right.

"If I'm to be your queen, I believe it's my job to order you not to. But that's for later. Come, we have work to do." She swept a hand out, indicating the chaos surrounding them.

"Right. Let me check on Wunik."

"I'll get someone to fetch towels."

Aven trotted back in to see if Wunik needed assistance, but it was clear Asten was doting on the old man like a prized warhorse. Through the window of light, he could see the horsemen had just reached the catapults, but mages on foot had emerged to engage them.

He didn't want to be separated from Miara for long, so he jogged out to find her again. His father was stabilizing somewhat, although his mother looked pale and almost… frail. Gods.

Miara strode up. "Come on. Things are stable down here. Let's figure out if Jaena and the others need help."

# 18 Titles

Miara took the steps up the tower two at a time, thigh aching and Aven following behind her. The air of the tower felt especially cold, having just left his arms, and part of her wanted to turn back and kiss him, to finally rest, but the mages might need their help. Another thunderous boom and tinkling rain filled the air as they neared the passage onto the ramparts. Derk, Jaena, and a man with a white streak in his black hair that Miara didn't recognize came into view. The man's arms were circling Jaena's waist as she leaned against him, eyes closed.

"Jaena!" Miara called.

Her eyes opened. "Miara!" Jaena left the man for a moment and threw her arms around Miara in an embrace.

"You made it, thank the gods. What are you two doing?"

"Her idea," Derk grunted. "We're slowing down or deflecting their shots."

"And shattering them, when I'm able," Jaena said with a determined smile.

"It should be almost over," Aven said. "The riders should have reached the catapults. Do you need our help?"

"Me? Need help?" Derk smirked at him, then stopped. His eyes flicked to their clasped hands, then back to Aven's for a long moment. "Yeah, actually, I could use some help."

Aven snorted, squeezed Miara's hand, and joined Derk near the wall as he explained what to do.

"Another one's coming—hold on." Jaena gazed out over the city for another moment. Sure enough, a huge stone came hurling toward the city, off to the left of their tower.

"Let's send this one back at them this time," Derk said, voice strained. "You're so good at blowing hot air, why don't you put that to some practical use, eh?"

As the boulder crossed high above the city wall and reached its zenith, it slowed unnaturally, almost stopped. Then, slowly, it reversed. "Think we can light it up?" Aven said.

"Try it," Derk grunted. As the boulder picked up speed, it burst into flame, hurtling back toward the catapults faster than it had approached.

"Watch the riders," Miara barked, raising her eyebrows.

"Yeah, yeah," Derk grumbled.

They all stood holding their breaths as the fiery rock plummeted to the earth, smashing into the back two rows of catapults that the Panaran riders had not yet reached. At least five catapults splintered into flying shards of burning wood and scraps of metal.

"Another!" growled Aven.

"I'm Tharomar," said the unknown man, bowing slightly.

"Miara. Mage, formerly of Kavanar."

"I…" Tharomar frowned, searching for how exactly to introduce himself. "I'm a blacksmith, among other things," he said with a glance in Jaena's direction.

Miara raised an eyebrow as her smile grew to a grin. Among other things? She had a feeling she would be interested to find out what those "other things" were.

Jaena returned from the edge of the wall. "You won't believe this," she said, her voice low and clearly only for Miara. "After you freed me, I was working in the smithy the next day, like we'd planned. They brought in a new mage to enslave, but he fought them and ran. I was knocked aside and found the brand not three feet from me."

Miara cocked her head. "And?"

"I grabbed it and ran," she said, nearly a whisper now. "That's why I had to escape early."

"What… ? Gods."

"Later. You'll see. Hold on, one moment."

The mages slowed another boulder and volleyed it back at the catapults. "I think that's the last of them," Derk muttered. "I hope."

"Looks like the riders are making short work of the Kavanarian forces. I think he's right, that's the last boulder we'll be seeing from them," said Aven. "Should we go back down? Miara, I think we may have some more good news for you."

Miara frowned even as he came and took her hand again. "The vote? The vote! Did it happen?"

Aven nodded.

"What happened?"

"Everybody voted for him except those two trash-eating worms," Derk interjected from behind Aven.

"And then one of the Assemblywomen accused the vicious one of high treason. It was great!" Jaena laughed, but then sobered. "Well… until the catapult hit before we were able to imprison him."

"We'll find him, don't worry," said Aven. "But that's not the good news. Come on downstairs." As they began to head down the steps, Aven leaned close and whispered in her ear. "I also told them all I'm going to marry you, like it or not."

She raised her eyebrows. "Before or after they voted for you?"

"Before."

"Fool," she said, smiling.

"You seem to inspire a lot of very foolish behavior, what can I say?" He shrugged.

She struggled to contain a smile at that and failed as they reached the bottom of the tower. No immediate good news caught her eye, except that Samul was sitting up and definitely breathing.

"Miara Floren," Samul thundered. The jubilant feeling in the room and her heart faltered.

"Yes, my lord," she said, coming forward quickly and relinquishing Aven's hand yet again. The king looked deathly serious. Miara's heart pounded in her throat. Had he seen their hands clasped, could this be over such a small thing as that? Or perhaps he intended to make an example of her escape, if only verbally.

"Take a knee," he ordered, and she fell to one knee as instructed. "You are all witnesses. This mage has saved my life and my son's life. I daresay it's becoming a habit. For your bravery in combat and your martial ability, as well as your unflagging loyalty even as we doubted you, I declare you, Miara Floren, an Arms Master of the Realm of Akaria. I officially bestow upon you this title and all the respect that goes with it for your valiant efforts on behalf of our kingdom, my ancestors, and my family."

She rose, astonished, as applause went up around her. She glanced at the room, finding Wunik, Asten, Beneral all smiling.

And then her eyes caught on a familiar sight, an impossible face, no, two faces that didn't belong in Akaria at all. Her father and Luha waited quietly in the corner, beaming joyfully.

"Father!" She rushed to them and threw her arms around them. "How did you—?"

"Your 'friend' saved us," her father said, grinning.

"He's more than a friend," she said quickly.

"I gathered that."

She bent to squeeze Luha against her chest, whispering, "I was so worried. I missed you."

Luha grinned up at her. "Your friend clubbed Father in the head."

Miara blanched. "Um…"

"It was the Dark Master's fault, don't worry," Luha said. "Otherwise Father was going to club your *friend* in the head."

Miara mouthed a silent "Oh" and squeezed them all together again as someone approached from behind. She turned to see Aven hanging back and ushered him closer.

"You clubbed my father in the head?"

His eyes widened for just a moment before relaxing again. "The Masters were holding them and Tharomar in a palace about two hours' flight from here. We, uh... went and got them. Did quite a bit of damage, actually. I don't think we've heard the end of that. But at least we're safe for now."

"Indeed." She threw an arm over his shoulder and squeezed them all again.

"Uh, Miara? I can't breathe," squeaked Luha.

"C'mon," said Aven. "I think this calls for some mead."

"Wait," Samul's voice called again. Aven and Miara turned to face him. "Aven, I have one more need of you first."

"Yes?"

"Come here."

Aven strode to him and froze as Samul gestured toward the earth. "Kneel, Son of Akaria."

Miara's heart pounded, and she clenched Luha's hand in hers. Was she seeing what she thought she was seeing?

Slowly, Aven sank to one knee.

Samul rose to standing with difficulty, Elise rushing to his side to help him stay up. Why was he not fully healed? Perhaps they'd only had the energy to get him partway there. But that didn't make any sense.

From the door of the cellar, Dyon strode forward,

holding something. A circlet, she realized, a band made of a shining silver metal and studded with sapphires that glittered even in the dull firelight.

The room had fallen silent. Samul took the crown carefully in both hands. "In times of war like this one, when the wounded fall, shields shatter, and towers burn, the old must step aside," Samul said, his voice rough. He lowered the shining band onto Aven's brow. "In times such as these, we make room for the new." Samul regarded Aven for a moment, a smile like she hadn't seen before on his face. "Rise, Aven Lanuken, King of Akaria."

A cry rose up around Miara, a shout, a roar of triumph. A war cry.

Well. All things considered, this calculated risk had turned out far better than Daes could have hoped.

Daes glanced at Marielle, her form beautifully arrayed across the throne next to him. Perhaps the gods *were* on his side. Either that, or she'd been an immense stroke of luck. He could never have arranged something like this on his own, and even if he had, it probably wouldn't have gone off as planned.

Sure, they'd lost the brand, but they'd have a new one soon. His first scouting party should have reached Panar by now and attacked the location Lord Alikar had so dutifully supplied. His first mage squad was in the Akarian mountains. His assassins were still hard at work in Estun.

Everything that he wanted was in motion, hurtling him and Marielle toward victory.

He shifted on the hard marble. Leave it to that idiot Demikin to make a throne that looked grandiose but was horrifyingly uncomfortable. And *white*. Who made a chair out of marble anyway and didn't even put a cushion on it?

Oh, there were so many things to change around here.

He only sat on black chairs. He suppressed a grin. The doors to the throne room opened, and nobles filed in. Nobles that had once looked down on his half-noble birth. Nobles that had once mocked his post at Mage Hall as a child-minder to miscreants. Nobles he had manipulated carefully over the years.

Nobles that he would now rule.

The room fell silent. With appropriate gravity, the queen stood. She moved slowly, casually, as if to say, I could take all day to do this, and you would all wait and watch me as long as I willed it. And they would too. None among them would dare to challenge her.

Or more particularly, him.

A slight flick of her fingers summoned a servant carrying a red velvet pillow, on top of which rested a newly minted golden circlet studded with three rubies. She held the crown aloft, then glided gracefully to him and placed it on his brow. He bowed his head to accept it but never rose.

"Lords and ladies of Evrical, and of the kingdom of Kavanar, our finest realm in all the land," she said, facing the gathering. "May I present to you Royal Consort Daes

Cavalion. Abide him as you would abide me."

The nobles of Kavanar bowed before him, as did the queen, and Daes smiled.

Oh, there were *so* many things to change around here.

# About the Author

R. K. Thorne is an independent fantasy author whose addiction to notebooks, role-playing games, coffee, and red wine have resulted in this book.

She has read speculative fiction since before she was probably much too young to be doing so and encourages you to do the same.

She lives in the green hills of Pennsylvania with her family and two gray cats that may or may not pull her chariot in their spare time. If you hadn't noticed, fall is her favorite season.

For more information:
Web: rkthorne.com
Facebook: facebook.com/ThorneBooks
Pinterest: pinterest.com/rk_thorne
Twitter: @rk_thorne

Made in the USA
Middletown, DE
18 May 2018